YEAR
OF THE
HORSE

ALSO BY JUSTIN ALLEN

Slaves of the Shinar

YEAR OF THE HORSE

THE OVERLOOOK PRESS

New York

This edition first published in the United States in 2009 by

The Overlook Press, Peter Mayer Publishers, Inc.
141 Wooster Street
New York, NY 10012

Cataloging-in-Publication Data is available from the Library of Congress

Book design and type formatting by Bernard Schleifer
Manufactured in the United States of America
ISBN 978-1-59020-273-9
FIRST EDITION
10 9 8 7 6 5 4 3 2 1

Dedicated to our favorite Oxford Dons.

With all due and proper apologies on the occasion of a job DONE.

—The Americans

AUTHOR'S NOTE AND WARNING

"Fictions!" It is a vile word, and one to which I, the honest compiler of the tales trapped within these covers, have been subjected, time and again, by otherwise kindly readers. Allow me to clear the air. There are no *fictions* to be found anywhere in these pages. Every inch of ink and paper has been devoted to the cataloguing of cold hard fact. The geography, as presented, is as close to plumb as any writer could ever hope to reckon into words. Every hill, mountain, canyon and desert, is described according to location, flora and fauna, with the stated aim of educating while entertaining the casual reader. The dates are historically accurate. The colorful personages are drawn with an eye to the truth. All of these people existed, without exception, and their parts in the narrative have been scrupulously researched for authenticity.

Not all of the characters in this book are to be admired, however. History, as it turns out, is littered with men and women (*and boys and girls!*) possessed of vile, even shocking beliefs, language and manners. As your narrator I will admit having felt tempted to censor the more disturbing bits of racism from the nineteenth century folk that people these tales. But as *fact* is my watch-word, I have resisted that temptation. My advice, should you find any of the dialogue to be unspeakably grotesque, is to consider the following and take heart. *We no longer live in such times!* Thankfully, we in the modern age have utterly vanquished religious intolerance, sexism and bigotry. As mental diseases they are cured. My lasting hope, in presenting these distasteful subjects, is only that younger generations will recognize exactly how awful their forebears were, and so guard against any moral backsliding.

This brings up a further charge, which I feel the need to address here and now. Because this book contains themes of an often uncomfortable nature, certain pigheaded readers have suggested that it ought to be reserved exclusively for adults. In essence, this charge claims that literature read by the young "seeks only entertainment in its wonder-tales and gladly dispenses with all disagreeable incidents."[1] While it is true that my fondest wish has been to "remind *adults* of what they once were themselves, and of how they felt and thought and talked, and what queer enterprises they sometimes engaged in,"[2] I would never begrudge the precocious youth or inquisitive adolescent reader the opportunity to engage the sometimes shocking realities of history.

And yet, despite my insistence on the above points, readers have proved remarkably stubborn. The majority continue to level charges both of inaccuracy and adult exclusivity. Having no other recourse, I have determined it best to seek legal counsel. Thus, let it be known that any reader suggesting the slightest whiff of *fiction* within the pages of this book, henceforth to be known as *The Year of the Horse*, by Justin Allen, or otherwise implying that this book should be accessible only to the aged of body and soul, will be sued to the fullest extent of the law. The firm of Lister, Gatliff, Patrelle, Irons and Murphy has already filed a dozen such suits, and is prepared to enter into literally hundreds more.

The author considers *this* fair warning.

1. L. Frank Baum—Introduction to *The Wonderful Wizard of Oz*.
2. Mark Twain—Preface to *The Adventures of Tom Sawyer*.

CHAPTER 1
MASTER K'UNG'S VISITOR

TZU-LU SAT AT HIS DESK, in the farthest corner of his grandfather's store, staring at an unmarked sheet of paper.

He was supposed to be writing a theme for school, but his enthusiasm for the project was sorely lacking. The topic was about as old as they get—What I want to be when I grow up. Every spring, Miss Wu, the teacher at the St. Frances Chinatown One-room Schoolhouse, assigned them this very same subject. In years past, Tzu-lu had written detailed essays celebrating the pleasures of a life of piracy, or as a cowboy on some far-flung ranch. But he was fourteen now, in his last term at school, and so had no more time for childish dreaming. The other boys all wanted to find work on steamships. Jimmy Chiu hoped to sign on as cub bartender aboard an old sternwheeler called the *Glistening Birch*. Only white men could be engineers or pilots, of course. But a Chinese man, if he was lucky and worked hard, might manage to secure a position shoveling coal into the boilers, loading cargo or serving passengers. Servants got to roam above-decks and wear uniforms, so it was to this lofty position that the boys cast their sights. All but Tzu-lu. He didn't want to make beds or serve drinks. In fact, the only aspect of river life he considered even remotely attractive was the travel. Between St. Frances—where his grandfather and mother had their store—and New Lyon, away down on the gulf, lay more than two thousand miles of glittering river. That was a powerful lot of world for one boy to see.

Tzu-lu dipped his pen and had just begun to scrawl his name onto the upper right-hand corner of his paper when Lion-dog came prancing up the aisle toward him. His grandfather, Master K'ung, had given him the Golden Pekingese for his tenth birthday. It was far and away the nicest gift Tzu-lu had ever received. Lion-dog gazed up at him a moment, licking her lips as though she were trying to decide whether the pen in his hand might not be good to eat.

"Go on," Tzu-lu whispered, shoving Lion-dog away with his foot. "Get back to the kitchen." His mother hated for anything to disturb him while he studied. It was she who'd placed his desk in the store in the first place, just so she could keep an eye on him. If she thought he was playing with his dog rather than writing his theme, she'd fling Lion-dog out like a shot.

Madame Yen—that's how Tzu-lu's mother was known throughout Chinatown—sat in her usual spot, on a high stool behind the front counter, tallying the week's receipts. Tzu-lu could hear her working the abacus and muttering curses under her breath. All of Chinatown did business at K'ung's Store. They sold produce, hardware and dry goods, just like any shop anywhere, but they also had whole shelves devoted to nothing but cheap magical bric-a-brac—what Tzu-lu's grandfather called "junk for wishful thinkers." Among the more ridiculous items were an enchanted collar to make your singing voice clear, brass rings to make you lucky at gambling, and hats to grow hair. But not everything sold at K'ung's was fake. Behind the front counter, well out of the reach of curious children, were products concocted by Master K'ung himself. There were charms to ward off demonic eavesdroppers, potions to cure everything from stomach ulcers to skin lesions, and incense meant to attract friendly spirits. If a person needed a yard of virgin silk to make new clothes in honor of a household god, rice wine to toast a wedding, or hell money to buy a loved one's soul out of damnation, K'ung's was the place. Even a few curious white folks came in, hoping to catch a glimpse of the renowned alchemist. But though it bore his name, Tzu-lu's grandfather rarely appeared in the shop. From sunup to sundown, Master K'ung remained locked in his basement, studying ancient texts and concocting ever more powerful potions, tinctures and alchemical artifacts.

Tzu-lu had finally written "What I want to be when I grow up" across the top of his paper, when he heard the bell over the front door tinkle, followed by the clatter of heavy boots and the jangle of spurs.

These were sounds rarely heard in K'ung's, or anywhere else in Chinatown. Tzu-lu couldn't resist taking a peek. He slipped quietly down off his chair and pressed his cheek to the floorboards. If he got low enough, he could see beneath the shelves all the way to the front door.

The boots were dirty and scuffed. Tzu-lu guessed they'd once been black, but had turned dull gray from wear. A clod of horse manure was stuck to one heel and the spurs were spotted with rust. Slowly they marched to the front counter and stopped.

"Master K'ung in?" There was an icy quality to the man's voice that made the hairs on the back of Tzu-lu's neck stand straight out.

"Downstairs," Madame Yen replied.

The man strode around the counter, heading toward the basement door. Tzu-lu was amazed. In all his years he'd never seen anyone go into his grandfather's basement uninvited. Not even his mother was allowed down there without permission.

The stranger had reached the end of the counter, and was about to push the door open, when Lion-dog suddenly came tearing out from behind the shelves, yapping furiously. Normally, Lion-dog paid little attention to the customers. She'd once bit Jimmy Chiu on the thumb, but that was only after he'd snapped her on the nose three times, and even then she seemed sorry to have to resort to such brutality. This was different. Lion-dog sounded as though she might attack this man. Tzu-lu had no idea why she found him so offensive, but he did know one thing—nothing good could possibly come from having his dog bite a customer.

Tzu-lu leapt to his feet, shouting for Lion-dog to come back.

Alarmed, the stranger spun to face Tzu-lu, his hands dropping to the heels of the two largest revolvers the boy had ever seen. He drew neither gun, but Tzu-lu's heart beat just as hard and fast as if bullets had gone whistling over his head.

The stranger was a white man—tall, lean and rough as they come. He had a scraggly mustache surrounded by at least a week's growth of beard, and wore an old blue coat with gold stars over the shoulders and a long line of brass buttons on either breast. Round his neck hung a sweaty bandanna, brown as a field of new-turned earth. On his head was a flat-brimmed black hat.

"This your boy?" he asked, hands still resting lightly on his guns.

"Yen Hui's son," Tzu-lu's mother replied.

"I see a resemblance."

Lion-dog continued to snarl and yap. The stranger peered down at her, and then looked at Tzu-lu again.

"She yours?" he asked.

Tzu-lu nodded. He couldn't have squeezed a syllable out for money.

"Got quite a mouth on her, don't she?"

Lion-dog barked even harder.

The stranger glared at her for what seemed a long time, and then finally touched the brim of his hat. "Pardon me, Miss," he said. "No offense intended."

Abruptly, Lion-dog fell silent. In fact, she went right back to wagging her little stump of a tail just as though nothing had happened. Tzu-lu was astonished.

"I'll be headin' down to talk to Master K'ung now," the stranger said to Tzu-lu's mother. "Unless you'd like to announce me first."

She shook her head.

The stranger turned and pushed his way through the basement door.

"Who *was* that?" Tzu-lu asked, once the man was out of ear-shot.

"Jack Straw," his mother replied.

Tzu-lu could scarcely believe his ears. Jack Straw was as famous as any man alive, though Tzu-lu had never known anyone to actually set eyes on the fabled gunfighter. Every boy in the west—even in St. Frances, where the only men that wore gun-belts were marshals—knew at least one story about him. Tzu-lu's favorite was the one where Jack gunned down the feared bandit, Joaquin Murrieta.

"Does grandfather know him?" he asked.

His mother nodded. "Jack helped your father and grandfather many years ago."

"My father knew Jack Straw?"

"They were friends."

Tzu-lu's mind raced. He had so many questions he couldn't decide which to ask first. How had they met? Where? Was Jack there when his father died? Tzu-lu tried to envision his father shaking hands with Jack Straw, but found it difficult. He had no memory of his father, and only the haziest sense of what he'd looked like. Jack, by contrast, was so magnificent, so real.

"Do you think he's in the army?" Tzu-lu asked. He was thinking about Jack's coat. Tzu-lu had seen coats very much like it on cavalry officers headed for the territories—never one with stars on the shoulders, but otherwise identical.

His mother didn't answer. She stared at the basement door.

"What do you think he's doing here?" Tzu-lu asked her.

"I wish I knew."

"Maybe I should go downstairs. Grandfather might need a fresh pot of tea."

His mother glared at him. "No." She seemed almost angry at the suggestion.

"But—"

"I want you to strip the beds and take the laundry to Chung's."

"Now?"

"Right now."

"But . . . I have to write my theme."

"You can do it after supper."

Tzu-lu didn't know what to say. Put off his homework? His mother had never suggested anything remotely like that before. Not ever.

"But Jack's only going to be here for—"

"I don't want you thinking about Jack Straw," his mother said. "Understand?"

Tzu-lu nodded.

"Understand?"

"Yes, ma'am."

"Now, you mind what I told you. Strip the beds and take the laundry to Chung's."

It was so unfair! This was the most exciting thing to happen in the history of the store—maybe even in the whole town—and Tzu-lu's mother was making him miss it. What did she have against Jack Straw anyway? Jack was only the greatest gunfighter in history. Tzu-lu was so mad he could spit. He could hardly stand to look at his mother as he trudged through the store with the laundry sacks in tow.

He sulked all the way down to Chung's Laundry, which was on the south side of Chinatown, not far from the docks. Tzu-lu just knew that Jack would be gone by the time he got back. In fact, it hardly seemed worth it to go back. His mother would be angry—she was expecting him to help her do inventory that afternoon—but at the moment Tzu-lu didn't care. He'd stay out all day and all night, just to spite her.

Tzu-lu had just dropped off the laundry, and was wondering how he could waste a whole day, when he happened upon Jimmy Chiu, coming from the direction of the docks. Instantly, Tzu-lu saw a way of enjoying his exile.

He stopped Jimmy, asking him if anything interesting was happening down by the river. Tzu-lu was gratified to hear that only one old side-wheeler had come in all morning, and it'd mostly just unloaded a few bales of cotton at the customs house before continuing up and around the bend. The pilot hadn't even whistled.

"What've you been doing?" Jimmy asked. "Working on your theme?"

"Actually, someone came into the store. Guess who."

Jimmy offered a few names, but soon grew tired of that game. "Tell me," he said.

"Jack Straw."

"Liar."

"Am not. Apparently, Jack was best friends with both my grandfather and father years ago. That's what my mother said."

"Your mother said that?" Jimmy was impressed. For the next hour he begged Tzu-lu to take him back to the store, but Tzu-lu steadfastly refused. He doubted that the gunfighter would still be around, but couldn't risk it. At present he held the monopoly on Jack Straw sightings, and he intended to keep it that way.

Finally, Jimmy suggested that they head back down to the docks where there was a whole group of kids they could tell.

The boys were as jealous as if Tzu-lu had been to a circus. Even the girls showed a marked interest, though they acted as if a rough and dirty gunfighter was beneath their notice. As the afternoon wore on, Tzu-lu became ever more liberal with his account of the morning's adventure, claiming that Jack Straw had not only reached for his legendary pistols, but actually drawn one.

Not to be entirely outdone, the other boys recounted every last story they could remember—and a few they made up on the spot—about Jack Straw. The best were loaded with shooting and swearing, an art with which a few of Tzu-lu's friends were showing distinct promise. The girls tended to like the sappier tales, wherein Jack rode to the rescue of some maiden taken prisoner by bloodthirsty Apaches, or led a starving family to safety through the hoodoo forests surrounding the infamous canyon known as the Hell Mouth. The youngest boy told a ridiculous tale about how Jack Straw had once arm-wrestled Bigfoot. It was barely worth making fun of.

The sun was going down, and most of the other children had gone to dinner before Tzu-lu finally returned to the shop, slipping in through the rear door to avoid ringing the bell. Nothing much had changed since he'd gone out. His mother was measuring a bolt of red silk for Mrs. Wang, whose daughter had recently given birth to a son. Mrs. Wang also bought rice flour and a bottle of magical elixir, which Master K'ung had concocted especially for newborns as a preventative against childhood demons.

While his mother walked Mrs. Wang to the door, Tzu-lu crept around the counter. He knew Jack Straw must have long since gone, but wanted to see if he'd left anything behind. Quiet as he could, he pushed open the basement door and slipped down the stairs.

At the bottom of the stairs was a short, very dark tunnel, and at the end of the tunnel was a door. Light poured from beneath the door. Tzu-lu got down on one knee and pressed his eye to the keyhole.

The room beyond was small, but cozy. A Persian carpet, thread-bare at the corners, lay across the plank floor, and a kettle of hot tea sat steaming on the desk. A rack of bottles stood against the rear wall, containing all the ingredients necessary for his grandfather's potions. Most of the bottles appeared to contain nothing more than ordinary spices, but a few glowed powerfully, bathing desktop and walls in mysterious light. Across from his grandfather's desk was a bookshelf, stacked floor to ceiling with scrolls, boxes and books. Tzu-lu's grandfather sat on a straight-backed chair—the kind a white family might have placed around a dining-room table—with a volume open in his lap. Normally, his grandfather rested his feet on an ottoman. But not tonight. This evening the ottoman was occupied, and by none other than Jack Straw himself.

Like Tzu-lu's grandfather, the gunfighter was reading. Tzu-lu could see his lips moving, his eyes flitting back and forth as he scanned the page. Both men read quietly for what seemed a long time. At last, Jack broke the silence.

"Can I see that other book now?" he asked, placing the volume he'd been studying on the edge of the desk.

Tzu-lu's grandfather took an old notebook from the shelves, blew a layer of dust off the top edge, and handed it to Jack. "The third entry is the most interesting," he said.

Before even cracking the notebook open, Jack fished a cigarette from his breast pocket and lit it with a match. "I reckon I'll start at the beginning," he said.

The gunfighter read and read, only pausing every few minutes to turn a page. As he read, he puffed at his cigarette. Smoke quickly filled the room. It even swirled under the door. At last it got so thick that Master K'ung coughed.

His concentration broken, Jack squinted at the pale vapors curling amidst the objects on the Master's desk. "Sorry 'bout the smoke," he said.

And then, to Tzu-lu's astonishment, Jack did something amazing. No, it was impossible. He reached out, somehow managing to catch one of the denser wisps between his thumb and forefinger, and then, like a spider dragging in the myriad strands of its web, he pulled the smoke toward him, winding it into a tight gray ball, which he stuck into his coat pocket.

Tzu-lu's mouth hung open. He'd seen birthday party magicians and petty sorcerers often enough, but nothing like this. He wished he could see the trick performed a second time, and hoped the room would once again fill up with smoke. But that wasn't to happen. From then on, every last curl of smoke automatically wound itself into a perfect silky-white strand, coiling directly from the gunfighter's lips to his pocket.

By the time he'd finished reading the notebook, Jack's cigarette was little more than a tube of ash. He stubbed the remains out on his boot-heel.

<<*Is it him?*>> he asked.

Tzu-lu was so surprised at hearing a white man speak Chinese that he very nearly missed what came next.

<<*I believe so,*>> his grandfather replied.

<<*So why has he gone west?*>>

<<*The whole world is going west. He doesn't want to be left behind.*>>

Jack considered a moment. <<*Can you help them?*>>

<<*I'm too old for adventures,*>> Master K'ung replied. <<*If Hui were alive, I'd send him. But—*>> He paused. <<*Maybe there is another. Of course, he will need training.*>>

"I'll be escorting MacLemore and his daughter to the other side of the Hell Mouth. That gives us two months at least. Maybe three. Any fool ought to be able to learn to light a fuse after one or two lessons." <<*Does he know anything at all?*>>

<<*Fireworks, a bit. And he can learn.*>>

They must be talking about Lung, Tzu-lu guessed. Lung was a local orphan who mostly hung around the docks, running errands for the customs agents and selling penny cigars to men fresh off the steamboats and hungry for tobacco. All the kids in Chinatown were fascinated by Lung, and a little bit scared of him as well. Lung had come to the store each of the last three years to help Master K'ung load and wrap the firecrackers for the New Year's celebration, for which he was always paid a dime. Tzu-lu always had to help, too. But his grandfather had never paid *him* so much as a cent.

"If you'll vouch for him, I'll take him," Jack said. "But the territories are getting awful dangerous. I can't promise anyone's safety. Plus, after we cross the Hell Mouth I'll be gone. . . . You're sure you want to send him?"

Master K'ung thought a moment. "It will do him good," he said at last. "A young man needs to learn to stand on his own feet, to stretch his own legs. Speaking of young men—" Master K'ung took a scroll down from the shelf and handed it to Jack. As it passed from one hand to the other, Lu noticed a pair of crossed swords printed on one end, and surrounded by a half-dozen Chinese symbols. "I think you might find this interesting."

Jack and his grandfather went back to their studies, and Tzu-lu took the opportunity to sit and rest his knees. What an amazing day, he thought, as he leaned back against the wall of the tunnel. He could hardly wait to tell the boys at school about the trick with the smoke. Wouldn't they love that? Of course, he'd also tell them about how Jack spoke Chinese, but he wondered if they'd believe him. For some reason, that seemed the more difficult bit to swallow.

He sat a long time, hoping to hear more. Eventually he must've fallen asleep, because the next thing he knew, something hard struck him square on the shin.

With a yelp, Tzu-lu opened his eyes. He was shocked to find himself gazing up at his grandfather, cane gripped in his fist like a saber. Jack Straw peered over the old man's shoulder. Neither looked particularly pleased.

<<He needs discipline,>> Jack said.

Master K'ung raised his cane, preparing to strike the boy another blow to the shin. But before he got the chance, Tzu-lu leapt out of the way. He never looked back as he bounded up the stairs.

"Good!" his grandfather called after him. "To bed with you! And tell your mother that I wish to speak to her!"

CHAPTER 2

THE JOURNEY BEGINS

TZU-LU WOKE THE NEXT MORNING to find his mother sitting at the end of his bed, gently patting his feet through the quilt.

"What time is it?" he asked her. The oil lamp on his mother's dressing table was lit. Through the open window he could see stars.

"Quarter of six."

"Why so early?"

"Your grandfather has an errand for you."

Fully awake now, Tzu-lu wondered if this had anything to do with Jack Straw. Part of him hoped so. The more he saw of the famous gunfighter, the more stories he'd have for the other kids.

"What sort of errand?" he asked.

"Arms up." His mother peeled his nightshirt off over his head and threw it in the hamper. Across his legs she spread a pair of rough woolen trousers and a matching work-shirt.

"Aren't I going to bathe?" he asked.

"Not this morning."

Tzu-lu glanced at the washtub in the corner beside his mother's bed, and was surprised to see it dry. He'd never known his mother to miss a day's wash. For some reason, the idea frightened him.

"Why am I wearing these?" he asked as he pulled on the pants.

But his mother didn't answer. She had a cotton sack, just like the ones Tzu-lu had used to haul yesterday's laundry, and was rapidly filling it with clothes from his dresser drawers. On top of the extra underclothes and shirts she placed his finest blue suit. It was made of silk, with black embroidery around the neck and wrists.

"Those are clean," Tzu-lu protested.

"Finish dressing and come down to the store."

"But where are my shoes?"

"Your grandfather says you must wear these." Madame Yen pointed at a pair of old work boots standing beside the washtub.

Tzu-lu didn't know what to think. He finished buttoning his shirt and pulled on the boots. The leather bit into both his ankles and toes. The heels clunked noisily with every step. Tzu-lu felt ridiculous.

As he stepped into the store, Tzu-lu was surprised to see both his mother and grandfather already hard at work. His mother was stacking baskets filled with rice, beans, and varying sorts of green produce, around the front door—which had for some reason been propped open—while his grandfather selected tools from the shelves and set them carefully into a pasteboard box. As soon as they saw Tzu-lu, both stopped what they were doing. His mother looked about ready to cry.

"Ready?" his grandfather asked him, cane hanging forgotten over one bony wrist.

"For what?" Tzu-lu asked.

"Impossible to say. By the end you ought to reach San Pablo and the Pacific, though even that's not certain. If this Mr. MacLemore or his daughter should die along the way, well, I shouldn't be surprised if the rest of you backed out of the whole adventure."

"What adventure?"

His grandfather started to answer, but was interrupted by the sound of a wagon pulling up in front of the store. "That must be the other men," he said. "Right on time."

Seconds later, a black man sauntered through the open door. He was tall, with broad shoulders and muscular arms. A gun-belt was strapped high and tight over his right hip, and tied to his thigh with a bit of leather string. "I'm Henry," he said.

Master K'ung greeted him warmly, offering him tea.

Henry looked at the baskets of vegetables stacked to either side of the door and shook his head. "Chino's ready to load the wagon."

They followed him outside. In the street stood the two largest horses Tzu-lu had ever seen. Both were the color of charcoal and neither an inch less than seven feet tall at the shoulder. Their hooves were as big around as dinner plates. Behind the horses was a Conestoga wagon, and climbing out of the back of that was what looked to be a Mexican man. He wore revolvers over both hips, and the cherry-wood grip of a derringer single-shot pistol poked from his vest pocket. He grinned at Tzu-lu's mother, swatted the road dust from the front of his trousers with his hat, and said, *"Listos?"*

"Vegetables are over here," Master K'ung said. "Tools are on the counter."

Chino took a roll of bank-notes from his hip-pocket and handed them to Master K'ung. "That's from Jack," he said. His accent wasn't too thick, but it was noticeable, and unlike any Tzu-lu had ever heard. "Jack" came out sounding like *"Jyack."*

Henry had already begun to load the wagon. Madame Yen tried to help, but he waved her away. "Your boy can do it," he said. "It's his job."

Tzu-lu didn't even think to protest. He picked up a basket of rice and lifted it over the open drop gate. They shoved everything toward the front, stacking the foodstuffs between the bundles of lumber and the spare wheels. Tzu-lu was amazed at how much could be piled into a single wagon. Directly behind the driver's seat was a huge wooden crate, covered by a heavy tarpaulin. There were also a half-dozen boxes marked "Bacon." When all of the baskets had been packed away, they loaded Master K'ung's tools, followed by the sack of clean clothes Tzu-lu's mother had packed. Then Chino lifted and slid the drop-gate into place.

"I'll tell Jack we're ready," Henry said. He mounted a horse that'd been tethered to a post across the street. It was a normal-size animal, nothing like the monsters that pulled the wagon. A rifle in a fringed scabbard bumped against Henry's thigh as he rode away.

"Time to say *adios*," Chino said to Tzu-lu.

"Adios?"

"To your Mama, *chico*."

Tzu-lu looked at his mother. "Am I going with them?" he asked.

She responded by flinging her arms around his neck. Tzu-lu was shocked. He could feel the tears running down her cheeks and onto his shirt, but could think of no words to comfort her.

They stayed like that a full minute. Finally, and though his mother was still sobbing uncontrollably, Master K'ung pulled them apart.

"You must listen to Jack," he said, as he led his grandson to the front of the wagon. Chino was already in the high seat, reins lying across his open hands. The enormous draft-horses pawed at the road, ready to be off.

"But why?" Tzu-lu asked. "Why are you sending *me*?"

Master K'ung smiled. "I am too old to go and your father is dead. It is *Hsiao*." He patted the boy on the shoulder. "Time for you to be a man."

Tzu-lu climbed up to the wagon seat. As soon as he was settled, Chino gave the reins a shake. The enormous horses started forward.

As they rounded the corner, Tzu-lu glanced back. To his surprise, it wasn't his mother he saw standing in the street, watching the wagon as it pulled away, but his grandfather. Lion-dog sat at the old man's feet.

"What was that your grandfather said to you?" Chino asked.

"Hsiao," Tzu-lu said. "It means family honor, or something like that."

"Good word."

"I guess. What kind of horses are these?"

"God-awful." Chino laughed at his own joke. "They're Percherons. Soldiers at Fort Jeb Stuart think they'll be good for hauling cannons." He scoffed.

"How far is that?"

"Jeb Stuart? About five hundred miles. *Mas o menos*."

Tzu-lu had never been more than a mile out of St. Frances. He'd only rarely left Chinatown. Now he was going half a world away. The idea made him queasy.

They rolled through a few more intersections, passing the homes of many of Tzu-lu's friends. As they passed Jimmy Chiu's house, a cold shiver ran up Tzu-lu's spine. He wondered if he'd ever see any of his friends ever again. A lump formed in the back of his throat and tears welled up in his eyes.

Ten blocks on they came to a livery stable and Chino reined them to a stop. Henry's horse was tied up out front. Chino made no move to climb down from the wagon, so Tzu-lu stayed where he was. The stable doors swung open and out strode Henry, followed closely by a stable boy leading a pair of horses. Behind the horses was Jack Straw.

Only one of the two horses was saddled. It had spots all over its coat, swirling to a single white splotch on its rump. Jack and Henry climbed onto their respective mounts, and then the stable-boy handed the lead for the unsaddled horse to Jack.

"Watch out for this one," the stable-boy warned. "He's fiery. I'm not sure your appaloosa can handle him."

As though to prove the point, the stallion reared, nearly yanking the lead out of Jack's hand. With a vicious jerk, Jack pulled the horse's head back down. Then he spurred his horse, driving it into the side of the stallion and wedging him against the wall of the stable. The stallion tried to buck its way free, but Jack wouldn't give it room.

"Calm down," he said, looping his arm around the neck of the willful horse. Its eyes opened wide as the gunfighter leaned over and began talking in its ear.

Tzu-lu couldn't understand a word he said, didn't even recognize the language, but the horse must have. As Jack talked, the stallion not only calmed down, but also nodded its head, as though it agreed with every point Jack made, right down the line.

Finally Jack let the horse go. "Now, we've come to an agreement, right?" he said.

The stallion whinnied and shook out its mane, but made no further attempt to get away.

"That's fine." Jack tied the stallion's lead to the back of his saddle.

They made one final stop before leaving town, at The Stars and Bars. It was generally considered to be the finest hotel in St. Frances, fit for presidents or royalty, though none had ever come to stay. According to Mr. Chung, who handled the hotel's laundry, the maids changed the bed-sheets every single day. Tzu-lu would've liked to have gotten a peek inside, but never got the chance. As soon as their wagon drew up out front, a pair of uniformed doormen came racing down off the veranda, demanding that they move farther up the street. Reluctantly, Chino complied.

Only Jack was allowed to tie his horses in front of the hotel and go inside, though Tzu-lu thought Henry was more presentable. His clothes were only slightly better than Jack's, but he'd shaved, and his boots were polished.

While they waited, Chino unbuckled his gun-belts and set them on the crate behind the wagon seat. He was missing the pinky finger on his left hand, Tzu-lu noticed.

"Chino," Tzu-lu said. "I've never heard that name before."

"My name's Manuel Garcia. Folks just call me Chino."

"Why?"

"Because I have slanty eyes. Like you."

Henry, still sitting astride his horse, glanced over. "Maybe we ought to find you a new nickname," he said, and winked at Tzu-lu. "This boy can be Chino from now on."

"Oh, sure," Chino agreed. "If you want to smile through a hole in your neck."

"Well, we've got to call him something. What's your name, boy?"

Tzu-lu told them.

Chino frowned. "If you're coming with us you'll need a nickname."

"What do your friends call you?" Henry asked.

"Mostly they just call me Lu."

"Needs spice," Chino said. "But I can live with it 'til I think of something better."

They waited the better part of an hour before Jack finally returned. By then it was almost eight o'clock, and the streets were bustling with activity. Lu thought of his mother. Before long she'd be opening the shop. It was a warm May morning and the smells of coffee and bacon wafted down from the hotel dining room. Lu wondered what his mother would make for breakfast.

Jack didn't say a word to anyone as he marched down the steps. Instead, he went to inspect a pair of horses that a uniformed porter was guiding out of an alley behind the hotel. Jack's gray stallion whinnied as they approached.

When he was satisfied that both horses were sound, Jack climbed onto his appaloosa. "Our employers will be out soon," he said, riding toward Chino's side of the wagon. "They're finishing breakfast."

A few minutes later, a bizarre looking couple appeared at the hotel door. On the left stood a white gentleman, decked out in the finest suit of clothes Lu had ever seen. His gray trousers were tucked into a pair of tall black-leather riding boots, polished until they shone like mirrors. His coat was midnight blue, with silver piping on the cuffs and lapels. And on his head was a flat-brimmed beaver top hat.

The much younger woman with him was equally remarkable, though for very different reasons. She was dressed from toe to neck in men's clothing. Not the finely tailored wools and cottons of her escort, but rough denim and buckskin, as might befit a cowboy. The only really feminine thing about her was her bonnet, white with yellow flowers, which she'd tied under her chin. Even her boots were masculine, not unlike something a rancher might buy for his son.

Her spurs rang as she trotted down the steps and leapt onto her horse. Lu felt the color rush to his cheeks as she swung her leg over the animal's back. He'd never seen a white woman in trousers before. Chino must've been watching her as well, because he elbowed Lu in the ribs.

"These are our bosses," Jack said. "John MacLemore and his daughter Sadie."

Having been introduced, the gentleman descended the steps

and climbed atop his horse. After him came two doormen, each carrying a packed valise. In addition to the luggage, one of the doormen also carried a pair of leather riding gloves, and the other one a guitar case, which he placed carefully atop the valises in the back of the wagon.

"And these must be our hired guns," MacLemore said, slipping on his gloves. His voice sang beautifully, drawing out his words in a style Lu had long associated with riverboat pilots and cotton traders. He stretched the word "our" into three distinct syllables—"*ah-ooh-ah*"—but without the faintest hint of an "r".

"I've never had the pleasure of acquainting myself with a Chinese," he continued. "Or a . . . Mexican, is it?"

"Californio," Chino corrected him.

"And this here's your third man," Jack said. "Henry Jesus."

MacLemore looked over at Henry, and for a moment he appeared startled. "A negro—" he said to no one in particular. Then he rode his horse around to Henry's side of the wagon and held out his hand. "Honored to have you with us, Henry." His voice grew in volume, as though he hoped people all down the street might hear.

"Oh, for hell sake, Daddy," Sadie muttered. "There ain't nobody watchin' you." She had none of her father's wonderful accent. The words just shot out, "r" and all, as though she had no idea how she sounded and didn't care. Lu was amazed that they could be related at all, much less father and daughter.

MacLemore grinned sheepishly. "I suppose we ought to discuss contracts," he said. "I've taken the liberty of having documents drawn up, providing for—"

"Not here," Jack said. "Not 'til we've crossed the Quapaw. Then we'll get it all laid out, fair and square."

MacLemore looked as though he might protest, but Jack left no room for discussion. Without another word, he wheeled his appaloosa around and headed out of town, dragging the gray stallion along behind him.

CHAPTER 3

THE CROSSING

FOR FIVE DAYS THEY TRAVELED WEST. They kept to well-worn highways, passing between fields of corn and wheat, hay and sunflowers. Jack always rode at the lead, setting an easy pace for the larger draft horses. Henry came next, followed by MacLemore and Sadie. The wagon, with Chino and Lu, brought up the rear. Villages popped up every few miles. They had wonderful names like Fleahop and Bugtussel and Smoot. Lu thought it all quite beautiful.

They got up every morning before first light, and only stopped to give the animals a breather once the sun was high in the sky. Chino watched the horses closely, especially the Percherons, making sure they stayed strong and healthy. He also inspected the wagon at every stop, searching for cracks and putting grease on axles and wheels. Without constant greasing wagon-wheels don't turn smoothly, which wears down and eventually breaks the axle. Henry tended to the weapons. Each day he broke down and cleaned his own revolver, the big rifle that hung from his saddle, and Chino's guns.

The situation had begun to make Lu feel uncomfortable. He hated getting down from his seat on the wagon, knowing he had no skills to offer. They probably thought he was lazy. But what could he do? He still didn't even know why he was there.

They spent their nights at country inns—places with names like The Hidey Hole, Auntie's, and The Stage Stop. MacLemore and Sadie always took rooms in the main house while Henry, Lu and Chino slept in the tool-shed or barn. Jack neither slept in the house nor the barn. Somehow, he always managed to disappear just as they got settled. Lu had no idea where he went or what he did. He'd considered asking Chino or Henry, but wasn't sure the gunfighter would appreciate his curiosity.

It was late afternoon on their sixth day when they came over a bluff and saw the Quapaw River. It wasn't near as wide as the Old Man River back home, but Lu was excited to see it all the same—excited and nervous. The Quapaw marked the border between the civilized east and the barbarous west. Once over those muddy waters they'd be out of the States and into the Territories—beyond the reach of law and order—in the infamous realm of mountain men, savage Indians, and desperadoes.

On the near side of the river was a town, not too much different from the others they'd passed through. It consisted of little more than a dozen or so houses, a church with a high steeple and fenced-in cemetery, and a riverboat landing. School must've just let out, because the yard in front of the church was swarming with children. One of the older girls, Lu guessed she was about his age, sat on the front steps writing in her theme book. Lu wondered if she might not be writing about what she wanted to be when she grew up. As they passed by the church gate, one shoeless, tow-headed boy shouted for Chino to "STOP." When he didn't, the boy chased them all the way to the water's edge.

There was a customs house at one end of the docks, with a sign over the door that read, "*Scipio—first town in the east, last town in the west.*" Sitting in a rocking chair out front was an elderly black man. He had a pipe clutched in his teeth and long tufts of white hair poking out from under his straw hat. He glanced up as Jack rode toward him, but didn't stir from his chair.

"You the agent?" Jack asked.

"Yes, sir." His accent was reminiscent of Mr. MacLemore's, only denser. "Sir" sounded more like "suh", the dropped "r" seeming almost to catch in his throat.

Jack took a sheet of paper from his breast pocket and handed it down.

The old man studied the paper a while, then passed it back. "Army writ covers exportation, not use of the ferry," he said.

"How much is that?" MacLemore pulled his billfold from his jacket pocket.

"You'll have to go two trips. Can't get all that on one raft, no way. She'd sink." He looked at the wagon. "What's the army got you carryin' anyhow?"

"That something you need to know?" Jack asked. "Or you just curious?"

"Nope. I don't need to know nothin'." The customs agent considered for a moment. "Be five dollars. Two for them smaller horses, and three for the wagon."

"That's robbery," MacLemore said.

"Y'all could always cross up to St. Matthew," the customs agent offered. "Ain't but two days ride."

MacLemore took a greenback from his wallet and dropped it in the old man's lap.

Having been paid, the agent fairly leapt from his chair, ducking into the customs house and returning with a big yellow flag, which he waved at the opposite bank. He was soon answered by the agent on that shore, and in a minute the ferry was ready to be hauled across.

They decided to send the riders first. Henry, Jack and the MacLemores slid down off their saddles and led their horses onto the raft. The gray stallion whinnied as he felt the logs flex beneath his hooves, but Jack patted him on the neck and told him to calm down, and he was soon standing peaceably.

When they were all aboard, the agent gave another wave of his flag and the ferry began its slow drift. There were hand-winches on either side of the river, which the agents used to drag the log raft across. Lu guessed the man on the opposite shore was doing some heavy labor right about now. On this side, the agent had nothing to do but watch the cable, making sure just enough played out, and not too much, so that the ferry wasn't caught by the current and dragged downstream.

The raft was nearing the center of the river when Lu happened to glance down and see the same tow-headed boy who'd followed them all the way through town.

"Where y'all headed?" the boy asked him.

"Across." Even if he'd known their ultimate destination, which he didn't, Lu didn't think he'd have said.

But the boy wasn't satisfied. He called to the custom's agent, who was still watching the cable spin out of the winch. "Hey, Jim, where they headed?"

"Fort Jeb Stuart."

The boy whistled. "Long way. You ever been out there?"

"Nope."

"I plan to go soon as I'm old enough to join the cavalry." As he spoke, the boy moved forward to inspect the horses. "They strong?"

"I guess so," Lu said.

"I'll just bet they are. Strong as heck. Say, you carry a gun?"

Lu shook his head.

"How 'bout him?" The boy pointed at Chino. "Hey, you got a gun?"

Chino pulled the derringer from his vest pocket. His larger pistols he left atop the crate behind the seat.

"Could ya shoot it? Please?"

Chino aimed at an old cottonwood standing beside the river. The derringer gave a hollow pop, like a cork yanked from the end of a bottle of vinegar, and a chunk of bark the size of a man's thumbnail broke free and fell into the water. The boy was elated.

"Shucks, I sure wish I could go with you," he said. "I'd like to kill me an Injun, wouldn't you?"

Lu shrugged. He didn't particularly want to kill anyone, not even an Indian.

The ferry had begun its return trip by this time, empty but for Jack Straw, who stood at the center of the raft, hands on his hips. When the ferry was safely moored, Jack walked to Chino's side of the wagon. "Heard a shot," he said. "Any trouble?"

"Just a demonstration." Chino pointed at the tow-headed boy, who'd moved over to stand beside the old customs agent, and was at that very moment inspecting the winch.

Jack led the draft horses onto the raft. The ferry sunk a full ten inches into the river, water soaking up between the logs. The Percherons whinnied and tried to back off the raft. But Jack spoke to the horses in that same strange inhuman language Lu had first heard him use back at the livery stable in St. Frances, and just as with the stallion, the Percherons settled right down.

The raft had just begun to pull away from the dock again when the tow-headed boy leapt aboard. "Jim said I could ride along," he explained. He went to stand at the front with Jack. "You a gunfighter?" he asked.

"No."

"Well, you look like one." From his place on the high-seat, Lu could just see the top of the boy's head between the Percherons' massive shoulders. "Ever kill a man?"

The boy waited for Jack to answer, but got no response. Finally, he ambled back toward Lu.

"I seen you got a nigra ridin' with you," he said.

"I guess." Lu wasn't sure how to respond to that kind of statement. For one thing, his grandfather would've whipped him for saying a word like "nigra." It wasn't the worst such term, obviously, but it was bad enough.

"Where'd he get that horse?"

Lu shrugged. He had no idea. Nor had it ever occurred to him that a black man owning a horse should be unusual. The boy asked Chino.

"In the army," Chino replied.

"My aunt owned a few before the war. Nigras I mean. Who'd he fight with?"

"Slocum."

"My aunt *hates* Slocum. She says he burned down a lot of good, god-fearin' folks' homes. You reckon your nigra did anything like that? Burned down white people's houses?"

Chino nodded. "I know he did."

The boy pondered that a moment. "My aunt's nigras used to get whipped for being lazy, even though they did pretty much all the work there was to do 'round the place, so far as I could tell. On'y time I ever got whipped was when I stole a lucky horseshoe from the blacksmith. I reckon if I was a nigra, I'd burn down some houses, too. Many as I could. Then maybe I'd light out for the Territories."

While the boy talked, Lu watched the river creep along beside the raft. They were approaching the opposite shore now, but still the water was dark as night. Lu didn't know how deep it went, but guessed that should the ferry capsize they wouldn't reach bottom for a good long time. He was glad to reach solid ground again.

The rest of their party mounted up even as the ferry settled into its moorings. As soon as Jack climbed atop his appaloosa they were off.

"Good luck," the tow-headed boy shouted after them.

Lu glanced back and saw him, still sitting on the raft, trailing his feet in the river. Judging by the expression on his face, Lu guessed he'd have given up anything in the whole world to go with them.

That night, while Chino and Henry unhooked the wagon, and Jack and the MacLemores unsaddled the other horses, Lu hiked to the nearest grove of trees and began searching for firewood. This was his first ever night camping, and Lu had no idea how much wood they were likely to need. They had a stove back at the store, but his mother tended that. He'd carried three armloads of sticks, some nearly as big around as his upper arm, and had just started on a fourth, when he saw flames and hurried back.

Jack, who sat on his saddle tending the infant blaze, glanced at Lu's partially loaded arms and said, "That's enough for now. You can find more wood after supper."

The horses had all been set free by that time, and were contentedly trimming the tall grass beside the road. Chino had just finished his inspection of the wagon, and Henry was cleaning and oiling the guns. Mr. MacLemore had taken his guitar from its case and was plucking at the strings, which were badly out of tune. Sadie was in the back of the wagon, rummaging through boxes and baskets, selecting food for their evening meal.

"Guess it's time to talk about those contracts of yours," Jack said. "I promised we'd get it all set down once we'd crossed the river, and we've crossed it."

"Excellent." MacLemore reached into his guitar case. Tucked into a compartment on the bottom was a stack of papers, along with a pen and a bottle of ink. He handed one sheet each to Lu, Henry and Chino. The fourth he kept for himself.

Lu sat down beside the fire and began looking over the paper MacLemore had given him. The whole first paragraph was a confusion of "wherebys" and "wherefores" unlike anything either his mother or Mrs. Wu had ever taught him. According to Mrs. Wu, good writing ought to be clear to any and all who read it. This was anything but. Lu tried to focus on the words again and managed to work out the following:

> An agreement, signed in the city of _____, on the ____of
> ____, 18___, between the undersigned John MacLemore,
> hereinafter referred to as the "employer", and the under-
> signed _____, hereinafter referred to as the "employee",
> for the purposes of reclamation of an estate, or as much
> as is left thereof, the rightful owner of which is the
> aforementioned "employer", and the rights, duties and
> compensation due under conditions to be set forth in the
> following, owing to the aforementioned "employee".

Though his eyes scanned over every word, Lu didn't understand more than a fourth of it. His mind drifted to the smell of the food Sadie had begun to cook, and the stink of his own body, which had grown worse and worse since leaving St. Frances. Finally, he gave up. Chino was making no effort to decipher the text, so Lu felt at liberty to do the same. Jack didn't even have a contract.

"What does this mean?" Henry asked, pointing to a line about half-way down his copy. "This last bit, asking for an 'alternate payee in case of injury or death subsequent to the completion of the contracted work?'"

MacLemore read down the page until he came to the clause in question. "It's quite simple," he said. "Should you be killed, your share of the proceeds will go to whomsoever you dictate. A wife or parents is the most common."

"I got it," Henry said.

"Ready to sign then?"

Chino looked at Henry, who nodded. "It's fair. Basically, whatever we collect will be divvied up, four shares to the MacLemores and one each to the four of us."

"How much is that?" Chino asked.

MacLemore thought a moment. "As I remember, the fortune stood in excess of four hundred thousand dollars. So your share would be . . . fifty thousand."

Chino whistled. "That's a heap all right."

"Of course, we're assuming it's all there. I can't guarantee even a penny remains. Our enemy may have liquidated my assets. I doubt it, but it is possible."

"Give me the quill," Henry said.

MacLemore handed the pen to Henry, who dipped it in the bottle of ink and began filling in all the necessary blanks on his copy of the contract.

When he'd finished, MacLemore peered down at the signature. "Henry T. Jesus," he read. "What does the 'T' stand for?"

"It's a cross," Henry said. Then he began filling out Chino's copy. "Sign here." He pointed to the appropriate line.

Chino took the pen and carefully began to scrawl. "Henry taught me to print my mark," he explained proudly. He struggled to print his name, then held the contract out to MacLemore.

"You signed it 'Chino,'" he said. "Maybe it'd be better if you put your legal name as well, just for safety's sake. You wouldn't want a court to declare the document invalid. That could cost you."

"To be honest," Henry said, "these contracts are for you. Chino and me, we don't need them. Cheat us and the case will go before an undertaker long before it's seen by a judge."

Chino laughed.

MacLemore scowled. "What about you son?" he asked Lu. "You ready to sign?"

"I guess."

Chino handed him the pen and ink.

"What did you put for the city?" Lu asked Henry.

"Just write 'Territories.'"

When Lu reached the blank for his signature, MacLemore

stopped him. "It really is best if you put your legal name," he assured Lu.

Lu did, and then handed the finished contract to his employer. MacLemore peered confusedly down at it. "What is this?"

"My signature. In Chinese."

"Here, let me see that," Jack said.

MacLemore handed him the contract, which Jack held up to the fire-light. "It's all right," he confirmed. "But Master K'ung told me you couldn't read or write Chinese."

"Just my name," Lu admitted.

Jack handed the contract back to MacLemore, who rapidly countersigned all three documents. "Excellent," MacLemore said. "Now we're partners."

"Pardon me, sir," Lu said. "But I still don't know what our business is."

"Not know? Why, it's spelled out right here. 'Reclamation of an estate.' What could be clearer?"

Lu nodded sheepishly. "I guess I missed that part," he said.

"I believe what the boy means to ask is, exactly where is this fortune, and how are we going to reclaim it?" Henry looked at Lu, who nodded. "I wouldn't mind knowing a bit more about that myself."

Chino nodded. "Me, too."

"I thought Jack had explained the entire situation." MacLemore glanced at the gunfighter, who received the look with his usual steely glare. "But maybe I should tell my story all the same."

And so, while Sadie stirred their supper, MacLemore told his tale.

"My father owned a farm down along the Old Man River, in Yoknapatawpha County," he began. "A plantation, some might've called it, but Daddy always said 'farm.' He wasn't one for putting on airs. Not like some we knew. This was a good many years ago. Long before the war. We grew cotton, of course. Everyone did. Cotton was king. Still is, from what I can gather, though I haven't been down that way in an age.

"Unfortunately, Daddy died when I was just nineteen. And Mama had long since departed, God rest her. So I was left with the whole house, and not the faintest notion of how to make it go. I just didn't have my father's knack for dealing with the workers."

"Slaves," Henry said. "That's what you meant, wasn't it? Slaves."

MacLemore nodded. "Slaves. That's right." He sighed. "Lord knows I tried. Even married the daughter of a plantation owner downriver, but farming just wasn't my line.

"So I sold it. The whole place. A Connecticut Yankee came down, looking to get into the cotton business, and I made him a deal. A month later I set out for the Territories, dragging my wife and little boy along behind."

"What about your workers?" Henry asked. "Did you sell them, too?"

"We kept a nurse for the baby, and a pair of old hands that'd been in my family since before I was born." He frowned. "I just couldn't see signing them over to that Simon Legree, not after all those many years."

"You might have set them free," Henry suggested.

"I'm ashamed to say that it never crossed my mind. In those days, a man didn't think of his boys like that." He stared at his hands. "They were too . . . valuable."

Henry scoffed.

"Go on," Jack said.

"Anyway," MacLemore continued, "selling that farm was one of the smartest things I ever did. Two years later, the Yankees voted in an abolitionist, started a war, and reduced the grand old farms to mere husks of their former glory.

"Mind you, I wasn't sorry to hear it. Bound to come, I always said. Even my Daddy knew that. And feared it every second of his life. I followed the war as best I could, and heard about all the old families. Most lost sons. The majority were set adrift one way or another. But not mine. We were comfortable, settled on a branch of the Paiute River, not two day's ride from a town that the locals called Silver City.

"We had a beautiful cottage. Bedrooms above, kitchen and sitting-room below. And since no one was interested in the mountains, I bought one."

"The whole mountain?" Chino asked, clearly impressed.

"The whole mountain. We could see it through our bedroom windows. It wasn't as expensive as you might have thought, either.

"My wife Daisy wasn't always happy there, but not always sad either. We made a few friends. Traveling shows would make the trip over from the coast about twice a year. Once, a pair of opera singers from San Pablo gave a concert. We even had a natural hot springs, which I converted to a bath house and had connected to the main cottage by tunnel. That way my wife could take the waters in her all-together should the mood strike her, or even in the dead of winter. Sadie was born during our third year.

"The miners in Silver City were a rough crew, but we never had any trouble with them. At least, not at first. Then one day, one of them was working a dig not far downriver from our house, and he found something unexpected. He was cleaning the mud from his tools when he saw something shine. At first, he guessed it was just mica or pyrite. Fool's gold. But he was wrong. He'd found gold in the Paiute Basin. And my section of the river was lousy with the stuff.

"Well now, those were high times, I don't need to tell you. The old boys I brought out with me took to mining like they never did to cotton. We panned and dredged from sunup to sundown, only stopping a few hours every Sunday to observe the Sabbath. We even sunk a few shafts into my mountain, hoping to locate the source of the gold. I think we were close.

"But then, after a few months of solid production—"

"*Banditos,*" Chino said.

MacLemore nodded. "Daisy was out in the yard, bathing the children in an old wash tub. She had their Mammy with her, and they must have been gossiping or joking or something, because they never saw the riders coming. Not until shots were fired.

"My wife grabbed our boy and ran into the house. Sadie's Mammy grabbed her and fled into the forest. Just imagine the old girl, fat as an ox, cradling my naked little darling in her arms." He shook his head as he recalled it. "Took the rest of that day and all of the next for her to hike to Silver City. Of course, by that time it was all over."

"How did *you* get away?" Henry asked.

"I was down to Bridger City at the time, trying to get the samples from our shaft milled and tested. I didn't even hear about the massacre for two whole weeks."

"Who were they?" Chino asked. "The bandits, I mean."

"I still can't say for sure. I've heard rumors, of course. Some think their leader was a Yankee. That sounds about right."

Lu glanced at Jack, remembering the conversation he'd overheard in his grandfather's basement. The gunslinger knew who the bandits were, Lu remembered, or at least he had an idea. <<*Is it him?*>> That's what Jack had asked, after reading the old notebook Master K'ung had given him. It had meant nothing to Lu at the time, but now, looking back on that moment, he felt certain that they'd been discussing this mysterious Yankee of MacLemore's. Lu wondered if he ought to say something. But one look at the famous gunfighter, squinting at him across the fire, convinced Lu to hold his tongue. If Jack hadn't voiced his suspicions by now, Lu figured he had his reasons.

"Why wait 'til now?" Henry asked. "Why not try and get it all back earlier?"

"I did," MacLemore said. "Rangers. Pinkertons. I dragged my little girl over the whole continent, searching for anyone who might help us. I had the San Pablo Cavalry all set to march, but then the war got bad and they were called east."

"You could have started your own army for the money you say you've got."

"Most of my gold is still at that house. I'd made one or two tiny shipments, but they barely paid for equipment."

"Don't look like you're starving to me," Chino muttered.

MacLemore glanced down at his coat. "I owe a heap of money to Sadie's uncle," he explained. "And he wants it paid. He never forgave me for taking his only sister into the Territories. Besides—" His mouth twisted into a grimace of pain and fury. "Those villains killed my wife. They killed my son. They don't deserve my gold as well."

"What makes you think it's still there?" Henry asked.

MacLemore smiled. "Most of it was hidden."

"Where?" Chino asked him. "Where'd you hide it?"

"You'll see when we get there."

Sadie began to dish up the stew. "Ain't but pork-belly and mustard-greens," she said. "But if you don't like it, you can starve."

She handed a bowl to Lu. It smelled good. He stirred it with his fork, searching for a piece of bacon, and was about to take his first bite when a thought suddenly leapt into his head. "What about me?" he asked.

They all looked at him.

"I mean, am I just supposed to ride along and collect firewood?"

MacLemore stared. "Why, you're our explosives expert, of course. Chosen by the great Jack Straw himself. Isn't that right?"

Lu was stunned. The closest he'd ever come to working with explosives was when he helped his grandfather roll firecrackers for the New Year's celebration. Until now, he'd completely forgotten that part of Jack and his grandfather's conversation. At the time he'd been so convinced they were talking about Lung that Lu had allowed all the rest to wash right over him without sinking in. He was about to say as much, but before he got any words out, he looked at Jack.

Instantly, Lu felt as though a steel lock had snapped closed over his tongue. He tried again, but couldn't even manage to unclench his jaw. Jack had done something, Lu felt certain. It was some kind of enchantment. The gunfighter had taken hold of his voice, just as surely as he'd grabbed that smoke out of the air. And Lu couldn't even protest.

Jack lit a cigarette. As he inhaled, his eyes bore down on Lu. The intensity of his glare made Lu break out in a cold sweat.

"That's right." Jack blew a cloud of smoke over their campfire. "Selected by me. But 'til you reach the mine, and can dazzle your new employers with your blasting skills, you have a different job."

"What's that?" Lu croaked.

"To learn."

CHAPTER 4
ON YOUR FEET

LU'S LESSONS BEGAN BEFORE SUNUP the next morning and continued clear through their whole journey.

Each day began with cookery, and by the end of a week he felt like an expert. Lu could bake biscuits in a Dutch oven, stir sow-belly into a pot of mushy stew, and burn coffee to an undrinkable tar as well as any cowboy who ever rode the range. After breakfast Lu did the dishes, and then accompanied Chino in his thrice daily inspection of the wagon and animals.

That first morning, Lu wondered how in the world they were ever going to find the horses. There'd been no sign of them in hours—not since shortly after they'd been set loose the night before. Lu asked, but Chino just said to "leave it to Jack." Sure enough, as soon as they were ready to start saddling, the gunfighter performed another of his minor miracles. He whistled. That's it. He pursed his lips, let out a single sharp blast, and not even a minute later in came the horses. Jack's appaloosa was first, though the gray stallion was close on its heels.

When the stock was all present, saddled, and harnessed, the day's long march began. Back in the States, before they'd crossed the Quapaw River, Lu had spent his days lazing on the high-seat, daydreaming as the landscape drifted past. No longer. Chino made Lu drive the team. It wasn't hard work, but it did keep him facing forward. Hour after hour they trundled through the tall grass prairie. Lu might have gotten bored if not for Chino, who was constantly on the lookout for wildlife. They saw prairie dogs, jack-rabbits, kangaroo rats and ground-hogs in abundance. Less frequent, though by no means rare, were mule deer and pronghorn, the latter of which Chino said was the fastest animal in the Americas. They hadn't seen any buffalo yet, but Chino said there would be huge herds as they got closer to the fort. He also said they'd likely see a grizzly bear or two, and mountain lions if they were lucky. Chino seemed to know everything there was to know about nature, and he had a real gift for description. According to him, a mountain lion could drag a full-grown man right off his horse—a grizzly could knock down a tree as big around as a man's thigh with one swipe of its paw. Lu thought they'd be luckier not to see either one, but didn't say so. He didn't want Chino to think he was a coward.

On their fifth full day out of Scipio, their trail was joined by a second, more deeply-gouged road from the north. That was the road to St. Matthew, Chino explained. Wagon-trains went that way, hoping to cross where the river was wider and shallower and so avoid paying for the ferry. Sure enough, there was a line of wagons just ahead of them, which they passed later that same day.

It wasn't much, as wagon-trains went. Lu had often seen groups of twenty or thirty wagons heading west out of St. Frances. Some of the richer wagon-trains even had whole herds of cattle, bound for the grazing lands of the northern Big Sky Territory. This was just six old prairie schooners, each with its requisite team of oxen and a driver. At least one woman followed after each wagon, and sometimes more. There were also dozens of dirty children, tears running down their faces from the dust. A pair of young gunfighters rode with the train, while a third scouted the path ahead, presumably hired to protect the wagons from marauding Indians and stampeding buffalo. Chino didn't so much as glance at these outriders, so Lu ignored them as well. They waved to the children and drivers, however, and wished the women good luck. One of the older men invited them to camp with the train, but Jack refused.

When they'd passed the last wagon by, Lu asked Chino about it. "Why didn't we camp with them?"

"Because they're settlers," Chino said. "Nice enough folks maybe, but Jack can't stand settlers."

"Why not?"

"Well, because at heart they're thieves. They come to the Territories hoping to get somethin' for nothin'. One of them families will find a meadow, build a cabin, and declare the whole land around settled. Might be land the Indians have grazed their horses on for generations, but all at once it belongs to them what took it. Jack can't stand that. I hate it myself."

They camped that night on a bluff overlooking the trail. In the distance, Lu could see pinpricks of light from a half-dozen fires, and guessed it must be those same settlers. He wondered where they were going. Didn't hardly matter, he supposed. Lu had once heard that twenty-five percent of the folks who start out on a wagon-train never survive the trip. Now he knew why. A few of the younger children had already looked done in. He wondered if they missed their friends, or their old schools, back in whatever towns they'd left behind forever. Lu felt sorry for them, and sorry for himself. At least they have their families with them, he thought, as he laid down and tried to go to sleep.

The next morning, Jack excused Lu from wiping down the breakfast dishes. He said that Lu had passed muster in both dish-cleaning and wagon-driving, and was being moved on to bigger and better things. Excited, Lu trotted over to where Chino was inspecting the wagon and asked him about it. But Chino said that if it had been up to him Lu would be driving the wagon another week, maybe two. That's when Lu saw Sadie, waving at him from across the camp. He didn't have to be asked twice.

"Daddy says I have to teach you to saddle," she said.

"You?" Lu was taken aback. The idea of having a girl not much older than himself taking over as his private schoolmaster hadn't occurred to him. He wasn't sure he liked it. Plus, for whatever reason, Sadie had left her buckskin jacket in the wagon and Lu couldn't help noticing how bosomy she was. He found it all very uncomfortable.

"How many times you ridden?" Sadie asked.

"Once," Lu lied. The closest he'd ever come to riding a horse was a year ago, when he'd climbed onto Mr. Chiu's donkey. It brayed, leapt like a flea, and sent him head first over the nearest fence. Lu hadn't been in too big a hurry to ride since.

"What breed?"

"Appaloosa." Lu winced. It was the only breed he could think of, other than Percheron, and even a city boy knew that sort of lie wouldn't serve.

"Well, we ride quarter-horses," Sadie said. "That one there is Cody. And this here's Cinnamon."

"Nice horses," Lu offered hopefully.

"Be quiet and listen." Sadie shook her head. Lu guessed she'd rather do anything besides teach him. "You always start with the bridle." Sadie grabbed Cinnamon's chin, forcing her thumb and forefinger into either corner of the horse's mouth. Magically, instead of tearing her whole arm off to the elbow, its teeth parted and she slipped in the bit. "See that?" Sadie asked.

Lu nodded.

"Next, you got to smooth the hair on her back, making sure there's no stickers." Sadie ran her hands over Cinnamon's shoulders. "Lay the blanket on nice and high. Then the saddle." Lu noticed for the first time that her saddle was emblazoned all over with tiny flowers—daisies, just like those on her bonnet. "I don't know what sort of tack you're used to, but this here's a California saddle. Sits right over the withers. If it were English, you'd fix it lower. But it ain't. Remember that. I don't want to turn my head and see no bonny prince Charlie ridin' up behind me. Understand?" She reached between the horse's front and rear legs and pulled a padded leather strap tight against its chest. "Look at how she puffs up." Sadie gestured at her horse's belly. "She don't like the girth too tight, so she tries to fool me." Sadie gave the horse a vicious kick. "But I can't be fooled." She looped the leather strap through the rings in her saddle and cinched it down. "Now your turn."

Lu looked over the equipment for Cody. He reached for the blanket.

"Bridle first," Sadie corrected him. "That way, if you should need to tie him off you can."

Lu picked up the bridle. His horse eyed him warily.

"You got to talk to him," Sadie said. "So he'll know you're comin'."

It felt foolish, but Lu did as he was told. "Hello, Cody." He didn't know what to say after that, never having conversed with a horse. "Hello," he said again. "You're a pretty boy. A pretty boy. Pretty boy. Pretty boy."

"He's a horse, not a parrot," Sadie grumbled.

Lu reached for Cody's mouth. Predictably, the horse turned away.

"Grab a hold of his chin," Sadie whispered. "He's got to know you're in charge. Otherwise he can't trust you to protect him."

It was all but impossible to imagine an animal as large as this needing protection, but Lu didn't say so. With a trembling hand he took Cody by the muzzle, drawing his lips to the waiting bridle. The hairs around Cody's mouth were as soft as warm butter.

"Now, just like I shown ya," Sadie said.

Lu put his fingers at the edges of Cody's mouth and squeezed. Amazingly, the horse's jaw opened up and the bit slid right in.

Feeling more confident, Lu smoothed out Cody's hair and placed the blanket on his back. Sadie watched, never saying a word. Lu got the saddle on and situated, fastened the girth, and then stepped back for her to inspect.

"Here, let me show you how to cinch." Sadie heaved at the girth, tightening it by five full inches.

"Not bad for your first time," Jack said, riding over on his appaloosa. "Now climb aboard."

"The horse?" Lu looked at the wagon. He was surprised to see MacLemore sitting in his usual spot on the high seat.

"Either that or walk."

Cautiously, Lu put his foot into the stirrup and swung himself up.

By the time they stopped for the night, Lu's backside was bruised and beaten beyond recognition. He didn't so much dismount as fall out of the saddle. His knees were so sore he could barely stand. His crotch was raw as a new-born calf. Jack let him beg off his chores that night, but said he'd have to do all the cooking the next day.

Soon as he'd downed a bowl of stew, Lu rolled over in the grass and went to sleep. He guessed he'd feel better in the morning. He was wrong.

Lu woke to the worst pain he'd ever felt. The previous evening's agony was only a preview of the real torment. Just sitting up was misery. His hip bones felt as if they'd been ground down to the nerve. Cooking breakfast was torture.

By midway through that second day, Lu sincerely hoped Cody might trip and cast him headfirst against a stone, ending the misery. The pain in his crotch, knees and hind-quarters had all emigrated to his lower back. Lu had to grip the saddle-horn with both hands to keep from falling off. He knew that if he did, he'd never be able to get back on.

Sadie must have seen him grimacing, because she rode up alongside him. "I reckon your stirrups could be let out a bit," she said, after studying him a few moments. "But I don't think that's going to put an end to your pain. You got to *ride* that horse."

"What do you mean?" Lu moaned.

"Gee whiz. You're slumped up there like a sack of fertilizer. Get on your feet. Sit tall. Look at Henry."

Still gripping the saddle-horn with both hands, Lu peered ahead. Henry was reaching into his saddlebag for a stick of jerky. His back was as straight and rigid as a board, and his feet were firmly planted in his stirrups. He wasn't standing in them exactly, but not sitting either.

Lu tried to do the same, and surprisingly, the pain in his back lessened. It didn't go away, but it did ease up a bit.

"That's better." Sadie smiled. "Just keep sittin' like that. Ridin' ain't hard, but it does take some effort. You'll get used to it in no time."

She was right. It took three more days, but Lu eventually became accustomed to riding posture. He learned to keep his toes forward and his heels down. Sitting a trot was still beyond his abilities, but he knew he'd get there. At least now he could bounce off the saddle each evening without moaning or falling down. That was progress.

They were a full two weeks beyond Scipio—nine days since Lu's first lesson in horsemanship—and were camped for the night along a bend of the Clark River, when Henry suddenly strode over to where Lu was sitting by the campfire and told him it was time he learned about guns.

"I'm ready," Lu said. For a long time he'd wondered whether Jack would ever let him handle a weapon. Lu figured every man ought to know how to use a revolver, especially in the Territories. The only question was whether Jack would consider Lu *man* enough to learn. "When do we shoot?"

"That's up to you." Henry handed his rifle to Lu. Surprised at its considerable weight, he nearly dropped it.

"It's heavy," Lu said.

"I'm going to show you how to clean it."

"Clean it?" Lu was disappointed. "Shouldn't we fire it first?"

"When you learn to clean to my satisfaction, I might let you shoot." Henry took a can of gun-oil and a set of coarse brushes from his saddlebags.

Resigned, Lu watched as Henry inspected and oiled his rifle, explaining each part as he came to it.

While they studied the gun, MacLemore took out his guitar and began to pluck. He was good. Since taking over Lu's place on the wagon, he'd grown ever more liberal with his strumming, sometimes playing for a full hour before lying down to sleep. Of all the songs MacLemore knew, Lu's favorite was *Home on the Range*. It had the same throaty hush as the wind whistling over the grass. He also liked *Yellow Rose of Texas*, *Streets of Laredo* and *Rose of Alabama*. The only song he didn't much care for, and which MacLemore took up now in full voice, was *Clementine*. It was too repetitive. It stuck in your mind like cockleburs stuck in your pant-legs.

When the rifle was thoroughly oiled and brushed, Henry

began meticulously wiping down the metal, both inside and out, with a piece of hide.

"How can you tell if it's clean?" Lu asked. It was a dark night. If there was a stain on the weapon, he doubted they'd be able to see it.

"It doesn't need to *look* clean," Henry said. "It needs to *feel* clean." He handed the rifle to Lu. "How does it feel?"

"Slick."

Henry nodded. "Look down the barrel. Hold it to the fire so you can see."

Lu did as he was told.

"See the rifling?"

"That corkscrew bit at the end?"

"It goes all the way down."

"What does it do?"

"Sets the bullet to spinning, so it flies straight and true." Henry took a cartridge from his saddlebag and set it in Lu's palm. It was as big around as his middle finger, and heavy. "I'll show you how to load it." He held up a hollow tube, about a foot long, the only removable part that he hadn't fitted back into the rifle. "This is called a magazine." Henry took a fistful of bullets from his saddlebag and pressed them, one after another, into the tube. When it would hold no more, Henry slid the magazine into the stock of his rifle. "And that's it," he said, once again handing the weapon to Lu.

"All I have to do is pull the trigger?" Lu asked.

"You'd have to thumb back the hammer first."

"Is this a powerful rifle?"

"Powerful enough."

Lu sighted down the barrel. "What kind is it?"

"Spencer .56-.56. Tomorrow you can clean it yourself."

"And then I can shoot?" Lu asked hopefully.

"We'll see."

The next night, while Chino built the fire and Jack sliced their bacon and rolled the last of their cornmeal into balls, Lu cleaned the rifle. They were already out of vegetables, unless they wanted to chew grass, and would soon be at the end of the flour.

There was one last box of bacon, but that too would go fast. Very soon they'd be reduced to a diet of rice and beans. Lu liked the rice just fine—he'd eaten rice two meals a day for most of his life—but wasn't crazy about beans. Sadie complained about the food, and MacLemore suggested that as soon as they saw a buffalo they ought to replace their dwindling supply of meat. Henry paid them no attention. His eyes were fixed on Lu and the rifle.

"Not bad," Henry muttered, inspecting the weapon for excess oil. "You could stand to brush the hammer seating a bit more, and the magazine spring is sticky, but—"

"I can shoot it?" Lu asked.

"Let me think it over."

Lu woke the next morning before sunrise to find Henry standing over him. The eastern sky had already begun to lighten—just enough to see a few hundred yards down the road in either direction. Chino was still sound asleep under the wagon, and the MacLemores were still bedded down beside the fire. Jack was nowhere around.

"Ready to shoot?" Henry whispered.

If Lu had been tired, he wasn't anymore. He bounced to his feet, casting his blanket aside.

Henry led him down the road a short distance, and then pointed at a pair of trees leaning over the river. "There's your target," he said.

"One of those trees?" They were easily fifty yards away. From there, the trunks looked about as thick as one of Lu's wrists.

"See the tree on the left?" Henry asked. "There's a branch sticking out."

Lu squinted. "The little dead one?"

"That's right." Henry handed him the rifle. "First, get down on one knee." Lu did as he was told. "Now, hold the butt flat against your shoulder. Put your elbow on your bent knee. Can you still see that twig?"

"I can see it."

"Good. Sight down the barrel. Put the twig into the 'v' of the sight closest your eye, and directly behind the post of the one furthest away. Got it?"

For some reason, Lu couldn't seem to hold the rifle still. He wondered if there was something wrong with him. His hands had never seemed so shaky before. He squeezed tighter, trying to bring the weapon under control, but the sights just wouldn't stay on the branch.

"Don't strangle the gun," Henry said. "Just hold it. Cradle it. Try taking a deep breath. When you feel calm, fire."

Lu took a deep breath, then another. The rifle settled down a bit. He jerked the trigger, but nothing happened.

"Forgot to cock it," Henry said. He leaned over Lu's shoulder and eased the hammer back. "Now, try again."

This time, when Lu pulled the trigger, the gun seemed to catch fire in his hands. Smoke belched from the barrel. The rifle jumped, striking him on the shoulder and cheek bone and nearly sending him over backward. The roar was deafening. Lu came close to dropping the gun, but didn't. Good thing. He doubted Henry would have let him shoot again if he had.

"Good." Henry patted him on the back. "Very good."

Lu squinted at the tree. "But the twig is still there."

Henry nodded. "You'll have to try again."

Lu got into position, this time holding the rifle even tighter to his shoulder. He'd drawn back the hammer, and was sighting down the barrel, when Henry whispered in his ear. "This time, squeeze the trigger. Don't pinch. Squeeze."

The gun roared for the second time. It hurt his shoulder again, and set his ears to ringing, but Lu was ready for it now.

"Better," Henry said.

"I missed again," Lu groaned. He'd felt certain he would hit it that time.

"But you were closer."

"Maybe your sights are off." The words were barely out of Lu's mouth, and already he wished he could take them back.

Henry stared at him, clearly surprised. "All right, let's see." He took the rifle out of Lu's hand, cocked it, brought it to his shoulder and fired. All together it took about two seconds. In the distance, the dead branch blasted into wood chips, one long piece spinning into the river.

"Sights seem fine to me," Henry said.

"I'm sorry. I didn't mean to—"

"No offense taken. Tomorrow we'll see if you can hit another limb. Two shots each morning. You'll get it eventually."

"Maybe pistols are more my speed," Lu suggested hopefully. Henry just laughed.

Days passed, and still they headed west. All told, Lu guessed they'd been on the road a little more than a month. It was easy to lose track, busy as he was. One day, Chino put new shoes on the MacLemore's horses, and Lu helped. Henry cleaned the pistols, even though they hadn't been fired, and Lu helped. MacLemore sang songs around the campfire, and Lu joined in. He wasn't much of a singer, but MacLemore was still glad to have accompaniment. None of the others so much as hummed. It was an exhausting schedule, but it did keep his mind off his mother and the kids back home. Lu almost began to feel glad he'd come along.

Then one morning Lu awoke and saw, far ahead of them, something white hanging between sky and earth.

"It's snow," Chino declared. "That there is Stuart's Peak. You'll see it better in a few days. *Es muy grande*, huh?"

"Is it part of the Hell Mouth?" Lu asked. Jack had told his grandfather that he was planning to leave them as soon as they'd crossed the canyon. Lu wondered how much time they had left.

"It's the nose," Chino said.

"Do we have to climb it?"

"Naw. Our path goes round the southern side. We'll get a close look though."

They put the draft horses into their harnesses and then Lu began saddling Cody. Sadie didn't even watch him anymore.

"You're still shooting that buffalo gun every morning," she said.

"Two bullets a day," Lu acknowledged. It was a tender point for him. Thus far he'd managed to miss every target Henry set. Finally, one day, he'd shot the trunk of a tree, just to make sure a bullet was actually exiting the barrel.

Lu had just finished cinching down Cody's saddle when Jack rode into camp. "We'll see buffalo today," he announced. "Not much of a herd, but everyone should stick together anyway."

Along about noon, they rode past a half-dozen sickly-looking bison, standing on the edge of the river. The bison watched the wagon as it rattled past, but otherwise made no move. Henry drew his rifle from his scabbard, but didn't fire.

"I thought they'd be bigger," Lu said to Chino. All his life he'd heard of the massive herds of the plains. No story had ever mentioned so sorry a crew of skin and bones as what they'd just passed. It was disappointing. "I don't guess we'll see any more now, what with the mountains and all."

Chino laughed. "See that cloud a few miles ahead of us?"

It was a kind of black haze, hanging against the ground.

"Bad weather?" Lu asked. This was the time of year for storms, though so far they'd seen nothing much to write home about. A few light rains, just enough to refresh the spirit during a long ride, but nothing startling.

"Dust. *Those* are the buffalo."

Lu looked again. The cloud stretched from the northern horizon all the way to the southern, without a break. If it really was a herd, then it must have consisted of hundreds of thousands of beasts. Millions maybe.

"What should we do?" Lu asked.

"Do?" Jack glared at him. "We ride through."

An hour later, they came over a small rise, and there, all at once, was the herd. Lu was struck dumb. These were not the undersized, malnourished animals they'd seen along the river. They were massive, larger than any horse or even an ox. Their heads were easily as big as Lu, with two curving horns as large as a man's forearm. The bison seemed to be all torso, with very little leg. Even so, they moved with a surprising fluidity. The herd was like a river overflowing its banks. As the closest animals started to run, parting before the slow moving wagon, Lu found himself shaking.

"What if they decide to charge us?" he asked.

"They won't," Henry assured him.

Lu wasn't comforted. "Are you going to shoot one?"

"Not yet. Not 'til we're closer to making camp."

"But they'll be gone by then."

"We'll see."

Lu needn't have worried. They saw buffalo throughout the rest of the day. Sometimes they drove straight through the center of the herd. Other times they passed along the outskirts of the great sea of beasts. Henry kept his rifle at the ready, but made no move to kill any of them.

Late in the afternoon, Jack called for them to make camp. It was early, but Lu didn't complain. He was about to unsaddle his horse, but Henry stopped him. "Come with me," he said.

"Can I come, too?" Sadie asked.

"If you like."

The three of them rode back up the trail they'd just traveled.

"Are you going to shoot one?" Lu asked.

Henry nodded.

"Can I?"

"I don't think that's a good idea. I want to be sure we get a clean kill."

They'd only ridden a few hundred yards when Henry called for a stop, and climbed down from his horse. Lu and Sadie did likewise.

There were no buffalo in sight, but the haze of dust was intense. Henry slowly brought his rifle to the ready.

They had to wait nearly a quarter hour, but finally the buffalo came into view, moving southwest at a diagonal to where they stood watching. "Hold the horses tight," Henry whispered, handing his reins to Sadie.

Just then, a half-dozen bison came rushing toward them. The one in the lead was enormous, the largest Lu had yet seen. It snorted and roared as it tore over the ground, leading its lesser brothers and sisters right at them. Lu bit his lip. He couldn't imagine Henry missing his shot, but still had visions of all three of them, and their horses, being trampled to death under the onrushing hooves. "Shoot it," he whispered.

Henry's rifle gave its usual roar, and the largest buffalo sank face first into the dust, skidding for a half-dozen yards before lying perfectly still. A hole the size of a man's fist was punched clean through one eye. Blood turned that whole side of the animal's head a fiery crimson. The other bison turned just short of where the enormous bull now lay dead, and melded once more with the herd.

"Tell Chino and Jack to bring their knives," Henry said, gesturing back toward camp.

"Daddy can help, too," Sadie offered. "He's a fair field butcher."

"Good. The sooner we get the choice bits off this carcass, the sooner we can get to smoking the meat." As he spoke, Henry took the clasp knife from his belt.

Lu looked around, but could see not so much as a single tree. He didn't even know if the river was still close by. "What'll we use for the fire?" he asked. "There's no wood."

Henry kicked a buffalo turd, one of the thousands that lay on the ground all around them, dry as week-old cornbread. "The two of you can gather them up after seeing to the horses. Burns like charcoal."

Neither Sadie nor Lu spoke as they rode back to camp. A small fire was burning and a pot of beans set over it to boil. Lu told them what Henry had said. Chino borrowed Sadie's horse Cinnamon, MacLemore mounted Cody, and Jack climbed atop his appaloosa. As soon as they were gone, Lu and Sadie began gathering buffalo chips to feed the fire. By the time the men returned with the meat, there'd be a pile waist high.

"He's hell for shootin', ain't he?" Sadie said, as they carried the first load of fuel into camp.

"Henry? He sure is."

"Reckon he'd let me shoot with y'all? Just a bullet or two one mornin'?"

"Can't see why not. Ask him."

Sadie smiled. "I just might."

CHAPTER 5
CIVILIZATION

IT TOOK THEM THREE MORE DAYS to reach Fort Jeb Stuart, but Lu didn't mind. The prairie was green, the mountains purple and white, and he enjoyed the company of his traveling companions a little more with every passing day. He'd even managed to hit one of the targets Henry set for him. Sadie turned out to be a far better shot, but that was an irritation he'd soon got over. In fact, the only downside to travel, so far as Lu could see, was the food. They had run out of everything but beans and buffalo, neither of which he particularly liked. He ate both, of course, huge plates-full every time they stopped. But he dreamed of a bit of spicy beef over noodles, the kind his mother made, with garlic and brown sauce, and a hot cup of tea.

Finally, late one afternoon, when their camp had been set up and the beans were boiling over the fire, they saw something twinkling, far away in the foothills.

"That'll be Jeb Stuart," Jack said. "We'll reach it tomorrow."

They were all very excited. MacLemore said he planned to get a shave and a haircut, eat a beefsteak, and spend a lazy evening in a saloon, enjoying what he called "civilized drink." Chino and Henry were more interested in gambling, though Chino thought he might also buy a bottle of whiskey or a plug of chewing tobacco. Sadie fancied a long soak in a hot tub and a night in a soft bed. Lu thought all of those things sounded fine, but was more excited to see the town. He wondered if there'd be any real live mountain men, or maybe even a gunfight.

Lu woke up that night with an icy chill creeping up and down his spine. At first he blamed it on nerves. Just excited to get into Fort Jeb Stuart, he thought. But the chill refused to subside. The strangest part was that this was the most humid night they'd spent on the prairie yet. Lu scratched the back of his neck and found his hair sopping wet. No one else seemed to be suffering. Henry was fast asleep, his rifle tucked under one arm. MacLemore was rolled up in his blanket, snoring loudly. Sadie groaned and rolled onto her side, but gave no sign of waking.

At last, the creeping feeling got so bad that Lu decided to get up. Maybe if he took a short walk he'd be able to go back to sleep. Without even thinking, Lu started down the trail toward the mountains. Ahead of him, the lights of Fort Jeb Stuart burned as bright as ever.

After a half-mile or so, Lu noticed someone standing in the road ahead. It was Jack. He was smoking a cigarette and staring at the mountains. The gunfighter turned as Lu approached, squinted down at the boy for a moment, and then blew out a cloud of white smoke.

"Am I bothering you?" Lu asked him.

"What are you doing up?"

"I had a chill." Lu stood next to Jack, crossing his arms in imitation of the older man. "What are you looking at?"

Jack pointed at Stuart's Peak. "Watch," he said.

Lu began to feel the same chill running up his spine, only stronger. He was about to say as much when he saw five glistening points of light fly up over the snows on top of the mountain.

They were on fire, whatever they were, and moving fast. Sparks bounded off to either side as they raced down the slope, building speed. As they neared the tree-line, Lu winced. He half-expected to see the whole range blaze up like a bonfire.

As the points of light drew closer Lu imagined he could hear a gang of cowboys cursing their horses. He couldn't tell whether the sounds were coming from up on the mountain or from inside his own mind. He was about to ask Jack when, all at once, the flaming specks turned sharply and went racing across the foothills.

They blasted along until they came to a gully, and then turned and cut back up and over the ridge. When they'd reached the top, and had no more mountain to climb, they shot skyward, scaling a puff of darkened cloud.

And then, just as instantly as they'd appeared, the dots of light were gone.

Lu sighed as the chill in his back receded. "Was it lightning?" he asked hopefully. "Or shooting stars?"

"Wish it were," Jack said. "Those were ghost-riders."

"What?"

"Demons. Servants of darkness. Only the innocent and the damned can see them."

"What do they do?"

"Mostly they search for sinners. Locate weak souls for their masters."

"And then what? What do they do to them?"

"Well, ghost-riders can take human form if they're particularly riled. But that's unusual. For the most part they don't do anything. They watch and listen. That's it."

"They must have a lot to watch for."

"Territories are full of sinners," Jack agreed. "Fort Jeb Stuart included."

They stood a while longer, Lu wondering all the time if the ghost-riders would reappear.

"Do you think they might've been looking for us?" he asked finally.

Jack shrugged. "Never can tell who or what the ghost-riders might take up with. Could be they're working for MacLemore's Yankee bandit. I wouldn't be surprised."

Another shiver ran up Lu's spine. He looked down at his boots, hoping Jack hadn't noticed. "Can I ask you something else?" Lu asked.

"Shoot."

"Do you know who the bandits are? The ones that stole MacLemore's gold, I mean." He waited, but Jack just stared at him. "I wondered, because I heard you talking with Grandfather and—"

"Better not to talk about that just yet," Jack said. He pointed at the mountains. "Evil's always listening. Remember that. It's their ears that are the real problem, much more than their eyes. Say the wrong name and the ghost-riders *will* find you. Especially at night."

"So you *do* think they're working for the Yankee."

Just then, from behind them they heard the approach of footsteps. It was Sadie. Her eyes were still mostly closed and her hair was sweaty. She looked at Jack and Lu, and yawned. "Did y'all feel it too?" she asked. "I wouldn't have guessed there could be such a cold wind on such a hot night."

They rolled into Fort Jeb Stuart not long after mid-day. MacLemore went to the barber, Sadie to the hotel, and Chino and Henry to the saloon. The hotel and saloon were actually the same building, Lu observed, though with separate entrances. Jack tied both of his horses to a post and then climbed onto the wagon. He was about to drive off when he noticed Lu, still sitting astride MacLemore's horse.

"What about you?" Jack asked him

Lu had no plans. This town wasn't as exciting as he'd hoped. It was only two blocks long and sparsely populated. A few ladies stood on a balcony over the saloon/hotel, brushing their hair and waving at the odd passerby—one even waved at Lu—but he wasn't particularly interested in them. A dry-goods store was open across the street, and it had jars of hard candy in the window, but Lu had no money and didn't much like sweets anyhow. His mother stocked all sorts of candies in their store back home. Being able to eat it anytime he liked, candy just didn't seem like a treat.

"Well, come along with me then," Jack said.

Lu followed Jack and the wagon out past the edge of town, finally reining to a stop in front of a pair of log cabins with iron bars over the windows. An American flag had been run up a pole between the two buildings. It hung lifeless in the stifling midday air.

"This must be the fort," Lu thought, as Jack leapt down off the wagon and strode into the smaller of the two cabins. He emerged a few minutes later with a cavalry officer.

The officer had a felt hat perched rakishly atop his head and long golden curls that cascaded over his shoulders. Lu had never seen so much hair on a man before. Jack led the officer to the back of the wagon and yanked down the drop-gate.

"There's the Hotchkiss," he said, pointing at the crate they'd hauled all the way across the plains. "You'll need help to unload it. The damn thing's heavy."

The officer strode to the door of the other cabin and shouted for help. Six soldiers filed out. Not one so much as glanced at Lu, but they all took a hearty interest in Jack.

The soldiers climbed into the wagon, pushing aside tools and lumber, and then shoved the big crate back toward the drop-gate. Grunting, they lifted it out of the wagon and set it on the ground. The long-haired officer used a claw hammer to pry off the lid.

Lu crowded in amongst the soldiers, as interested as they were in what the crate might contain. He was surprised to see the barrel of a cannon, packed in amidst a sea of balled-up paper and wood shavings.

"Looks like it's in fair shape," the officer said. "Those heathens will be damn sorry to see this coming at them."

The soldiers lifted the cannon barrel out of the crate and carried it to a shed behind the fort. Then they broke the crate into kindling and piled it in a bin beside the barracks door. The packing material they left lying in the yard.

Meanwhile, their officer had moved to the head of the wagon and was inspecting the horses, beginning with their hooves.

"Dragged this heap all the way from St. Frances, did they?" he asked. He didn't wait for an answer, but moved on to inspect their front legs and teeth. "They look strong enough. We'll buy them."

"I'd just as soon trade for a mule team," Jack said. "Save me a stop."

The officer thought the proposition over. "How many mules?"

"Six. Plus harness."

Judging by his smirk, the officer clearly thought he was getting the better of the deal. "You want them hooked to the wagon?" he asked.

Jack nodded.

"Fine. They'll be ready tomorrow morning, along with your cargo."

"Good enough." Jack beckoned to Lu. They untied Cody from the post where Lu had left him, and started back toward town.

They'd only gone a few steps when the officer called out. "Just one other thing," he said. "Were you ever in the army?" He was looking at Jack's coat. Lu was so used to seeing the gunfighter in it that he hardly noticed it anymore.

"I was," Jack replied. "During the war."

"You wear stars. Were you a General?"

Jack shook his head. "The General gave me this coat a few years back."

"And which General was that?"

"*The* General," Jack said. Then he turned and stalked away.

The cavalry officer stared after him, a look of profound disbelief etched over his face. Lu hadn't the foggiest idea which General Jack was referring to, and didn't have the guts to ask. Jack considered such things as the identities of Generals to be common knowledge. Lu would've been ashamed to admit he didn't know about something so simple.

Back in town they went first into the dry-goods store, where Jack bought provisions, and then to the hotel. Sadie was sitting in an armchair in the lobby. She told them that there was only one bathtub in the whole town, and it was being used by a gambler from back east. She also said that the gambler had invited her to share, but that she'd refused. Lu didn't really believe that, but he blushed all the same.

As usual, Jack paid not the slightest attention to Lu or Sadie. Casual conversation simply didn't interest him. He went right up to the front desk and asked the proprietor if there were any letters for him.

"As a matter of fact, there is one," the hotel-keeper said. He was an apish man, with a round belly and waxed mustache. He took an envelope from a drawer and handed it to Jack. "Came three weeks ago. I'd have thrown it away by now if it'd been addressed to anyone else."

Jack tore the envelope open and read the note inside. Lu couldn't tell from looking at him whether it contained good news or bad. Jack had a sort of permanent bad-news expression, which got worse once in a while, but never seemed to get any better.

"Jeb in town?" he asked.

The hotel-keeper nodded. "I expect he's looking for you."

Jack signaled to Lu. "Come with me," he said. "Jeb will want to meet you."

They walked to the end of the block, turning right on the only cross-street in town. At the end of that road stood a rough house, half sunk in the earth, with mud and wattle walls and a plank roof. They were only about half-way to it when the front door swung open, and out stepped the largest man Lu had ever seen.

He had arms like a grizzly bear and a beard to match. His clothes were well-worn buckskin, decorated with claws, teeth, and bits of bone. Atop the man's head was what looked to be the rear two-thirds of a beaver, its flat tail hanging down to brush the man's enormous shoulders. He mounted the steps leading up from his front door and crossed his arms.

"Jack Straw," he growled. "Glad you finally saw fit to drop by. You've only seen everybody else in the whole dern town."

"How are you, Jeb?" Jack asked.

"Mean as a snake." Jeb peered down at Lu. "And who in blazes is this?"

"Tzu-Lu," Jack said. "He's K'ung's grandson."

"Well now, *that* changes everythin'." Jeb took Lu's hand and gave it a hearty shake, nearly dislocating his shoulder. "How is your granddad?"

"He's fine, sir," Lu squeaked.

"Sir?" Jeb laughed. "That's a new one on me. What'd old K'ung used to say?" He paused to think. "*'To learn, and at due time to repeat what you have learned, is that not a pleasure?*

Like an old friend come from a long journey.' Your Granddad still say that?"

"Whenever I complain about my schoolwork," Lu said.

Jeb roared with laughter. "K'ung used to say I was the most un-teachable, uncultured lout he'd ever met. I guess we've got somethin' in common."

They followed Jeb into his house. Judging by the outside, Lu had expected it to be tiny, barely even a shack. He was surprised to see that it was not only large, but clean and well lit. And it wasn't just a house—it was a trading post, as well. In one corner, piled floor to ceiling, were skins taken from just about every animal that walked, loped, scurried or swam through that part of the world. Jeb also had traps of all sizes, including a set of steel jaws large enough to pinch a full-grown man in two. Along the walls were shelves stacked high with boxes of ammunition, saddles and tack for a dozen horses, and replacement parts for rifles of every make or description.

"Look here, Janey!" Jeb called as he stomped inside. "Jack Straw's come for a visit. And he's brought a youngster."

Jeb led his visitors to the back of the house and into a comfortable sitting area. There were two chairs to one side and a bed on the other. Jack and Lu took the chairs while Jeb plopped himself down on the bed, its wood frame groaning under his considerable weight. An Indian woman in a blue gingham dress came bustling through a door in the back. She was carrying a pitcher of beer and four glasses.

While she poured, Jeb kicked off his boots and flung his hat on a table in the corner, revealing a head as bald as an egg. "Now then," he said. "What can we do for you?"

"Look at this." Jack tried to hand him the letter, but Jeb waved it off.

"Can't read a lick," he said. "Never cared to learn."

"It's from Pap Singleton."

"Is that right? How is old Pap?"

"He's been having some trouble."

"Is that big trouble, or just the ordinary kind?"

"Hard to say. He wants me to come down and take a look."

"Well, I guess you'd best get to it then. Pap ain't one to cry wolf."

Lu sipped his beer. He found the conversation difficult to follow. Lu had no idea who Pap Singleton might be, or what sort of trouble he might be having. Nor could he see what any of this might have to do with their mission.

"It's a long trip though," Jeb muttered. "Too bad Bill ain't around. That border was his area, warn't it?"

Jack nodded.

"So what's your plan?"

"I'll head down there as soon as I can. But first I've got to deliver a gang of treasure hunters through the Hell Mouth." He motioned toward Lu. "That's where he's going."

"The Hell Mouth? That'll shorten your ride considerably, if you make it. Haven't been that way in years myself." Jeb shook his head. "It's grown dangerous. If you want to know about pathways through, you'll have to find Joseph."

"I figured as much," Jack said. He turned to Jeb's wife. "Janey, do you have any idea where he is?"

"It's summer, so I expect he's up in his pastures." It was the first time she'd spoken, and Lu was surprised. He'd read a good many stories about Indians, and considered himself well educated in the halting, studied manner of their speech, especially when talking to a white man. But Janey had no trace of accent. None whatever. If he hadn't been looking right at her, Lu might have thought she was from St. Frances, or even further east.

"Can I find him?" Jack asked her.

"If he wants you to," Janey said. "My guess is that he'll want to see you."

"I know he will. I brought a wagon this trip."

Janey's eyebrows raised. Though she didn't ask what might be *in* the wagon, Lu got the distinct impression that she knew only all too well. He was beginning to get the feeling that everyone in the world knew more about their adventure than he did.

They talked a great deal more, about the Hell Mouth, MacLemore and his Yankee problem, and various people they'd known over the years. Lu didn't have much to contribute, but he listened contentedly. By the time they'd finished, the sun was sinking into the mountains, bathing the snows atop Stuart's Peak in orange light.

"Wait just one minute," Janey said, as they were about to step out the front door. She disappeared into her kitchen, emerging with a small bundle wrapped in cheese-cloth.

"This is for you," she said, handing it to Lu. "It's cake, for after dinner. Give some to that girl you're riding with. But don't let Chino see. He's got a sweet tooth."

"And tell Henry and Chino that we expect to see them both before you set out," Jeb added. He shook Lu's hand again, so hard it rattled his teeth.

"We'll bring the wagon by at first light," Jack promised. "I'll need supplies."

"Anything special?" Janey asked.

"The usual."

Jeb laughed. "Same old Jack."

As they walked back through town, Lu thought over the conversation he'd just sat through. "Who is Pap Singleton?" he asked Jack.

"Pap? He's a friend of mine. A former slave, as a matter fact. He started a little town down along the border. It's a kind of sanctuary. A place where freedmen can live without interference from whites . . . . He also keeps an eye on the border."

"What sort of trouble is he having?" Lu asked.

Jack glared at him. "Is that something you need to know? Or you just nosy?"

Lu shook his head. "Just asking."

They were passing the hotel when Lu thought of another question. "Who's Joseph?"

"Janey's brother," Jack replied.

"And he knows how to get through the Hell Mouth?"

"Maybe." Jack grinned. "I guess we'll find that out soon enough."

They found the other four members of their party already in the saloon. MacLemore sat beside the piano player—a blonde lady Lu had seen on the balcony earlier—singing *Jeannie with the Light*

Brown Hair. Judging by the timbre of his voice, Lu guessed he'd already had a few civilized drinks too many. Sadie sat at a nearby table. Her hair was damp and hung to her shoulders. A half-empty glass of beer sat in front of her. Henry and Chino were farther back, playing cards with two other men. Henry had a good-size pile of chips at his elbow. Chino was down to a dollar or two.

Lu took a seat opposite Sadie. "Janey Stuart sent this for us," he said, setting the cake down on the table.

Sadie peered under the cheese-cloth and grinned. She pinched off a bit of the yellow cake and dropped it on her tongue. "It's good." She held the rest out to Lu, who also took a pinch.

Jack asked the bartender about supper and was told that he'd have to go next door, but that the hotel would bring over their food as soon as it was hot. While he was gone, MacLemore and the piano player started in on a rousing rendition of *Dixie*. They were so boisterous that a few of the other saloon ladies came downstairs to see what the racket was all about. Most stayed to join in the singing.

> *O, I wish I was in the land of cotton*
> *Old times there are not forgotten*
> *Look away! Look away!*
> *Look away! Dixie land!*
>
> *In Dixie land where I was born in*
> *Early on one frosty mornin'*
> *Look away! Look away!*
> *Look away! Dixie land!*
>
> *O, I wish I were in Dixie. Away! Away!*
> *In Dixie land I'll make my stand*
> *To live and die in Dixie*
> *Away! Away! Away down south in Dixie!*

That was as much as anyone else knew of the song, so MacLemore had to continue on alone, singing ever louder to take up the slack.

Lu was surprised at the words that followed, and judging by the looks on the upstairs ladies' faces, he wasn't the only

one. What MacLemore sang was unlike any portion of *Dixie* Lu
had ever heard. Its tone was no longer gay and airy. In fact, it
was downright dark. Whoever wrote these words had done so
clearly intending to shame the Union, if not to pose an outright
threat. The only one who seemed oblivious to this fact was
MacLemore himself.

> *Hear the northern thunders mutter!*
> *Northern flags in South winds flutter!*
> *Look away! Look away!*
> *Look away, Dixie land!*

> *Send them back your fierce defiance!*
> *Stamp upon the cursed alliance!*
> *Look away! Look away!*
> *Look away, Dixie land!*

By this time, Lu had begun to seriously question the wisdom
of allowing this song to continue. He couldn't help thinking of
that long-haired cavalry officer and all his soldiers, stationed just
a short walk down the road. Lu guessed they wouldn't like this
song one bit. Northern soldiers, especially those stationed in the
Territories, were known far and wide for their intolerance of
rebel sympathizers. The war might be over, but it hadn't been forgotten. Not by anybody.

Lu glanced at Sadie. She seemed to be thinking the same thing.
Casually, as though nothing were wrong, she stepped toward her
father. But she wasn't in time to prevent the next two verses.

> *Fear no danger! Shun no labor!*
> *Lift up rifle, pike and saber!*
> *To arms! To arms!*
> *To arms, Dixie land!*

> *For faith betrayed and pledges broken!*
> *Wrongs inflicted, insults spoken!*
> *To arms! To arms!*
> *To arms, Dixie land!*

At last, Sadie convinced the piano player to quit tinkling the keys. MacLemore looked as though he might continue singing, music or no, but then he too fell silent.

Unfortunately, the damage had already been done. Just as Sadie regained her seat, the bat-wing doors swung wide and a trio of soldiers sauntered in. They were young—younger even than the soldiers Lu had seen that afternoon—and full of newfound manhood. The army-issue rifles they carried were polished and oiled 'til they shone like blue lightning. Their mustaches and sideburns were trimmed with an attention to detail suggesting a newfound love of the barber's arts.

"We heard music," the first one through the door said. His mustache was waxed and twisted up at either end. He seemed to be their leader. "Ain't that right, Will?"

The man to his left nodded. "Heard somethin' all right."

"You hear it too, Jim?"

"Sounded like a dern Reb anthem to me."

"That's just what I thought, though I could scarce believe my ears."

"We was just havin' a sing, Tom," the piano player explained. "Nobody meant no harm. Honest they didn't." But the soldiers took no notice of her explanation.

"I'll tell you boys," Tom said, further twisting up the ends of his mustache as he talked, "this town gets sorrier ever' day. But I'll be darned if I thought I'd ever come into our saloon and see this. Near as I can tell we got a drunken Reb at the piano, a coon playin' cards with a Mexican, and a Chinese sitting right out front, beer and cake on his table just as though he was a white man. That's one too many for me. Hells bells, I start to wonder if my horse didn't kick me and I'm dreamin'. What say boys? Have I gone plumb out of my mind?"

"Could be," said a voice from outside.

Startled, all three soldiers spun around. Jack Straw glared at them over the top of the swinging doors.

"And just what do you want?" the soldier on the left asked. His voice quavered. He brought his gun up, covering his chest with the stock.

"Thought I'd wet my whistle," Jack said, "but you three have the door blocked."

He elbowed his way into the saloon. Lu could feel the tension rise with every step the gunfighter took.

"No beefsteaks," Jack said, taking the chair next to Sadie's. "I told the cook we'd et nothing but beans since before any of us could remember, so we'd take anything else she might like to heat up."

The soldiers watched, fires blazing in their eyes, as Jack discussed supper, ignoring their very existence. At last, Tom spoke up. "You bring him in here?" he asked, gesturing at Lu with his rifle.

Jack glanced over, as though surprised to see the same trio of soldiers still standing in front of the door. "Who? Him?" He pointed across the table at Lu, who wanted nothing so much as to sink through the floor and out of sight. "I guess he brought himself. This is still a free country, isn't it?"

That last comment must have puzzled the soldiers somewhat. They looked at each other. Not even Tom seemed able to think of anything to say.

"Tell you what, why don't you boys have a drink?" Jack suggested. "It's clear you've had a rough day. Take the edge off."

"We don't drink with no Rebs," Tom grunted. "Coons neither."

"Suit yourselves." Jack waved to the bartender, who immediately began pouring him a beer.

The soldiers glared. Not one of the three moved from his post beside the door.

"Seems to me that if you're dead set against having a drink with the folks that are in the saloon, you'd best run along," Jack said.

Still, none of the three moved.

"Now look," Jack said, "I've asked nicely—" As he spoke, a pistol appeared in his hand. Lu didn't see him draw it. In fact, he *didn't* draw it—Jack stuck out his hand and the revolver snapped out of thin air. It happened so fast the soldiers didn't even have time to flinch. "I don't want to have to start shouting," Jack finished.

The whole saloon seemed to hold its breath.

"Cheese it," Tom said at last. "This ain't much of a party anyhow. 'Sides, we'll have us a real good rip next week, after we've finished off them Green Woods Injuns. C'mon boys."

They shoved their way back through the bat-wing doors.

Soon as they were gone, Jack holstered his pistol.

"Lucky you came back when you did," Lu sighed.

"Yep. Much more lip and Chino would've shot those boys."

Lu looked toward the back of the room. Henry was shuffling cards, peaceful as ever. Chino, on the other hand, sat with his arms crossed, staring at the still swinging doors. The expression on his face was pure scorn.

"Let's have some music," Jack called to the piano player. "But keep off the war songs. Just a nice peaceful tune."

"Make a request?"

"Can you play *My Old Kentucky Home?*"

The piano player could, and did. MacLemore joined in on the second verse.

The next morning, Lu stepped out of the hotel to find Chino sitting high on the wagon seat, just as he had for so many weeks. The only difference was that now, instead of two enormous horses he had a team of six mules to pull it.

"What's in the back?" Lu asked.

"Take a look." Chino's smile stretched from ear to ear.

Lu walked around to the tail-gate and peered over. The entire bed was covered, wall to wall and front to back, with rifles. Lu guessed there were at least a hundred of them, maybe more. There were also the same old tools, lumber, and even the laundry bag with Lu's fresh clothes, still untouched. But all of that sat atop a sea of weaponry.

"Where'd they come from?" Lu asked.

"Soldiers got new guns, so they traded these to Jack."

"Do they work?"

"Of course they work."

"What'll we do with them all?"

"Do? Why, we'll trade 'em. What else?"

Lu wondered to whom they could possibly trade a wagon-load of old rifles between here and the Hell Mouth, and for what. But before he had a chance to ask, Chino gave his reins a flip and the mules began dragging the wagon down the road. "Follow me up to Jeb's," he said. "We got more to load yet."

Janey was standing on the front steps when they arrived. "Here are your cartridges," she said, pointing to a dozen or more boxes stacked in front of the door.

Chino picked up as many as he could carry. Lu did the same. He was surprised at how much a carton of bullets weighed.

They'd deposited the first load in the wagon, and were just about to go back for a second, when Jeb emerged from the cabin. He had two wooden apple boxes, one under each arm.

"Guess these are yours, Lu," Jeb said, handing him one of the boxes. It was heavy for its size, but not nearly as heavy as the cartons of rifle-shells. "Don't worry, this here's prime material," Jeb assured him. "You've got my word on that." They set both boxes carefully inside the wagon.

"Thanks," Lu said. Standing up inside each box were four tin cans. There was also a bundle of greasy string. Lu hadn't the foggiest idea what it was.

While he was looking at the boxes, Lu noticed something else, glinting from beneath the pile of dull gray rifle barrels. Digging it out, he discovered a pistol. It was very much like the ones Jack wore, only made of brass instead of steel. Lu dug down again and came up with a holster. The leather was partially rotted away, but more than enough remained to hold the gun.

He was still admiring his find when Henry rode up.

"It's a counterfeit," Henry explained. "A copy of a Union sidearm. Navy style. Confederates made them during the war. I've heard some were fairly decent guns."

Lu buckled the holster around his waist.

Jack arrived with the MacLemores a few minutes later. Mr. MacLemore looked as though he'd been sick during the night, and planned to remain sick throughout the day. Sadie had changed into a clean shirt and bonnet.

"What did you find?" Jack asked, pointing at Lu's gun.

"It was under the rifles." Lu drew the revolver and held it up for Jack to see. "Can I keep it?"

"Can't see why not. Just don't fire it until Henry's had a chance to look it over. A gun like that could be dangerous."

"I won't," Lu promised. "Heck, I don't even have any bullets."

Sadie laughed.

THE AIR GREW COOL as they climbed into the mountains. Mornings they woke to find the grass, trees, and even their blankets sodden with dew. Cooking, once considered the most odious of chores, was suddenly desirable. Sitting closest the fire, hands over a steaming pot, was a fair way to spend the evening. Boiling the morning coffee was even better.

In no time they'd skirted the southern edge of Stuart's Peak, and were winding through alpine valleys corralled by pine trees and dotted with wildflowers.

One morning—it was MacLemore's turn to stir the breakfast—Jack came trotting into camp, his horse already streaming sweat. As usual, the gunfighter had spent his night alone. MacLemore offered him a cup of coffee, but Jack refused it.

"There's a boulder," he announced, reining his appaloosa to a halt behind the wagon. "It must've broke loose last winter. At first, I thought we might float the wagon around it, but I doubt the mules'd survive." He looked at Lu. "We'll have to remove it."

"We?" Lu asked.

Jack reached into the wagon, taking out a sledgehammer, an old bucket, a steel rod, and one of Jeb Stuart's mysterious boxes.

Lu watched, mystified.

"Go on then," Jack said. "Saddle up."

"But what about the others?"

"They'll follow." Jack handed the rod and bucket to Lu.

By noon they were riding along the banks of a river. It was by far the angriest stretch of water Lu had ever seen. Every inch was churning foam, dotted here and there by jagged shards of granite, broken off from the sheer slopes that rose to either side. This river was as little like the Quapaw as a sparrow was like an eagle. The roar of the water was enough to send cold shudders up his spine.

"Here it is." Jack had to shout to be heard over the roaring stream.

A chunk of stone as large as a sharecropper's hut blocked the trail ahead. A horse and rider might climb around it, but the wagon certainly couldn't.

"How do we move it?" Lu asked.

Jack slid down off his horse. "You'll have to blow it up."

"Me?"

"You're our explosives expert."

"But . . . I mean—"

"First, get down off that horse." Jack waited until Lu was on his feet. "Now, put your hands on the stone. Feel anything?"

"Like what?"

"Your Granddad used to say he could feel the veins running through a rock. Tried to teach me, but I could never feel a thing."

"Grandfather taught you?"

Jack nodded. He must've noticed the look of disbelief on the boy's face because he laughed. "You didn't think I was born knowing how?"

Lu started. The idea of anyone teaching Jack Straw how to do anything was strange enough—so far as Lu was concerned, Jack knew and could do EVERYTHING, and better than anyone else, too—but imagining him as a newborn baby was just too much.

"Try thinking your way into the rock," Jack suggested. "Old K'ung would close his eyes and sort of reach out to the stone."

Lu did as he was told. The boulder felt dusty beneath his outstretched fingers.

As he ran his hands over the surface of the rock, Lu wondered what he should be searching for. "Veins," Jack had said. Lu tried imagining the boulder as a living being. To destroy it, they'd have to reach down past its skin, right to its heart.

Almost instantly, Lu felt something smooth and warm brush by under his fingers. He tried to find it again, but couldn't seem to locate the right spot. Discouraged, he opened his eyes. A bit of mica jutted out of the boulder directly in front of him. He touched it, expecting to find the glassy rock cool. But it was warm. Hot even. "I think we should try here," he said.

"Feel something?" Jack asked.

Lu shrugged.

"Well, let's give it a go." Jack handed him the steel rod. It was about two and a half feet long, and as big around as a grown man's thumb.

"What is this?" Lu asked.

"A bit," Jack said. "We'll have to drill."

Lu held the bit while Jack heaved the sledge. It was nerve-wracking work. Every time Jack swung the hammer over his shoulder, Lu's rational mind told him to drop the bit and get his hands out of harm's way. It only took a half-dozen good swipes before his palms were singing, his wrists numb. That he avoided dropping the bit seemed to him miraculous. Jack's portion of the work was no less difficult. Sweat ran down his face as he repeatedly lifted and then let the hammer fall. By the end of an hour, the bit had reached to a depth of about two feet.

"Gather some sand," Jack said. He was breathing hard.

Lu took the bucket and began scooping handfuls of grit from the riverbank. The sand was littered with small stones, sticks and other bits of rubbish. When the bucket was half full, he dragged it back to the boulder.

"Time to set the charge," Jack said. He took one of the tin cans from Jeb's box and handed it to Lu. "Dump that in the hole."

"What is it?"

"Blasting powder."

Lu did as he was told. As soon as he'd finished, Jack handed him the bundle of greasy string. "Cut enough fuse to reach the powder," he said.

Using Jack's knife, Lu cut the fuse and snaked it down the hole.

"Good." Jack pointed at the bucket. "Now, pack in the sand."

"It's full of stones."

"Doesn't matter. Put it all in."

When the sand was in the hole, Jack handed Lu the drill bit again. "You've got to pack it down," he said.

Using the back of the bit, Lu rammed the sand down into the rock.

"Now what?"

Jack handed him a match. "Soon as you've lit it, run."

"Where?"

The gunslinger pointed back up the gorge, in the direction from which they'd come. He was already walking away, the box of blasting powder cradled under one arm, and the sledge and drill bit in the other. The horses followed him.

Lu eyed the fuse trailing from the boulder. It was only an inch long. His fingers shook. What if he'd made a mistake and the rock exploded before he got away? He turned to look after the gunfighter. Jack stood a hundred yards distant, lighting a cigarette. The horses stood behind him.

There was nothing else to do, so Lu struck the match. Immediately, the fuse began to spark and hiss. Needing no further urging, Lu turned and ran. He'd only just reached Jack when he felt the charge go off. Air, pushed so hard it felt almost solid, struck against his shoulders and neck, followed a split-second later by the sound of the explosion.

When the smoke finally cleared, and the gravel had all fallen out of the sky, they saw that the boulder was blocking the trail just as completely as ever it had. Lu was crestfallen. "It didn't work," he muttered.

Jack strode back to the work site. "You expected too much," he said. "That charge broke half the stone. One more good blast and it should be passable. Back to work."

Actually, Lu wound up setting two more charges before the path was clear, and even then they'd had to throw a lot of granite into the river by hand. But still, Jack was right. Lu had done it. By the time Chino and the others reached the gorge, the boulder was utterly destroyed, leaving only rubble as evidence that it'd ever been.

"Look at all that smoke," Chino said, as he passed by in the wagon.

"So how'd he do?" MacLemore asked.

"Fine," Jack said. "He did just fine."

They reached the end of the gorge later that same day. The river, so recently a churning ribbon of deafening whitewater, emptied onto a peaceful valley, forming an oblong lake of crystalline blue surrounded by verdant grass.

Jack afforded them only a short rest before guiding them across the valley and into the forest beyond.

Lu was amazed by the colors. The needles on the trees were darkest green. Their trunks were gray, red or golden. He saw, deep beneath the shadows of the towering firs and pines, his first blue spruce, its needles as tough and prickly as those of a porcupine.

They'd gone a little more than a mile when Jack signaled for a stop.

"What are we stopping for?" MacLemore asked.

"We're being watched," Chino whispered.

"Watched?" MacLemore peered suspiciously at the shadows beneath the trees.

Jack took a cigarette from his shirt pocket. He lit it and took a long drag. As he exhaled, Lu heard the first sounds of approach. He reached for his pistol. There were still no bullets in his gun, but Lu felt better holding it.

"Put that away," Jack said.

"But what if—"

Jack glared at him, and Lu slipped the pistol back into its holster.

No sooner was his weapon stowed than an Indian boy—not much older than Lu, if a shade taller—rode out of the trees directly ahead of them. His buckskin shirt was decorated with animal teeth, and dyed in streaks of crimson and ocher. Round his neck hung a string of white beads. His hair was adorned with feathers.

The Indian gave only cursory glances to the rest of their party before riding over to Jack. When they were side by side, Jack handed him the cigarette he'd so recently lit. The boy took a puff and handed it back.

"Father sent me to find you," the boy said. "He says you are late."

"There was a boulder," Jack explained. "Took us a while to remove it."

"We heard."

After that, Jack spoke to the Indian in his own language. Lu listened close, but couldn't tell whether Jack and the Indian boy were friends, enemies or just casual acquaintances. Their whole conversation blended into a stream of indecipherable noise, punctuated by questions, grunts and meaningful silence. He felt the way he imagined a white person must feel whenever his mother and grandfather began to argue in Chinese. It was a suspicious, fearful sensation.

And then, all at once, the Indian boy wheeled his horse about and gave it a kick. Jack was right behind him.

They followed the Indian boy deep into the forest. At long last, they saw smoke floating amidst the tree-tops. Lu wondered where they were being led. He'd heard that Indians were masters of camouflage. A war party could be anywhere, he figured, just waiting to spring their trap.

His fears seemed to be realized when, passing through a grove of enormous sugar-pines, they came face to face with a delegation of Indian warriors. Lu counted forty-seven, each mounted and ready for battle. Behind them, arrayed along the banks of a shallow stream, was an Indian village. A few brave souls peered out of the tipis. One elderly squaw stood right out in the open, hands on her hips, waiting to see what would become of the confrontation.

Jack greeted the men in their own tongue, but received no reply. The Indian boy also spoke, but was quickly rebuffed by a stern-faced warrior sitting at the center of the formation. Neither Jack nor the boy bothered to translate. It was clear to all that the warriors would not willingly let them pass through the village.

The Indian boy tried once more, pleading with his elders to allow them entry, but was once again shouted down. Strangely, it was Jack himself that the Indians appeared to find most offensive. One went so far as to point an arrow in the gunfighter's direction.

Jack was not amused. He shouted and gestured at the wagon with both hands. But his every word was met with stony glares. Worse, ever more of the Indians were putting arrows to bows.

Just as things seemed most dangerous, they heard new voices coming from the direction of the stream.

An Indian couple stepped from amidst the trees. The woman wore a long buckskin dress and matching moccasins. In her arms was a simple basket, loaded to the brim with fresh-caught fish. On the man's shoulders perched a little girl, her bare heels kicking playfully against her father's chest.

The Indian man smiled when he saw the standoff at the edge of the village. He spoke to his wife, and then they strolled over to stand between the opposing groups.

"You're late, Jack Straw," he said. "I sent my son to find you hours ago."

"Hello, Joseph," Jack replied. "There was a boulder."

Joseph gestured at the warriors standing guard over the village. "You must forgive Ollokot. My brother is normally more hospitable. But times have grown hard." He looked at Jack's coat. "And as usual, you come under the sign of war."

After that, Joseph spoke to the warriors. It took a bit more convincing, but eventually Ollokot gave the command to disperse.

"Now we may enter the village as friends," Joseph said. He spoke to his wife, who turned and led the way.

Jack dismounted and followed them. Henry, Lu and Sadie did likewise. MacLemore even climbed down from the wagon. Only Chino remained seated, driving the mules very slowly through the village.

They stopped at one of the smaller tipis. Joseph said something to his wife and she disappeared inside.

"Janey arranged for me to bring you a gift," Jack said, gesturing at the wagon.

"How is Janey?"

"Prosperous. Happy, I think. She worries about you."

"You're still riding my horse, I see." Joseph patted Jack's appaloosa on the neck. He spoke to it in his own language and the horse pawed at the ground.

"I've brought you another." Jack handed over the gray stallion's lead. "He'll make a fine stud."

Joseph inspected the stallion. "Good legs. What do you want for him?"

"The horse is a gift. But for transporting the rifles and ammunition we'll need two saddle-trained mounts. One for Chino. One for the boy. And I need information."

"You plan to cross the Hell Mouth."

"If we can."

Joseph looked at the sky. The sun was quickly sinking behind the trees. "Our Feast of the Sun begins at dusk. When it is over we shall discuss the canyon."

"How long does this feast last?" MacLemore asked.

"Only three days."

"Three days?"

Joseph looked MacLemore in the eye. "You've waited years to reclaim your gold," he said. "Is three days more so long a time?"

"How do you know about my gold?" MacLemore asked suspiciously, but Joseph just smiled.

Joseph's wife poked her head out of the tipi.

"*Alikkees* says you must wash for dinner," Joseph translated. "And that this little one must help serve." He set his daughter down and she scampered inside. "My son, *Chuslum-moxmox*, will take you to a place where you may scrub away the road."

"This way," the boy who'd guided them through the forest called. He pointed at the creek. "There's a good spot with plenty of sand."

When they'd reached the water's edge, Lu found himself kneeling beside their young guide. For some reason, the Indian boy kept staring at him.

"Are you really Yen Hui's son?" he asked finally.

Lu nodded. "How did you know that?"

"My Pa. He knows pretty much everything. You'll see." The

boy grinned. "He also says that your Pa was a good friend of his. Is that true?"

"I don't know. My father died before I was born."

The Indian boy frowned. This wasn't the answer he'd been hoping for.

"Can I ask you a question?" Lu asked. The boy nodded. "What was your name again?"

"Chuslum-moxmox. But you can call me "Little Joseph." The white soldiers all do. All but Jack."

"I'll try to call you by your real name," Lu said. "Chuslum-moxmox." If Jack thought it important enough to call him by his Indian name, Lu felt sure he ought to follow suit. "Can I ask you something else?"

"Sure."

"How come you speak English?"

"Pa taught me. He and Aunt Janey grew up at a convent school in San Pablo. They've been speaking it since they were five or six."

"Were they captured?"

Chuslum-moxmox shook his head. "Grandpa sent them. He believed the whites had powerful magic, and wanted his children to learn it so they could bring it back to the people." He'd finished washing, and was drying his hands on his shirt. "Grandpa must have been right, because Pa's the most powerful headman of all the *Iceyeeye niim Mama'yac.*"

"What's that?" Lu asked.

"It's the name of our people. What we call ourselves."

Lu remembered hearing the soldiers in Fort Jeb Stuart talk about "Green Woods Injuns." It'd never occurred to him to think they might have another name.

"What does it mean?" he asked.

"Children of Coyote," Chuslum-moxmox replied. He leaned toward Lu. "Can I ask you a question?"

Lu nodded.

"Is that a girl?" He gestured toward Sadie.

She was bent over the river, scrubbing the trail dust from the back of her neck. Her bonnet lay on the grass and her long honey-blonde hair dragged in the stream. Lu was surprised. With her face wet, and her hair illuminated by the setting sun, Sadie was quite beautiful.

"She's a girl," he said. "I swear."

"Good." Chuslum-moxmox sounded relieved. "That's what I told my uncle and the other warriors."

"Did they think she was a man?"

"They wondered. None of them had ever seen a white woman in trousers before."

CHAPTER 7

DAYS OF PLENTY

THEIR THREE DAYS AMONG the Iceyeeye niim Mama'yac flew by. The feast of the sun was, above all, a time of rest, and the travelers were more than willing to indulge.

Each morning began with an icy bath in the creek. The Iceyeeye niim Mama'yac bathed religiously. From youngest to oldest, none escaped. It was as social as it was hygienic. For the better part of an hour, the men occupied a broad sandbar a quarter of a mile downstream from the village. There they gossiped, told dirty jokes, and complained about their wives, who had their own swimming hole a mile or so upstream. Only Chino refused to get in the water. He said it was too cold for human occupation, declaring it a health hazard and predicting epidemics of every known disease from pneumonia to foot fungus. Lu ignored his warnings. After more than a month of dirt and sweat, it felt good to start each day fresh.

Once everyone was scrubbed and clean, the women prepared breakfast. Over the course of a little more than three days, Lu tried five varieties of stream trout, elk, rabbit, badger and squirrel. All were delicious, but he preferred the badger. Elk was too strong, and squirrel too tough. Rabbit was good, but not as sweet as badger.

After everyone had eaten, the Indians told stories, each with some sort of moral or lesson. Lu's favorite by far was the story in which Coyote first encountered a family of humans, starving in the wilderness. He showed them which fruits and vegetables were good to eat, taught them how to hunt, to dress and preserve their meat, and how to cook it over a fire. Eventually, the family got so strong they tried to hunt Coyote himself. In retaliation, he killed the oldest member of the family. The description of that first ever death was as delightfully bloody as any Lu had ever heard.

There were also games. The most popular consisted of little more than throwing arrows through a series of gradually more distant hoops. Henry proved a crack shot, capable of threading the smallest hoop at nearly thirty paces. Only Ollokot did better.

When they tired of games, the Indians napped or did chores. Lu chipped in wherever he could. One afternoon he accompanied Chuslum-moxmox and his mother on a hunt for mushrooms. They found only a handful, not even enough for one person. But the trip was by no means a waste. On the way back to the village, Alikkees stumbled onto a patch of wild strawberries. They picked all afternoon, eating as much of the sweet fruit as they saved.

After the evening meal, the Indians prayed and sang songs. At dusk, a few of the oldest men went into what they called a sweat-lodge, where they built a small fire and sat for hours on end, roasting in the heat and smoke. MacLemore tried it, and was cooked after only a few minutes. Jack went the distance, emerging only when the fuel was gone and the sweaters ready to retire to their various tipis for the night.

For their last evening in the village, Joseph invited the whole party into his tipi for supper. It was a rare honor. They'd eaten every meal with the headman and his family, but never inside. Truth was, not one of them had so much as ducked his or her head through the door.

Lu's other clothes were worn and stained from constant use, so he changed into his blue silk suit, the one his mother had packed for him. He wished now that she'd thought to send the shoes that went with it.

Joseph and his family met them in front of the tipi. Alikkees wore a new dress, and her braids were wrapped in strips of beaver fur. She looked quite beautiful. Ollokot stood beside her, his face set in its usual grimace.

"Welcome," Joseph said, then repeated it in his own language.

They exchanged pleasantries, MacLemore doing most of the talking while Joseph translated, and then Alikkees motioned for them to go inside. Lu entered last, ducking through the flaps behind Chuslum-moxmox. As they took their seats around the fire, Lu noticed the other boy staring at his suit.

"It's silk," he explained. "My mother made me bring it."

"Silk," Chuslum-moxmox repeated. He touched Lu's sleeve. "It's soft."

"Worms make it."

"No! Worms?"

"They spin it. Like a spider-web."

"Your clothes are made of webs?"

"Sort of." Lu wasn't entirely sure of the process himself, so he didn't elaborate. Fortunately, he didn't have to. Before Chuslum-moxmox could ask any other questions, his mother arrived with the food.

MacLemore clapped when he saw it. On one end of the platter was a roast—venison probably, though it might have been elk or moose—and on the other was a heap of steaming vegetables. Lu recognized wild potatoes, carrots and onions. Alikkees had also baked a loaf of *kehmmes* bread. Khemmes was a kind of root bulb that Joseph's people ground up and served with every meal. It didn't taste much like bread, but it was as close as Alikkees could get, and slathered with honey it wasn't too bad.

It was a fine meal. The food was good and the conversation friendly. The Indians chatted in their own tongue, while their visitors talked amongst themselves in English. Jack went back and forth, never missing a beat. Chuslum-moxmox told his uncle about the silk-worms and was immediately bombarded with questions, which he passed along to Lu. Ollokot wanted to know if the insects spun the fabric in colors, or if it was dyed. He also wondered whether the silk could be fashioned into anything other than clothes, such as bowstrings or rope. Lu did his best to answer all these questions, and when he didn't know something he guessed. Ollokot seemed satisfied either way.

When the food was gone, Joseph announced that he had yet another treat for his guests.

He drew a long pipe from a fringed leather sheath, along with a small pouch of pipe-weed, which he packed into the bowl and lit with a twig from the fire. A cloud of iridescent green smoke swirled around his head as he got the pipe-embers going.

Lu thought the smoke quite beautiful. He watched it swirl lazily up and through the open top of the tipi. It might have been nothing, a mere trick of the imagination, but Lu would've sworn he saw the smoke coalesce, forming into the shape of a man's face, mouth bent in a deep frown, just before it was caught by the breeze and dispersed.

Joseph handed the pipe to Ollokot.

"Do we all have to smoke?" Lu whispered to Chuslum-mox-mox. The war chief was sucking rapidly at the pipe, sending little puffs of green vapor out over the fire.

"You don't want to?" Chuslum-moxmox asked.

"I never have."

"Never?"

"Well, once," Lu lied. "But I didn't care for it."

"Just take a tiny bit and hold it in your mouth." Chuslum-moxmox took the pipe from his uncle and demonstrated. "You'll like it, I promise." After taking a deeper drag, he handed the pipe to Lu.

Seeing no way around it, Lu lifted the pipe to his lips. The mouthpiece tasted strangely spicy, and it made his lips tingle. He wondered what sort of plants the Indians smoked. It didn't smell like tobacco.

"Go ahead," Chuslum-moxmox urged. He made sucking motions.

Lu drew a tiny bit of smoke from the pipe and was surprised to find it sweet. He'd expected the taste to be bitter, but this was more like fresh cut grass or green hay. Encouraged, he took another puff, this time drawing the smoke into his lungs. The coughing fit he'd anticipated never came. In fact, Lu felt surprisingly calm. His lungs, rather than rejecting the foreign substance, actually seemed to welcome it. He wished he'd taken more when he'd had the chance.

"Good?" Chuslum-moxmox asked.

Lu nodded enthusiastically.

The pipe made its way around the circle. When it was his turn, Jack sucked deeply at the pipe not once, but three times. The clouds of vapor that escaped his mouth were as dense and radiant as liquid emeralds. Only Henry begged off.

When everyone had smoked, Joseph tapped the charred remains of the pipe-weed into the fire. It flamed up, for an instant turning the whole inside of the tipi pale green, and then was gone.

"And so ends the feast of the sun," Joseph said.

That night, Lu dreamt of home.

He dreamed he was kneeling outside his grandfather's sanctum, just as he had on that fateful evening so many weeks ago, peering through the key-hole. It was late, Lu felt that instinctively, but his grandfather was still hard at work, mixing some kind of potion. It must have been complicated. Master K'ung had a scroll open on his desk and consulted it numerous times. Lion-dog was sound asleep beneath his chair.

Happy to see them both alive and well, Lu snuck upstairs to his mother's room. She was in bed, so Lu took a quick look around.

The room had changed since he left. His books, usually piled atop the dresser, were gone, replaced by a mirror and a set of lady's combs. His bed was gone as well, disassembled, and the mattress shoved into the corner behind his mother's bathtub. Lu was angry. He'd been gone little more than a month, and already his family had eliminated all signs of him. Lu was about to shake his mother awake and tell her what he thought of her, when he noticed something clutched beneath her arm. It was a doll. Lu had loved it dearly as a little boy, dragging it behind him until its clothes—a suit of blue silk—were frayed and dirty. Lu was still pondering the doll, wondering where his mother had hid it all these years, when he felt a hand close over his shoulder.

"Wake up," Chuslum-moxmox whispered.

Lu opened his eyes. It was still dark. "I was dreaming of home," he mumbled, not yet fully awake. "I was dreaming of my family."

"Of course you were," Chuslum-moxmox said. "You smoked Father's pipe." He grinned. "But now get up."

"What do you want?"

"Come with me."

"Where?"

"It's a surprise."

Reluctantly, Lu rolled out of his blanket. The rest of his companions were still sleeping soundly. Jack was missing, but that was no great surprise. "Just let me put on my boots," Lu whispered.

Chuslum-moxmox guided him through the village, silently creeping past Joseph's tipi and a handful of others before stopping at the trailhead, right where they'd first encountered Ollokot and his warriors. Joseph was waiting for them, as was Ollokot. The war chief held the leads on three horses.

"What is this?" Lu asked. He didn't know if they'd been caught sneaking around or if Chuslum-moxmox knew his father and uncle would be there. "What's happening?"

"I want to give you something." Chuslum-moxmox took one of the horses from his uncle and pulled it toward Lu. "This is my horse," he said. It was a pinto, white with large brown spots. "His name is *Elaskolatat.*"

"I don't understand." Lu looked at the older men, hoping for an explanation.

"My son wants you to have his horse," Joseph said.

"But why?"

"We have only a few horses that can wear the white man's saddle," Chuslum-moxmox explained. "These three are the best."

Lu inspected the pinto more closely. Compared to the MacLemores' horses, it was short, spindly-legged and barrel-chested. Its hooves were broad and thick. In fact, it looked exactly like one of the old nags that pulled the plows through the fields west of St. Frances. Worst of all were its eyes. The top half of each was black, just like those of any other horse, but beneath that was a lighter area, like cream poured into strong coffee.

"Can it even see?" Lu asked

"He sees fine," Joseph assured him. "When a horse is born with such eyes, we call him a spirit horse. They are prized companions."

Lu was unimpressed, but didn't dare say so. "Good-looking animal," he offered.

"No he's not," Chuslum-moxmox countered. "He's ugly and skinny and short. But he's sure-footed as a goat. You'll be glad to have him in the Hell Mouth."

"I can't take your horse," Lu protested. "You'll need him."

"No I won't." Chuslum-moxmox beamed. "I'm getting a new horse. And a rifle. I'm to be a warrior."

"Oh." Lu was surprised. Standing beside his uncle, Chuslum-moxmox looked so young and hopeful. He was just a boy. It was all but impossible to imagine him riding into battle, maybe even to kill another man. But Lu could also see how proud of his new status Chuslum-moxmox was. Lu forced himself to smile. "Congratulations," he said.

"Here." Chuslum-moxmox thrust his horse at Lu again. "I want you to ride him."

Seeing no alternative, Lu took the pinto's lead. He guided it in a circle, watching it walk. The horse hung its head as though worn out. "What about a saddle?" Lu asked.

Chuslum-moxmox raced to the nearest tipi, Ollokot's, reappearing a moment later with a cavalry saddle and matching blanket. The leather, both on the seat and skirt, was well-worn, but still very serviceable.

"Where'd you get it?" Lu asked.

"Ollokot took it." Chuslum-moxmox pointed at the blanket. There was a brown stain on one corner. Lu was no expert, but guessed it must be blood.

Together, the boys placed the blanket and saddle onto the pinto's back. When it was cinched tight, Lu climbed aboard. Instead of a bridle and bit, the Indians steered their mounts with a nose harness. It wasn't so very different, really. Lu guessed he could get used to it in no time. After all, he'd only been riding a few weeks.

Lu trotted the horse a short distance into the forest, then galloped back. He was surprised to find its gait smooth. Much smoother than Cody's. The horse was well-trained, too. He responded to every kick and nudge as though Lu had been riding him forever.

"He has a nice trot," Lu said. "What's his name again?"

"Elaskolatat. It means, 'Animal that runs into the ground.'"

"I thought you said he was sure-footed."

"He is. It's a joke."

"Well, I can't call him that. I need something shorter." Lu thought a moment. He didn't want to change the horse's name completely, just make it easier to use. "I know, I'll call him Crash."

Chuslum-moxmox looked pleased. "So you'll take him?"

"Which of those others are you giving to Chino?"

"Both are Jack's," Joseph said. "Which Chino might choose to ride, I can't say."

"I don't understand. Jack traded for two horses, not three."

"My son gives that horse to you as a gift. It is *yours*."

Lu looked at Chuslum-moxmox, stunned. "A gift? But why?"

"Because we're friends."

There was no question of refusing now, not that he would have anyway. Lu scrambled down off his new saddle and shook Chuslum-moxmox's hand. "I never owned a horse before," he said. Lu was so happy and proud he thought he might cry. A lump even formed in his throat. "I really appreciate it," he said, forcing the words out. "I really, really do."

By the time they got back to camp, the other travelers were up and preparing to leave. A fire had been lit and a pot of coffee set over it to burn. Chino was especially busy, distributing supplies amongst the half-dozen mules, now strung together in a single-file line. MacLemore helped. Sadie and Henry saddled the horses. Jack gave coffee to Ollokot and Joseph. Chuslum-moxmox placed the saddle he'd brought—twin to the one Crash wore, minus the blood-stained blanket—beside the fire. Jack offered him coffee as well, but Chuslum-moxmox refused.

"Are these the new horses?" Jack asked.

"They're fine animals," Joseph assured him.

Jack nodded. "That mare especially. But what about this other?" He pointed at Crash.

"He's mine," Lu said.

"Is that right?"

Joseph nodded. "It is a gift from my son."

"He any good?"

"The best," Joseph said.

The coffee was nearly gone by the time Chino finished loading the mules. In addition to their food—pemmican mostly, a mixture of animal fat, nuts and berries, which the Indians ate whenever they were traveling—Chino had packed a dozen large water-skins. They hung empty round the necks of the mules, like scales from a molting snake.

"What's with all the empty skins?" Henry asked.

"Going to be dry," Chino explained. "After we cross the canyon there won't be water for miles and miles."

"And just how do you know that?"

Chino grinned, but refused to say any more.

Jack gave Chino his choice of the two horses, and Chino selected the mare. She was at least a foot taller at the shoulder than Crash, and no doubt outweighed him by two hundred pounds, all of it muscle. Chuslum-moxmox offered to place the saddle on her, but Chino wanted to do it himself. "I like a firm ride," he said.

All that remained to be packed was MacLemore's guitar, which he carefully tied to his own saddle, right behind the seat.

"Guess that about does it," Jack said.

Lu glanced around the remains of their camp. The wagon they'd driven all the way across the plains, and up the eastern slope of the mountains, sat to one side. Its canvas top, and much of its wood, had been stripped away for fuel, or to construct packing harnesses for the mules. What remained was a skeleton.

"It's been a real pleasure," MacLemore said, shaking hands with Joseph, Ollokot and Chuslum-moxmox. "All we need now is that map."

"Won't be necessary," Jack said. "I know the way."

"Since when?"

"Last night."

"I'd still feel better if we had a map." MacLemore looked at Joseph. "You think you could draw up something? I've got a pen and paper in my suitcase."

"I'm sure Jack knows the way," Joseph responded.

"I can't see how that's possible. Just yesterday he told me we needed directions. Now he's an expert?" MacLemore looked at Joseph, then at Jack. Neither offered an explanation. Disgusted, MacLemore shook his head. "I sure hope you know what you're doing," he grumbled. "I'd hate to get all the way to the bottom of that canyon with no way out."

"Mount up," Jack said.

Lu was about to climb onto his own horse when he noticed his bag, the white cotton sack his mother had packed for him, tied to the back of one of the mules. He quickly unfastened it and carried it to Chuslum-moxmox.

"I'd like to give you something," he said, reaching into the bag and drawing out his blue suit. "It's not much, but—"

"Silk. Made by worms." Chuslum-moxmox held the suit out in front of him as though it were gold. He said something to his uncle, who touched the fabric and smiled.

Lu scrambled atop his horse. The cotton sack, now all but empty, he shoved into one of his saddle-bags.

"I'll do my best to care for Crash," he promised.

Chuslum-moxmox smiled. "He will take care of you."

That night, they camped on the banks of a high mountain lake, beneath the broad boughs of a sugar pine. The tree's enormous cones, each as long as a man's forearm, made excellent fuel for the fire, and its trunk provided shelter from the wind. They didn't make camp until well after dark, so instead of cooking they decided to try the pemmican.

Unlike most Indian cuisine, which Lu liked tremendously, this was awful. It was beyond greasy. Even the currants, which had been mixed generously throughout, did little to cut the gaminess of the fatty paste. And Lu wasn't the only one who thought so. Sadie and her father both complained.

"A ball of fat only gets so tasty," Henry remarked.

"Makes beans sound darned good, don't it?" Chino added.

No one had much to say after that. Choking down their supper was hard enough. Talking about it would have been too much.

When they were finished, Jack went for a smoke. Lu followed him. They circled the lake, staying always a half-dozen strides from the water. The banks were stony, and Lu tripped numerous times, but always managed to right himself before falling down. Jack never faltered.

"What do you want?" Jack asked finally. They'd gone far enough for the campfire to resemble nothing so much as a bright star in the inky darkness.

"Can I have a smoke?" Lu asked.

The gunfighter reached into his shirt pocket, took out another cigarette and lit it off the first. "Here."

Lu took a drag and coughed. This was nothing like what he'd experienced the night before. After a single puff his tongue felt as dry as week old bread, and tasted half as appetizing. He took another drag, but it wasn't much better.

"You'd best enjoy that, because it's the last you'll have 'til you reach a town," Jack said. "It's a disgusting habit anyway."

"But you do it."

"Exactly."

"Can I ask you something?"

"Shoot."

"Well, you gave a cannon to the cavalry, and then delivered rifles to the Indians."

"So?"

"Who'll win?"

"Cavalry." Jack paused to stub his cigarette out on his boot heel. "Though it might take them a good while. That Hotchkiss gun isn't likely to do much good amidst all these trees."

"What makes you think the Indians will lose?"

"All peoples get the chance to taste defeat sooner or later," Jack answered. "For Joseph's tribe, that time's now."

"What'll happen to them?"

"Get shipped off to a reservation, I expect."

"Isn't there anything they can do?" Thinking about these mountains without the Indians in them made Lu sad, nearly as sad as when he thought about the Indians without the mountains.

"They could die fighting. You reckon that'd be better?"

Lu considered a moment. "I don't know."

"Me either." Jack shrugged. "I offered to fight with them, but Ollokot refused. I guess he's right. This is their battle to lose, not mine."

They wandered down to the shore. Jack rinsed his hands and face in the cold water.

"Couldn't they just run?" Lu asked him.

"They'll try."

"But they won't make it?"

"Where would you run, supposing you had to?" Jack asked. "And dragging along a whole passel of children and old folks? Where would you go?"

"I'd . . . I don't know."

"Neither do they."

"Did Joseph tell you how to navigate the Hell Mouth?"

"Not exactly."

"Then how do you know the way? You didn't before."

Jack looked at him. "What was your grandfather doing last night?"

"Grandfather?" Lu started. "He was . . . mixing a potion. Lion-dog was curled up under his chair."

"And how do you know that?"

"I . . . I don't want to say." But in his mind he knew the answer. It was that strange green smoke. There'd been some enchantment in it. Through the smoke, Joseph had showed them what they most wanted or needed to see. Lu guessed that Jack had wanted to see the safest path through the Hell Mouth.

"Fair enough," Jack said. He pointed at the cigarette in Lu's hand. A long tube of gray ash hung from the end. Lu had completely forgotten he was holding it. "You plan to finish that?" Jack asked.

CHAPTER 8

A CHANGE IN THE WEATHER

BY THE TIME THEY'D FINISHED their circuit of the lake, the rest of the company had bedded down for the night. All but Chino, who sat close to the fire, one of the mule harnesses spread across his lap and a stack of pinecones between his feet.

"What're you doin'?" Jack asked him.

"There's a hole in this strap. Figured I might patch it somehow."

Jack looked at the harness, and at the puncture in question. "Why don't you get Lu to help you?" he suggested.

Chino peered over at Lu, who'd begun spreading his blanket beside the fire. "You want to help me with the stock, *niño?*"

"I don't know how to mend a harness," Lu said. "Besides, I have to cook, and wash the dishes."

"Sadie can do that," Jack said. "Chino's going to need help. Especially once we reach the Hell Mouth."

Lu sighed and began refolding his blanket. He was sleepy, but knew it was useless to resist. Once Jack gave you a task you were stuck.

"Not tonight," Chino said. "Sleep. Tomorrow you do man's work."

Sadie was less than thrilled to discover that she'd been assigned permanent kitchen duty. In fact, she threatened both

Jack and Lu with food poisoning. She calmed down only after Henry invited both her and Lu to resume rifle practice, starting the following morning.

Breakfast consisted of reheated beans and cold jerky—Lu began to seriously regret relinquishing the role of cook—but at least the coffee was good. He had two cups before Chino called him away.

"Now, mule-skinnin' ain't a science," Chino said, leading him toward where their equipment had been piled up the evening before. "Not an art neither. You just got to keep your eyes peeled and your mind on the stock, and it all comes out easy. Got it?"

They gathered the mules, harnessed them, and then Chino showed Lu how to string all six into a single-file line. After that, they lashed the uncooked foodstuffs to the harnesses, followed by the tools and other equipment. Personal items and ammunition went on last. "Have to spread the weight evenly, to make sure none of our mules is overloaded," Chino warned. "We don't want one coming up lame."

When the last sack had been tied, the last coffee cup bagged and stowed, Lu and Chino saddled their horses. The rest of the party was already mounted up and waiting.

"You want me to lead them out?" Lu asked, as he finished saddling Crash.

"For now you just ride at the rear," Chino said. "These mules'll want to lollygag. Your job is to make sure they keep up. Cut a switch and don't be afraid to use it."

As they rode out of camp, Lu tore a dead branch from an old pine tree. But he never did swing it. There was no need. As soon as Crash understood that he was expected to walk at the very back of the train, behind even the mules, his disposition took a turn for the worse. He'd have galloped right back to the front if Lu would've let him. But Lu kept him reined in tight, which only served to further irritate Crash. Fortunately, he took out his anger on the mules. If they slowed down for even an instant, Crash gave the nearest mule a fiendish bite. That got their attention better than any switch. By sundown they'd covered more than thirty miles, the farthest they'd gone in a single day since crossing the Quapaw. Chino was thrilled.

After choosing a campsite, Lu and Chino began unloading the gear.

"This is the most important part of a skinner's job," Chino explained, as they released each animal, beginning at the rear of the string and moving forward. "We got to carefully inspect each mule."

As they unbuckled and removed the harnesses, Chino gave each animal a thorough rub down, from hooves to ears. He paid particular attention to any spots that might've been worn raw by the leather straps. When he saw the numerous bite marks, especially on the rump of the rearmost mule, Chino shot Lu a curious look. But he offered no complaint. If anything, he seemed amused.

While Sadie boiled dinner, Lu and Chino inventoried the remaining supplies. Beans and buffalo jerky were both running low. They had a week's supply of each, two if they stretched, after which they'd be stuck eating the pemmican. Jack promised the fat balls would keep them alive and healthy, but no one was anxious to test that theory. After everything had been mentally catalogued, Lu split the supplies into six piles of roughly even weight, ready to be tied onto the mules the following morning, thus beginning the whole process over from scratch.

By the time he'd finished his work, and eaten a few of the parboiled beans, Lu was ready for bed. Unfortunately, Henry had other ideas.

"We start practicing again tomorrow," he said.

Lu stifled a yawn. "So?"

Henry handed Lu his rifle. "Before you turn in for the night, I expect you to give that weapon a good cleaning."

The next few days raced by. The paths they followed were narrow, but easily navigated, and the terrain was more or less level. Lu did his work, morning and evening, and spent the whole of every afternoon half-asleep in the saddle, while Crash kept the mules in a state of nervous agitation. According to Jack, they were drawing nearer the Hell Mouth, but Lu had thus far seen no sign of the infamous gorge. He did observe a slight change in the rocks and soil, however. Where before it'd been almost exclusively granite and quartz, giving the path a cold grayish tint, now there was a decidedly reddish hue sprinkled generously throughout.

The trip over the high plateau did include one moment of real importance, however. At least, it was important to Lu.

It was just before dawn on their sixth day out of the Indian village and Lu was sound asleep, dreaming of a bowl of hot egg-drop soup, the kind his mother made on cold winter days. Lu was about to bring the steaming bowl to his lips when Henry gave his shoulder a firm shake and whispered at him to get up. Lu rolled over and opened his eyes. In addition to his rifle, Henry had slung a coil of heavy rope over one shoulder. It was one of the longer pieces, normally used to string together the mules.

"Ready?" Henry asked, handing Lu his boots.

"Just let me wake Sadie."

"Not this time. Today's lesson is just for you."

Lu was both surprised and pleased. He'd gotten somewhat better at shooting over the last few days, and could usually be counted on to hit the closer targets, but Sadie was still much handier with a gun. Lu knew that if he were ever to catch up to her, he'd need a few extra sessions.

Silently as they could, Lu and Henry crept through the grove of stately ponderosas that formed their camp's western border, and then crawled up a hill. Jack was waiting for them at the top.

"He still there?" Henry asked.

Jack pointed. A whitetail buck stood in a thicket, not thirty yards down the other side of the hill, nervously plucking the leaves from a huckleberry bush.

"Do you want to shoot him?" Henry asked, handing the rifle to Lu.

"Me?"

"Think you can hit him from here?"

"Any closer and he'll get wind of you," Jack warned.

"I can try," Lu said.

"It's already loaded," Henry whispered, as Lu brought the rifle up to his shoulder.

Lu thumbed back the hammer. "What'll I aim for?" he asked. His mouth was dry, making it hard to talk.

"Aim just behind the shoulder."

The buck must have sensed something, because it raised its head to look around. Blood pounded in Lu's ears as he squeezed the trigger, and the rifle gave its usual deafening roar. The deer blasted over backward, its body crashing through the thicket and then disappearing in the tall grass.

"You hit him," Jack said.

"It was a good shot," Henry said.

They hiked down to where the buck lay in a twisted heap, better than five feet from the bush on which it had lately been grazing. The slug from Henry's rifle had torn clean through its upper body, sheering off one of its forelegs and vaporizing a good portion of its ribcage. Lu could barely stand to look at the wound, it was so big and dirty and red. At least the deer wasn't suffering, he thought.

Henry drew his knife from the sheath on his belt and handed it to Lu.

"Not much left of the shoulders," Jack said. "Make sure you get the hind-quarters at least."

"You want me to butcher it?" Lu asked.

"If you're man enough to shoot it, you're man enough to dress it." Lu must have looked a touch green because Jack gave him a pat on the back. "Don't worry, Henry'll show you how."

"What about you?" Lu asked.

Jack turned and started back toward camp. "I'll make sure Sadie saves you some breakfast."

"You're sure you want me to do this?" Lu asked, trying to hand the knife back to Henry. "I might mess it up."

But Henry wouldn't take the knife back. "Start here," he said, pointing at the patch of white fur where the buck's rear legs came together. "Nice and easy. That's right. Cut right up the belly. We'll take his skin off just as if it were a fur coat." Henry watched as Lu made the first incision. "Careful," he warned. "Intestines are likely to pile out on your shoe tops."

For the next hour, Henry instructed Lu in the intricacies of butchery. It was thirsty work. By the time they'd finished, both men were bloody to the elbows and Lu had seen filth he never even knew existed. Once the deer had been skinned and gutted, they tied its rear legs together and hauled it up a tree. After that,

Henry slit its throat and they stood back as the blood poured out. Flies came from miles around to feast on the stinking offal.

While they waited for the carcass to drain, Lu returned to camp. Chino had already finished his breakfast, so they got busy loading the mules. When that was done, Jack handed Lu a pair of burlap sacks. "Go get your meat," he said.

"But I still haven't had breakfast yet."

Sadie handed him a plate of re-cooked beans, leftovers from the previous night's supper. They weren't even hot. Lu thought about complaining, but one look at Sadie changed his mind.

"There ain't no more," she spat. "And you can damn well wash that dish yourself."

Chastised, Lu carried the beans back over the hill. After they'd polished off their meager breakfast, Henry helped Lu lower the carcass, and then showed him how to remove the deer's hind quarters. There was a surprising amount of tugging and sawing necessary. When both legs had been shorn off, Lu wrapped them in the burlap sacks and he and Henry carried them back to camp. Chino lashed them to a waiting mule.

For the rest of that morning, and all that afternoon, Lu stared at those seeping burlap sacks. By evening, the smell of blood had turned his stomach. He didn't throw up, but felt as though he might at any moment. Crash was equally put off by the stink. Instead of nipping the tails of the mules in front of him, he maintained a cautious distance. They kept the train in sight, but only just barely.

That night, MacLemore showed Lu how to spit the hindquarters and roast them over the fire. Apparently he'd done a fair bit of hunting, back when he'd first come to the Territories, and knew just how to pass a spit through a venison flank without striking bone or getting it stuck in gristle. Lu didn't think he'd be able to eat any, but the rich smell soon won him over. It was sort of amazing. Slow-cooking it over a smoky wood-fire had turned the aroma of the meat from horrible to mouthwatering. They swallowed steaming venison by the fistfuls, carving chunks of meat straight off the bone. Chino ate the most, as was usual, but Lu wasn't far behind. When every member of their party had eaten his or her fill, and maybe a few bites more, Chino cut up the remaining flesh and packed it away. Cooked, the deer would last them near a week, a fact that greatly lifted everyone's spirits. Even Jack was in no hurry to eat pemmican.

After the utensils had been washed and put away, Jack offered cigarettes to any that wanted one. Only Henry and Chino refused, though for very different reasons. Henry wasn't a smoker, and Chino preferred to chew, which he did, cutting a chaw off the plug he'd bought at Fort Jeb Stuart.

"Figured this was a good time to celebrate," Jack said, lighting his cigarette with a burning twig from the fire.

"Indeed." MacLemore held his cigarette aloft. "To Lu, our great Chinese hunter."

"To Lu," Henry echoed.

"And to the Hell Mouth," Jack said.

The other members of their party stared.

"What do you mean?" MacLemore asked.

"Took us near two months," Jack said, "but we've reached it at last."

"Where?" Sadie turned back and forth as though she might spot it, winking at her from around one of the tree trunks.

Jack pointed. "Mile or so farther up the path."

"Really?" Sadie looked at her father. "Can we go see it? It's only a mile. We can walk."

"Is it safe?" MacLemore asked.

Jack shrugged.

"I'll go with you," Lu offered.

"You still have a rifle to clean," Henry reminded him. "And my knife could use a good sharpening as well."

"Can't I do it when I get back?" Lu asked.

"I'll help him," Sadie offered. "I can sharpen the knife while Lu cleans the gun."

"Fine," Henry relented. "But I don't want to hear either of you complain about being tired in the morning."

No one else was interested, so the two youngest members of the team set off alone. They were just barely out of earshot of the camp when Sadie slapped Lu on the elbow, hard enough to make his whole arm sing.

"So how was it?" she asked.

"How was what?" Lu groaned, still rubbing his stinging limb.

"Shooting that deer."

"Oh . . . All right, I guess. Actually, it turned into a lot of work."

"Why didn't you wake me?"

"I wanted to, but Henry said to leave you be."

Sadie mulled that over for a few minutes. "You reckon I could've hit it?" she asked finally.

"Can't see why not. You're a better shot than me."

"Dang right. I wonder why they let you shoot it at all."

"Well, if you'd have been there I probably would have let you take the shot."

"What for?"

"I don't know." Lu shrugged. "Maybe that's why Henry didn't want me to wake you. I need the practice."

"You're right about that," Sadie said. "So where'd you hit him?"

"In the shoulder. The bullet tore off one of its front legs."

Sadie whistled. "That must've been somethin' to see."

"It was pretty gruesome, actually."

"I'll just bet it was." She sounded positively delighted.

Sadie asked many more questions about the deer: how it had looked when it was skinned, how they'd skinned it, how much meat they'd left behind, and what they did with the guts. Lu answered all her questions, though he found the topic unpleasant. Fortunately, just as Sadie got to asking about the flies, they passed between a pair of spindly scrub pines and stopped.

Even in the dark, on a cloudy and moonless night, it was awe-inspiring. Lu leaned over the edge, but could only make out one single tiny bend of the Moreno River, winding its course along the bottom of the gorge, passing innumerable ashy terraces and monoliths of naked stone. In the dark, everything seemed to be painted in hazy shades of blue, purple and black. Just like most everyone in America, Lu had read dozens of descriptions of the Hell Mouth, but none had prepared him for the grandeur of the thing.

"Can you make out the other side?" Sadie asked.

"Sort of." Lu squinted. "It's dark, but . . . It looks—"

"Tall," Sadie said. "Taller than this side anyhow. How far do you reckon that is?"

Lu shook his head. He couldn't even hazard a guess. Truthfully, if someone had told him that the Hell Mouth was fifty miles wide, he'd have believed it. Even seventy-five. A hundred miles he'd have known was too far, but that was as much of his brain as he could wrap around the problem. And he was no better at guessing the canyon's depth. It looked deeper than Stuart's Peak was tall—a fact that, all by itself, was enough to set the mind reeling—but how much deeper? Who knew?

"Reckon I could hit that cliff with a rock?" Sadie asked, pointing at one of the numerous formations that stuck up throughout the length and breadth of the Hell Mouth.

Lu shrugged. In fact, he doubted very much whether anyone could pitch a stone that far. He'd already caught onto one of the great truths of the canyon—distances were nearly impossible to judge with any sort of accuracy, and nearly always appeared shorter than they actually were.

"Well, I'm going to try it." Sadie picked up a stone and flung it with all her might. It sailed into the inky sky, losing only a little elevation at first, and then seemed to fall straight down and out of sight. She tried again and again, but never managed to throw a stone more than about half-way to her target.

"It's a long way," Lu offered. "I don't think anybody could hit it."

"I know what let's do," Sadie said. "Let's roll something over the edge."

They settled on a smallish boulder, perched just a few strides from the edge of the chasm. It was only knee high, but heavy. They had to work together to move it at all.

As soon as they had it positioned—balanced half-over the yawning maw—Sadie gave the boulder a good hard kick. And then both of them watched as it bounded downward, digging deep furrows through the few straggly plants that clung to the canyon's upper slopes.

Lu held his breath as the boulder soared over the edge of the precipice and disappeared, followed a second or two later by the sound of an explosion, echoing up from the depths of the gorge.

"Did you hear that?" Sadie asked. "Loud as a gunshot. Imagine how deep it must be. I can't wait to see it tomorrow."

"I guess we ought to be getting back," Lu said. "I still have to clean Henry's rifle, and morning comes darn early."

They stood a moment longer, staring at the rocky chasm, and then turned and retraced their steps toward camp.

"I'll bet it's pretty in the daylight," Sadie said. "Don't you?"

"And deep."

The next morning, Lu was up and ready to move with the sun. He bolted his breakfast, shot at the targets Henry set for him without really looking at them, and tied their tools and supplies to the mules almost haphazardly. Sadie was just as excited. Seeing the canyon in the dark had only whetted their appetites. Even a meal of weak coffee and burnt venison couldn't douse their enthusiasm.

When they finally rode between those last scraggily pines no one spoke. Even Sadie and Lu, who'd last stood on that very spot just a few hours previous, had no words to describe their feelings. With the morning sun pouring into it, the Hell Mouth was both larger and grander than it had appeared the night before. It was gigantic. Just gazing into it made Lu feel dizzy and afraid. And yet he couldn't look away. The Hell Mouth was also beautiful. And colorful. And sublime. Yellow, red and burnt-orange stripes of sandstone, lime and shale were piled, one atop another, forming ripples and wrinkles, mounds and monoliths. The hazy purple shapes of the previous night were replaced by an almost unnatural complexity of forms. Any description would be a lie. All comparison was empty. Lu saw boulders as large as mountains, resembling both altars and armchairs. He saw stone waterfalls, and fins of rock that stuck up like enormous hands of cards. Far in the distance he saw what appeared to be a perfect natural bridge of blood-red stone, spanning the river at a dizzying height.

"I've heard folks call this the eighth wonder of the world," Jack said, breaking the silence. "But I think that gives too much credit to the other seven."

Lu nodded in agreement.

"We're pretty close to the center," Jack continued. "From here, the Hell Mouth runs about five hundred miles due north."

"How far south?" MacLemore asked.

"Four hundred fifty, give or take a dozen miles."

"How do we get down?" Sadie asked.

"We'll have to cut north a shade," Jack said. "Even then it'll be steep."

"South looks easier," MacLemore suggested. "Not so many sheer walls."

"It's no good that way."

"Why not?"

"It's just no good."

For the next hour, Jack led them north, skirting the edge of the abyss. It was a fine ride, offering excellent views. Plus, it was warm at the top of the canyon. Lu wondered what the temperature might be like once they got down amidst all those shadows.

They stopped at noon, so that Lu and Chino could make one final check of the mules. The harnesses were all snug, the supplies tight, and the lines untangled. Sadie cut a few hunks of roast venison for each of them, while Henry and Jack inspected the saddles. They chatted only in short bursts, never taking their eyes off the Hell Mouth. At last, Jack said it was time to move on.

"Over we go," he said. "Everyone hold on tight."

They spent the rest of that afternoon in the saddle. For the most part, the trail turned out to be surprisingly decent. It zigzagged back and forth along the tops of sheer cliffs, wound around boulders and monoliths, and cascaded down the steep sides of terraces, but always offered good footing for the stock, and by and large steered them away from the most blood-chilling precipices.

Eventually they came to the first of what would turn out to be innumerable forks in the road. The scarier of the two paths led over one of the sandstone fins Lu had seen earlier, though the alternative wasn't much better—it was nothing more than a narrow ledge winding along the side of a cliff. To Lu's relief, Jack chose the cliff. From then on, the trail was a muddle of splits, forks and divergences. Lu didn't know how he did it—excepting that it had something to do with the magic smoke from Joseph's pipe—but Jack seemed always to know exactly where he was going. He selected paths as confidently as one might choose the road to a corner store.

They camped that night on a wide shelf of granite, overlooking the river. According to Jack, they were a little more than halfway down. By the next night, assuming all went well, they ought to have forded the river and be camped on the western bank of the Moreno.

There was very little wood that deep into the canyon, so they had to make do without a fire. They still had most of a leg of roast venison, and plenty of water to drink, so no one complained. No fire meant no morning coffee, but Lu guessed they could do without for a day. Coffee was beginning to run short anyway.

After hobbling the horses and mules, they began to settle in for the night. As they did, a cold wind started whistling up the canyon from the south. Their thin blankets were no match for it, especially when coupled with the cold granite beds. Lu was soon chilled to the core, and he wasn't the only one. He could hear someone's teeth chattering. Fortunately, Lu was also bone-weary, or else he might not have gotten a wink of sleep all night.

He was still sleeping soundly when Jack shook him awake. "Get up," the gunfighter said. "There's work to be done."

"What work?" Lu sat up and looked around. "What's happening?"

"Help Chino with the animals."

Lu squinted, but could only make out the gunslinger's eyes and the ember of a burning cigarette perched between his lips. "It's still dark," he complained.

"And likely to stay that way." Jack pointed. Thunderheads as dense and black as nuggets of coal had begun settling over the canyon. The worst of them were still far to the south, but spreading fast.

It took them just fifteen minutes to get packed, but already they'd run out of time. No sooner had they mounted up than Lu felt the first cold drops splash on the back of his neck. He glanced back at the storm clouds and shivered.

"Rain," he called. But no one answered.

The downpour commenced soon after, and didn't let up for the rest of the day. Jack did his best, and always managed to find the right path, but the process was slow and miserable.

Water streamed down the rock wall beside them, exploded against the narrow ledge along which they trailed, and then dove over the edge of the cliff and disappeared. Lu had never been so scared. His heart beat so that he thought it might burst through his ribs. Over and over, Lu imagined one of their horses slipping, its legs wrenched out from under it by the rushing water. It was so awful a thing to contemplate that he could hardly stand to keep his eyes open at all. And even worse was yet to come.

They'd been in the saddle for a little more than four hours, and were soaked clear through to the soul, when the first bolts of lightning began lancing their way into the canyon, thunder riding close on its heels. Crash had to bite the mules again and again to keep them moving. Like Lu, the mules were terrified. But stopping in the middle of a narrow ledge was no answer.

At last, after five hours of misery, even Jack Straw could take no more.

"Damn storm's gettin' worse!" he shouted.

"Any ideas?" Henry asked him.

"Just one."

"Well?" MacLemore urged. "What is it?"

"There's a cave. It's out of our way, but—"

Jack was interrupted by an earsplitting boom. The whole earth shuddered. Stones that hadn't moved one iota since before the time of the Pharaohs seemed suddenly ethereal. The air smelled hot and electric.

"We can't take much more of this," Chino shouted. "One of these mules is like to throw itself over the edge."

Jack nodded. "Stay close," he said. "It's not far."

At first, their decision seemed a good one. Lu imagined stripping off his wet clothes and spreading them on the cave floor to dry. They'd have no fire and no hot soup, but one couldn't have everything. Even the mules must've sensed an end to their tribulations, because they followed Chino's lead without complaint.

It was then, just as Lu was feeling most hopeful, that tragedy struck.

A bolt of lightning shot the whole length of the canyon, striking one of the mules and sending the rest hurtling over the edge of the cliff.

The animals wailed, a high-pitch whinny of agony and horror unlike any Lu had ever heard, or even thought possible. As they tumbled through the murky darkness, the mule that had been struck by the lightning somehow managed to catch the others on fire. Blue flames erupted from their manes and tails, casting a hideous glow over the rocks they passed in their awful plunge to the Moreno. Lu watched, mesmerized in spite of his fear, as the fires grew ever brighter, fanned by the winds as the falling mules gained speed, only to be doused when they struck the foaming waters of the river.

Shocked, speechless with terror, Lu looked for his friends. He was amazed to see that the lightning, in addition to what it had done to the mules, had also struck the stone path on which they had been perched. The damage to the rock was incredible.

Lu screamed as the greater portion of the ledge, nearly twenty feet of solid granite, suddenly gave way. Chunks of stone the size of churches collapsed into the abyss. The sound was very much like what they'd heard the night before, when he and Sadie rolled their "boulder" into the canyon, only amplified a thousand times. Lu put his hands over his eyes, unable to contemplate the destruction for even a moment longer.

"Hey, Lu," Chino shouted, once the collapse was finally over. "You OK?"

Lu wiped his eyes. He could just barely see through all the steam and smoke. There was only one mule left, the one that had been closest to him. All the rest were gone. Swallowed by the Hell Mouth.

"Are you hurt?" Chino shouted again, waving to draw Lu's attention.

Lu shook his head. "But the mules. . . ."

Chino held up his hand, the one with the missing finger. His palm was bloody. "Ripped 'em right out of my hand," he said. "Lucky I didn't have 'em tied to my saddle. You sure you're all right?"

"What'll I do now?" Lu gestured at the still-smoking chasm separating him from his friends.

"Stay there."

Chino called to Jack, who dismounted and came back along the ledge to see what had happened. Henry, Sadie and MacLemore came with him. Their faces were ashen.

All were relieved to see Lu alive and well. But that relief proved short-lived, as the reality of the situation set in.

"How'll I get across?" Lu asked.

Jack looked at Chino, who looked at Henry. No one had any ideas. The gap was much too large to jump, and the cliff face too sheer to climb. There was no way across. Worst of all, another bolt of lightning could strike at any moment. They had no time to study the problem fully.

"You'll have to go back," Jack said finally.

"Back? Back where?"

"Find Joseph. Tell him what happened. Then go home."

"But, you need me to—"

"We'll make do."

"Don't worry," MacLemore said. "You've earned at least a buyout share of the gold. I'll make sure you get it."

Lu couldn't see how he'd earned much of anything yet, but didn't argue. Getting paid wasn't even the smallest of his concerns at present. "But how'll I find the way?" he asked.

"Your horse will know how to get home," Jack said. "Just tell him where you want to go. Give him his head."

"But I don't want to go back."

"There isn't any other way."

Lu hung his head. That was it, he'd been dismissed. Tears threatened to roll down his cheeks, but Lu quickly wiped them away. He hoped none of the others would notice.

"Good luck," Sadie called.

"I'll pray for you," Henry added.

Chino didn't say another word, though he looked more upset than any of the others.

Jack spoke to the remaining company—something Lu wasn't meant to hear—and all five returned to their horses. Lu watched, tears coming to his eyes, as they mounted up. He didn't guess he'd see any of them ever again.

Lu spent the next few minutes getting Crash and the remaining mule turned around. It wasn't easy, especially as his hands wouldn't stop shaking, but he managed. He tied the mule's lead—a broken piece of leather harness was still attached to the end—to his saddle. It seemed foolish after what had just happened, but he could see no other way. He couldn't possibly drag a mule all the way to the top of this canyon by hand.

It rapidly became apparent that the lion's share of the storm was yet to come, and that Lu was marching directly into its teeth. Even seeing the trail ahead was all but impossible, to say nothing of landmarks. Lu was shivering cold, alone and scared half out of his mind. Left to his own devices, he might have given up. Fortunately, Crash seemed to know exactly where he was going. Twice they'd come to forks in the road, and he was able to sniff out the right path each time. But as the storm intensified, even Crash found the going difficult.

They needed to find shelter, and quick. Lu began to wonder if there might not be other caves in this canyon, places even Jack Straw knew nothing about. It was possible, he guessed. Jack didn't know everything.

At the next fork in the road, Lu waited for Crash to choose a path, and then reined him in the opposite direction. Lu knew there were no caves on the trail they'd come down. If they were to find shelter, they'd have to go another way.

Crash whinnied in protest, but eventually assented. Lu just hoped he hadn't made a fatal mistake.

Hour upon hour they searched, over ledges so narrow, beside cliffs so sheer, that Lu's knees were scraped to bleeding on the canyon walls. More than once they came around a bend and, seeing the path ahead, Lu's heart skipped a beat. It just didn't seem possible for a horse to hug close enough to the wall to keep from falling. But somehow, Crash always did. At last, just as the storm was its nastiest, they came around a bend and saw a cave. It was only a shallow indent, but large enough for their purposes. Lu dismounted and led Crash and the mule inside.

"Well, at least it's dry," Lu muttered, standing between the steaming bodies of the animals. He took off his boots and dumped out the water that had collected inside.

They stayed there the rest of that day, watching as the rain beat against their stone doorstep.

After moping and cursing his fate for the first couple of hours, Lu began to feel hungry. A quick inspection of the mule showed that he'd managed to get away with some of the pemmican, a small sack of oats, two boxes of bullets for Henry's rifle, one of the MacLemores' valises, and a half-dozen of the extra water-skins Chino had taken from the Indian village. Lu was amazed at it all. He decided to name the mule "Lucky."

After feeding Crash and Lucky some of the oats, Lu ate a bit of the pemmican. It didn't taste so bad any more. Hunger had spiced it very nicely. Then, because he had nothing else to do, Lu unpacked the valise. Inside he found two bonnets, two pairs of men's trousers, a cotton shirt, a union suit, and a set of surprisingly frilly ladies' underclothes. He also found a gingham dress and a pair of rawhide gloves.

Lu was about to pack it all away again when he noticed something else. At the bottom of the bag, folded inside a navy blue handkerchief, was the smallest revolver Lu had ever seen. It was larger than the derringer that Chino carried in his jacket pocket, but not by much. It did have one thing to recommend it, however. Unlike his own brass pistol, this gun was loaded. Lu stuck it in his pocket.

By the time he got Sadie's clothes folded and put away, darkness had begun to descend over the canyon. Lu wasn't tired, but figured he may as well lie down. Normally he used his saddle for a pillow, but that night Lu rested his head on Sadie's valise.

He must've been sleepier than he thought, because a moment later he was out. And he didn't wake up 'til morning.

CHAPTER 9
A BILL COMES DUE

THE STORM MUST HAVE BLOWN itself out sometime during the night, because when Lu woke up the next morning all was bright and beautiful once more.

He was stiff and groggy as he stumbled out of the little cave. The sun was just beginning to peek over the walls of the canyon, but already it was hot. Lu splashed through the puddles that had collected on the narrow piece of ledge surrounding the cave entrance, right to the edge of the precipice, and was shocked to see the river not even a thousand feet below. He was even more surprised when he glanced to his left and saw the very same red and burnt-orange stone bridge he'd marveled at two mornings before, and with a path leading up to it as surely as if it were the finger of god pointing out, with no uncertainty what-so-ever, exactly where he needed to go.

As he chewed a bit of pemmican, Lu concocted a plan. He'd cross that bridge—if such a thing were even possible—and then head north along the opposite wall of the canyon until he found his missing friends. He laughed out loud as he imagined the looks on their faces. They'd be hungry, he guessed. Unless one of them had thought to squirrel something away in a saddlebag, Lu had all the remaining food. Henry would bless the day he'd first met Lu. Chino would swear up a storm of happiness. And Sadie would want to shower him with kisses.

The march to the bridge was a good deal farther than Lu had first reckoned it—he'd forgotten about the difference between actual and apparent distances in the canyon—but he managed to reach it at least one full hour before noon.

Looking across, Lu began to seriously question the wisdom of his undertaking. It wasn't that the bridge lacked strength. Even at its narrowest, the stone arch was at least ten feet wide. Compared to the ledge on which the rest of the mules had met their end, this was a veritable highway of stone. And it was as thick as a pair of railway engines, stacked one atop another. A hundred horses wouldn't have weighed enough to break that estimable stone beam. But as a bridge it had one major flaw. It was round. And not gently round either. Seen from above, the whole span resembled nothing so much as the pointy end of a chicken's egg. Crossing it would be something along the lines of walking over the peak of a barn roof. Lu guessed he could manage well enough, but Crash's hooves were another matter all together. It was impossible to imagine a horse balanced on a barn roof, even one as sure-footed as Crash.

But Lu couldn't resist giving the bridge a closer look. Seeing the faces of his friends again, tears of joy running down their cheeks and kisses at the edges of their rosy lips, was just too much to give up. The very least he could do was to walk the bridge himself. Maybe once he felt it underfoot, he'd decide that it wasn't as peaked as he'd thought.

So Lu climbed down from his saddle and started across. The first few steps were easy. The bridge was constructed entirely of sandstone, and so offered plenty of grip for the soles of his boots. It was nothing to skip over, but it was crossable. Fortunate that it was, too, because Lu had gone no more than halfway across before Crash decided to follow. And since his guide rope was fastened to Crash's saddle, Lucky was being dragged along as well.

That decided things in a hurry. Lu guessed he might find some way to get both animals across that bridge, but turning them around, or backing them over it, would be impossible.

It took the better part of fifteen minutes for the three of them to slink across, during which time Lu stared at nothing apart from the stone that lay directly in front of his feet. Thinking back on it, there were undoubtedly places where he might've taken a quick look around. And in retrospect, he probably should have. But he didn't, and so he was heartily surprised when suddenly, and with not more than ten yards left to cross, Crash let out a loud whinny and refused to go even one step farther.

"Don't stop now," Lu said. "We're darned near the other—"

He was interrupted by a growl so deep and rumbling that Lu's first thought was of thunder. When he looked up and saw two luminous gold eyes peering at him out of a tawny face, he wished it had been.

A mountain lion lay sprawled across the far end of the bridge. If it'd had a mind to, it could have covered the distance between itself and Lu in a single leap. Fortunately, the lion seemed content to do little more than pant and flick its tail.

"Shoo!" Lu hissed. "Go on."

The lion stared at him. It looked neither hungry nor violent, but Lu couldn't take any chances. He needed to get Crash and Lucky across this bridge, and he couldn't do it so long as a mountain lion was blocking the path. Really, he had no choice. Very slowly, Lu reached for the revolver in his pocket.

"I don't know what sort of a pea-shooter you got stashed, but I'd leave it set if I was you."

Lu turned toward the voice. A cowboy, sitting atop a mottled gray charger, moseyed out from behind a fin of red stone. He wore a gray Stetson and rawhide chaps. A cigarette dangled from his bottom lip. His hair was the color of sunburned wheat.

"There's a lion," Lu said, fingers still gripped tight to the heel of the revolver in his pocket.

"Her?" The cowboy squinted at the mountain lion. "Pshaw. Why, she ain't nothin' but a pussycat. Wouldn't hurt a fly. Would you, Sweetheart?"

"Do you think she could get out of the way then?" Lu asked. "Just for a minute?"

The cowboy grinned. "Git along now, Sweetheart. Quit teasin' the boy."

Reluctantly, the lion rolled to her feet.

"She looks fearsome, I'll grant you that, but there ain't no accountin' for looks."

As soon as the lion had gone, Lu grabbed Crash's reins, dragging both he and Lucky the last few meters to safety.

"That's a fine lookin' horse you got there," the cowboy observed. "Wish I could 'a seen the squaw what sold him to you."

"Crash is better than he looks."

"Must be."

Lu stared at the cowboy, not sure whether to thank or curse him.

"Well, mount up then," the cowboy said. "We got a mile or two to cover yet."

"You . . . You want me to come with you?"

"Lookin' for that group of pilgrims, ain't ya?"

"Pilgrims?"

"Them that nearly got blown up in the lightning storm."

"Those are my friends," Lu said.

"Well, you're sure never gonna find 'em settin' on your heels."

Lu wasn't sure what to do. On the one hand, this cowboy seemed to know exactly where his friends were, and how to reach them. But he was also a complete stranger. He could be dangerous. "I'm not sure I ought to go with you," Lu said at last.

"Not go?" The cowboy guffawed. "You got some better option I ain't aware of?"

Lu shook his head. He didn't.

"Well then, get onto that nag of yours and let's move."

He waited until Lu was in the saddle, and then wheeled his horse around south.

"But aren't my friends to the north?" Lu asked.

"Don't worry, son, you'll catch 'em." The cowboy gave his horse a kick. "Home, Widowmaker."

Lu trailed after that cowboy for the rest of the afternoon, until the sun had disappeared over the canyon walls. Days were short this deep in the Hell Mouth, shadows dark and ominous.

Lu might have liked to talk to his strange new guide, but the cowboy offered little in the way of opportunity. His horse was a miracle of energy, alternating between a trot and a canter for hours at a clip. Crash managed to stay within shouting distance, but Lucky made even that difficult. The mule was sweating freely, droplets running off his long ears, foam bubbling around the straps of his harness.

At last they reached their destination. It was a cave not unlike the one in which Lu had whiled away the previous night, though with the opening boarded over to resemble an ordinary cottage. There was even a length of tin chimney pipe jutting through a hole over the door.

"This here's my house," the cowboy said, sliding down off his horse. "There's a hitchin' rail round that corner yonder, and a bale of fine green hay under an old overturned trough. I'd be obliged if you'd feed Widowmaker while you're at it. I'll start dinner. Like biscuits?"

"Sir?" Lu stammered.

"Somethin' wrong?"

"My name's Tzu-lu." He held out his hand. "But my friends call me Lu."

They shook.

"Bill," the cowboy said. His hand was as rough and horny as a snakeskin boot. "Take care of your gear, Lu. Must be wet as the grave in them bags."

When he'd finished looking after the stock, Lu knocked on the cottage door. Bill shouted at him to "come on in."

The cave was deeper than Lu would have guessed. Inside was a desk, a stove, a four-poster bed covered with a rag quilt, a stocked bookshelf, and a pair of oil lanterns dangling from hooks that'd been drilled into the stone ceiling. At the center of the room was a table and chairs. Fine porcelain dishes, tea cups and saucers included, were set on the table as though in expectation of friends, though Lu doubted anyone had visited in at least a score of years.

Bill stood over the stove, stirring a bubbling pot of stew. "Hungry?" he asked.

"Yes, sir."

"Well, grab a seat then."

Lu pulled out one of the chairs. He was about to sit down when he noticed a rattlesnake curled up in the seat, its head reared back to strike. The shock was enough to make Lu curse, which he did, painting the entire cave, floor and ceiling included, with multiple coats of the vilest swears he knew. Not to be outdone, the snake joined in the ruckus with a half-dozen hard shakes of its tail, a noise which in no way calmed the nerves of its discoverer.

"That's Hank," Bill explained, once the profanity had dissipated. "Just push him off the seat. He knows he ain't supposed to be up there. You hear me? Git along now Hank. Your place is in the hole under the bed, and you know it."

The snake made no move to abandon the chair, and Lu had absolutely no intention of pushing him. He'd just take another chair, preferably as far from Hank as possible.

Bill set two steaming bowls of stew on the table, one for himself and the other for Lu. A third he set outside the door for Sweetheart.

"Like rabbit?" he asked. "Partial to it myself. Tastier 'n chicken. Not so heavy as a beefsteak." Bill took a forkful of stew and crammed it in his mouth. "T'ain't bad." He was about to take another bite, but instead slapped his palm down on the table. "Dang. Near forgot the biscuits." He yanked the oven door open, pulled out a pan of golden brown biscuits, and deposited it on the table along with a tin can brim-full of what appeared to be bacon grease. "Just you slice one of these here open and slather on some drippins," Bill instructed. "Finer eatin' than you'll get in any Frenchie dive."

Bill had little to say for the next quarter-hour. He shoveled away that first bowl of stew before Lu had fairly tasted his portion, and went back for seconds. Lu liked the rabbit stew, though he didn't think it was any better than chicken. The biscuits, on the other hand, were the best he'd ever eaten, light and fluffy and delicious. He slathered on some of the bacon grease, as Bill had suggested, and thought it tasty enough, but guessed he'd just as soon take his biscuits straight from then on.

As soon as Bill had polished off his second helping—Lu was still only half through his first—he took a cigarette from his breast pocket and stuck it in the stove. When it was lit, he sucked a voluminous cloud of smoke into his lungs. Bill was no man for half measures.

"Now then, what exactly are you folks doin' in my stretch of canyon?" he asked.

"Just passing through," Lu said. "We're headed for a mining town called Silver City. Ever heard of it?"

Bill shook his head. "Must be one of them new jobbies that're poppin' up all over. Folks tryin' to strike it rich without doin' no work." He spat on the floor. "That what you're after?"

"Sort of. Chino, Henry, Jack and me were hired by Mr. John MacLemore. A gang of bandits killed his wife and son, and moved into his house. Mr. MacLemore wants to turn them out." Lu considered telling Bill about the gold, but decided against it. Jack would have skinned him for telling this much. Besides, Lu figured Bill would be able to guess the rest without being told. Bill was quick.

"Must be one fine house," Bill remarked.

Lu shrugged.

"What about these bandits? Y'all know who they are?"

"Jack does. At least, I think he does."

"But he won't tell you."

Lu shook his head.

"Nope. Just like him," Bill said. "Born poker player."

"You know Jack?" Lu asked.

"I guess I know him 'bout as well as anybody. 'Course, that ain't sayin' much. Jack Straw plays close to the vest. Has for years beyond countin'. And I don't reckon he's likely to change anytime soon."

"Do _you_ know who the bandits are?"

"Might." Bill pondered a moment. "You ever heard of Lucifer?"

Lu nodded.

"Well, just remember this. No matter who you find in that house, it ain't Lucifer. Not by a long shot. There's a whole passel of underhanded devils out there, but not a one of 'em has half the power he pretends. Mostly they just use simple tricks. Find ways for folks to damn themselves. Nope. Not Lucifer by a mile. You get me?"

Lu stared. If there was any way to respond to such a wild and outrageous statement, he didn't know what it was. There didn't even seem to be any questions to ask. Lu gave serious thought to laughing out loud, but decided that wouldn't do any good at all. So he just sat there, a look of puzzlement plastered over his face. He tried to think of some way to change the subject.

"Maybe we shouldn't talk about this," Lu said. "Jack thinks the ghost-riders will hear. He thinks they're probably working for MacLemore's bandit."

"Ghost-riders?" Bill scoffed. "Those rascally fiends? They don't have any power in *my* house."

"Why not?"

"They don't because I say they don't. That's all." Bill spat each word out as though it were a wad of over-chewed tobacco. "Who's the girl?"

"What girl?"

"The one ridin' with Jack."

"Oh, that's just Sadie. She's MacLemore's daughter."

"Good rider."

"Great rider. A good shot too."

"Let me see your pistol."

Lu pulled it out of his holster and handed it across the table.

"Confederate," Bill said, turning the revolver back and forth in his hands. "Copy of a navy colt." He squinted at the underside of the barrel. "See this mark?" He held it up for Lu to see. There was an X, stamped inside a rectangle, directly in front of the trigger guard. "The man that owned this gun was probably from the Heart of Dixie. That's their usual mark. How does it shoot?"

"I never shot it," Lu said, and hoped it was too dark in the cave for Bill to see him blush. "I don't have any bullets."

"No bullets? Well, that's a heck of a note."

Bill went to his desk, opening all six drawers before finding what he was looking for. It was a pistol, exactly like Lu's, except made of steel instead of brass. Bill laid it on his desk-top, then reached into the drawer once more, pulling out a holster to fit the gun. A dozen shells were pressed into the loops on either side of the buckle. Bill thumbed the bullets into his palm. As he did so, Lu noticed that there were letters tooled into the leather across the back of the gun-belt. They spelled out a name. "Sue."

"Load your piece," Bill said, dropping all twelve shells into Lu's lap.

Lu did as instructed, and was pleased to see that the bullets did in fact fit. He was about to slide a sixth bullet into the cylinder when Bill stopped him.

"Always leave the chamber under the hammer open," he said. "Five bullets are enough to kill any man. And if they ain't, a sixth isn't likely to turn the trick."

"I notice you don't wear a gun," Lu said, as he shoved the remaining shells into the pouch on his holster.

"Nope," Bill agreed. "Guns have a funny way of goin' off in your hand. Carry one long enough and you'll wind up shootin' somebody. If you hate him, so be it. But if you don't?" He whistled. "Nowadays I keep my pistols under my pillow, and my rifle in a case atop the bookshelf. I dig 'em out once a month or so, to impress the Injuns mostly, but I never load 'em. Not no more."

Lu remained silent a moment. "Who's Sue?" he asked finally.

"My wife." A smile stole over Bill's lips, but not a happy one.

"Is she gone?"

"Long gone . . . And far away."

Bill obviously took no pleasure in discussing his wife, so Lu changed the subject. "Think we'll be able to find my friends tomorrow?" he asked.

"Tomorrow?" Bill shook his head. "Couple days is more likely."

"Days?"

Bill grinned. "You've miles to ride afore you see Jack Straw again. But you'll make it. Yep, you'll make it."

✪

Lu didn't get much sleep that night. He stretched out on the floor beside the stove, his head resting on Sadie's valise, and was as warm and comfortable as if he was in his bed at home. But he couldn't seem to relax. The last thing Bill had said to him, just before climbing into his own bed, was that Hank liked to slither around the cave in the middle of the night, "just to keep his blood movin'." Bill said not to worry, that Hank was as quiet and personable a sleeping companion as a body could wish for. Lu had his doubts. In fact, just imagining that big old rattler wandering the room was enough to keep his eyes pinched open the whole night through. Lu may have slipped off for a moment, now and again, but his dreams were chuck-full of creeping, slithering bodies. More than once he came wide awake, convinced that Hank was crawling up his pant leg.

Lu was relieved when the sun finally peeked over the canyon wall and Bill said it was time to ride. They ate the leftover biscuits, drank a cup of bitter coffee, and were off. Crash and Lucky were glad to get back to the trail, too. They'd had almost as nerve-wracking a night as Lu. Bill assigned his mountain lion, Sweetheart, to watch over and guard them from any thieves or predators that might happen along. She sat with them from sundown to sunrise, but somehow they felt no safer for all her diligence.

To Lu's surprise, Bill brought his rifle along for the ride. It was an older gun, oiled and polished until it gleamed like a star on a clear night, but it wasn't loaded. Lu wondered if the cowboy even had bullets, or had pawned them off on some other traveler in need of munitions.

Their trail led due south and descended to the very edge of the river. It was a fine path, nothing like the rocky cliffs down which Lu and the others had made their descent. Even the river seemed calmer, though he'd never gotten so good a look at it before, and so had only limited impressions with which to make a comparison. In places it resembled a lake, the normally churning waters settling into a deep green. Why had Jack taken them north? Lu asked Bill, and was surprised at the answer.

"Avoiding the Mimbrachua, I expect," Bill said.

"Mimbrachua?"

"Injuns. Warriors. Control the whole southern half o' the canyon. Rocks ain't the only dangers in the Hell Mouth, you know. Ain't even the worst."

"I don't think I've ever heard of them."

Bill shrugged. "Well, you'll see 'em tonight."

"Maybe we should go another way," Lu suggested. "If Jack was afraid—"

"I never said he was afraid. Jack and the Mimbrachua headman just never saw eye to eye, that's all. Speakin' of which, I wouldn't mention Jack Straw in their camp if I was you."

"What should I say?"

"Say whatever you like. Just don't mention Jack."

They trailed the river's edge for hour upon hour, climbing around boulders and through thickets of brush and scrub as thorny as a barbed-wire fence. Around noon they came upon a waterfall, trickling from the high granite cliffs that overhung this particular bend of the Moreno River. It wasn't much, as cascades go. The fall was too long for the water to actually reach the surface of the stream. In fact, by the time it reached bottom it barely qualified as mist. But what the waterfall lacked in power it more than made up for in beauty. The mist was fertile soil for the cultivation of rainbows. Lu sat limp atop his horse, staring openmouthed at all the rich colors. The rainbows looked, from a distance at least, nearly as solid as the stone bridge over which he'd come the morning before. He wished his mother was there to see it. She hated rain, but loved rainbows.

"Like it?" Bill asked. "That there's one of the wonders of the Hell Mouth. The Tears of Uruk. Beautiful as Lucifer's Leap, if I do say so myself."

"Who's Uruk?" Lu asked.

"Uruk was a hunter and warrior. This was way back, before anyone paid much attention to heroes, lessen they became kings or the like. He's all but forgotten now. Just as we'll all be, sooner or later."

"What about Lucifer's Leap?"

"Hell son, you crossed it yesterday. Lucifer's Leap is where I found you."

"The stone bridge?"

"None other."

They sat a while longer, marveling at the rainbows. Then Bill climbed down from his horse. "This is as good a spot as any to water the stock," he said.

Lu guided Lucky and Crash to the river. While they drank, he took a quick look around. The path they'd been following came to an end at the waterfall. Lu asked Bill about it and received back a look of scorn.

"Don't guess a little mist'll hurt you none," he said.

They rode straight through the waterfall, coming out the other side wet but refreshed. Lu licked his lips, and was surprised to find the water sweet. If he'd known, he might have used the short break to fill his water-skins. He suggested the idea to Bill, but the cowboy was unmoved. "Plenty of water up ahead. Leave Uruk his tears at least."

The rest of that day was spent in the saddle. Dust from the trail stuck to their damp clothes, turning to mud and then drying and cracking in the sun. Lu's shirt was nearly solid with the stuff, as was Crash's mane. Lucky looked a nightmare. He was entirely covered in mud, but didn't seem to mind.

By the time the sun had disappeared into the Hell Mouth's western bank they'd covered close to twenty miles. Lu wondered if they'd be stopping any time soon, but Bill said they still had a mile or two yet to ride. Before long it was full dark. Fortunately, a waxing moon illuminated the path well enough to keep them on the trail. Without it, Lu might have been scared. He was a little bit scared anyway. Lu did wish they could stop and rinse off at least one or two layers of trail dust, but Bill said that wasn't necessary. "These Indians aren't likely to mind a bit of grime."

And he was right. The first Mimbrachua they saw sat perched atop a boulder, at least a mile from the main camp. He had on a long shirt of dark blue wool, and atop his head sat a cavalry officer's broad-brimmed hat. Lu recognized it by the gold tassels. As soon as he saw them, the scout leapt from the rock and went running up the path, easily outstripping the tired horses.

A few minutes later, a delegation of boys descended upon them, chattering animatedly in their own tongue. They'd clearly sprinted down from the camp, hoping to be among the first to stare at the strangers, but not a one of them was out of breath. The boys maintained a safe distance, jogging just far enough ahead so that they could see and be seen, but not close enough to grab. Lu counted five of them. The youngest was naked from the soles of his feet right up to the hair on top of his head. The oldest wore a shirt very much like the one they'd seen on the scout, undoubtedly a hand-me-down from a father or older brother. The other three boys were possessed of a motley haphazard of clothing bits and pieces, giving them the appearance of tramps or story-book pirates. Each and every one of them was at least twice as filthy as Lu himself, though they seemed as proud as if they were kings.

The Mimbrachua camp was alive with activity. Women, most with babies bound loosely to their breasts, were either hunched over cook-fires or kneeling over grinding blocks, turning maize into meal. The younger children, not one of whom was possessed of a single thread of clothing, or an ounce of modesty, crouched at their mothers' feet, making dirt cakes and mud pies. The older boys and girls, including the ones Lu had seen on the path, hauled water from the river for the herd of mangy horses that occupied the far side of the camp, or else tended the fires. Dogs, each and every one of them starved near to death, skulked at the edge of the shadows, heads lowered and tails between their legs. Only the men seemed truly at ease. They sat around the smaller fires, in groups of five or six, smoking their pipes.

The instant they rode into the camp, Bill was yanked down off his horse. Lu was too. He tried to protest, but the Indians wouldn't listen.

"Don't worry," Bill assured him. "They're just havin' some fun. It's their way of welcoming us into camp."

While the boys led their horses off to join the herd, the girls dragged them toward one of the cook-fires, where women forced bowls of steaming corn mush into their hands. Lu hated to scoop it up with his filthy fingers, but saw that there was no other choice. The women stared at him the whole time, smiling and nodding proudly every time he took a bite. The mud on his fingers didn't make much difference, as it turned out. At least a third portion of the mush was just ground up sand, no doubt a result of their method for grinding corn.

"Awful, ain't it?" Bill said. "They make me eat this mess every time I come. I used to try to tell them 'no,' but they'd hear none of it. Even tried to get them to let me wash up first, but the idea was as foreign as a fork or spoon." He scooped up a finger of mash and stuck it in his mouth. "Once, I made a whole pan of good biscuits, just to show them what could be done. But you know what they did? Took my good biscuits, ground 'em down to nothin', and made more sandy porridge."

Lu laughed. Over Bill's shoulder he could see a pair of Indian women roasting ears of corn over a fire. "Maybe we could get them to give us a roasted ear," he suggested.

"Try it," Bill said.

Lu gestured to the girls crowded around them, asking for one of the roasted ears. It took a while, but eventually they saw where he was pointing. Immediately the ears were brought. The woman who'd been so carefully roasting them over her fire held the steaming corn up for Lu and Bill to see, then took them right over to the grinding stones and started turning them to paste. Bill howled with laughter.

When they'd finally finished eating their tasteless mush—Lu could only think to describe the flavor as "gray"—the Indian girls took Bill and Lu by the arms and dragged them toward one of the many rings of pipe-smokers. The oldest of the men, a haggard scarecrow of what Lu guessed to be about 210 years old, and with fewer than four teeth, motioned at them to sit. As soon as he was settled, Lu was given a pipe and instructed to smoke. He took a long suck at the mouthpiece, expecting a breath of smoke something like what he'd had with Joseph, but was disappointed to find it a choking mixture of tobacco and something else, he dared not guess what. He was still coughing as he handed the pipe to Bill. For all their friendliness, these people in no way resembled Joseph's fastidious village. Even so, Lu didn't dislike these Mimbrachua. Not at all. If anything, he thought them the jolliest bunch of ragamuffins he'd ever heard tell of.

Bill took his turn at the pipe, making a far better show of himself than Lu had, and passed it along. "Where's Gokhlayeh?" he asked, smoke still puffing out from between his lips.

The Indians looked at each other.

"Gokhlayeh?" Bill tried again.

"I am here," a voice boomed over the heads of the seated men.

Out of the gloom padded the most grim and downcast individual Lu had ever seen, Indian or otherwise. He wore a shirt of black cloth, speckled over with dust, and his long hair was tied up in a bandanna cut from the same material. Cinched round his waist was a leather belt studded with rings and disks of silver. From one hip dangled a pistol, and on the other was a bowie knife, the sheath of which he had decorated with scalps. Gokhlayeh wore tall leather boots, tied over his knees with lengths of horsehair rope. As he strode into the firelight, his gaze was fixed on Lu and Bill. He seemed almost angry at them, Lu thought. Or maybe he was wondering how their scalps might look next to the others on his belt. Either way, Lu wished they'd never come.

Gokhlayeh said something in his own language, a long string of words that sounded to Lu like vile swears. He'd heard much of the same lingo from the boys they'd met on the trail, and the women chattered constantly, sounding lovely whatever they might be saying. But from this man the language seemed harsh and cruel.

Bill waited until Gokhlayeh was finished, then said, "I've told you before, and I'll tell you again, I don't savvy none of that gibberish. Jack Straw might, but I sure as hell don't. I've no mind for languages and no intention of acquiring one just so I can talk to the likes of you."

For an instant, Lu thought Gokhlayeh would reach out a hand and strike Bill dead. Then he laughed. "You do not visit enough, Bill," he said. "I never tire of your stupidity."

The other Indians scooted apart and Gokhlayeh sat down. As he did, Lu noticed a young woman. She must have been standing there the whole time, but he'd completely overlooked her. No longer. As Gokhlayeh took his place in the circle, she was for the first time fully illuminated by the fire. Lu gasped. He couldn't help it. This young woman might have been pretty once, but never would be again. Her nose had been hacked off at the root, leaving not even a bump. All that remained was a blunt scar, spread cheek to cheek, lip to eyes, and a pair of rough holes for breathing.

She crouched in Gokhlayeh's shadow, disappearing once more from sight. But Lu's mind kept the image of her ruined face solidly in place. He knew that in different parts of the world they hung murderers, castrated rapists, and cut the hands off thieves. Had this girl committed some crime? What crime could possibly explain such woeful treatment? Cruelty, that's all this was. It made Lu's eyes water to imagine the sheer hatefulness of the devil, be it man or woman, who'd done it.

"What do you want?" Gokhlayeh asked, once he'd taken his turn at the pipe.

"Escortin' this here boy," Bill said.

"And where are you taking him?"

"Up top."

"Back to the Pecos?"

Bill shook his head. "He got separated from his people. I aim to put him back."

Gokhlayeh looked Lu up and down. "And just who are his people?"

"I'm with the MacLemore party," Lu explained. "We're going to Silver City. To shoot some bandits."

"With that?" Gokhlayeh pointed at Lu's pistol.

"We've got other guns."

"And just where are these other guns?"

Lu shook his head. "I don't know exactly."

"I see." Gokhlayeh leaned forward, his black eyes focused exclusively on Lu. "Were those your mules we found floating down the river?" he asked.

"You found them?"

"Nothing comes through the Hell Mouth without my knowing it."

"They were struck by lightning and fell."

The headman didn't seem particularly interested in Lu's story. "Who else is in your party?" he asked.

"Well, there's Henry and Chino, Mister MacLemore, Sadie and me."

"Sadie? A girl?"

"Sadie's a girl, but she's a heck of a shot, too."

"Anyone else? A famous gunfighter perhaps?"

Lu looked at Bill, and then shook his head. "Nope. Nobody else."

Gokhlayeh smirked. "And what have you brought for me?" he asked.

"For you?"

"This is my country. My canyon. You don't think you can just ride through without offering some kind of tribute? A white man would pay in blood."

"Well, what do you want?" Lu asked, suddenly feeling very nervous.

"What do you have?"

Lu thought a long time. He'd give up his guns if he had to, but only if he could think of nothing else. He looked at Bill, hoping for guidance, but the cowboy just shrugged. Should he give them Lucky? Better to give them a gun, he thought. Gokhlayeh glared at him during the whole of his deliberations, which didn't help. Lu had just decided to give them Sadie's revolver when another thought leapt into his mind. "Let me grab something," he said. "It's on my mule."

Gokhlayeh waved at him to go.

Lu raced to where the animals stood, chewing the bits of thorny brush that lined the hillside. Crash and Lucky were still tied together, the contents of the mule's bags apparently untouched. Quick as he could, Lu untied Sadie's valise. It was covered in mud, as was everything else, but when Lu looked inside he saw that the contents were clean.

Valise in tow, Lu raced back to the fire.

Both Bill and the Indians watched with interest as Lu unpacked the riding gloves, shirts and trousers, folding them carefully and stacking them on a rock. At last, toward the bottom he found what he'd been searching for.

"Here," he said, and handed Gokhlayeh one of Sadie's extra bonnets. It was the pale yellow one, with the tiny white flowers.

Gokhlayeh stared at it, puzzled.

"For her," Lu explained, gesturing at the girl huddled in the headman's shadow.

Apparently mystified, Gokhlayeh turned toward the girl, the bonnet dangling limply from his fingers. At first, she tried to duck back into the shadows. She only came out when Gokhlayeh explained that she was meant to have this strange frilly bandana.

Slowly, as though fearing some trick, the girl took the bonnet and held it up to the light. When she saw the flowers embroidered over it, she smiled.

"She can wear it on her head," Lu said, and Gokhlayeh translated.

The girl put the bonnet on, tying the strings under her chin. She'd put it on backward, so that the lace went across the back of her head, but Lu didn't correct her.

"And there's more," he said, pulling out the frilly ladies' underclothes and handing them to the girl. At first, she didn't want to take them directly from Lu's hand, but with Gokhlayeh's encouragement she managed.

Lu was far too embarrassed to explain the use of the bloomers, and so was gratified to see that the leg holes made an explanation unnecessary. Right out there in front of the whole world, the girl hiked up her skirt and stepped into her gift. Watching her pull them up was almost too much for Lu. He hesitated to give her the last of Sadie's garments, but decided that a thing once begun had to be finished.

He took the gingham dress from the valise and held it up for the girl to see. This time she needed no urging. She took the dress and pressed it to her face.

After she'd cradled it a moment, she put it on. Fortunately, she slipped it on over the rough Indian skirt she was already wearing, thereby saving Lu from further embarrassment.

When the buttons had all been fastened, the girl turned to show Gokhlayeh. The look of hope in her eyes was heartbreaking. The headman said nothing. He just looked her up and down, and then gave her a pat on the cheek. She said something to him in their language, and he responded. It must have been nice, because all at once the girl went skipping across the encampment. Every man in the smoking circle watched her go. If anything, the girl's terrible scar was made even more prominent. Lu had no doubt that the other girls would continue to make fun of her, if they did so now, but at least she'd had a moment of vanity. For one instant, the wreck of her face was overcome, in her own mind at least, by an interest in something as worthless and unnecessary as a white woman's dress. At least for tonight she'd be a different sort of curiosity among her tribe.

The same thoughts must have been running through Gokhlayeh's mind. "This payment of yours is worthless," he said. "One bullet. One water-skin. Even a single grain of corn would do more for my people than this . . . dress." He frowned. "It is so valueless that I can not offer even one of my warriors to escort you to the top of the canyon."

"That's all right," Lu began. "If you'll just point us to the path—"

"No," Goklayeh cut him off. "I will take you myself."

CHAPTER 10
OUT OF HELL

THEY PLANNED TO LEAVE EARLY the next morning, making for a trail Lu and Bill had passed by in the dark the night before. The Mimbrachua women were up before dawn, and had hot corn mush ready even as the first rays of sunlight slithered down the western wall of the canyon.

Lu and Bill choked down their breakfast and had just begun to saddle their mounts when Gokhlayeh came galloping into camp. Apparently he'd spent the better part of the previous night scouting, and had startling news.

A party of military surveyors, fourteen in all, had begun the slow descent to the canyon floor. They were heavily armed and possessed a full train of pack mules. As soon as they heard, the Indians began to break camp.

"I guess we'll have to go on without you," Lu said to Gokhlayeh.
"Why?"
"You'll want to stay with your people. Won't you?"
"They will be fine for a day or two."

Lu didn't know whether to be pleased or disappointed. Gokhlayeh was far and away the most frightening man he'd ever met. The cold rage that hung at the corners of his mouth was as hard to look at as the sun. But Lu was intrigued by the headman as well.

"So you'll come with us?" he asked.

"Of course. Unlike a white man, I keep my word."

It took no more than a quarter of an hour for the whole tribe to be packed and ready to move. About half of their horses—to Lu they looked even mangier in the light of day—were saddled for use by the warriors. The rest of the animals dragged simple log sledges, each piled to maximum density with the most diminutive bits of junk and flotsam Lu had ever seen. The Indians took everything. Not just food and equipment, but river rocks and random sticks. Even the ashes from their fires were dug up and hauled away. Whatever wouldn't fit onto the sledges they tied to their dogs. It was the most ramshackle, disorganized outfit Lu had ever seen. But it worked. In the time it took him to finish saddling Crash and harnessing Lucky, the Mimbrachua had completely dismantled their lives. The only sign of their ever having occupied this stretch of river was a mud-pie one of the children had made and left to dry on a boulder beside the river. And then even that was destroyed. A boy, one of their escorts from the night before, took the pie and flung it into the swirling waters of the Moreno.

When all was bound and packed, babies included, Gokhlayeh sent his people away. The men rode at the front, rifles across their knees, while the women and children footed it at the rear. Last to depart was the young woman Lu had taken an interest in the night before, still wearing her yellow bonnet and gingham dress. In the morning light, her face was even more heartbreaking. She gazed longingly at Gokhlayeh, obviously wishing she could go with him, then waved to Lu and raced away.

"Where will they go?" Lu asked.

"There is a good camp only a day's march to the south," Gokhlayeh said. "They will wait for me there."

"How far do you think you'll have to go? To escape the soldiers, I mean."

"Escape?" Gokhlayeh scoffed. "It is the soldiers who should think of escape. We think only of blood."

When his tribe had all gone, Gokhlayeh mounted his horse, the same rickety old plug he'd ridden into camp, and motioned for Lu and Bill to do likewise.

Gokhlayeh set an easy pace, not wanting to stress the animals unnecessarily. The way up was not as easy as the way down, Bill explained. If they weren't careful, the horses could be injured by the climb.

"Fortunately for us, that mule of yours will quit before there's any real danger. A mule does as much as it can and not a bit more. They're smarter than horses that way."

Bill and Lu chatted off and on during the ride. Lu told Bill all about his mother and grandfather—he got the impression that Bill had at least heard of Master K'ung, if not actually met him—and about his friends from school. Bill told Lu about his mountain lion, Sweetheart, whom he'd once saddled and ridden to satisfy a bet. Lu didn't believe the story, but didn't entirely discount it either. Bill was full of tall tales. He even knew a few about Jack Straw.

Gokhlayeh seldom spoke, but he did listen. And not just to Bill and Lu either. In fact, if Lu didn't know better, he'd have guessed the Mimbrachua headman was listening to words only he could hear. Whenever the breeze picked up, as it so often did in the canyon, Gokhlayeh would cock his ear. Sometimes, after listening for a few minutes, he'd turn toward Lu and grin, displaying a full set of straight white teeth. Other times he'd gaze back at Bill with a hideous scowl. For some reason, Lu found the headman's smiles vastly more disconcerting. It was hard to imagine Gokhlayeh taking pleasure in much of anything, unless it was the suffering and misery of a white man.

They stopped at least once every hour, to let the horses catch their breath, but they still climbed at a fantastic rate. By late afternoon they'd covered nearly thirteen miles, and had risen better than six thousand feet. The change in elevation was so abrupt that Lu began to feel sick. Twice he leaned over to throw up, but managed to clench his jaw and weather the storm. The third time he couldn't help retching a little, and was unsurprised to find that the Indian mush came up nearly as easy as it went down.

When Gokhlayeh called a halt, Lu didn't even bother to unsaddle his horse. He just lay at the side of the trail, head propped on a rock, sucking air.

"Chew this," Gokhlayeh said, pulling a sprig of gray leaves from under his belt.

"What is it?" Lu asked. The leaves were sweaty from being pressed against the Indian's belly.

"Medicine. Chew it."

Lu put the leaves in his mouth. The leaves were so bitter it made him want to scrape the skin from his tongue with a sharp rock. But Gokhlayeh was watching, so Lu kept right on chewing.

"Feel better?" Gokhlayeh asked after a few minutes.

Lu nodded. He couldn't actually tell for certain whether he did or not. The desire to throw up was as strong as ever, though Lu guessed that could be as much a result of the bitter leaves as the elevation.

When he could take no more, Lu dug a hole and spat the vile leaves in. Bill and Gokhlayeh had gone in search of firewood, so Lu didn't much worry about being caught spitting out valuable medicine. The bitter taste stayed with him for a good long while, only subsiding when he took a pull from one of his water-skins. After that, he really did start to feel better. In no time he felt well enough to unpack Lucky and unsaddle Crash.

For supper, Gokhlayeh had brought along a small pot of corn mush, which he boiled over the fire. Lu offered to supplement it with a pinch or two of pemmican, but Gokhlayeh flatly refused.

"Mimbrachua do not eat such filth," he said.

"I don't know about pemmican, but a beefsteak would taste pretty darn good right now." Bill smacked his lips. "And a hot biscuit to soak up the juice."

"Biscuits," Gokhlayeh spat. "Chokes me just to think of them."

"Ever et one with bacon drippin's and coffee?"

"In prison. The biscuits were moldy. The bacon rotten. And the coffee muddy."

"Prison? Why, no wonder you've got no taste for 'em. Derned things prob'ly destroyed your buds." Bill took a finger of mush from the pot and stuck it in his mouth. "Still, I reckon a moldy biscuit'd still taste better than this muddy cow-plop you savages are so fond of."

"Was that girl your daughter?" Lu asked, changing the subject. "The one with the . . ." He made a slashing motion across his nose.

"She is an orphan," Gokhlayeh said.

"How long has she been like that?"

"Since she was little. Eight or nine."

"Why? I mean, what did she do?"

Goklayeh glared at him. "How old are you?" he asked.

"I'm . . ." Lu stopped. "Do either of you know the date?"

Bill and Gokhlayeh looked at each other. Gokhlayeh shook his head.

"Feels like July to me," Bill mused. "Don't it feel like July?"

"Then I guess I must have had a birthday," Lu said. "A week or two ago."

"Well dang, happy birthday." Bill slapped Lu on the back. "How old are you?"

"Fifteen."

"Darn, that's a good one. I met my Sue when I was just fifteen. At least, I think I was fifteen. It's gettin' harder and harder to keep the years straight. The older I get, the more time seems to want to twist out from under me."

"I killed a white man when I was fifteen," Gokhlayeh said. "My first."

"What did he do?" Lu asked.

"I do not know."

They started again at first light.

"Your friends have finally crossed the river," Gokhlayeh told Lu as they saddled their horses.

"Really?"

The headman nodded. "But they are on a difficult path. One of the worst in all of the Hell Mouth. I doubt they will reach the top any time soon."

"How do you know all this?"

Gokhlayeh smiled. "I told you. Nothing happens in the Hell Mouth without my knowing."

Lu looked at Bill, who shrugged.

It was a fine day, sunny but cool. The trail climbed at an even steeper angle, but Lu suffered no further bouts of nausea. By noon they'd reached the eastern edge of an enormous plateau. There was one last slope still to climb, and it looked to be fairly steep, but Lu guessed a day's ride, day and a half at the outside, would more than do the trick. By sundown tomorrow he'd be clear of the Hell Mouth.

"See that finger of stone?" Gokhlayeh pointed to a sliver of pale rock, rising like a knife from the opposite end of the plateau. "The path you need begins at its base."

"Aren't you coming?" Lu asked.

"It is time that I return. There are white soldiers down there waiting to be killed." He smiled and Lu's blood ran cold.

"You will be safe from here," Gokhlayeh continued. "We have reached the end of Mimbrachua lands. There are no more warriors ahead. No scouts."

"Did you see any scouts?" Lu asked Bill.

"Pair of roughnecks 'bout a mile back," he said. "The one had a nice rifle, though he held it too far down the stock."

"You saw them?" Gokhlayeh sounded surprised.

"Knew they'd be around." Bill shrugged. "Ain't much to it. Just got to keep your eyes peeled."

Gokhlayeh sniffed, clearly annoyed. "Good luck," he said to Lu, extending his hand for the boy to shake. "I hope you kill your bandits."

"Thanks." Lu considered saying something about the soldiers Gokhlayeh and his people planned to ambush and murder, but decided against it. He just couldn't bring himself to wish death on someone he'd never met. "Thank your people for me," he said. "I really enjoyed meeting them."

Gokhlayeh nodded. "And tell Jack that the next time he tries to pass through my canyon, I *will* kill him."

Then, without muttering a single word to Bill, he wheeled his horse around, gave it a swift kick in the ribs, and was gone.

"Well, let's get along then," Bill suggested.

"Do you think it was him that cut that girl?" Lu asked.

"Nope," Bill said. "Can't say who done it, but I don't guess it was him. I'd bet whoever did do it was mighty sorry when old Gokhlayeh caught up to him, though."

"Do you think he did? Catch up to him, I mean."

"Yep. And I reckon you could hear that scoundrel's screams from miles away."

They camped that night at the base of the rock Gokhlayeh had pointed out to them. What Lu had taken for a mere sliver of granite turned out to be a monolith thirty feet wide and more than a hundred feet tall. A pair of red-tail hawks had built a nest at the top. As Lu and Bill settled down for the night, the male flew in with a rabbit carcass dangling from his talons.

"Darn," Bill said, still chewing the pemmican Lu had given him. "Animals eat better than we do."

The next morning, Bill guided Lu to the base of the slope, showing him the path he was to take. "All you have to do is follow it up and remember to stop ever-so-often to rest your stock. When you get to the top, head north. There's a stand of pines a couple of miles away, perched right at the edge of a cliff. Your friends will happen along there eventually."

"Are you going home?" Lu asked him.

Bill nodded. "Sweetheart must be gettin' powerful hungry by now. She fancies herself a hunter, but without the stew I give her, I reckon she'd starve. But don't tell her I said so."

"I won't."

"Just one more thing," Bill said. "You make sure Jack tells you all about this Yankee bandit you're after. Don't let him get away without spillin' his guts."

"Sure."

"And don't waste those bullets I give you. There's only twelve, and I know you'll be tempted to blast them at trees and what-have-you. You're just fifteen, and the temptation'll be strong. But don't give in to it. Those aren't no ordinary shells. You'll see. If you feel you just have to blast somethin', use that pea-shooter in your pocket. Save Sue's bullets for when you really need 'em. Hear me?"

Lu nodded.

"Hear?"

"Yes, sir."

"Good. You're a fine boy and I'm right glad I give 'em to you. My Sue, she'd 'a been proud, too. That's no lie. Sue couldn't stand no lies. Remember that. She had ways of forcing the truth to come out." Bill grinned. "You'll see."

They shook hands.

"Say 'hey' to Jack for me," Bill said.

And then, with a tip of his hat, Bill was gone, galloping back across the plateau, hell-bent for leather.

Lu watched him for a few minutes, until he could just make out the figure of a man atop a horse, racing along at the center of a cloud of dust. When Bill was out of sight, Lu thought back over everything that the strange cowboy had told him. Most of it made no sense. At least, it didn't make any sense *yet*. But Bill was more than he seemed. That much was obvious. Suddenly, Lu remembered something that struck him odd. Bill had said to make sure Jack told them all about the *Yankee* bandit they were after. Had Lu ever told him that the bandit was a Yankee? He didn't think so.

Lu shook his reins, gave Crash his head, and began the long slow climb to the top.

Two days later, Lu was lounging against one of the pines Bill had directed him to, when he heard voices. He grabbed his shirt off the branch over which he'd spread it, and yanked it down over his head. It was still damp, but not uncomfortably so. There was a stream a few yards from where he'd set up camp, so he'd kept busy washing his clothes, the equipment on Lucky's harness, and even Crash and Lucky themselves.

Soon as he had his shirt tucked in, Lu ran to the edge of the canyon and peered down. The voices were coming closer. After a few minutes he spotted them. All five, alive and healthy, and Jack at the lead. Lu could tell him by the brass buttons on his coat.

"Hello!" Lu shouted. "Hello!"

He was answered by a bullet striking the tree directly behind him.

Lu dove to the ground. Above him, a hole the size of a man's head had been punched half-way through the trunk of a ponderosa pine. That was Henry's rifle, no doubt about it. And it was likely a warning shot. If Henry had wanted to kill him, Lu knew he'd be dead, and probably headless to boot.

"Don't shoot!" Lu screamed, standing up and waving his arms over his head. "Don't shoot!" He could almost feel Henry sighting in on his face or chest, but resisted the urge to flinch. Lu just kept waving his arms, hoping he looked sufficiently harmless. It must have worked. No more bullets were sent after that first.

It took two hours for them to wind their way up to the surface. Jack appeared first, easing over the lip of the canyon with one pistol drawn and cocked. When he saw who was waiting, his face went as blank as a white-washed fence. It was the first and only time Lu ever saw Jack truly surprised.

"It's me," Lu said.

"Well, I'll be danged." Jack slid down off his appaloosa and shook Lu's hand. "I never thought to see *you* again."

The others were equally surprised and happy to see him. Chino was so overjoyed he got tears in his eyes. Sadie didn't actually kiss him, but she did give him a friendly punch on the arm, which was almost as good coming from her.

They demanded to hear Lu's story, and asked a fair number of questions as he told it. Lu was more than happy to oblige. He told them all about crossing the stone bridge, meeting Bill, and being taken to his strange little cave cottage. He told about the trip to see the Mimbrachua and their frightful headman, Gokhlayeh. He even told them about the scarred girl, and how he'd given her Sadie's dress and bonnet, though he made no mention of the lacy bloomers. Sadie was less than thrilled to hear that Lu had rifled through her private possessions, and worse, given some of them away, but she eventually forgave Lu his trespasses, as that was the Christian thing to do. Lu didn't tell them everything, however. He made no mention of his sleepless night in Bill's cottage, nor of how Hank had chased him away from his chosen chair. Likewise, he said nothing about how he'd gotten sick during the long ascent. In short, he did his level best to make himself out a hero.

For some reason, Lu also stayed quiet about the bullets Bill had given him. He didn't know why exactly, he just didn't think he ought to say anything. And unlike the western models that Jack and Chino wore, Lu's army holster had a fully closable ammunition pouch rather than open bullet-loops, so no one was likely to notice his newfound wealth.

After his story had all been told, Lu led his friends to the stream, where he set out a small feast of pemmican and water. Normally they'd have turned their noses up to such as that, but no longer. A few days of starvation rations had taught them to appreciate food in all its forms.

While the others ate, Lu cared for their horses. He unsaddled Henry's, Jack's and MacLemore's in turn, setting them free to graze on the long grass at the water's edge. Then he went to unsaddle Sadie's horse, and was startled. It wasn't Cinnamon. He looked at MacLemore's horse again, and recognized Cody for the horse he'd ridden across the plains, but Sadie's horse was nowhere to be seen. Her saddle, with all its flowery leatherwork, had been strapped onto the extra Indian horse Jack had traded Joseph for.

"What happened to Cinnamon?" Lu asked.

His question was met by hard stares.

"Gone," Sadie said at last. "And good riddance to her."

"Where'd she go?"

"Fell down crossing the river and broke her leg," Sadie spat. "Can you believe that? Her hoof went over a rock and bang! Dang near bashed my skull in while she was at it. I'm better off, though. That there Indian horse is better than Cinnamon ever was."

Lu could see she was lying, but knew enough not to say so. He didn't tell her he was sorry either, though he hoped she'd be able to read as much from his eyes. Lu really was sorry, too.

During the long trip across the plains, Lu had ridden untold miles next to Sadie and her horse. He'd always considered it a fine animal. Cinnamon had a way of lifting her front legs whenever Sadie spurred her to a gallop that Lu admired. He'd tried to get Cody to do the same, but always failed. Now Sadie was stuck on an Indian gelding only slightly more attractive than Crash. It just didn't fit somehow.

"Does your new horse have a name?" Lu asked her.

Sadie shook her head.

"Its coat is a sort of a funny orangish color. How about Carrot?"

"That's dust mostly," Sadie said. "But still. Hey, Carrot!"

The only horse that didn't look up was the one Sadie was shouting at. Even Lucky turned to see what all the noise was about. It must have struck Sadie just right, because she let out a deep belly laugh, and went right on laughing for the next few minutes, until tears started running down her cheeks.

"That decides it," Sadie said, once she'd got control of herself. "Carrot it is."

CHAPTER 11
DESERT BREEDS

"HEY, LU," SADIE WHISPERED. "You awake?"

"What is it?" Lu poked his head out from under his blanket. It was still dark, and very cold. The western bank of the Hell Mouth was higher than the eastern bank, and once the sun went down the temperature dropped precipitously. The night before, Lu got so cold he'd nearly wet his bed. He woke up feeling a dire need to make water, but hated to leave the meager warmth of his blanket long enough to do it.

"C'mon," Sadie said. "Get up."

"What for?" Lu looked around. The sun wouldn't rise for two hours at least, and Henry was still sound asleep beside the smoky remains of their fire.

"I want to talk."

Lu slipped on his boots and followed Sadie out of camp. They walked along the creek until they were out of earshot of their sleeping friends, and then Sadie turned and stared Lu in the eye. She was breathing hard, as though she'd just run a race. Puffs of white vapor spewed from her mouth like dragon smoke.

"Find anything else in my valise?" she asked. She didn't even wait for Lu to answer. "You found my bonnets. My gloves. My dress. Find anything else while you were snooping?"

"Trousers," Lu stammered. He figured she was asking him about the lacy bloomers, but Lu was too modest to say so. "I guess I found everything."

Sadie reached into her jacket pocket and pulled out a navy blue handkerchief. "Anything else?" She waved the handkerchief in his face. "Did you give it to that killer?"

Lu took the tiny revolver from his pocket and held it out to her. "It's right here."

Sadie snatched the pistol out of his hand just as though it was made of butter and Lu's hand was a hot skillet. She shoved it in her jacket pocket, then wound up and slapped Lu across the face. Her palm struck his cheek so hard it sent him spiraling to the ground.

"Never touch my stuff again," she growled.

Lu shook his head. He wouldn't. Not for anything.

"Never!" Sadie turned on her heel and strode back toward camp.

Lu watched her go, wondering if the handprint on his cheek would disappear before the others woke up.

"She got you a good one," Jack said, striding out of the bushes on the other side of the creek. "I saw it all."

"Glad you liked it," Lu muttered.

"Don't take it too hard. You just learned something about women, that's all. They don't much care for a man invading their delicates."

"I saved her little gun," Lu said. "She should have thanked me."

"You did save her gun," Jack agreed. "I'll give you that much."

"I might have given it to Gokhlayeh, too. He told me he wanted it."

"No, you did just fine. Took guts, too. I reckon Gokhlayeh was about as likely to tie you to a stake and burn you alive as lead you out of that canyon."

"Bill wasn't scared. He rode right into the Mimbrachua camp just as calm as if he owned it." Lu's comment was intended to sting Jack's pride, but he didn't think it worked. The expression on the gunfighter's face remained as cool and aloof as ever.

"Tell you what," Jack said. "You gather an armload of sticks and I'll light a fire. It's cold as hell up here."

"Starting fires is Sadie's job."

"Well, tell her to do it then."

"That's all right," Lu said. "I'll gather the wood."

Their horses had been saddled, and Lucky the mule harnessed and packed, when Jack called them all back to the fire.

"It's time we filled the water-skins Chino brought," he said. "Desert's coming. Never can tell when the next stream is likely to show."

"One mule can't carry all that," Chino remarked. "Not with the baggage he's already got."

"There are six skins," Lu suggested. "If we each take one—"

"Good enough," Jack said. "But there's something else. The five of you have got a decision to make. I agreed to lead you across the Hell Mouth. You're across. My job's done."

"But—" MacLemore stammered. "Where do we go from here? Is there a road?"

"Might be a game trail through these hills. I can't say. I expect Chino could find his way if he was so inclined. Only problem is, you're short on food."

"So what do we do?"

"Your other choice is to follow me. I'm going south. It'll take you out of your way, but I might be able to scare up one last acquaintance. Could mean the difference between life and death."

MacLemore looked at Henry and Chino. Neither offered an opinion. Henry merely shrugged. Chino stared into the rapidly diminishing flames.

"How far out of our way will we have to go?" MacLemore asked.

"Not far," Jack said. "Three hundred miles, maybe. Four at the outside."

"I say we go with Jack," Sadie said. "He's brought us this far."

MacLemore crossed his arms. "How much is this going to cost me?"

"No charge," Jack said. "So long as you don't hold me up, I reckon it's no skin off my teeth."

They rode for two straight days, barely leaving their saddles long enough to spread their blankets on the ground. If anybody slept, Lu wasn't aware of it.

Jack led them along an old game trail. In the beginning, it stayed fairly close to the edge of the canyon. But by the evening of that first day, the trail had begun shading off to the west. Lu was glad of that. He didn't know if the Mimbrachua ever wandered up this high, and didn't care to find out. Meeting Gokhlayeh once had been plenty.

Leaving the canyon also meant ascent. Every step took them higher. Soon they'd reached elevations beyond which not even the heartiest pine and fir trees could grow. These were miserable old mountains, Lu thought. Rocky and dead. As little like the verdant range on the other side of the canyon as heaven is from hell. Things didn't look to be getting better, either. According to Jack, on the other side of these mountains was a vast desert. Mister MacLemore found that particularly disconcerting, but Lu didn't see how things could get much worse. Or much drier. In two days they'd come upon exactly one creek, and that was barely wet enough to darken the bottom of their horses' hooves. This land was desolate in every sense of the word. They saw no game, not even rodents, though they kept their eyes peeled and guns at the ready just in case. There were still a few pounds of pemmican in their gunnysacks, but that wouldn't last much longer. Lu guessed they'd be eating snakes before long. Chino said he'd eaten lizards and found them tasty. Lu thought he could eat one, if it became absolutely necessary, but didn't particularly relish the idea.

They finally crested a pass on the afternoon of their third day, and got a good look at the desert. It was laid out below them for as far as the eye could see, and undoubtedly a whole lot farther than that. When Lu heard that they'd be traveling through a desert, he'd imagined an endless sea of yellow sand. But this wasn't that sort of desert at all. If there was sand down there, it came only in patches. This desert was mostly rock.

"Does anything grow out there?" Lu asked Chino.

"Sure," he said. "Stickers. Lots of 'em."

They rode down the other side of the mountains, picking their way between heaps of jagged stones, each sharp enough to cut through a pair of brand new boots, to say nothing of the tender feet beneath. As the elevation dropped, they began to see plants again, though of a variety and type Lu had never before imagined. This desert was a good deal more complex than his first view had given him to believe. He recognized a few of the cactuses from story-books, especially the giant saguaros, arms reaching skyward like a teller at a bank hold-up. More interesting by far were the twists of thorn-ridden vine that stood, sometimes ten feet tall, in the shade of the rock-piles. Chino called them *ocotillo*, and claimed they made good fire-wood. Every plant they saw had spikes. Some appeared to be all spikes, with just enough plant underneath to hold it all together.

"Watch out for the pears," Jack shouted back.

"Pears?" Lu asked.

Sadie pointed to a bunch of green pincushions lying to either side of the path. "Prickly-pears," she explained. "Purple are the worst. Get one in your hand and it'll fester awful. The fruits make good jelly though."

They camped that night in a clearing surrounded by thorns, spines, briars, stickers and thistles. It was warm, but Jack still cut wood for a fire. Actually, he dug it up. He found a bush he called a "honey mesquite," and used his knife to dig out the roots. Just a few of those sticks and they had a fire that lasted nearly all night, with hardly any smoke.

"I don't know how you can stand to sleep in boots," Lu said to Sadie. She was sprawled out with her feet just a few inches from his nose. "My feet cramp if I leave my shoes on overnight."

"Can't stand the thought of scorpions climbing in and laying eggs."

"Do they do that?"

"They could, I guess."

Lu put his boots back on.

He was just closing his eyes when a bloodcurdling moan suddenly broke from the thicket. Lu had never heard a sound like it in his life. His first thought was of a werewolf, prowling at the edge of the camp.

"He's close," Chino observed. "Could be watching us through the bushes."

"Is it a wolf?" Lu asked.

"Naw. Just a little ol' coyote. Probably searching for scraps."

"Strange that he wants to be so near camp," Henry said. "Coyotes are usually solitary creatures. Something's got this one riled."

"Maybe Jack," Chino said.

Lu sat up. Sure enough, the gunslinger was nowhere to be seen. His bedroll was spread, his appaloosa hobbled and standing with the other horses, but Jack was gone.

"Where is he?" Lu asked.

Chino shrugged. "Scouting, I guess."

Another long howl froze the blood in Lu's veins.

"Don't worry," Chino assured him. "Jack's safe. No coyote alive is mean enough to get the best of him."

"What about us?"

"We're safe, too. I promise."

Jack didn't show up until morning. The first glow of new-risen sun had just started to break over the eastern peaks when the gunfighter came striding into the clearing, his boots chalky with dust. He rolled up his blanket, grabbed his saddle by the horn and slung it over his horse's back.

"Get ready to ride," he said.

The path continued its slow descent of the mountains. By noon, Henry judged that they'd come down nearly ten thousand feet, from pass to basin. Lu could certainly tell the difference. He'd already sweated clean through his shirt, and his pants weren't exactly dry. Henry took his jacket off and tied it around his waist. Sadie and Chino both followed suit. Only MacLemore remained fully dressed, and he claimed to be perfectly comfortable.

"It's a dry heat," he said. "Dry."

"I guess that's right," Sadie remarked. "Though it's got you about as wet as if you'd been dropped in a pond."

Despite the oven-like temperatures, Chino never stopped naming and describing the uses of the various plants they passed. He pointed out one type of pink flower, the stem of which was covered in spines as long as a ten-penny nail, and called it "Spanish Needle." Then he pointed at another flower, identical in color and armament, and called it "Apache Plume." Lu doubted whether he could remember a quarter of what Chino told him, and was glad he wouldn't be tested. During the course of that afternoon they encountered yucca, fishhook barrels, beavertails, prickly-pears and cholla enough to stab holes through the fingers of every man, woman, and child on the continent. Lu's favorite flower was one Chino called "cowboy's fried egg." It looked about like it sounds, white with a big ball of yellow at the center, but was supposed to be as poisonous as a coral snake. According to Chino, just one petal, ground up and mixed in a barrel of beer, was powerful enough to murder a whole ranch full of vaqueros. Sagebrush was the most common plant they saw, though grease-wood and creosote came close. Mesquite lent the whole desert a scent like a pit barbecue on a summer evening.

They also saw birds and reptiles of all sorts. Woodpeckers, roadrunners, and wrens twittered amongst the cactuses and thorn-bushes as happy as any robin in a yard back home. Golden eagles and turkey-vultures turned on heat waves in the pale blue sky. They even saw a horny toad—though Lu thought it looked more like a fat lizard with scaly eyes—and about sixteen thousand snakes, rattlers chief among them.

Taken all together, the desert was a fascinating place. It might have even been enjoyable, except for the sun. All through that day, Lu stared at the horizon, hoping in vain to see a cloud. He wasn't particular. It didn't have to be a storm-cloud. Any old puff of white would do, so long as it came between him and the sun for a second or two. But no cloud was to be had. Not one.

It was while Lu was staring at the horizon that a large fur-covered pig broke from the brush and went charging across the path. Quick as lightning, Henry yanked his rifle and set it to his shoulder.

"Don't—" Jack shouted.

Henry's finger was on the trigger, but he didn't fire. "I can take it clean."

"No. Leave it."

"But—"

"It doesn't belong to us."

Henry thrust his rifle back into its scabbard. Jack offered no explanation, nor did Henry ask for one. They rode on.

"I didn't know there were pigs in the desert," Lu said, squinting down at the hoof-prints as they passed.

"*Javelina*," Chino corrected him. "Good eatin'. But if you see one comin', get out of its way. Darned things got teeth like chisels."

They found another clearing just before sunset, and decided to set up camp. Lu and Sadie gathered wood for their fire. As soon as it was lit, Sadie handed around the pemmican. Lu only ate a tiny bit. Their provisions had dwindled alarmingly. Two or three more days and they'd be completely out.

Jack didn't even wait for supper. He put his saddle down, told the others to sit tight, and strode up the path.

"Are you leaving again?" Lu called after him.

Jack looked back.

"Can I come with you?"

"No. Stay here. Don't go *any*where."

A coyote began howling as soon as it was full dark. It sounded suspiciously like the same one that'd haunted their camp during the whole night previous. On a whim, Lu let out his own high-pitched whoop. Sadie thought she could do better, and MacLemore guessed he'd like to try as well. After that, barely a second went by when one or another of them wasn't yowling at the moon. Chino liked to finish his howls with a bark. Lu thought that made him sound more like an old bloodhound than a coyote, but he didn't guess Chino would much care for his saying so. Henry's howls had a vibrato quality, like a lady singing hymns in church. Sadie laughed at that, but Henry didn't seem to mind.

When they'd had enough of howling, Chino told a joke. It wasn't funny, but it got the ball rolling. MacLemore told a story about a man who traveled about washing ladies' underclothes, but could never get them quite fresh. Lu wasn't sure he understood, but laughed anyway. Sadie recited a poem about a lass from Nantucket, which she'd heard from a ranger down on the border, and which Chino thought about the funniest thing he'd ever heard, but which must have embarrassed her father somewhat. Lu knew no jokes, so he told the only funny story he could think of. It was the same story all the kids back in St. Frances had made such sport of, about how Jack had arm-wrestled Bigfoot. Henry said it was just like Jack, to take credit for something he'd done himself. Sadie wondered if there really was a Bigfoot, and Chino said he knew for a fact that there was, as he'd seen the beast himself. Henry voiced some doubts about that, but didn't deny Chino's claim outright. They had such a merry time, talking and telling lies, that not one of them even noticed when the coyote stopped howling.

Jack wandered into camp just after midnight, and was surprised to find the whole group awake and alert. Slung over his shoulder was a dead javelina. It had already been skinned and gutted. Jack dropped it beside the fire and got a drink from one of the water-skins.

"Let's get that thing on to roast," he said. His shirt was soaked with blood.

"Who field dressed this carcass?" MacLemore asked.

"Why? Is there a problem?"

"None. Only it looks like its throat was chewed out—" MacLemore pointed at the ragged flesh around what remained of the javelina's neck, "by a wolf or a big—"

"Maybe it was." Jack took another long drink from his water-skin.

A few minutes later, the meat was sliced, skewered, and roasting over the fire. The fattier bits Chino placed on flat rocks over the coals, frying it 'til it was crispy like bacon. Lu ate a few pieces. The meat needed salt, but was still a whole world better than the pemmican they'd been getting by on for so long.

"I have to make," Sadie announced, as they were finishing their late night snack. She got up and headed toward the bushes.

"Stay in the light," Jack told her.

"What am I supposed to do, squat right out here in front of everybody?"

"I don't care how you do it," Jack said. "Just make sure you stay in the clearing."

"Can everyone turn their backs at least?"

Jack nodded.

Sadie strode to the furthest edge of the clearing, unbuckling her belt as she went. "Well, go on then," she commanded. "Turn your heads."

Lu untied his blanket from his saddle and spread it beside the fire. There were only a handful of hours left before morning, and he was suddenly very sleepy. Before long, all of them had bedded down. All but Jack, who sat up, smoking and staring at the darkness. No sooner did Lu's head touch his saddle-seat than he was out.

He woke an hour or two later to see Jack, standing over the fire with his palms resting lightly on the butts of his pistols, a cigarette poking from the corner of his mouth. All the rest of the camp was asleep. Chino was snoring.

Lu had to relieve himself, and so quickly made his way to the edge of the clearing. He saw the spot where Sadie had gone hours before, and decided to rewet it. He'd already undone his pants and started the flow, when a flash of movement caught his eye. Lu squinted, trying to see what it was. At first, he thought it was just another javelina. Then he saw what it really was and leapt backwards.

"What's wrong?" Jack asked him. "What'd you see?"

"I thought I saw . . ." Lu shook his head. "It was a face, only—"

"What'd it look like?"

"Sort of like a big dog with a mouth full of sharp teeth. Except its eyes were blue and—"

"Was it a coyote?"

"I don't know. Looked like a dog to me."

"Get on back to bed," Jack said.

"But—"

"Go on."

Lu turned and started back toward the fire. Their chatter

must have woken Sadie, because she was sitting up staring at him.

"What's wrong?" she asked.

"I think I saw the coyote," Lu said. "Or something."

"Was it big? Dang, I wish I'd seen it."

Lu wished he hadn't. He just knew he'd be seeing its teeth in his dreams. And those eyes.

"Are you feelin' all right?" Sadie asked him. "You look pale."

"I guess. Yeah, I'm all right. Just startled me, that's all."

"Well, close your pants then. And try to get some sleep."

Lu looked down and saw that his trousers were still gaping open. He turned his back, feeling the blood rush to his cheeks as he fumbled with his buttons. When he looked at her again, Sadie was asleep—or at least her eyes were closed. Lu felt sure he could hear her snickering. He wondered if she'd seen his dingus, or just his open fly. Somehow, it didn't seem fair. If she was going to look at him, he ought to be able to look at her. The worst part was, he couldn't even complain. After all, he was the one who'd gone walking through camp with his dangle hanging out.

Fortunately, acute humiliation drove all thoughts of the coyote from his mind. Instead of nightmares about wild beasts, Lu dreamt he was naked and running down the streets of St. Frances. That wasn't much of an improvement.

The next day went much as the two previous, except that they had bacon for breakfast, and spent a few of the hottest, driest hours tapping barrel cactuses and refilling their water-skins. It wasn't all that difficult, once they'd shaved off all the spines. Chino simply drilled his knife through the meat of the plant, creating a hole as big around as a man's thumb. After that, water trickled out for minutes at a time. They only had to tap three large cactuses before all six skins were full.

It was late afternoon and they'd been in the saddle for three straight hours, when they came upon a crossroads and Jack whistled for a stop. Lu hoped he just needed a moment to determine which path they ought to follow, but feared the worst.

"That there's my road," Jack said, pointing down the fork to the left. "And this one here is yours."

"You're leaving us?" MacLemore asked.

"I've spent too much time with you already. I've got my own business."

"But I thought we were going to meet your friend. I thought you knew someone who might help us across the desert."

"How much help do you want? He's already given you javelina meat enough to last a week. I had to all but get down on my hands and knees and beg for that."

"And we appreciate it," Sadie said. "We just hate to see you go, that's all."

"This is your expedition. It's about time you took control of it."

"But we don't even know where we're going," MacLemore complained. "Or who we'll find when we get there."

"Go west."

"Bill says you know the man we're after," Lu said. "The Yankee."

Jack glared at him. "I have my suspicions."

"He also said not to let you leave until you'd spilled your guts."

"Bill's mighty sassy for a man hiding out at the bottom of a hole."

"So, will you tell us?"

Jack took a quick glance at the sun. It had begun its descent to the horizon, though it showed no hurry about getting there. They had at least three more hours of brutal heat before it'd set. That was plenty, so far as Lu was concerned. But Jack didn't seem to agree.

"I don't want to say anything out loud," he said. "There might be safe places to talk in this world, but here and now ain't one of them."

"Then what'll we do?" Lu asked.

Jack reached into his saddlebag. "Take this." He rode over to Lu and handed him a package. It was wrapped up in a piece of pearl-white silk, and bound with a string. A charm, just like those his mother sold in their shop back home, was tied to the knot.

<<*A dragon?*>> Lu asked. He turned the package slightly, so that the sun shone directly upon the charm. Instantly, the dragon changed from dark gray to pale blue, and its eyes blazed fiery gold. <<*Is this Shen-Lung?*>>

Jack nodded. <<*A powerful spirit. Guardian against the eyes and ears of demons.*>> He pointed skyward. <<*All demons.*>>

Lu could feel the other members of their band staring. He hadn't meant to speak Chinese. Seeing the charm had just brought it out of him.

"Open it tomorrow at noon," Jack said. "Read it, and then pack it away just as you found it." He pointed at Lu. <<*And don't forget the dragon.*>>

MacLemore took the package from Lu, glanced at it, and then handed it back. "I can't read anything but English," he said.

"Don't worry," Jack said. "This is as American as Yankee Doodle Dandy."

"What'll we do after we read it?" Lu asked.

"Remember it. If you can."

"Anything else we should know about this desert?" Henry asked.

"It's wide, and you've barely scratched the surface. Use every drop of good water you find. There's a creek not far from here. Drink all you can stand, and fill your skins. You never know when there'll be more. And don't kill any animals, *especially* not coyotes. If you feel you just have to shoot something, shoot each other."

"I still wish you'd come with us," MacLemore said.

"You'll be all right. Chino knows the way."

And with that, Jack gave his horse a firm kick and went galloping away. It took only seconds for him to disappear amidst the sagebrush and mesquite.

"Well, I guess that's that," MacLemore grumbled.

"Yep," Chino agreed. "That's that."

"He didn't even wish us luck," Sadie said.

"Who knows?" Henry said. "Maybe Jack will show up again sometime. He has a way of doing that."

"I sure hope so," Lu whispered.

"Go on, then, open it up," MacLemore urged.

Lu sat cross-legged in the shade of a giant saguaro, Jack's silk-bound package in his lap. "Is it noon yet?" he asked nervously.

"A little past," Henry said. "Open it."

Fingers trembling, Lu untied his grandfather's charm and set it aside. The dragon glowed for an instant as he lifted it away from the pearl-white silk, its eyes turning a most unsettling red. Then it faded until it was the same flat gray as the rest of the charm.

Lu hesitated, half-expecting demons, maybe even ghost-riders, to come blasting out of the desert all around them. But nothing happened. The string that bound the package was tied in a simple bow. Lu tugged at one of the ends and the string fell away.

"It's an old notebook," Lu said, holding it up for all to see.

"Careful with that material." Chino motioned toward the silk covering. In his haste, Lu had allowed it to slide out of his lap. Sadie picked it up, brushed it off, and stuck it in her jacket pocket.

"Does it say whose it is?" MacLemore asked.

Lu turned the notebook back and forth, but there were no words on the cover. "I think it may belong to my grandfather," he said. "I saw Jack reading it before we left."

"Well, open the darn thing," Sadie suggested. "Read the first page."

The spine creaked as Lu thumbed the book open. On the inside cover was a poem he knew well. It was something his grandfather had taught him when he was little. Master K'ung said it was a nursery rhyme from England, but that English speakers the world over knew it. Whoever had written the poem into this book possessed a fine hand. The letters were clear, but not flowery. There were no lines in the book, but the spacing was even and exact. Master K'ung, who took great pride in his own calligraphy, would have admired this. For a moment, Lu wondered if his grandfather hadn't penned the rhyme himself. But the more he studied the letters, the more he became convinced that this was the work of someone else entirely. Master K'ung always wrote English so that the letters went straight up and down. Whoever had copied this poem gave his words a decided bent to the left.

To either side of the nursery rhyme were lines of Chinese characters, written top to bottom as was proper. There could be no doubt that Master K'ung had written these. He had even signed them.

"Well?" MacLemore asked. "What is it?"

Lu held the book up so that everyone could see. "There's some Chinese written here and here," he said. "And there's a poem down the middle."

"Those bits in Chinese sort of surround the rest, don't they?" Chino observed. "That's interesting."

"What does the Chinese say?" Sadie asked.

Lu shook his head. "I only know a few characters. This is my grandfather's signature." He pointed at the figure in question. "The rest I don't know."

"You can't read your own language?" MacLemore asked him.

"It's very difficult," Lu said. "Not like English."

"I think reading English is difficult," Chino muttered.

"Why don't you read it to us?" Henry suggested. "The parts you do know."

"Me? Are you sure?" Lu had never much liked reading aloud. He was a good reader, but whenever he tried to read anything out loud he jumbled the words. "How about Mister MacLemore reads it?"

"Why me?"

"Give to Caeser what is Caeser's," Henry said.

"And what's that supposed to mean?"

"It means, you're the leader of this little expedition," Sadie said. She took the book from Lu and handed it to her father. "So read."

Reluctantly, MacLemore took the book. He held it at arm's length, touching it with just his fingertips. He looked like an old bachelor holding a baby with a dirty diaper. "Well, if I must," he said.

He opened the notebook and looked at the inside cover. "I know this."

"Read it out loud," Henry reminded him. "So we can all know what it says."

MacLemore cleared his throat.

"Taffy was a Welshman, Taffy was a thief,
"Taffy came to my house and stole a leg of beef.
"I went to Taffy's house, Taffy wasn't in,
"I jumped upon his Sunday hat and stuck it with a pin."

"That's what it says?" Henry asked.

"Exactly."

"Who is this Taffy?" Chino asked.

"It's a nursery rhyme," Henry explained. "A poem mothers teach their children."

"Strange thing to teach a child. What's a Welshman?"

"A man from Wales," Sadie said. "It's also someone who doesn't pay his debts."

"Unlike the other man in the poem," Chino said. "He pays his debts."

"Or his trespasses," Henry agreed.

"Can I continue?" MacLemore turned a page. The yellowed paper crackled under his fingers. "The handwriting's not as clear, but I think I can make it out."

"Do the letters bend to the left?" Lu asked.

"No. To the right. Looks like this writer was left-handed. My own mother was a lefty. You can always tell."

MacLemore cleared his throat again, then read the following:

"November 5th, 1799. Tarry Town.

"Six long years have I trod the miserable paths of these northern woods, searching for proof, or at least goodly sign, of the Adversary, which some men call the Devil. But all my efforts have come to naught.

"Despite several brushes with sorcerers, ghosts, minor demons, and other beings of the weirdly supernatural, I have yet to see the Dark One face to face. Still, I refuse to give up hope. I will see him. I swear I will."

MacLemore shrugged. "Still no name," he said, turning another page. "Creepy, though, isn't it?"

"Keep reading," Sadie said.

"This next entry looks like a long one." MacLemore flipped a couple more pages, searching for the end. "Real long."

"That's all right," Chino said. "We've got time."

MacLemore continued:

"November 11th, 1799. Tarry Town.

"In previous journals I have often remarked upon the tendency of certain petty criminals to use the supernatural as a ready explanation for crimes otherwise all too human. The time I have wasted in chasing after such humbugs has been considerable. But never have I beheld so laughable a fraud as that which I uncovered during this past week, whilst investigating the disappearance of an upstate schoolmaster, Ichabod Crane.

"According to reports read prior to my journey, Crane was abducted by the ghost of a decapitated Hessian cavalry officer. Having lost his head to cannon fire during the revolution, this headless horseman rides the lanes and fields of the surrounding lands searching for a replacement. His

weapon of choice is a saber. But the Hessian has also been known to make use of a charmed gourd, an enormous pumpkin filled with the fires of hell, which he flings at his victims, knocking them from their mounts and sending them tumbling through the gates of damnation.

"Aroused by the strangeness of this tale, I hastened to investigate.

"For the better part of two days did I tramp upon the scene of the crime, a hollow spooky of countenance and much given to mists and fog, but no concrete evidence could I unearth. At last, late on my second day, whilst inspecting a patch of blackened ground, I was approached by a farmer of the nearby village, one Hans Van Ripper. Mister Van Ripper claimed to be well-versed in both the comings and goings of the headless spectre, and having got wind of my expedition, bade me come to his home. There he showed me the moldy corpse of a pumpkin, claiming to have discovered it upon the very spot wherein the aforementioned teacher breathed his last.

"Excited by such excellent and tangible evidence, I spent the next day at a local tavern, a hall without proper name but possessing a strangely muddled portrait of George Washington over the door. My aim was to interview other locals, those most commonly purported to have first-hand knowledge of the spook, and so to develop a more complete understanding of both his whereabouts and the intervals during which he was most likely to be seen.

"But the meetings I took with the villagers who frequented this inn, far from clearing any murk from the waters, further confounded my understanding of the case. When together, their stories of the haunting ran in a singularly picturesque vein, each man or woman adding his or her own bit of yarn to the rich tapestry of legend. Indeed, after the first such gathering, I was convinced. 'Truly,' said I to myself, 'there is a deep evil residing in this Sleepy Hollow.' But subsequent interviews proved my optimism groundless.

"When taken individually, the villagers presented wildly divergent histories of the galloping Hessian. His mode of

dress. His methods of dispatch. Even the breed of his horse. No detail of the ghost could be agreed upon. When I inquired into the shards of pumpkin, shown to me by the good farmer, Hans Van Ripper, no fewer than eleven of the villagers claimed to be the actual discoverers of the broken gourd. Eight offered to show me the shards, which they had kept safe in their cellars, attics, or even beneath their children's beds.

"On the morning of my fifth day, I interviewed the worthy Baltus Van Tassel, in whose home the missing schoolteacher was last seen. He presented me with certain clues as to the true character of the crime. According to Mister Van Tassel, Ichabod Crane had developed a fondness for his daughter Katrina, a fact which mainly served to stoke the flames of hatred in her numerous suitors, and especially a local tough by the name of Abraham Van Brunt, but who most of his fellows called simply 'Brom Bones.'

"With this newfound intelligence, I hastened to the home of Master Van Brunt, newly promised the hand of that same Katrina, and inquired as to his knowledge of the galloping Hessian. At first he claimed no personal knowledge of the schoolmaster's disappearance. But with cajoling, he offered up a vivid tale of a chase, the schoolmaster fleeing for his life from the 'headless' horseman. Listening to it, I at once ciphered the truth from the myriad lies and fables.

"I cannot say with any certainty whether the schoolmaster yet lives, and occupies some other village schoolhouse, or has been cruelly murdered, as seems more likely, and his body hidden away in any one of the innumerable 'haunted spots' that surround this superstitious village. In either case, his disappearance is without doubt the result of a woefully human source, most likely Brom Bones himself, and thus no business of mine."

"Wait a minute," Sadie said. "He didn't even report Brom Bones to the authorities?"

MacLemore read the last few sentences again. "Apparently not. I guess he didn't think Crane's murder was any of his business."

Sadie whistled. "That's what I'd call cold-blooded."

"Maybe he's the man we're after," Lu said. "Maybe he's the Yankee."

"Could be," Henry said. "He is uncommonly interested in demons."

Lu nodded. "And Jack thinks the Yankee is somehow using the ghost-riders. It all fits."

"But we still don't know the man's name," Sadie said, "or what he looks like."

"There's more, if you'd like to hear it," MacLemore said. Lu couldn't tell whether he was anxious to continue, or somehow irritated by the tale.

"Go on," Henry said. "Let's have it all."

MacLemore read:

> "One finds it difficult to imagine how these villagers can continue to believe in their local spook, whilst all evidence points to murderers most foul. But I shall chalk it up, yet again, to an earnest desire to BELIEVE. The denizens of Sleepy Hollow sincerely wish to see the Devil's face, peering at them from behind every tree and bush, and at the center of every bit of low-lying fog, and so they do. And yet, woe unto me, I hope to see that evil face laid bare, and in the light of day, but have as yet been foiled.
>
> "Still, my trip was not a total loss. I did hear one tale of remarkable interest, whilst interviewing the denizens of that aforementioned tavern. And had I not spent the vast majority of my time investigating the cheap humbug that was the headless horseman, I should have very much liked to look into it further. No doubt it too would have proved without foundation, but I shall give the particulars here all the same.
>
> "Toward the end of my third evening in Sleepy Hollow, whilst the hopes of a demoniac discovery were still alight in my breast, I chanced to speak with an elderly gentleman possessing of a singularly untamed bush of graying chin-whisker, and going by the name Rip Van Winkle. He lived with his grown daughter, whom he had brought to the tavern that

night, and who confirmed the bare facts of the story as he related them.

"According to Van Winkle, twenty-five years previous, whilst hunting squirrels in the Kaatskill Mountains, he was met by the ghost of Hendrick Hudson.

"The famed explorer led him a merry jaunt over hill and dale, only stopping once they had arrived at a wide glade populated by the hobgoblin remains of Hudson's crew. There Van Winkle was offered a flagon of powerful liquor, which he accepted gratefully, and refilled numerous times. The result was that Van Winkle fell into a bewitched sleep—A sleep from which he did not wake for fully twenty years!

"When at last he did alight, the poor man discovered that all he'd previously known was gone. Even his country had changed. He was now a citizen of the United States of America, where before he had been a loyal subject of the King.

"His daughter readily confirmed the lengthy disappearance, and avowed a complete faith in her father's tale. I asked many questions, and came to believe that Van Winkle was at least no teller of base fibs. There may have been some more ordinary cause of his lost years—a blow to the head perhaps, resulting in acute loss of memory—but if there was, Van Winkle knew nothing of it.

"When questioned as to the details of the day leading up to his encounter with Hendrick Hudson, however, Van Winkle showed extraordinary powers of recollection. Apparently, he had been in that self-same tavern, conversing with friends, when his wife, a terrible shrew of a woman, stormed in and began cursing the whole assemblage. She had even cursed the most august member of their circle, one Nicholas Vedder, a man whom the other villagers called simply 'Old Nick.'

"Suffice to say, Van Winkle's mention of that name fairly halted the proceedings. As any educated person will attest, 'Old Nick' is nothing less than the third or possibly fourth most commonly used cognomen for the Devil. It is his 'NICK-name,' as it were. I don't mind saying that I was positively agog. Could this be mere coincidence? Or evidence of chicanery on the part of Van Winkle and his daughter? I cannot say for certain. But it seemed to me then, and still does now, a remarkably uncanny bit of information. I pressed Van Winkle to continue.

"According to his tale, Van Winkle begged his wife to retire, which she reluctantly did, though only after extorting from him a promise of fresh meat for their stew-pot. Van Winkle agreed to go that very afternoon to the Kaatskill Mountains and hunt for squirrels. It was during this trip that he encountered Hendrick Hudson.

"When Dame Van Winkle had finally gone from the tavern, 'Old Nick' expressed his extreme dismay at being so callously treated. Van Winkle apologized, saying that his fondest wish was 'to wake up one morning and find his wife dead, so that he might discover what life could be like without her.' I thought that bit extraordinarily interesting, and had Van Winkle repeat it a number of times.

"The other aspect of Van Winkle's tale which I found remarkable was his description of Hendrick Hudson. Van Winkle described the ghost as square-built, short, and possessing of a thick black beard. I asked if the beard wasn't parted at the center, much as portraits of our Savior Jesus Christ show his beard to have been parted, and Van Winkle came almost out of his seat in surprise.

"I then asked if Hudson favored one leg. To this Van Winkle replied in the negative. Still, I can't help but wonder if the old man wasn't the victim of a rather more powerful spirit even than that of Hendrick Hudson.

"If I can but find the time, I really must send a letter to Nathaniel, describing the above and inviting him to continue the inquiry where I left off. It is not so very far from Salem to Tarry Town, after all, and he may deem the Van Winkle matter of particular interest. His successes in the case of Goodman Brown, as well as the prodigious level of detail he has managed to unearth relating to the

*demoniac possession of the infamous Parson Hooper, sug-
gest him as a most fitting replacement."*

"Strange bit of fiction, isn't it?" MacLemore turned the page.
"Ghosts," he scoffed.

"Isn't there any more?" Lu asked.

MacLemore nodded. "Two other entries."

"Read them," Henry said. "We still need that name."

"November 13th, 1799, Tarry Town.

"I am trapped.

*"The sloop, which was scheduled to depart at dawn,
bound for the island of the Manhattos, has not arrived. What
has delayed its passage from Renssalaer, none can guess.
Fortunately, I still have my room at the inn, though the keeper has installed a roommate to share my bed. At first, I considered this insufferable. Upon meeting the man, however—
one Philip Traum—I quite readily altered my opinion.*

*"He is of a genial nature, handsome and clean of appear-
ance, with a pale skin that fairly radiates decency, and possessed of a knowledge regarding matters demoniac nearly as
deep as mine own. Like me, he is a traveler. He calls himself
a 'salesman,' and is in fact also on his way to the Manhattos,
where he is to meet with a shopkeeper who has agreed to sell
health potions on Mr. Traum's behalf. He also admits to dab-
bling in usury, and claims to have money lent out at various
rates of interest throughout the whole of New England.*

*"For reasons unknown, I have felt compelled to describe
to him the nature of my years-long hunt in almost embarrass-
ing detail, and Mr. Traum, gentleman that he is, has listened
politely all the while. After hearing my description of the
cases at Sleepy Hollow, he asked why I did not stay to investigate the Van Winkle matter. I explained that there were
tales of a more recent vintage in the southern states, which I
thought more likely to bear fruit. To this, Mr. Traum inquired
as to whether I had not myself ever attempted to summon the
Dark One, since I had such a thirst for direct confrontation.*

I admitted that my efforts in that vein had ever come up empty. 'But perhaps if we were to try together,' he suggested. And I readily gave my consent.

"That evening, after a hearty dinner, we set about attempting to conjure the Devil. After much discussion, we settled on a pentagram and candles, that being the way in most of the stories we had read, and quickly began collecting the necessary implements. Whilst I went to the local school to obtain chalk, Philip went in search of a half-dozen tallow candles. We met back in our shared room, where I had already cleared the floor in preparation.

"I was astonished to find that he'd brought not only the candles, but also a hen's egg, the shell of which was marked by a spot of purest black. I quizzed him as to the egg's purpose, but Philip would not at that moment say. He merely set it down at the center of the chalk pentagram, which I had already drawn on the floor, and then went rapidly about the circle, lighting the candles. I suggested that the pentagram was easily large enough for the both of us, but Philip said he thought the spell would work better with only one inside, and kindly allowed me the honor. Careful not to obliterate any of the chalk markings, I stepped into the ring.

"'Pick up the egg,' Philip told me. And so I did. 'Now say the name.' I recited as many cognomens of the Devil as I could remember. 'Crack the egg.' Having nothing else handy, I cracked the egg on the knuckles of my right hand. 'Now, drink the contents.'

"I admit to balking at this last instruction. First, because I had never heard that eating an egg was a part of the conjuring spell. And second, because I had a natural revulsion to raw food. But at Philip's continued insistence, I did as bidden, opening the shell into my mouth and swallowing the contents without chewing.

"We waited. Traum sat in a chair, just outside the pentagram, watching me curiously, whilst I waited patiently for the appearance of the demon. Hours we spent, saying nary a word to each other, until the candles were close to burning out. At last, out of patience, Philip asked me whether I hadn't yet seen anything, and how I felt. I felt fine, and told him so. 'What do you want to do now then?' he asked. I replied that I should still wish to see Old Scratch, face to face, to which he smiled.

"'We will try again on the Manhattos,' Philip promised. And with that, the first candle guttered and went out."

"November 14th, 1799. Island of the Manhattos.

"The sloop arrived even as Philip and I were casting our failed spell. We sailed at dawn, with a strong southerly breeze. I enquired as to what had caused the ship to be tardy, and was told that a dense fog had covered the port in Renssalaer, making it impossible to depart on time, and that similar hindrances had cropped up at every port they came to. One sailor said that he thought it was the Devil himself, holding them back.

"No such complications marred our passage this morning. In fact, I have never before experienced so rapid a descent of the Hudson. I wondered if the sailor I spoke to earlier would credit the Devil with the good weather, but did not ask.

"We arrived in port shortly before five, nearly an hour ahead of schedule. After saying goodbye to Philip Traum, I beat a rapid path to the door of my solicitor, that most excellent gentleman, Geoffrey Crayon. I bid his man, Mister Irving, a hearty good evening, and was led to the master's chambers.

"Crayon offered me tea, for which I have little taste, and toast and jam, which I relish, and then presented me with papers necessary for the withdrawal of a small fortune from my inheritance. After I had signed, Crayon gave me the requisite funds, having withdrawn the money from his own accounts on the understanding that it would be repaid by what he withdrew from mine. Whilst handing me the gold, he asked if I was absolutely sure I wanted to go south. 'Where will all this chasing lead?' he asked.

"I explained that I had got some very substantial information, and even told him about my new acquaintance, Mr. Traum. Upon hearing that name, Crayon shuddered. I asked if he wasn't feeling all right, and he said that he was, but that he'd be staying inside more now that the weather was turning chill. I wished him a fine winter, and then raced to my own rooms, in a house overlooking The Bowery.

"Along the way I purchased a box of chalk, a gross of tallow candles, and a dozen eggs. The shells were a uniform brown, but I took them anyway.

"When I arrived at the house, my landlady was in the downstairs hall waiting. She was upset about a package that had been delivered a few moments before, from Philip Traum. I gave her no explanation, saying simply that Mr. Traum was a friend, and that I would be going to visit him later that evening.

"Once locked inside my rooms, I opened the letter accompanying the mysterious package and read it through. Traum had finished his business with the shopkeeper, to their mutual satisfaction, and would expect me at his house on Whitehall just before midnight. He also said not to open the package until we were together. It is fiendishly difficult to follow his instructions on this last point, but I shall endeavor to do so.

"His letter concluded with a strange statement. 'I hope you still _wish_ to see me,' and the word 'wish' was underlined. Of course I still wanted to see him, and thought it a peculiar thing to ask. I would want to see anyone who could get me even an inch closer to my goal, that to which I have devoted the whole last years of my life.

"I leave in a few moments.

"Midnight is still hours away, yet I feel certain that Traum will both understand and forgive my excitement.

"Much more to write tomorrow, I am sure."

MacLemore turned a page, then another.
"What's wrong?" Sadie asked him.

"The rest of the notebook seems to be blank." MacLemore flipped through page after page, but could find no other entries. "There isn't any more to read." He was just about to give up when a strip of yellowed newsprint fell out of the notebook, landing in his lap.

"What's that?" Henry asked him.

"A death notice. For a Master Diedrich Knickerbocker, historian. It says he was found dead, lying on the floor of his room overlooking The Bowery, on the morning of November 15, 1799, apparently of acute apoplexy of the brain. His solicitor, and only known friend, was named executor of his estate."

"Do you think that's our writer?" Chino asked.

Sadie and Henry both said that they thought it must be. Lu was somewhat less certain. Mister MacLemore offered no opinion whatever. He just sat there, frowning as he flipped once more through the pages of the notebook.

"I wonder if he ever made it to Traum's," Lu said. "The notebook writer, I mean. Whoever he was."

Sadie nodded. "And what was in that box?"

"It's an evil story." Chino made the sign of the cross. "I'm sorry we read it."

"Seems just a longwinded yarn to me," MacLemore said, finally breaking his silence. "I never put much stock in these Yankee ghost stories. If you've heard one, you've heard them all."

"Jack must've thought different," Sadie said.

"Well, I've begun to have my doubts about Jack Straw. Can't see how his guidance has gotten us very far."

"He got us across the Hell Mouth."

"True," MacLemore admitted. "But that wasn't so very hard, was it? I have no doubt but what we could have done it ourselves."

"Jack thought we should know what was in that notebook," Henry said. "I for one am going to remember it."

Chino nodded his agreement. "Jack's smart about devils and such."

MacLemore shrugged. "Do as you like. Far as I'm concerned, we've just wasted the better part of a day on ridiculousness." He scoffed. "Old Scratch."

Lu glanced at the sky. MacLemore was right about one thing. The afternoon was rapidly slipping away. "I don't think we ought to talk about this anymore," he said. "It'll be dark in a few hours. Jack was always cautious about talking after sundown."

"Fine by me," MacLemore said, and tossed the book to Lu.

It bounced off his knee and landed in the dust, the back cover flopping open to reveal another piece of the Taffy poem MacLemore had read earlier.

"Wait." Lu picked up the book. "There's one more thing."

"What is it?" Henry asked him.

"Another nursery rhyme, written in the back cover. And it's surrounded by more of my grandfather's Chinese."

"What does it say?"

Lu read:

"Taffy was a Welshman, Taffy was a liar,
Taffy came to my house and set my roof on fire.
I went to Taffy's house, Taffy lay in bed,
I took the pistol from my belt and shot him in the head."

"Jesus y Santa Maria," Chino whispered. "That is one evil book."

CHAPTER 13

A PRICKLY SITUATION

THEY CAMPED THAT NIGHT on the trail. Lu thought they'd probably find a clearing if they rode another hour or two, but the time
they'd spent with the notebook couldn't be made up. Their horses
were too tired.

After they'd unsaddled and watered the stock—their water-
skins were running dangerously low again—Sadie passed
around the meat. It'd been only two days, but already the bacon
was gone.

"Mustard," MacLemore muttered, as he chewed up his piece.

"What's that, Daddy?" Sadie asked.

"Oh, nothing. . . . It's just that we've been eating this charred
pork for two days, breakfast and supper. For the longest time I
thought it needed salt. Then pepper. Now I know. It's mustard I
want. I'd give anything for a pot of good German mustard."

"How 'bout your share of the gold?" Chino suggested.
"Would you give that?"

"I don't know about mustard," Henry said. "But I'd give his
share of the gold for a carrot. Or even a green bean."

Chino and Henry both laughed. MacLemore eyed the men
suspiciously.

They were too tired to dig mesquite roots, so Lu and Sadie
gathered a heap of dry brush, including a few small tumbleweeds
that'd wandered into camp, and Sadie lit a fire. She built it larger

than normal, using nearly a quarter of their fuel just to get the flames going, but no one complained.

Chino offered to stand the first watch. He took one of his pistols from its holster, thumbed back the hammer, and laid it at the ready in his lap.

Lu woke hours later, nudged out of deep sleep by a sound he hadn't heard in weeks—silence. The whole desert had gone still. Lu listened, expecting to hear a coyote wail. But none did. No crickets sang either. Even the wind, which hadn't stopped blowing for one second in all the time they'd been in the desert, offered no complaint. The rustling of the foliage, a noise so constant and monotonous as to become silence, had given way to the real thing. It was the creepiest sort of racket Lu had ever heard.

He sat bolt upright, heart pounding in his chest, and was shocked to see a hairy little man standing over the remains of their campfire.

Lu screamed. It wasn't very manly, perhaps, but he didn't care. Reading Diedrich Knickerbocker's notebook had gotten him pretty nervous, to say nothing of his encounter with that coyote two nights before. He hollered until he ran out of air, took a deep breath, and then started in again. Given the chance, Lu probably would've shouted himself hoarse. But after his second round of bellowing, the hairy little stranger cut him off.

"Be quiet!" he snapped. "Let your friends sleep."

And sleep they did. All of Lu's carrying on hadn't disturbed his friends in the least. Henry lay stretched out not three strides from the horses, hat propped over his face like a cowboy in a painting. Chino sat upright beside the fire, just as Lu had last seen him. Only now, instead of standing guard he was snoozing, his chin resting lightly on his chest. MacLemore lay curled up beside his daughter, both so far under they might have been dead. Even the horses were dozing, though they did so standing up.

"Are they all right?" Lu asked.

The stranger put a finger to his lips. "Whisper," he said.

He was the most peculiar creature Lu had ever seen. For a hat, the man wore what appeared to be an old coyote skin. The flea-bitten remains of the animal's skull sat perched atop his head, while the rest of the pelt dangled down his back for a cape. He also had a bit of dusty fabric wrapped around his haunches, and an old rawhide belt. The rest of him was naked. Tucked under his belt was a pair of dead jackrabbits, both skinned and gutted. Some of their blood had gotten on the man's belly fur, making it look as though he'd been stabbed in the side. So far as Lu could determine, he carried no weapon of any kind. But dangling from one wiry fist was an empty water-skin.

"Am I dreaming?" Lu asked him.

"No."

"It's so quiet. We've sat up a lot over the last few days. Usually coyotes howl all night long. I wonder why they've stopped."

"The coyote howls for the darkness. And for the moon."

"They do? Why?"

"Because it is cool, and they are ready to hunt. Only foolish *men* go out under the hot sun. Night is the time for life in the desert."

As he talked, the stranger dug through the smoldering remains of their fire. When he found a cinder still possessing a tiny kernel of orange life, he plucked it out. Lu winced, but for whatever reason the man was able to hold the hot coal between his fingers without being burned. Very carefully, he placed it into a nest of dry twigs, gleaned from amidst the brush Sadie had collected. Lu felt certain that it would go out. But the stranger blew onto the dying ember, lightly at first, later with more force, and in no time, yellow flames were dancing amid the ashes. When the fire was large enough to sustain itself, he set about skewering the rabbits.

That done, he got up and trotted silently into the thicket, returning a moment later with a handful of prickly pears. If the spines irritated his skin, Lu could see no sign of it.

For the next few minutes he sat, pulling bristles from the cactus pads and tossing them into the fire. As soon as he'd got one clean, he added it to the skewers.

Lu asked him what he was doing.

"You need vegetables," he answered.

The rabbits were beginning to sizzle on one side, so he turned the skewers. When he had them set up to his satisfaction, he looked at Lu.

For the first time, moonlight shone full in the stranger's face, and Lu gasped. His eyes were the palest shade of blue Lu had ever seen. In fact, they were nearly white. Odder still, Lu felt certain he'd seen those eyes somewhere before, and not so very long ago. For some reason, as he looked into them, he couldn't help shuddering.

"Jack sent me to find you," the man said. "He is worried."

"Jack? Really? Why?"

"You don't have enough water." He picked up the empty skin from where he'd dropped it, and tossed it to Lu. "You need to collect more."

"We're doing all right."

"No. You have too many horses." He pointed at Lucky. "That one is strong. He will live. But the rest?" He shrugged.

"Who are you?" Lu asked.

"This is my land." He smiled, showing a mouth full of brilliant white teeth. Again, the sensation that he had seen them before, and recently, prickled up and down Lu's spine.

"It used to all be mine," the man continued, waving his arms at the horizon. "The whole hump, east to west. My plants. My animals. My people. Only this is mine now. This desert. It is all I have left."

"I see." Lu peered more closely at the man. He was only a trifle shorter than Lu himself, but much thinner. At first, Lu had taken him for an Indian. Now he wasn't so sure. His skin wasn't white, but nor was it the same coppery brown Lu had seen amongst Joseph's or Goklayeh's tribes. Plus, he was hairy all over, and had a thick beard. The more Lu stared at him, the less sure he felt. A person such as this seemed not to fit in anywhere.

"You're nearing the Lake of Fire," the stranger continued. "You must be fully stocked with water before you cross. Even then, I don't think you will have enough. Do you drink a lot?"

"Not too much."

"You must drink less. *Much* less."

"When will we reach this lake?" Lu asked him.

"I might reach it in a day. But I'm on foot and very fast. You?" He pursed his lips. "You are slow."

"You can run faster than a horse?"

Instead of answering, he got up and brushed the dust from his legs. "Your friends will wake soon." He pointed at Sadie. Her mouth had fallen open. Drool hung from her lower lip.

"What should I tell them?"

"Tell them to kill a horse. Roast it for meat. Save the water."

"I'll tell them," Lu promised. "But I'm not sure they'll listen."

The stranger nodded. "You howl good," he said.

"Me?" Lu was taken aback. He remembered howling at the moon. But that'd been more than two days ago, hadn't it? In the excitement over Jack's departure, and the subsequent reading of the notebook, the whole event had slipped his mind. "How did you hear me?" he asked.

"You *all* howl good. It is good to howl."

The stranger bent to turn the skewers one last time. It took him only a moment, and when he was done he turned and trotted down the path.

"Where are you going?" Lu called after him.

"I'll tell Jack you're alive. For now."

"Wait." Lu felt as though he should ask something more. He knew an opportunity was passing him by, he just didn't know what it was. "What about this Lake of Fire?" he asked finally, stalling for time.

The stranger grinned, once more showing two rows of long healthy teeth. "Be careful," he said. "Conserve." Then he turned and loped away.

As he passed the horses, the stranger dropped onto all fours, his slow lope turning into a four-legged sprint. Then he leapt between the twisting coils of an ocotillo and was gone. It may have been nothing more than a trick of moonlight and shadows, but as he bounded into the thicket, Lu felt certain that he saw a long bushy tail sprout from beneath the man's loincloth.

"What was that?" Sadie asked, knuckling the sleep from her eyes.

"Did you see him?" Lu asked hopefully.

"I saw something. Was it that coyote again?"

The image of the man's pale blue eyes and long sharp teeth flashed through Lu's mind. "I don't know what it was."

"Have you been sitting up all this time? Aren't you sleepy?"

"A little." Lu pointed at the fire. "There are rabbits cooking if you're hungry. And prickly-pears."

Sadie stared. "Did you do that?" she asked.

"He did." Lu looked over his shoulder, at the spot where the stranger had disappeared into the brush. "He also said that we're drinking too much water. And that we ought to kill one of the horses."

"Kill a horse?" Sadie scoffed. "Maybe that old mule."

Lu shook his head. "Lucky's the strongest one."

Sadie inspected the rabbits. Another minute or two and they'd be ready. "You sure we can eat these pears?"

"I suppose so. He said we needed vegetables."

"Reckon it couldn't hurt to try." Sadie cut a bite from the pear closest the flames. "Well, it ain't exactly delicious," she said. "You want to try one?"

"Not right now. I'm going back to sleep. When he wakes up, tell Chino we're coming near the Lake of Fire."

"What's that?"

Lu shrugged. "I think Chino will know." Then he settled back, head on his saddle-seat, and went to sleep.

Crickets chirped, wind rustled through the brush, but Lu slept on. He didn't even hear the howl of the lone coyote, racing along the path behind them, lifting its plaintive call to welcome the morning.

"But I still can't see how we slept through it," MacLemore said. They'd got everything packed, and were watering their horses in preparation for the day's ride. "You're sure you weren't dreaming?"

"What about the rabbits?" Chino asked him. "They taste like a dream to you?"

"And he sure didn't dream this." Henry held up the extra water-skin.

"All right then, why does he see everything?" MacLemore looked accusingly at Lu. "Can you tell me that? Why him?"

"Maybe it's because he's nice," Sadie said.

"I'm nice," her father grumbled. "And I never met any savage war-chiefs, or coyote-men, or anything else."

"Maybe that's your problem, right there," Henry suggested. "Lu probably didn't call Gokhlayeh a savage. He may have thought it, but he didn't say so. Did you, Lu?"

"Heck no. I smoked when they told me to smoke, ate what they told me to eat. And when he asked me for a present, I gave him one. There wasn't anything to it."

That's what Lu said. But the truth was, Lu had begun to feel mighty proud of himself. As they rode out of camp, he thought over his adventures. He wished the boys back in St. Frances could see him now. They'd be so jealous they'd die. Jimmy Chiu would give anything he had just to hear one of Lu's stories. Lu reveled in that thought all morning long. He'd begun pondering all the ways he might add a touch of gunfire to his adventures for style, when Sadie rode up alongside him.

"You think you're mighty smart, don't you?" she said.

"Maybe," Lu replied.

"I saw the ghost-riders, too, you know."

Lu looked at her. "Did you?"

"Well, I felt 'em anyway. And I heard you and Jack talking."

"Oh."

"And I saw that feller last night."

"You didn't talk to him though."

"No, but I saw him."

"Good for you."

"I just don't want you thinkin' you're always the only one. The rest of us see things too, you know." And with that, Sadie galloped back to the front of the line.

Lu hated her for saying that, and went on hating her all afternoon. Chino kept trying to interest him in plants and animals, but all Lu could think about were the things he might say to her. A few were awfully mean. He even planned to talk about Sadie's hair, which was as dusty as an old rag. It gave him a secret thrill to ponder all the ways he might hurt her feelings. But as the day plodded on, and Lu's energies went more toward sweating than scheming, he began to lose hold of his anger. Spite just wasn't in him. Finally, he gave up.

It was late afternoon when they came upon a small creek, the first moving water they'd seen in days, and Chino said they ought to set up camp for the night.

The creek was only an inch and a half deep, tasted of moss, and barely moved over the flat ground. But they drank it up just as though it were lemonade. When the water-skins were full to bursting, they led the horses a short distance downstream from camp, and set them loose. Chino promised they wouldn't go anywhere, and he was right. Crash and Lucky stood in one spot for hours, alternately sucking up water and nibbling at the brittle grass that lined the stream banks.

With the balance of their day at leisure, Chino decided it was high time they replenished their stores.

"*El Lago del Fuego* is coming," he said. "Best we stock up now, before it's too late."

"What is it?" Lu asked him.

"The Lago? Just more desert. But harder than this. And hotter. If we're lucky, we can get through in a couple of days."

"Hotter?" Lu could hardly believe his ears. How could anything be hotter?

"And what happens if we aren't lucky?" MacLemore asked.

"Death," Chino said. "But we'll be lucky, I think."

"Death? From the heat?"

"And the desolation. It's a lonely place, the Lago. Lonely and thirsty."

"Enough talk," Sadie said. "Let's get these chores done. I still want to wash up before bed."

Chino gave each of them an assignment. He and Henry were to gather firewood. Mesquite grew everywhere, thick enough to build a bonfire a thousand feet high, but Chino wanted only the roots. Without a shovel, or even a hatchet, digging them up promised to be hard work. Henry whittled a couple of pointy sticks and got started. Sadie offered to help, but Chino had another task for her. Near the creek he'd found a stand of dark green weeds, which he called "Saint's Tea."

"It's strong medicine," he explained. "Good for the liver. We'll likely need it sooner or later." He showed her how to cut and bundle the shoots, which looked fairly simple to Lu. Sadie's main problem would be finding the stuff. Chino said she'd probably have to wander up and down the creek for miles. "And watch for snakes," he warned.

"Can't I take my horse?"

"The horses need rest," Chino said. "You'll have to walk."

Lu could hear her grumbling under her breath as she wandered away. "What about Mister MacLemore and me?" he asked.

"Prickly-pears," Chino said.

He led them up the path, passing a half-dozen smaller plants. At last, seeing one he liked, its big green pads fairly bursting with juice, he stopped.

"Now, this here's called *napolito*." Chino pointed to one of the fresher pads. "It's what we ate for breakfast." He searched over the rest of the plant until he found a bright red fruit. "And this is *tuna*. But it isn't ripe. I only want you to cut the napolito."

"But that's the spiny part," MacLemore protested.

"Yep. You'll have to use gloves."

"But I don't have any gloves," Lu said.

Chino took a pair of canary yellow cavalry gauntlets from his jacket pocket. A line of fringe ran from the little finger all the way to the middle of the forearm. "Henry said you could use his. He got them in the army." Chino laughed. "I think he used to wear them for parades."

Lu felt ridiculous as he pulled the gloves on. They were a couple of sizes too big and the fringe slapped against his wrists. "Do I have to wear them?" he asked.

MacLemore clapped him on the shoulder. "I think you look smart." He pulled on his own gloves, the very same pair he'd worn on the day they left St. Frances. "Now then, let's get to work."

At first, as they sawed the prickly pears from the bush, Lu was miserable. His one and only thought was of how glad he was that none of the kids back home could see him now. But Henry's gauntlets proved invaluable. MacLemore's fashionable riding gloves weren't half as good. Barely a minute went by without his yelping in pain. Finally he asked if Lu wouldn't like to trade, but Lu had decided he liked Henry's gloves after all.

They'd cut more than half-a-bag of napolitos before Lu devised a method for processing the pears more rapidly. With his heavier gloves, Lu sawed the juiciest pads from the bushes, while MacLemore plucked out the spines and stuck them in the sacks. Both were happy with the arrangement, and in no time they'd filled one whole bag. Every few minutes they had to go in search of a new plant, but that was the only thing that slowed them down.

While they worked, they talked. Actually, Mister MacLemore did the lion's share of the talking. Once in a while he'd ask Lu a question about his family or school, but mostly he told stories. He told all about his mother and father, and funny things he remembered from his boyhood on the farm. Lu listened to all of it with interest. Eventually he started talking about Sadie's mother.

"I wish you could've met Sadie's mother," MacLemore began. "She was a fine woman. And I'm not just saying that, either. She really was. A credit to her race. And not prejudiced in the least. Why, she cared for everyone just the same. Black, yellow, red, green or purple. She was mighty white that way. Handsome, too." He chuckled to himself. "I can remember my Daddy calling women 'handsome' when I was a boy, and I always thought it strange. Handsome. Still sounds sort of funny when you think about it. But that's what my Daisy was. Handsome as any woman you'd ever like to meet." MacLemore grinned. "Her beauties were the sort a woman gets from aging, not the adolescent prettiness of a girl in a school-yard. Nope, Sadie's mother was an upright *woman*. And she had a way of dealing with our farm hands, too. I don't believe I ever heard her resort to baseness. Not once. Daisy never called a spade a spade, if you see what I mean. Sadie favors her mother, thank God. Spitting image. Though she has but little of her mother's style. My Daisy liked to wear the most *beautiful* dresses. And here I can barely convince Sadie to pack one in her suitcase, let alone put it on. All my fault, I suppose." MacLemore shook his head. "It's no wonder she has more interest in horses than boys. She's spent more time with the one than the other, Lord knows. Don't guess she'd recognize a corset if she saw one. But maybe that's for the best."

"I think Sadie is just about the most wonderful girl I ever knew," Lu remarked. He hadn't actually meant to pipe in, and certainly not on such a potentially disastrous subject. But MacLemore didn't seem to mind, so Lu continued. "You ought to be proud of her."

MacLemore stared at him a moment. "That's mighty kind of you," he said at last. "And I am proud. I just wish I could get a *real* boy to take an interest in her."

Lu didn't say anything for a while after that. MacLemore hadn't meant to hurt his feelings, Lu was sure, but he had all the same. So Lu stayed quiet, busying himself with the pears while Mister MacLemore told stories about Sadie's childhood. If he ever noticed how silent his young friend had become, he didn't show it.

They harvested until after dark, and managed to fill all four bags. Lu guessed they might have forced another pear in somewhere, but all he could find were shriveled up old pads. And purple ones. Those he steered clear of. Chino never said a thing about the purple prickly-pears, but Lu reckoned they were sick somehow. Even Lucky turned up his nose when they came upon one in the path. And he'd eat anything, stickers included.

MacLemore still had a few more spines to pluck out, but that only took him a second. When he was done, he looked at the gunnysacks, full near to bursting, and grinned. "Dang, Lu," he said. "You're a regular pear-carving machine."

"We'd best get back. The others are probably wondering what happened to us."

MacLemore tied the last bag closed. Then he and Lu slung them over their shoulders, two to a man, and started back toward camp. Lu was pretty well tuckered out. After hours of staring at prickly pears, his eyes wanted nothing more than to go shut. He was so sleepy that he didn't even notice the javelina blocking their path until MacLemore grabbed his arm.

It was staring right at them—an enormous pig, fully three feet at the shoulder, with hair bristling up at least another six inches. Its snort, as it looked them over, was deep and sonorous.

"What do you think we ought to do?" MacLemore asked. "Chino seems to think these things can be dangerous."

"Let's just go around it," Lu said.

"Wait. I have a better idea." MacLemore dropped his two gunny-sacks and reached into his jacket pocket. Lu wasn't entirely surprised to see him pull out a revolver. It was a shade larger than the one he'd found in Sadie's valise, but definitely of the same family. "I'll fire a couple of shots," he said. "That ought to scare it."

"I don't think that's such a good idea," Lu said. The javelina had a look in its eyes that he didn't care for in the least.

"Tell you what. I'll fire twice. If the pig doesn't run away, we'll go around."

It still sounded risky to Lu, and he said so. But MacLemore had his heart set on shooting. He aimed and fired, the bullet plunking into the dust a couple of yards in front of the javelina. It gave a snort, but otherwise held its ground.

"Maybe you ought to quit," Lu suggested.

"Just one more." MacLemore fired again. This time, his bullet struck a rock, smashing it into a thousand pieces.

Surprised, the javelina backed away.

"See that?" MacLemore crowed. "One more shot and it'll run for sure. Did you hear the way it squealed?"

But Lu wasn't so sure. The pig looked surprised, and a little confused, but it also looked as though it might get angry any second. When those bits of exploded rock bounced off its chest, the javelina did squeal, but Lu wasn't sure he'd heard fear in its voice so much as outrage.

"I think we ought to forget the whole thing," he said.

But MacLemore wasn't listening. He brought up his little revolver again and prepared to shoot.

As he cocked it, Lu reached for his own gun. He just had the feeling that this javelina wasn't going to put up with any more shooting. And he was right. As soon as MacLemore fired, the javelina charged, teeth bared in wild-eyed attack.

It took only seconds for it to cover the distance between itself and the two men, just time enough for Lu to thumb the hammer on his revolver, advancing the cylinder to a live round, and pull the trigger.

The resulting blast was a surprise, and in more ways than one. First, it was louder than anything Lu had yet heard, or was ever likely to hear. Much, much louder. It was so ear-splittingly noisy it made Henry's rifle seem like a pop-gun. And it had a kick to match its roar. The recoil knocked Lu clean off his feet.

Next thing he knew, MacLemore was leaning over him. "My God, son," he said. "Are you all right?"

Lu could just barely hear him over the ringing in his ears.

"Jeeminy! Dropped you like a ton of bricks, didn't it?"

"What happened to the javelina?" Lu asked. He sat up, expecting to see a carcass, and was almost disappointed to see nothing.

"It's gone. You must've scared it though. Darned thing raced through the middle of that mesquite yonder, and I don't reckon it's stopped yet."

"What'd I hit?" Lu asked.

"Cactus." MacLemore pointed at a nearby saguaro. A hole as big as a man's fist had been punched straight through the trunk, about five feet off the ground. "What kind of gun is that anyway?"

"I'm pretty sure it was the bullet." Lu slid the pistol back into his holster. "Bill gave them to me. They belonged to his wife." He hadn't intended to say that, but the words came out before he could stop them. For some reason, he still didn't want his friends to know any more about his bullets than was absolutely necessary.

"His wife?" MacLemore whistled. "That must have been quite a gal."

The rest of their party stood up as Lu and MacLemore strode back into camp. Henry looked worried. "We heard gunshots," he said.

"Just an old javelina," MacLemore explained.

"You didn't shoot it, did you? Jack said that—"

"Just scared it, thank god. I'd hate to think what that bullet would've done if it'd struck meat."

MacLemore told the whole story, even admitting to having

riled the javelina up with his own shots. "Earlier, I'd been brag-
ging to Lu about my wife," he said, blushing. "That got me thinking about my dead son, and how he'd be about as old as I was
when Daisy and I got married." He paused. "I guess I felt old,
and wanted to show off. Can't have these young fellers thinking
you're just an old so and so . . . even if you really are."

Lu was amazed at how forthright MacLemore was being. It
was as though the truth were forcing its way out. When he'd
finally finished talking, Henry demanded to see one of Lu's bullets. Reluctantly, Lu acquiesced.

"Looks plain enough," Henry said. "Brass jacket. Lead slug.
Can't see anything that ought to make it any more powerful than
any other bullet. What's this pink stripe?"

Lu said he didn't know, but did admit to getting the cartridges from Bill. After that, Chino demanded to hear the whole
Bill story again, with the gift of the bullets described in detail. For
some reason, Lu was still reluctant, even now that his secret was
revealed. When Sadie asked him how many bullets he had, Lu's
first inclination was to lie. "Ten," he tried to say. But the truth
came out instead. "Eleven, plus the one I already fired."

"Lu was quick on the draw, too," MacLemore said. "I don't
think Jack Straw himself could have done better."

"And it knocked you over backwards?" Henry asked.

"Dropped him like a ton of bricks," MacLemore replied.
"Wham, he was *down*."

"Did it hurt?"

"It made my ears ring," Lu said. "In fact, they're still ringing
a little."

"Take off your shirt. Let Chino see your arm."

Lu did as bidden, though he was mortified at having Sadie see
him bare-chested. Muscles weren't exactly dripping off him.

"He looks all right to me," Chino said.

Henry agreed. "Here, let me see that gun."

He inspected every inch of the barrel before handing it back.
"No cracks," he said. "But I'd leave a cylinder open if I were you.
Especially riding through this brush. If that gun is as powerful as
you say, you can't risk its going off by accident."

"I already do," Lu said. "Bill told me the same thing."

It was getting late, so they ate a little supper—more of the roasted javelina meat—and then Chino said he was going to turn in. "We have another long day tomorrow."

"I still need to wash," Sadie said. "So don't any of you wander down to the creek 'til I come back."

"You plan to wash that much?" her father asked.

"I figure it's my last chance. And I can't see getting my clothes all wet."

Lu watched her go. He was trying to think of some way that he might slip out of the camp unnoticed—he still owed Sadie for seeing him with his pants unbuttoned—but the minute she left, MacLemore sat down beside him and asked if he wouldn't like to sing a song. He sounded so hopeful that Lu just couldn't say 'no.'

They were only halfway through *Streets of Laredo* when Lu heard a splash, followed by a girlish giggle. It almost made him forget the words.

They got their first glimpse of the Lake of Fire shortly after noon the following day. Their path wound up and over a naked bluff, and there it was—a stripe of stark white stretched over the whole earth, north to south, and all the way to the horizon.

"Even the sky is white," Lu observed.

"That's the heat," Chino explained. "It bleaches everything."

"How big is it?" MacLemore asked. "I don't believe I can see anything beyond."

"Some places it's narrow as forty miles."

"And here?"

Chino shook his head. "No way to know."

"I don't see any roads," Sadie said.

"Nope. Never has been a road in the Lago. Don't reckon there ever will be."

"So how do you know which way to go?"

"That's easy. You head west."

"For how long?"

"Long as it takes."

CHAPTER 14
SALT FLATS

THREE STRAIGHT DAYS THEY RODE, sunup to sundown, and still saw nothing to break up the bone-whiteness of the land.

At first, as they'd ridden down off the bluff they'd passed a few old and withered sage-brush plants, and salt-grass enough to keep their horses in feed. But by the evening of that first day, even the salt-grass was gone.

It was a dreary thing, to stare hour after hour at a landscape so utterly devoid of interesting features. There wasn't a hint of color or shape anywhere. No stones to mark their passage. No trees or cactuses. Nothing that created shade. The horizon remained as featureless and out of reach as when they began. No matter how far they went, or for how long, it never felt like they were making any progress. It sapped the spirits like nothing in Lu's life ever had. He would have rather taken a good hard whipping than to spend another minute looking at those salt-white plains. The horses didn't like it any more than the people did. Even Chino's big mare, normally proud and spirited, hung her head. If he didn't know better, Lu would've said the horses were melting. The sweat a horse could produce over the course of a day was astonishing. Out on the Lake of Fire, even a slow walk was enough to work them to a lather. The humans sweated nearly as much, but it got trapped in their clothes and soaked up by the dust.

The Lago was composed almost entirely of dust—powdery

fine, salty dust. Bad enough if it were just lying out there, or happened on occasion to be kicked up by their horses' hooves. But this dust wasn't the lazy sort one might find in a house, relaxing on a bookshelf or lying casually atop a picture frame. This dust was active. And it was ruthless, too. No matter which direction Lu looked, the dust was always blowing straight in his face. Henry and Chino both wore bandannas, tied over mouth and nose like bank robbers. Sadie had her silk kerchief, the blue one she'd used to wrap up her little pistol. Unfortunately, neither Lu nor MacLemore had any way of blocking out the torture of the blowing salt. It chapped the lips, blistered the inside of the nose, and made the eyes stream. By the time they stopped, just after sundown each night, they were so crusted over they looked like snowmen. Sadie's hair caught the stuff by the pound.

Around midmorning of their fourth day on the salt flats, misfortune struck. Somehow, MacLemore's horse Cody found the only significant hole in the entire Lago and stepped right in. MacLemore was thrown and Cody rolled. The horse came up limping.

Chino inspected Cody's ankles and hooves. He had a minor sprain in his right hind-leg. Cody could walk, but he wouldn't be able to do any heavy work for a few days.

MacLemore, still sitting on the ground where his horse had flung him, wanted to know what he was supposed to do now.

"Put your saddle on the mule," Chino said. "He'll carry you easy enough."

"No MacLemore *ever* rode a mule."

"Walk then."

Grudgingly, MacLemore placed his saddle on Lucky, who seemed no more thrilled with the prospect than his proposed rider. It did look strange, Lu had to admit. Everything about MacLemore, from his riding boots to his beaver hat, spoke of money. His clothes, once the finest Lu had ever beheld, were now worn and dirty, but a touch of the quality still shone through. Even his saddle, while not decorated with near the detail of his daughter's, had the sheen of richness. He made quite a picture, poised atop a lumpy, short-legged mule.

By sundown, Cody was stumbling over rocks that weren't there, and falling in holes too small to hide a thimble. He wore Lucky's harness, but Lu didn't guess that could possibly be the trouble. The harness weighed less than half as much as a saddle. Their remaining firewood added a few pounds, of course, as did the sacks of prickly-pears. But all together that didn't amount to a fraction of what MacLemore weighed.

The wind was blowing so hard that a campfire was impossible. So they sat in the dark, heads huddled between their knees, as Sadie handed out shares of the roasted javelina. Lu complained about the size of his piece, but stopped when he saw Sadie upend the sack and fish out an even smaller bit for herself.

"Y'all had best enjoy it," she said. "Tomorrow we're back on pemmican."

"How much pemmican is left?" Henry asked.

"Enough for a day. Two if we stretch."

"We'd better stretch then," Chino remarked.

"What about that grass you had me pick?" Sadie asked.

"We'll get to it as soon as we're done with the pemmican."

They broke camp early the next morning. Lu felt sick, but knew it couldn't be anything he ate. There was nothing in his stomach but a few swallows of warm water. By noon he was so hungry he thought he might pass out. MacLemore asked if they couldn't eat a few prickly-pears, just to take the edge off, but Chino flatly refused. The pears were for the stock. If they ran out of everything else, water included, Chino said they might gnaw up a few. Until then, they'd just have to tighten their belts and grit their teeth. In the meantime, he offered each of them a cut of his tobacco. Sadie and her father both accepted. Lu refused. Even the smell of tobacco spittle was enough to make him want to throw up. And that was the last thing he needed.

Cody tripped and stumbled his way across a good fifteen miles of open desert before finally refusing to go a step farther. Sadie yanked and pulled at his reins, but the horse wouldn't move.

"You don't think he's broke something, do you?" MacLemore asked.

"Naw." Chino shook his head. "He's just playin' possum. I seen it before. Figures if he acts sick, we'll give him an extra bit of food."

"Can we?"

Chino pondered that a moment. "Well, all right. But just one prickly-pear. I don't want the other horses gettin' any ideas."

MacLemore searched through their remaining supplies, finally coming up with a particularly large and juicy chunk of pear flesh, which Cody swallowed almost whole.

"Go on," Chino said to Sadie. "Give him a tug."

The extra nourishment must have done the trick. Cody followed her lead all the rest of that day without once tripping or falling in a hole. In fact, he barely limped at all. Lu judged the experiment a success.

By the next afternoon, however, he'd come to think differently. Once again, Cody was stumbling. Sadie cursed and screamed, but her threats didn't seem to do any good. Eventually, Cody flat refused to move. This time, Chino wouldn't be duped. He rode around behind the willful horse, drawing his pistol as he went. As soon as he was directly behind it, Chino let off a shot. Cody and Carrot both crow-hopped, leaping first sideways and then straight ahead. It was so sudden and unexpected a jolt that, for an instant, Sadie looked as though she might be thrown. If she was any less a rider, she would've been.

When both horses had calmed down, Chino told Sadie to get going. She did, and managed to drag Cody a whole mile without stopping. Then Cody dug in his front hooves again. Chino swore a blue streak.

For the rest of that afternoon, Chino rode directly behind the rebellious horse, kicking it, whipping it with his reins and firing his guns. It was a slow method of travel, and a difficult one. Come evening, Chino was as exhausted as the horses.

"Tomorrow," he said, slumped beside the glowing remains of their fire. "I'm going to lead that horse. And if he tries to stop, I'll jerk his derned teeth out."

Chino was as good as his word, and the next day they managed to cover twenty-eight miles. All told, Henry estimated that they'd traveled one-hundred-sixty-two miles. And still they saw no sign of the Lago's western end.

For supper that night, Sadie offered up the last of the pemmican.

"I reckon it's about time we started in on that tea stuff you're so dern tight with," she said. "Ain't nothin' left now but prickly-pears, and one or two chaws of tobacco."

Chino opened his saddle-bag and took out the bunch of stiff weeds Sadie had collected along the creek. "Bring me your water-skins," he instructed. He got them to stand in a line, and then went from one person to the next, breaking up the shoots and dropping them down the necks of the bags. Sadie eyed the whole process with derision.

"Hell," she muttered. "You could've done *that* five days ago."

"It'll work better now," Chino said. "Less water to dilute the tea."

Sadie took a sip and grimaced. "It's awful."

"But healthy. From now on we take nothing but tea. The horses'll eat the pears."

"Sounds like a lot of foolishness to me," Sadie said.

The hunger with which they began the following day was almost more than Lu could bear. The gurgling in his belly was the worst. When he couldn't take it any longer, he took a swig of tea. Sadie was right, it was truly awful. To Lu it tasted like moldy bread. But it did take the edge off. One swallow was enough to keep him from being thirsty for a whole hour. The only problem with it, other than the revolting taste, was that it made him want to urinate.

Chino was still dragging MacLemore's horse, and they were making decent time. By noon they'd covered almost nine miles. Soon after, Henry, who always rode way out front, gave a shout.

"Water!" he yelled, and pointed at the horizon.

Lu squinted. He saw heat-waves, and even a bit of corn-flower-blue sky away to the north. Then he saw it, a shine amidst the chalky dust. "I think I see it," he shouted. "It is water, isn't it?"

Sadie and her father were equally excited. Only Chino remained unmoved.

"It's no good," he muttered. "You can't drink it. Can't even wash with it."

"How do you know?" Sadie asked.

"It's salt. Or worse. Same as everything else out here."

"I still think we should look it over," MacLemore said. "Just in case."

They adjusted their course, and were soon riding along the edge of a small lake. At the center stood an island of pure salt, dried into strangely shaped monoliths, some as much as five feet tall, and covered over with a thick layer of dust. Where the water had come from, only God knew. There were no streams leading into the lake, nor any that led out. Drinking it was out of the question. Even at a distance of a hundred yards the smell was enough to turn your stomach. Worst of all, a steely gray scum, something like the bubbles on a sink of old dish water, drifted across the surface, collecting on the windward side of the island.

"Bad water," Chino said. "There are pools like this all over the Lago. It'd kill you as surely as if—"

They never heard the rest. All at once, and for reasons none of them would ever understand, Cody broke free and went racing toward the lake. He was standing knee-deep in the water before anyone even knew what'd happened.

"I'll get him," Sadie offered.

Chino shouted at her to stop, but Sadie wasn't listening. She galloped right to the edge of the water, and nearly flipped over Carrot's head as he sunk his front hooves into the sandy bank. By that time, Cody had waded chest deep in the muck, and was trying to go even deeper. Once she'd regained her seat, Sadie gave her horse a slap on the haunches, and set her spurs to his ribs, but Carrot refused to take another step.

"You're lucky he's an Indian horse," Chino said, riding up beside her. "They're too smart to wander into such as that."

"What are you talking about?"

"Look."

In his effort to reach the deep water, Cody had disturbed something in the mud on the bottom of the lake. Gray bubbles popped all around him, though Cody didn't seem to have noticed. Amazingly, he was drinking the foul-smelling water. Lu guessed he'd probably drunk about a gallon, and was rapidly sucking in even more, when all of a sudden Cody let out a terrified whinny, reared and started thrashing his way back toward shore.

"What's he doing?" Sadie asked.

"The water's boiling his guts," Chino said.

They watched in terrified silence as Cody struggled to reach the edge of the lake. He'd made it only half-way before foam began to spurt from his mouth and nostrils. It was gray, just like the lake water, though now flecked with blood.

"Wouldn't be right to let him suffer," Chino said.

Henry reached for his rifle.

"It's my horse," MacLemore said. "I guess I'll be the one to shoot him."

Without a word, Henry passed him the gun.

MacLemore checked the hammer, making sure the rifle was cocked, and then brought it up to his shoulder.

Cody shuddered. The foam pouring out of him was no longer flecked with blood, but more or less composed of it.

"Take him down," Chino urged. "Do it now."

The rifle gave its usual roar and Cody collapsed. He convulsed a moment longer, blood spurting from the bullet-hole in his neck, and then slipped beneath the surface of the pond. Pink bubbles burst over the spot where he'd last stood.

"He was a good horse once," MacLemore said, handing the rifle back to Henry.

Lu nodded. He wondered if he ought to say something. Cody was the first horse he ever rode.

"No use bawling over it now," Chino said. "Haven't got water enough to piddle away in foolish tears." Chino gave his horse a nudge, turning her away from the lake. "Time we put a few more miles behind us."

Sadie glared daggers at him. But either Chino didn't notice, or didn't care. They had just over an hour of sunlight left, and he meant to use it to good purpose. He gave his mare a sharp kick, forcing her to a trot. In no time at all the lake was behind them, and then lost to sight.

As they rode on, Lu realized for the first time the true enormity of what had happened that day. The last of their wood had been tied to Cody's back, as were the prickly-pears for feeding the stock. They had no fuel, no food, and what was far worse, absolutely no prospects for collecting more. If they hadn't been carrying their skins looped over their saddle-horns, they'd have been without water too. Lu looked around at the others. Their faces were pinched and drawn. He guessed they were thinking the same things he was, but they were all too depressed to say anything.

The wind died as they made camp. For the first time in a week, Lu could breathe deeply, and through his mouth. It did nothing for his mood, however. He was angry and intended to stay that way. It was just like this darned old desert to give up blowing just after they'd lost their wood, he thought to himself.

Chino and Henry sat on their saddles, watching as the horses pawed through the salt. They spoke not a word. And yet, Lu thought they looked as if they'd come to a decision of some kind. Not an easy decision either.

"We're in trouble," Lu said to them. "Aren't we?"

Chino nodded.

"Is there anything we should do?" MacLemore asked. "Anything at all?"

"You a praying man?"

"Not anymore."

"Nope. Me neither." Chino sighed. "It was easier when I was. Feels good to put all the hard decisions on God."

"Like what?" Sadie asked. "What've you decided?"

"I figure we can wait 'til tomorrow night. But if we don't see any change in the landscape by then, we'll have to kill one of the horses."

"Kill? What in the world for?"

"Meat. And blood."

"Blood?" Sadie glared at the men. "What do you want with blood?"

"Mix it with some of our tea and the horses could drink it maybe. So could we."

Lu's mouth dropped open. "That's disgusting."

"Horse isn't too bad," Henry said. "We ate lots of it in the army. Never raw, of course, but—"

"Which horse do you plan to kill?" MacLemore asked them. Chino and Henry both looked at Lu.

"What?" he said. "Why are you looking at me?"

"Crash is a good horse, chico. Better than I'd have thought possible."

"But you can't kill Crash. He's still strong."

"I know he is. But it's either Crash or Carrot. I think Carrot will be able to carry you and Sadie together. Do you think Crash can do the same?"

"Sure he can. And what about one of your horses? Or the mule?"

Neither Chino nor Henry said a word.

"He can. I swear it. Crash is strong."

"All right," Chino said at last. "If it comes to that, we'll put down Carrot."

They all looked at Sadie.

"Fine by me," she spat. "Crash is a better horse anyway."

"We ought to kill Henry's horse," MacLemore observed.

"My horse?" Henry didn't sound angry, just surprised. His horse had been nothing but strong throughout the whole trip. It was the best horse they had left.

"He's the last of our original stock. I guess he must be bad luck."

Henry seemed honestly taken aback. "He's always been plenty good luck for me."

The next morning, as they were saddling up, Lu paid particular attention to Sadie. She'd been rubbing Carrot down for the better part of an hour, until his coat was entirely free of dust—no easy trick in the Lago.

"You all right?" he asked her.

"Sure. Just hate to see a horse shot, that's all." Sadie looked west, toward the emptiness that had dominated their every waking moment for the last week, and frowned. "Seems like nearly all the shootin' we've done this trip was to shoot our own horses. When Daddy said we were goin' to hire Jack Straw, I reckoned there'd be a whole heap of shootin'. But not our own derned horses.'"

Lu didn't know what to say. Sadie was a hard girl to under-stand. One minute she'd be swearing or spitting tobacco, and the next she'd say something as soft and tender as a snowflake.

"I guess we *had* to shoot Cody," he said finally. "He was suf-fering just awful."

Sadie shuddered.

"That lake was something." Lu shook his head. "We have a lake back home, in St. Frances, only it's not acidic. It's more of a pond really. Folks row boats on it in the summer. One year, the mayor invited my grandfather to put together a fireworks display for the Fourth and I got to help. There were white folks sitting on quilts all the way around the whole lake, eating fried chicken and deviled eggs. I'd never tried a deviled egg, so the mayor's wife gave me one. It was good." Talking about deviled eggs made Lu's stomach growl. "Anyhow," he continued. "That's it. Thinking of that lake made me think of the deviled eggs. Chinese people aren't usually allowed to go to picnics, you know. Not with other peo-ple. White people, I mean." Lu blushed. He'd meant to tell her about a nice lake, and suddenly here he was discussing deviled eggs. And with them starving, too. "I'm sorry," he muttered. "I didn't mean to . . . whatever."

Awkward silence hung in the air as thick as the dust. Sadie stared at Lu for a moment, and then began saddling her horse. Still blushing furiously, Lu turned and stalked away. He'd only just mounted up when Sadie looked over at him again.

"Deviled eggs," she said. "That's a peculiar name."

"Yep." Lu grinned. "That's exactly what I thought at the time."

They rode all day. Other than to comment on the heat, or curse the dust, no one had much to say. They just stared at the horizon and counted the hours. As the sun started downward, they were still looking at nothing but a blank white line.

It was growing late, but Chino didn't call a stop. Lu dreaded what was to come, and guessed Chino must feel the same. If he thought it'd do any good, Lu might have begged for a reprieve.

He just couldn't imagine shooting a horse as strong and good-natured as Carrot. He was still getting along so well. All the horses were, considering.

And then, just as Lu was about to speak up, Henry went galloping ahead.

"What in the hell?" Chino cursed. "Where's he goin'?"

They caught up to Henry a few minutes later. He'd dismounted and was standing over the skeletal remains of a deer. He looked happy.

"It's a mule deer," Henry said. He gave the deer's skull a sharp kick for emphasis.

"So what?" MacLemore asked. "Some old deer wanders into the desert and dies, and you act like it's your birthday."

"But wandered in from where?" Henry asked.

They all looked at the horizon again. Suddenly it seemed more hopeful than it had in days.

"Let's keep riding," Sadie suggested. "I'm not tired."

They all agreed. The horses were less energetic, but not a one of them balked or turned surly, as Cody had done.

All through the night they rode, maintaining a good pace even in the face of a stiff breeze. And then, suddenly, it appeared. The first rays of the sun peeked over the horizon at their backs and there, directly ahead of them, was a hill.

They rode toward it in high spirit. There was no vegetation of any kind on its chalky face, but they climbed up anyway. From the top they could see, not even a mile distant, a whole landscape of rolling hills. And beyond that, so far away that they seemed almost to hang over the land like angels, were mountains.

Crash was so exhausted that Lu decided to dismount and lead him the rest of the way on foot. The other members of their band did likewise. It was thirsty work, offering no opportunity for idle chatter, especially once they'd reached the hills. Up and down they went, seeing nothing apart from more and steeper slopes. Crash was really hanging back now. At the base of each hill Lu had to heave at his reins, and beg and plead with him to keep moving. Lu made promises of water to come. Crash peered uncertainly at him, but he always managed to summon the courage necessary to crawl up the next rise. Finally, just as the sun was beating down its hardest, they came over a bluff, and there, stretched out in a narrow valley below, was a whole thicket of sagebrush, surrounded on all sides by salt-grass. There was even one dusty old tree standing at the center. Lu didn't know what kind it was, and didn't care. After days without so much as a sprig of green anywhere, any tree looked fantastic. Crash proved less sentimental. As soon as he caught a whiff of the vegetation at the base of the hill he shoved Lu out of the way and went trundling down after it.

There was nothing for the humans to eat, of course, but that seemed somehow secondary. They still had a few swallows each of the Saint's tea, and while they were famished, they weren't yet in any serious danger of actually starving to death. Most importantly, they wouldn't have to shoot one of their horses. Not today.

While the horses grazed, Lu slept. He didn't even bother to unsaddle Crash before climbing into a hole beneath the biggest sage-brush he could find and settling his head on a rock. A rock! Lu chuckled to himself. He never guessed he'd get such a charge from a bit of old stone.

Lu was awakened, less than an hour later, by the titter of strange voices. At first he thought it was birds, then Sadie chatting with her father or one of the other men. But the more he listened, the more he thought it sounded like children.

Lu sat up. He didn't see anyone, but was sure he'd heard something. Quiet as he could, Lu crept out of his hiding place.

He'd gone less than a dozen yards when he saw two boys. Both had dirty-blond hair, and they wore matching blue chambray shirts. Lu snuck up behind them without being noticed, so attentive were the boys to whatever they'd spotted in the bushes.

"Is so," the younger of the two whispered. "You can just ask Brother Nephi. He's seen one before."

"Aw, I think he's just an old Injun."

"No Injun's got skin that dark. He's a black." The younger boy pointed. "That's the mark of Cain on his skin."

They were talking about Henry. He was lying right out in the open, head on his saddle, hat balanced on the bridge of his nose. One hand rested across his chest, and it was this that so interested the boys.

"Let's ask Ma," the older one suggested. "We'll just see what she says."

"She'll say it's the mark of Cain," his brother whispered. "You'll see."

"*Shhhh,* you're talkin' too loud. Do you want to wake him up?"

"He can't hear me. He's way over there."

"But I can," Lu said.

The boys yelped and spun around. The younger of the two—he was missing one of his front teeth—tripped over his feet and went sprawling.

"You'd better leave us alone!" the older boy shouted. He'd grabbed his brother by the shirt-collar, and was trying to drag him back to his feet. "Our Ma's right over yonder. Ma! Ma! Help!"

"What in the world are you two on about?"

Lu looked and saw a girl, eleven or twelve, marching down a narrow gully between the hills. She was just tall enough for Lu to see her head over the tops of the brush, but even that was enough to know she was their sister. Same blond hair. Same blue cloth for her dress.

"Sis!" the older boy shouted. "Tell Ma. There's Gentiles in the bushes."

The girl saw Lu about that time and froze. She stared at him, as if expecting Lu to turn into a wolf or grizzly bear, and then went racing back up the path, her bare feet sending up little clouds of dust. A moment later, they heard her scream.

In the meantime, Henry had been woken up by all the racket, and come to see what the shouting was about.

"And just what do we have here?" he asked. "What are your names, boys?"

Both stared up at Henry wide-eyed.

"Well? Cat got your tongues?"

Finally, the younger of the two found enough courage to answer. "He's Melvin. Ma called him that after our Pa."

"And what's your name?"

"Irus." For the first time, Lu noticed something odd about that boy. One of his legs was twisted, so that his foot pointed sideways rather than forward, and it had been wrapped and bound about as tight as a scrap of old wool could be tied. The boy saw Lu staring at his foot and grimaced.

Henry held out his hand for them to shake. "Pleased to meet you both."

"What's going on?" Sadie asked, pushing her way through the brush. MacLemore and Chino were right behind her. "Who's doing all that screeching?"

"It's just a couple of kids," Lu explained. "They were spying on us."

"Where are you from, boys?" Henry asked.

"Our house is right over that hill," Irus said. "All you have to do is go down the path. Your horses found us all right. They drank all the water from our goat's trough."

"Well, I'll be," Chino said.

"Where's your father?" MacLemore asked them.

"He lives in town with his first wife."

"His first wife?"

"Sure. Pa's only got two though. We don't got so much money."

Their conversation was interrupted by more screams from beyond the hills. "Irus! Melvin!" It was an older voice. Not the same little girl, but a full-grown woman. "Where are you?"

"Over here," Irus called back. "With the Gentiles."

The woman, she looked no more than thirty-five, though significantly worn and frazzled, came racing down the path between the hills. She had a wild look in her eyes. Lu half-expected her to take a swing at one of them, and hoped she wouldn't choose him. But she didn't hit anybody. Instead, she grabbed the boys and squeezed them to her bosom. "Are you all right?" she asked.

"Sure," Irus replied. "We're fine. These're friendly Gentiles."

The woman looked at the salt-crusted faces surrounding her,

still reluctant to let her babies out of her grip. "Who are you?" she demanded.

Mister MacLemore tipped his hat. Chalky dust slid off the brim. He introduced each member of their band, beginning with Henry and finishing with Lu. "We're just in off the Lago," he explained. "If you could spare a bit of food, I'm sure we'd be much obliged."

"The Lago? Why, you must be about dead."

"We are." Chino put a hand on Lu's shoulder. "Our boy here was as big as Goliath when we started."

The woman looked them up and down again. She didn't seem entirely sure of what she was seeing until she got to Sadie. Then her hard gaze melted.

"Normally, I don't have enough to feed my boys," she said. "But tonight we're hosting the Bishop, so I expect there'll be plenty to go around."

MacLemore tipped his hat again.

"Well, c'mon then." She gestured for them to follow. "Irus, Melvin, you boys run ahead. Tell your brothers to catch them horses and stick 'em in the corral. Then start hauling water from the well. We'll need four good-size pails. These folks will have to clean up a mite if they're to stay supper. And tell Sis to fill the tub in my room. We've a young lady here in dire need of a wash."

Both boys went off at a lope. Irus had a noticeable limp, but managed to keep his older brother in sight. Sadie noticed the younger boy's foot and gasped.

"Somethin' wrong?" the woman asked her.

"Your boy's foot," Sadie said.

"You should've seen it when he was first born. Turned right around backwards. I been twistin' and bindin' it since Irus was two. I figure in a couple more years I'll just about have it on straight."

"Must hurt him awful," Henry muttered under his breath. "Poor child."

"Yep. Irus used to howl somethin' fierce. He's got tougher in recent years. Barely complains at all now." She looked at the men and Sadie, and frowned. "Well, are you comin' or ain't you?"

"Just have to collect our saddles, ma'am."

"Get to it then. I don't have all day."

Chino, Sadie and her father pushed back through the bushes, while Henry made the short walk to his own saddle and grabbed it up by the horn. By the time they got back to where Lu was standing, the woman was gone. She wasn't a tall woman, but she was a fast walker.

"I guess she got tired of waiting," Lu said.

"Where's your saddle?" Henry asked him.

"Still on my horse, I suppose."

Henry frowned. He didn't have to say a word. Lu already felt guilty. Crash had been wearing his saddle for two straight days. It wasn't right for Lu to have gone to sleep without unsaddling his horse. That was no way to treat a mount as loyal as Crash.

"I guess we'd best get going," MacLemore said. "She didn't strike me as an especially patient woman."

"Nope," Chino agreed. "Say, did any of you catch her name?"

They all shook their heads.

"Well," Sadie said, "I'd call that peculiar."

"YOU MEN STRIP OFF THOSE SHIRTS and I'll fetch you some new."
The woman, Irus' and Melvin's mother, was waiting for them on
the front porch of her cabin as they hustled up the path. Lu was
relieved to see his saddle lying on the grass beside a pair of old
handcarts, the wheels broken and gone to rot.

"What about me?" Sadie asked.

"You just come along with me, dear." She took Sadie by the
hand, whisking her inside. "We'll get you fixed right up."

Lu, Henry, Chino and MacLemore stood in the front yard,
looking at each other. Buckets of icy well-water had been set up
along the edge of the porch, and there was a brick of lye soap for
them to share. Boys—five in all, each as blond as a corn tassel—
sat behind the buckets, clearly waiting for someone to do something fascinating. The oldest looked to be about sixteen. Irus, the
youngest, was five or six.

"Well?" MacLemore asked. "What now?"

"I guess we ought to wash," Henry replied, and stripped off
his shirt.

Just then, the cabin door banged open and the girl Lu had
seen in the thicket stuck her head out. "Ma says you boys are to
stay right here on this porch. If she catches any one of you tryin'
to sneak 'round back, she'll skin you all."

"Guess that tells us," Chino muttered.

The older boys laughed.

"What are your names?" MacLemore asked them. "We know Melvin and Irus, but what about y'all?"

The boys looked at each other. "I'm Louis," the oldest said. "That's Jesse, and the one on the end is Robert. There's also the baby. His name's Karl. But he stays inside with Ma."

"What about your sister?"

"Her name's Lovisa. But everybody calls her Sis."

"What's your mother's name?" Chino asked.

"Eliza Jane, but she always says she hates it. We had another baby sister once. Ma named it after herself 'cause she could see right off it was gonna die."

Lu looked at his companions. He could see that they all considered Louis's last statement odd. Henry went so far as to shake his head.

"And your father's named Melvin, too. Isn't that right?" MacLemore asked.

"Melvin Hammond," Louis said, nodding.

"Does he live far?"

"He lives in town. It's about six miles."

"Does he get out here much?"

"Ma says he comes just often enough to keep her pregnant, but it ain't true," Jesse ventured. "Pa comes at least once a week. He and Ma like to get their 'lone time."

"Does he usually spend the night?" MacLemore asked. "When he comes, I mean."

"Once in a while. Mostly he heads back to town to be with Alma."

"His first wife?"

"Yep."

Their conversation was interrupted by the cabin door banging open again, and the boys' mother stomping out. She had a whole pile of blue chambray shirts, and one lone towel. When she saw the men, still lined up in front of the porch, only one of them with his shirt off, and not a one of them wet, she stopped cold.

"You men are as bad as my boys," she said. She dropped the shirts in a pile and marched down the steps. "Arms over your head," she ordered, and grabbed Lu's hands to make sure he complied.

She stripped him of his old shirt as slick and fast as if he were a baby, and then tossed it to her oldest boy, Louis, telling him to put it in with the wash.

When she looked at Lu again she clucked her tongue. "Judas Proost, how did you ever get so dirty?"

Eliza Jane made him hang his head over one of the buckets of icy water while she scrubbed him down with the lye soap. It was humiliating. She even washed his hair, nearly yanking it out of his head in the process. Far from laughing, however, his companions seemed to recognize the peril they were all in, and got right to the business of scrubbing.

"Now, that's a lot better," Eliza Jane said, toweling off Lu's face. "I'm going to get each of you a slice of bread with butter."

"Well, that was wonderful," Lu said, once Mrs. Hammond was out of ear-shot. "You all ought to have given it a try."

"Just be glad she didn't take your pants off," Chino remarked. "That might've got real uncomfortable."

Lu grabbed the shirt she'd left for him and pulled it on over his head. As he did so, he happened to glance at Mr. MacLemore, who had just finished with the soap and was passing it on to Henry.

"You've lost weight," Lu said. He was surprised. Without the fat to hide it, MacLemore was actually quite a muscular fellow. His arms were as big around as one of Lu's legs, his chest deep and powerful.

"You ought to see yourself," MacLemore replied. "Lean and mean I'd call it."

They'd all washed and put on clean shirts by the time Eliza Jane came back, carrying a stack of sliced bread. She gave one each to the men and boys grouped along the porch. MacLemore asked if they might not have another, but she flat refused.

"Dinner's in a couple hours," she said. "I don't want you piecing. It'll just ruin your appetites. You can look after your animals until then. The boys will help."

She was just about to go back inside, presumably to start supper, when Sis stuck her head out the door, a look of astonishment on her face. "That girl," she whispered. "The one in the tub. She's . . ." Sis blushed so that Lu thought she might pass out from the blood rushing to her head. "She's naked!"

Her brothers were all so surprised that they didn't even think to laugh. The oldest ones looked at each other wide-eyed.

"That's just the Gentile way," their mother explained. "Take her a bathing sheet and show her how to put it on."

"Me?" Sis asked. "But I'll see her."

"Sounds to me like you've seen her already."

This time the boys did giggle.

Sis looked both nervous and excited as she backed through the cabin door. Lu couldn't entirely wrap his mind around the issue of naked bathing, but could see it was quite a scandal to this family. He considered asking, but decided against it. If it was taboo to be naked, even when bathing, it was undoubtedly taboo to talk about being naked.

"You boys get along now," Eliza Jane said, shooing them away from the porch. "Melvin left a bucket of oats in the shed. You can give 'em to the horses."

"Much obliged, ma'am," MacLemore said. His hat still lay on the porch where he'd taken it off, so he tipped the air in front of his forehead.

The boys led them along a path through the hills. They were a quiet bunch, by and large. Walking amongst them, Lu almost felt as if he'd joined the army. He even had a uniform. All of them, oldest to youngest, were wearing identical blue shirts.

"Your Ma must have bought a ton of this material," he observed.

"Pa likes the color," Irus explained. "Ma says it makes him look sharp."

"It is a nice color," Henry agreed.

The boys led them to a corral. Their horses were already safe inside, nibbling the salt grass that grew up around the log posts.

"Here are the oats," Robert said, running down the trail behind them, a rusty bucket bouncing against his shin. As with all the boys, he looked eager to help.

"You can feed them if you want," Henry offered. "Just share with your brothers."

"Can we ride them?"

"Maybe tomorrow. These horses are pretty tired."

The boys were clearly disappointed, but not one of them moaned or argued. They all proved capable grooms, as well. Even Lucky, who was normally a bully where food was concerned, got sent briskly away once the boys decided he'd had enough.

When the oats had been exhausted, Irus asked if they could brush the horses. Henry readily gave his consent. Quick as thought, Jesse and Melvin high-tailed it to the cabin to collect up their father's curry combs. In no time, the formerly withered and bedraggled horses looked good as new. At least, they no longer looked like prime subjects for the meat wagon.

By the time they were ready to head back in for supper, they were all the best of friends. The boys knew all of their names, and they knew the boys'. Lu found them to be surprisingly curious. They asked all sorts of bizarre questions about America, Indians, and the war. But more than anything, the Hammonds wanted to hear about their adventures. Lu told them everything that'd happened to him, and all the strange folks he'd met. They were prejudiced against any sort of supernatural activity, even the perfectly beneficial alchemy Lu's grandfather practiced, but at the same time they couldn't hear about it enough. They reveled in Lu's descriptions of the ghost-riders, and wondered aloud about what sort of "evil powers" Gokhlayeh and Joseph might possess. Lu even told them about Cody's death in the bad water. The older boys thought the idea of a horse melting in a pool of acid was amazing.

"But where are you going?" Irus asked. He sat on the top rail of the corral, swinging his deformed foot.

"Silver City," MacLemore replied.

"Our Pa goes to Silver City 'bout every year," Melvin said.

"Does he?"

"Sure. He helps drive cattle to the sinners. Pa says they make a fine profit."

"How far is it to Silver City?" Chino asked.

The boys looked at each other. It was clear by their expressions that they'd never been to Silver City, or anywhere else for that matter.

"How long is your Pa usually gone?" Henry asked.

"'Bout three weeks," Robert said.

"There and back again?" MacLemore was excited by the news. The boys nodded.

"That's just four days' ride," Henry estimated. "Maybe five. Who knows how fast they drive their cows."

"What're you going to Silver City for, anyhow?" Jesse asked. "You don't got no steers."

"I bought a house," MacLemore explained. "I'm thinking of moving there."

"Oh, you don't want to do that."

"Why not?"

"It's a bad place. Folks say the devil himself lives in Silver City."

"Do they? That's strange. What do you boys think?"

"I think they're right," Robert offered. "Treasure hunters are always going to Silver City, searching for gold. The greed turns their minds."

"Who told you that?" Henry asked him.

"Everybody knows it."

The boys had finished grooming the horses, and made sure the water trough was full to the brim, so it was time to head back. As they approached the cabin, Lu saw that there were three new horses tied to the porch rail.

"That's Pa's horse," Louis said. He pointed at a black gelding, the only one of the three to have been unsaddled. "And that one belongs to the Bishop. But the other . . ." He looked at his brothers. "Do any of you know whose that is?"

"Looks like one of Doyle Lee's to me," Jesse said.

"Were you expecting him?" Chino asked.

"No. But folks always travel in twos when they're on church business."

They'd just reached the end of the porch when the cabin door swung open and three men filed out. Two were blond, just like the boys. The other, a slightly older man, had hair as white as the salt plains themselves. It was this third man that attracted Lu's attention. The expression on his face was pinched and bitter.

"You must be Mr. MacLemore," the man at the center said, extending his hand. "I'm Melvin Hammond. We just had the pleasure of meeting your daughter."

Pleasantries were exchanged and introductions made. The other blond man was Jacob Higbee, Bishop of the local ward church. The white-haired gentleman was Doyle Lee, just as Jesse had predicted.

"We appreciate your hospitality, sir," MacLemore said. "Our horses were near collapsed. We were in bad shape."

"I don't wonder," Doyle Lee grumped. "Only a fool tries to cross the Lago in August."

"Or a sorcerer," Bishop Higbee said, grinning. To Lu it looked as though he might burst into laughter any moment, and was inviting MacLemore to do likewise. "You're not one of them, are you? A sorcerer?"

"No, sir. We got lost a ways back, and went across the middle of the Lago by mistake," MacLemore explained. "Fact is, we're still lost."

"You're headed for Silver City," Melvin Sr. said.

"That's right."

"What was that for again?"

MacLemore glanced at his companions. "I have a house there," he said.

"Your daughter said you planned to go into mining."

"That's why I bought the house."

"I see . . . Well, you're welcome here. Looks like my wife already gave you some fresh shirts. I do like that blue chambray."

They chatted a few more minutes, until Eliza Jane called to them from inside, announcing that dinner was almost ready. Melvin Sr. held the door while the whole bunch passed through, boys included. They were greeted by a vision Lu had never expected to have. There, standing at the end of a long table, husking corn, was Sadie. She wore a blue chambray dress and matching bonnet. Her hair was squeaky clean and her face had been scrubbed until it glowed pink.

"Why, Sadie," MacLemore said, staring at his daughter. "I'll be."

"My clothes are all wet," Sadie explained. "I washed 'em out while I bathed. Mrs. Hammond lent me one of her dresses."

"I'll not have a woman wearing trousers in my house," Eliza Jane said. "A girl ought not to show her shape like that. It's not right."

"Is it true you were naked in the tub?" one of the boys asked.

"Melvin!"

"It was Sis that said it. I just heard."

"It's true," Sadie admitted. "I'd never used a bathing sheet. To be honest, I can't quite figure what one might be for."

"It's to keep you modest," Eliza Jane explained. "We don't want our young women seeing themselves and having lustful thoughts."

Sadie seemed genuinely surprised. "I guess if I'd wanted to give myself a pinch," she remarked, "no sheet would've stopped me."

The boys all laughed, as did their father and his friends. In fact, only Lu and Mrs. Hammond seemed the least bit uncomfortable. Lu because he was embarrassed. Eliza Jane because she was disgusted, or wanted everyone to think so. Even Sadie's own father chuckled, though Lu thought it looked a trifle forced.

"How's dinner coming?" Melvin Sr. asked.

"Nearly ready," his wife said. "We just need to heat the corn. Sadie, do you reckon you could do that for me while I feed the baby?"

"You just want me to drop it in the pot?"

"That's it."

"Then sure." Sadie gathered up the husked ears and carried them to the big steaming pot on the stove.

Mrs. Hammond went to the cradle in the corner and lifted out a baby. He only fussed a little as his mother carried him to the back room and shut the door.

"That must be Karl," MacLemore said.

"Our youngest." Melvin Sr. smiled.

"How many children do you have, all together?"

"Fourteen."

"My word."

"It's a wonderful thing to bring so much love into the world," Bishop Higbee said. "Don't you think so Mr. MacLemore?"

"I suppose it is. But fourteen?" He whistled. "That is a heap of love."

As soon as Eliza Jane returned they took their places at the table. Melvin Sr. occupied the chair closest to the front door. Bishop Higbee took the chair directly opposite him. The rest of them piled onto benches to either side. There wasn't room enough for everyone, so the three youngest boys sat on the floor. Lu would've liked to sit beside Sadie, but got stuck in between Henry and Chino. Sadie was seated on the other side of the table, between Doyle Lee and Bishop Higbee. The Bishop must've looked at her at least once a minute throughout the entire meal. He even looked at her while talking to someone else. Doyle Lee did some looking of his own, but not at Sadie. He was focused on Bishop Higbee. And he didn't seem at all pleased with what he saw.

When they were settled, Melvin Sr. asked Bishop Higbee to give the blessing. Lu had known a number of Christians back in St. Frances, and seen them do a good bit of praying. So he knew the proper pose, and adopted it to the best of his ability. He only glanced up for a moment, as Higbee cleared his throat, and was surprised to see that the Hammonds, Lee, and even the Bishop himself, all had their arms wrapped around their bellies, just like a kid with a stomach-ache might do. Lu noticed that Chino had folded his hands, Henry too, so he gave them each a poke with his elbow. As soon they saw the way these folks got ready for prayers, they made the necessary adjustments. Neither Sadie nor MacLemore left off from their normal method of hand-clasping, but Lu had no way of poking them.

Bishop Higbee began. "Heavenly Father, thy grateful children thank thee for thy many mercies, and beseech thee to bless thy bounty to the nourishment of their bodies. Poor pilgrims have come to us through the purgatories of thy desert, and are hungry, both in body and spirit. We thank thee for sending them to thy Zion, where thy good news can fill their souls, even as Mrs.

Hammond's victuals lend them strength." He paused, and Lu took another quick peek around the table. For some reason, Sadie had turned away from the Bishop, and she didn't look especially happy either. Lu wondered what was wrong, but had little time to contemplate the change as Higbee started in on another round of "thee" and "thou." "Heavenly Father," he intoned. "We just want to thank thee again for all thy many blessings, and ask thee to take pity on us in all our future endeavors. Amen."

"Thank you, Bishop," Melvin Sr. said, and reached for a steaming plate of greens.

Lu took as much as his plate would hold, heaping mashed potatoes to one side and greens to the other. In the center he placed a chunk of meat he later learned to be goat, and covered the whole mess with spoonful after spoonful of dark brown gravy. On top of it all he laid a roasting ear, fresh from the pot and slathered with butter.

He attacked the corn first, and with gusto. But no sooner had Lu got the kernels all chewed off the cob than his stomach began to feel tight. After just half a plate, Lu was stuffed. He tried to force more down, knowing that he couldn't possibly leave so much uneaten, but found it increasingly difficult even to chew. Swallowing was torture.

His friends all seemed to be suffering. MacLemore belched, begged pardon, and then gave a low moan. Eliza Jane asked if he wasn't feeling poorly.

"I'm terribly embarrassed, ma'am. But it seems as if my companions and I have eyes bigger than our stomachs."

"I thought you said you were hungry."

"We are. Or were. To be honest, I feel primed to burst."

Moans of agreement escaped the lips of all five travelers. Lu couldn't even talk, he felt so sick.

"This is good food," Eliza Jane protested. "I even put grease in the gravy. You can ask my boys, that's not something we get ever' day."

"It's excellent food," MacLemore panted. "Best I ever ate, truly. But we haven't had a bite of solid food in three days. I'm afraid our stomachs have—"

But he failed to complete the thought. All at once, he rolled backward off the bench, clutching his stomach in both hands.

Lu knew without a doubt that he could hold the food down not a moment longer. He jumped up from the table and went sprinting toward the door, beating Sadie by only a step. Before long, all five of them were bent over the porch rail, stomachs empty once more. The boys came out to watch.

It was all over in less than five minutes, and they filed back inside. Lu and his fellows felt mighty sheepish as they returned to their seats. Mrs. Hammond looked as though she might just kill them all. But they were saved by Bishop Higbee.

"I had that exact thing happen to me once," he said. "This was twenty years ago, when the prophet first led our people to this Zion. The last two days I ate nothing but wild onions. When I finally shot a deer, the meat made me so sick I thought I'd die."

"What did you do?" Henry asked him

"Only thing for it, I'm afraid, is to keep trying."

Lu picked up his utensils and got back to work on the plate of food before him. He was in a good deal less hurry this time, however, and quit when he began to feel full. Painful cramps struck him in his belly, but fortunately he felt no need to leave the room. Lu didn't guess Mrs. Hammond would allow much more of her cooking to go over the porch rail, Bishop or no.

When dinner was over, and the last scraps of meat tucked away for sandwiches, Eliza Jane and Sis got to work on the dishes. Lu offered to help, but was told to stay seated. Apparently, Eliza Jane was as particular about her dishes as she was about everything else. She trusted no man to do them without chipping the rims.

"Besides," she said, "Bishop Higbee has come to read scriptures. You ought to be hungry to learn. Sis and me, we'll be listening mighty close, you can believe that."

So while the women worked, the men remained seated around the table.

"This is what we call family hour," Melvin Sr. explained, taking a book down from the shelf—the Bible, Lu guessed—and handing it to the Bishop.

"Are any of you Christians?" Higbee asked.

"I am," Henry said.

"What denomination, if you don't mind my asking?"

"None. I follow the scriptures on my own."

"I see." The Bishop furrowed his brow. "You'll permit me to offer up a bit of preaching here though?"

"Of course. And I'll be mighty glad to hear it, too."

"Excellent. Heavenly father loves all who come to him with an open heart, be they Gentile or Saint. Or even bearing the mark of Cain."

"My skin color has nothing to do with Cain," Henry said. "Nor Abel. Nor Seth either. I'm black because my father was, and his father before him."

"And all the way back to Cain," said the Bishop. Henry looked like he might protest, but Higbee didn't give him a chance. "Still, let's not get all bogged down in that," he said. "This is family hour, after all. Children are present. And Heavenly Father dearly wants us to be happy. Surely we can all agree on that?"

"No, sir," Henry said. "I can't agree."

"No?"

"Nope. I figure if God wanted us to be happy, he'd have planted green grass in that desert and given us cow stomachs to eat it with. No, God wants us to be *good*."

Doyle Lee gave a short laugh. Higbee, obviously less charmed by the suggestion, merely smiled.

"As to you," the Bishop continued, turning toward Chino. "You're one of Heavenly Father's chosen. Did you know that?" Chino shook his head. "Scripture tells us that Jesus will return when the Indians and their offspring find the one true church."

"Is that right?" Henry asked.

"It's from the works of a latter Prophet," Higbee explained. "Though I don't guess we're likely get into any of that this evening."

"Ain't we going to read at all?" Irus asked.

Lu turned to look at the boy, sitting on the floor directly behind him. The debate between Henry and the Bishop seemed to have unnerved him somewhat.

"Well, ain't we?" he asked again.

Higbee smiled. "Thirsty for the spirit. That's good. Fine boy you've got Melvin. And he's right." He opened the Bible and skimmed through, obviously searching for something in particular. "What do you say to a bit of Song of Solomon, Irus?"

"All right."

Higbee handed the book to Sadie. "Maybe you'd like to begin."

"You want *me* to read?"

"Just start at the beginning."

Sadie appeared less than thrilled with this turn of events, but bent over the book and read. *"Husband, let thee kiss me with the kisses of thy mouth."* A few of the boys tittered. Sadie pretended not to notice. *"For thy love-making is sweeter than wine. Delicate is the fragrance of thy perfume. Thy name is like aromatic oil, poured upon the body. And that is why all thy wives love thee."*

"Please go on," Higbee said, as she reached the end of the first verse.

"Draw me in thy footsteps," Sadie continued. *"Let us run. My husband has brought me into his rooms. He will be my joy and my gladness. My sisters and I shall praise his love above wine. How right it is to be loved by him."*

"Very good." Higbee's voice was low, almost a purr. "Pass the book on now, unless you'd like to read more."

Sadie passed the book to Doyle Lee, who spat out his portion of the scriptures just as if the words were cherry stones, the sweet flesh of the fruit long since devoured. And so it went, the Bible making a complete round of the table. Everyone read a verse or two, until the book came to Chino.

"Can you read Brother Chino?" Higbee asked him.

"I can make my mark, but otherwise not a word."

"Pass it on then. The good news is as pleasant to the ears as it is to the tongue."

Now it was Lu's turn. Unfortunately, he'd ceased paying attention to the flow of the poem. Lu had never had much of a taste for verse, especially when it didn't rhyme. He'd been a good deal more interested in watching Sadie, who greeted each successive reading with increasing disdain. Lu studied the book before him, searching for the bit he was supposed to read, but had no clue where to begin. Fortunately, Henry anticipated his difficulty and pointed to the correct spot on the page.

What he read was mystifying. *"While my husband rests in his own room, my nard yields its perfume. My love is a sachet of myrrh lying at my breast. My love is a cluster of henna among the vines of the goat's spring."*

Lu passed the book on to Henry, glad to be done with it. He had no earthly notion what a nard might be, or a sachet, or myrrh. None of it made sense to him.

"Do you read?" Higbee asked Henry.

"I read fine," Henry said. His bit wasn't much, but he read it, and then handed the Bible to Higbee, who finished the round with a spirited recital.

"How beautiful thou art, my love," he began. *"And how thou delightest me. Our bed is the grass. The beams of our house are the cedar trees, its paneling the cypress."*

It went on and on, Higbee's voice growing louder all the while. Lu found it a decidedly stirring performance, though he still thought little of the words. To him it sounded like the sort of poetry girls wrote in school, when they were trying to catch the attention of some older boy. Sadie must've thought the same, because she sulked through the entire presentation.

At last, breathing hard, the Bishop concluded. *"By all the antelopes and wild does of Heavenly Father's creation, do not rouse. Do not disturb my beloved before she pleases me."* And then, beaming, he snapped the book shut and set it on the table.

By this time, Eliza Jane had finished with the dishes. She and Sis were standing behind Sadie. Sis seemed almost transported by the oratory.

"That was some mighty fine readin'," Eliza Jane said. "I don't recall when I've heard the like."

"Thank you, Sister Eliza," Higbee said. "But I can't take all the credit. Solomon did some of the work."

"Well, it was mighty stirring. Mighty stirring. Now, for

dessert we've got berry cobbler." The children gasped in joy and surprise.

"That does sound good," Doyle Lee said. "I only wish I could stay to enjoy it."

Higbee scowled. "Where are you going?" he asked.

"I'm supposed to meet a courier from the Prophet. So are you."

"Gracious. I completely forgot. I'm awfully sorry Sister Eliza, but we'll have to cut this visit a trifle short. Church business."

"That's fine, Bishop. Church business always comes first. Besides, one of your wives is giving birth any day now, isn't she? I'm sure you'll want to see her. Which would that be again, Nellie or Myra?"

"Nellie. Myra's not due for a month."

"Well, you tell Nellie 'hello' for us. And let her know I'll be coming by to meet the little one as soon as she's got him out."

Lee and Higbee got up from the table. Melvin Sr. led them to the door.

"How long do you folks plan on staying in our Zion?" Higbee asked MacLemore.

"We'll be leaving as soon as our horses feel up to it," MacLemore replied. "Might be as early as tomorrow. Let's hope so. We'd hate to impose on these fine folks any longer than is absolutely necessary."

"But you can't go yet." Higbee looked at Sadie. "Lots more folks will want to meet you. And you've had a long trip. You need to renew your spirits."

"I'm afraid we're in a bit of a hurry," MacLemore said.

"You can stay with one of my wives. Any of them would love to have you."

"We appreciate the invite, but I don't think we'll take you up this time."

"Let's go," Doyle Lee muttered. "Much obliged for the grub, Sister Eliza. Tasty as usual." He nodded to MacLemore. "Pleased to make your acquaintance."

Higbee cast one final, lingering gaze at Sadie. Then they were gone.

Eliza Jane served up a large pan of berry cobbler. "I hope you five won't make as much a mess of this as you did my dinner," she warned. "I won't have much more of that foolishness."

"No ma'am," Chino said. "My dessert compartment's plumb empty."

For the next few minutes, the only sound in the cabin came from the scrape of spoons on bowls.

"So?" Eliza Jane asked finally. "How is it?"

"Oh, Ma," Irus said. "It's just wonderful."

"It sure is," Louis agreed.

"Well, thank your sister then, all of you. She made it."

They heaped praise on the girl. If it'd been water instead of kind words, she likely would've drowned. Chino went so far as to claim that the cobbler had made him forget English, it was that good. Sadie asked for her secret, though it was next to impossible to imagine Sadie ever making a cobbler, berry or otherwise. MacLemore asked if the girl didn't want a job as his personal cook. Sis beamed at the attention.

When the dessert was all gone, the pan scraped clean, Eliza Jane announced it was time for bed. "Sis, grab an extra blanket for Sadie, but be quiet. I had enough trouble getting Karl to sleep."

The children looked downcast, but marched off to their places just like little soldiers. The boys filed onto the porch. Sis went into her parent's room, returning with two quilts, one of which she spread on the floor as far from the stove as possible.

"Your boys sleep outside?" MacLemore asked. "What about when it's cold?"

"Cold?" Eliza Jane laughed. "I don't believe I've stopped sweating for one solid minute since Melvin built this place. I've asked him to move me to town, where there's dirt rich enough to grow a tree or two, but Alma says she'll shoot him before she'll live next door to the likes of me."

"Did you enjoy the reading?" Melvin Sr. asked, changing the subject.

"Don't guess I paid it much attention," Sadie admitted. "No offense, but your Bishop kept me on the dodge the whole time. Even during the blessing he was rubbing his knee against my leg."

Mr. and Mrs. Hammond looked at each other. "He does have a loving nature," Melvin admitted.

"I should've given you one of my older dresses," Eliza Jane said. "I've got one or two with no shape left at all."

"You don't like him then?" Henry asked them.

"The Bishop? Oh, he's all right. Just got a powerful interest in love. It's a common affliction among our more successful Saints."

"He won't be any trouble will he?" MacLemore asked, obviously deeply concerned by the information Sadie had just shared. Lu couldn't tell whether he was embarrassed, infuriated or nervous. He guessed it was a mixture of all three.

"I don't think so," Melvin assured him. "When he gets back to town, amidst all his children and pregnant wives, he'll likely forget all about your daughter."

"Maybe we should bed down, too," Henry suggested. "It's been a long day."

"Of course." Eliza Jane picked up the spare blanket from where Sis had dropped it. "You'll have to sleep in here," she said to Sadie, handing her the quilt. "I hope that's all right. With the stove it can get awful hot."

"I reckon I could sleep with both feet in the fire, and my head on a cactus," Sadie replied. She spread her quilt on the floor beside Sis.

"You men can grab spots outside," Melvin suggested. He and his wife were already heading toward their own room. Eliza Jane looked to be in a hurry. Probably nervous about the baby, Lu guessed.

MacLemore led the men onto the porch, but there was no place for them to stretch out. Every available inch was covered by sleeping boys.

So Lu and the other men took spots on the front lawn. Compared to the salt and dust of the desert, even sun-dry grass seemed cool and soft.

They were awakened, a few hours later, by the sound of a galloping horse.

"What in the world?" MacLemore said, sitting up. "Who would be riding out here at this hour?" He looked toward the boys, all of whom were wide awake and sitting on the porch, but not one of them said a word.

"I guess we'll find out soon enough," Henry said. He drew his rifle from its scabbard and made sure it was loaded.

A minute later, the horse came wheeling into the yard, nearly running Chino over in its haste. Atop it sat Doyle Lee, his hair glowing silver in the starlight.

"What's going on out here?" Eliza Jane must have heard the commotion and come to check on her boys. Her head poked just far enough out the cabin door for Lu to see the collar of her night-gown. It was pink with blue flowers.

"It's Higbee," Doyle Lee said. "He's taken a shine to that girl. Plans to make her his own. Tonight."

"I'll be dead before I let that happen," MacLemore said.

"You all will. Or worse. He's called for the Sons of Dan."

"Heavenly Father!" Eliza Jane said. "I saw him lookin', but never thought he'd go so far." She ducked back into the cabin, shouting at her husband to wake up.

"What is it?" Melvin called back. "What's wrong?"

"It's the Danites," she said. "They're comin' for Sadie."

"Who are these Danites?" MacLemore asked.

"The army of the Saints," Doyle Lee responded. "Protectors of the flock and killers of the wicked. If ever the Gentiles send an enemy into our Zion, you can be sure the Sons of Dan will use them up fast."

"They're the deadliest fighters on the whole continent," Robert said. Lu was sure he heard pride in the boy's voice.

Melvin Sr. appeared at the door a moment later. He had pants on, but no shirt. In one hand was an old repeating rifle, and in the other a box of bullets. "How far back are they?" he asked Doyle.

"Higbee's just stirring 'em up. I expect they'll ride out of town in an hour or two."

"Boys, saddle these folks' horses." His sons leapt off the porch, grabbing up saddles as they sprinted down the path to the corral. Louis, the oldest, took one in each hand. Robert, Jesse and Melvin

Jr. brought the other three. Irus, though he had nothing to carry, limped along behind his brothers as fast as he could manage.

"Take this," Melvin handed his rifle to MacLemore. "Those pistols of yours won't be much good against the likes of the Danites. Not out on these hills."

"I can't take your gun," MacLemore protested. "It wouldn't be right."

"Don't worry, I've got another. And I plan to tell them you stole it anyhow."

MacLemore started to argue, but was interrupted by the reappearance of Eliza Jane, still in her flimsy night-dress, a sackcloth bundle clutched under one arm. "The rest of the goat meat is inside," she said, handing it to Chino. "Along with some bread. You can make sandwiches when you get hungry."

Sis followed her mother down onto the grass. "Sadie's putting on her old clothes," she reported. "They're still damp, but she said that don't make no difference."

Sadie stomped out a moment later, working her heels down into her boots even as she finished buttoning her shirt. The skin on her belly was as white as the under side of a fish, Lu saw, nothing like the reddish brown of her hands and neck. She tucked her shirt-tails into the top of her trousers and did up her belt. "Let's get out of here," she said.

"I'll take you as far as the mountains," Doyle Lee offered. "After that you're on your own."

"I'm sorry," Eliza Jane said. "I thought this sort of thing stopped years ago."

MacLemore searched through his pockets, but came up with just one fifty-cent piece and five pennies. "I'd give you a few dollars," he said. "For the food and the gun—"

"We couldn't possibly take your money," Eliza Jane said. "It wouldn't be right to charge a hungry traveler for no more than what we got."

"But we have to give you something. Wait, I know." MacLemore took off his coat and hat. "Take these. They cost thirty-eight dollars just six months ago. That coat's the height of fashion among the Manhattos."

Eliza Jane looked at the clothes MacLemore offered her. They were dirty, but with a bit of cleaning might be fine garments once more. "What would I do with them?" she asked.

"Your sons can get married in them," MacLemore said. "However many times they do it, that coat will always look sharp."

"You can keep our old shirts, too," Lu suggested. "Mine isn't much, but it's still got some wear."

Eliza Jane smiled. "You're good boys," she said. "Your mothers did a fine job raising you." Then her face went hard again, and Lu wondered if she wasn't thinking about giving him another wash in the bucket. "Now *git*," she said. "I won't have the Sons of Dan killing you on my front porch."

DOYLE LEE LED THEM NORTHEAST, right along the edge of the salt flats.

Just getting close to the Lago again started the nerves in Lu's spine singing. Crash didn't much like their chosen route either. As soon as they came within sight of the white salt plain he started crow-hopping and tossing his head. It took every bit of Lu's horsemanship just to quiet him down. Protests were voiced, but Doyle Lee was unimpressed with any opinion other than his own. He held to the edge of the salt flats with a faithfulness bordering on paranoia. It was a miserable time to be out there, too. No sooner did their horses' hooves touch salt than the wind began to howl. Doyle Lee seemed to welcome the storm, while Chino cursed the wind in two languages. MacLemore and Henry kept their heads down and their eyes shut. Lu tried to do the same, but couldn't resist looking over his shoulder every few minutes. He was worried about their pursuers. The last thing Lu wanted was to be shot in the back while his eyes were closed. Sadie kept looking back as well.

"I'd sure hate to get shot," Lu said to her. The sun was just peeking over the eastern horizon, and the wind had responded by lowering to a mere gale. "Wouldn't you?"

"Better than being hung, I reckon," Sadie replied.

It was a debate much enjoyed by the boys back in St. Frances.

Half thought it'd be better to be shot, and could see no earthly reason why a robber would ever give himself up. The other half considered hanging preferable. Lu had always been on the shooting
side, mostly because folks said it was quicker, assuming that the
man who shot you was a good aim. Now he wasn't so sure. There
were powerful few hanging trees in the Lago, but bullets aplenty.

"Which do you think they'll do if they catch us?" he asked.

Sadie considered a while. "I've heard the Saints are big on
castrating men not of their faith," she said at last. "So I guess
that's what they'd probably do."

Castration made hanging and shooting both sound pretty
good. "What do you think they'd do to you?"

"Oh, I know just what they want to do with me. They hope
to take me back to their town, lock me in a room somewhere, and
preach at me 'til I want nothing more than to wear dresses and
bake pies." Judging by the tone of her voice, Sadie considered this
about on a par with castration.

The sun had been up over an hour, and their horses were
beginning to seriously feel the heat, when Doyle Lee finally called
for a rest. By that time, MacLemore decided he'd had enough.

"I don't know where you're leading us, sir," he said. "But we
certainly aren't getting there. If you don't know where the mountains are, say so now. I'll point them out to you." He didn't wait
for Doyle to answer. "There they are." MacLemore gestured
wildly. "Right there. Due west by any compass."

"You want to get free of the Danites, don't you?" Doyle
asked him.

"I can't see how wandering aimlessly will help us escape.
Maybe you could explain yourself."

"Their best tracker's not with them."

"So?"

"The wind's covering our tracks."

Lu looked. Sure enough, hoof-prints stretched out behind
them for a hundred yards or so and then began to fade, filled in
by the blowing dust.

"And just how do you know their tracker isn't with them?"
MacLemore asked.

"Because I'm their tracker," Doyle said.

"Do you think they'll find us?" Sadie asked him.

"Danites are what Gentiles call 'avenging angels.' They don't give up easy."

"These horses are near played out," Henry said.

"We'll rest again as soon as we reach those trees." Doyle gestured toward the mountains. Lu squinted, but could make out no trees whatever, just a vague sort of black-green velvet.

"What if they catch us?" Chino asked.

"Then you'll have to fight."

"Can we beat 'em?"

"I doubt it."

"Henry and me have been in tough scrapes before. We've always come through."

Doyle shrugged. He wasn't a man much given to talk. Lu remembered watching him at the dinner table, staring at his food. At the time he'd thought Doyle quiet, either because he was naturally shy or out of respect for his superior, Bishop Higbee. Now he guessed Doyle was one of those men who preferred to hoard up their thoughts, seldom letting more than one or two out at a time. Like Jack Straw, Doyle Lee never wasted words.

When the horses had caught their breath, Doyle struck out in a new direction. He guided them due west, following a trail only he could see. They kept to the low places between the hills as much as possible. It got brushier as they neared the mountains, but they pressed through. Finally, when they were within shouting distance of the tree-line, the sagebrush got so thick it acted as a sort of fence. There was no way through, so they took to the hilltops. It was then that Henry saw the riders.

They all paused a moment to look back. Lu squinted until his eyes ached, but still couldn't make out a thing. "Is it them?" he asked.

"Must be," Henry replied.

"I count twenty-five," Doyle said. "That's a pretty good number on such short notice. Comin' fast, too."

"Probably found our tracks and figure they got us treed," Chino remarked, though he didn't bother to look. His eyes were excellent for close-up work, as when studying a flower

222 / JUSTIN ALLEN

or leaf, but at a distance they were weaker than Lu's.

They urged their horses onward, forcing them into a stiff trot as they neared the tree-line. Lu didn't know what would happen once they reached the forest, but knew it'd be a lot better in amongst the trees than out on these bald hills. With sufficient cover, they might hold the Danites off for hours.

"How long before they catch us?" MacLemore asked.

"Half an hour," Doyle said. "Maybe more. There's a rock outcropping just a quarter-mile farther. If we can get on top of it, you still might manage an escape."

They galloped their mounts into the wood, coming at last to the base of a stony ridge. It wasn't more than twenty feet high, but stretched away north and south for as far as Lu could see. Best of all, there weren't but a half-dozen spots where a horse could climb up. To Lu, the ridge resembled the walls of a medieval castle.

Doyle gave his horse a sharp kick and was soon at the top. Henry and Chino raced up behind him, followed closely by Lu and Sadie. MacLemore, riding Lucky, came up last.

As soon as they were safe atop the rocks, Henry dismounted, drawing his rifle from its scabbard even as his feet touched ground.

"That's it for me," Doyle said. "I'm in no hurry for those men to see me."

"What if they already saw you?" MacLemore asked. "What'll they do?"

"You mean will they kill me?" He shook his head. "Not outright, I don't guess, though it may come to that by and by. They'll start by excommunicating me. I reckon I'll spend eternity in the outer darkness." His brow furrowed. It was clear to Lu that this "outer darkness" was a greater threat to Doyle Lee even than death.

"Why are you helping us?" Sadie asked. "No offense, but you seem more the kind to be with them."

"I have been, time and again. If you make it up that path yonder," he gestured down a game trail, leading away from the back side of the ridge—it was framed on both sides by trees, and mostly overgrown with skunk cabbage—"you'll come to a meadow. In it you'll see some of my handiwork."

"So then why help us now?"

Doyle frowned. "Two reasons. First, Higbee took one of my own daughters. She's the Nellie you heard Sister Eliza asking about. In the beginning he was just peaches and cream. But I don't believe he's been in to see her even one time since she got pregnant. I guess I don't take too kindly to that."

"What's the other reason?"

"I reckon these killings have got to stop. Gentiles are already sending lawyers to inquire into what they call *irregularities*. Cavalry will be along soon. Eventually, someone's sure to hang. Like as not, it'll be one of those men out there, killed for doing his duty. And the real instigators, men like Jacob Higbee, they'll find a way to wriggle free. They always do."

"Is this the way to Silver City?" Henry asked, pointing at the game trail.

"One of 'em. Follow it and you'll come to the middle-fork of the Paiute River. That ought to take you to Silver City all right."

MacLemore held out his hand. "We appreciate your help, Doyle."

They shook, and then Lee set his spurs to his horse and loped into the forest.

"Reckon he'll get away?" Sadie asked.

"One way or another," Chino said.

"How long do you think we have?" MacLemore asked.

"Five minutes," Henry replied. "Maybe ten."

They made a quick survey of their surroundings, locating a half-dozen defensible spots. The three best were behind large rocks, just a stone's throw from the game trail. Henry said they offered an avenue of escape, should the need arise.

"Lu, I want you and Sadie to take the horses a couple hundred yards down that path," Henry continued. As he spoke, he took two boxes of ammunition from his saddlebags. "Go 'til you're just barely out of sight. Hold them there. If we can fight these Danites off long enough, we might make a run for it in the dark. The three of us will take up positions here."

MacLemore untied the rifle Melvin Hammond had given him from his saddle. The box of shells he stuck in his pants pocket.

"Daddy?" Sadie's voice quavered.

"We'll be fine, honey. It'll be just like target practice."

Chino jerked his pistols from his holsters, spun the cylinders to make sure both were fully loaded, and rammed them back home. "I'm lookin' forward to it," he said. "My pistols have been quiet too long. They need exercise."

"I can stay, too," Lu offered. "I've got my revolver."

"No," Henry said. "It's a fine weapon, but you aren't proven with it yet. You've only fired the one shot."

Chino nodded in agreement. "This is no fight for you, chico."

"But I killed that deer."

"With my rifle," Henry said, "which I guess I'll use myself."

It was a bit of logic against which Lu had no defense. Clearly he could offer little in the way of experience, weaponry or marksmanship. To be truthful, Lu didn't much want to be involved in any battles. But he didn't want the other men to think him a coward either.

"We all know how brave you both are," MacLemore said. "But this isn't about bravery. Now, I want you to take these horses into the trees, just as Henry told you. In fact, I'm *ordering* you to do it. Both of you. You'll admit I've given very few orders so far. None in fact. But I'm doing it now. If you want to keep working for me, you'll take these horses to safety."

There was nothing else to say. Lu climbed onto Crash, took Lucky's reins and the reins of Chino's mare, and started up the path through the trees. Sadie was right behind him. As they rode away, numb and silent, Lu heard Henry talking.

"We'd best get into position," Henry said. "Try to shoot as many of their horses as you can. A man afoot will lose interest in chasing, I hope."

Lu and Sadie rode better than a hundred yards from the ridge, but could still see the blue chambray shirts of the men they were leaving behind. It wasn't until they'd reached a hard bend in the path, around which they discovered a fallen pine tree, that they finally got clear of the battle site.

"I guess we've gone far enough," Lu said, climbing out of his saddle.

There was a patch of green grass behind the fallen tree. Lu led the animals to it and then stood by while they grazed.

"He ain't my boss," Sadie muttered. "I don't have to follow no dern orders."

"He's your father," Lu said. "That's sort of like a boss."

Sadie glowered at him.

Just then, they heard the first of what was to be hundreds of shots. Lu and Sadie both recognized the source. Henry's rifle had a way of rumbling in the inner ear long after it had been fired, like thunder after a bolt of lightning. The horses nickered, but made no move to bolt. Henry's horse, having spent the better part of its life as a cavalry mount, didn't even perk up its ears.

The next shot rang out soon after, followed by a third. These must've come from MacLemore's rifle. A few more shots followed. Thus far, they'd heard no return fire. Lu guessed the Danites had been taken by surprise. That wouldn't last long. It'd only take a moment for them to determine where the bullets were originating from, and adopt the proper response. Unfortunately, Lu was right. In no time they were hearing the whine of lead slugs, ricocheting off the boulders behind which their friends were crouched, and clattering through the trees.

Sadie tied her horse to the fallen pine.

"What are you doing?" Lu asked her.

"I'm goin' to watch." She'd finished tying Carrot, and was rapidly doing the same with Henry's quarter-horse. "And you're comin' with me."

"No, I'm not. Your father ordered me to hold these horses, and I aim to do it."

"Well, I'm ordering you to come with me."

"You can't order me."

"Sure I can. Don't you remember your contract? It said you worked for the MacLemores. That means both of us, Daddy and me."

Lu paused. He didn't think that sounded right. It was months ago that he'd signed his name to that bit of parchment, but he didn't recall its saying anything about his working for *Sadie* MacLemore. To be honest, he didn't recall its saying anything about John MacLemore either. All he remembered was a long bit about the "reclamation of a property." He voiced his doubts, but Sadie just sneered.

"I tell you it was in there. Now tie off that horse of yours and let's get going."

Lu did as he was told, sure that he'd regret it later.

"How do you want to go?" he asked. "We can't just go sauntering down the trail. We'd be killed for sure."

"Let's just go 'til we see the others. We'll figure out what to do from there."

So they crept back down the center of the path, quiet as mice. It wasn't long before they saw a blue chambray shirt, crouched behind a boulder on the lip of the stone ridge. At first, Lu couldn't tell who it was. Then he saw the man stand up, a pistol in either hand, and send a half-dozen slugs blasting down the hillside. Chino shot so fast, Lu didn't see how he could possibly know where any of his bullets were going. He seemed content merely to fill the air with lead and let the chips fall where they may.

"What now?" Lu whispered.

"I can't see Daddy, but I think I hear his rifle." Sadie pointed through the trees to their right. "Let's sneak through there."

So they ducked and twisted their way amidst the tightly grown wood, coming at last to a place where they could see fully thirty yards of the stone ridge. Sadie was all for going on, but Lu held her arm.

"I still can't see him," she complained.

Lu pointed. A blue chambray shirt was just visible to their left, and it wasn't Henry.

"What's he doin'?" Sadie asked.

"Looks like he's reloading his gun."

For the next few minutes they sat, shoulder to shoulder, watching as MacLemore twice more loaded and fired his rifle empty. He was fast. Not as fast as Henry, maybe, but still a good deal quicker than Lu would've guessed. Brass cartridges littered the ground at his feet. Lu couldn't see the box, but figured MacLemore's ammunition must be at least half gone.

"I wonder if he's hittin' anything," Sadie whispered.

"I'll bet Henry is."

Just then, one of the Danites attempted to gallop to the top of the ridge. Lu and Sadie both held their breath as horse and rider leapt over the escarpment, nearly trampling Sadie's father in their rush. MacLemore barely got his rifle up in time, and likely wouldn't have if the horse hadn't reared. But it did, and MacLemore blasted him.

The bullet tore through the lower leg of the rider, a man of no more than twenty, dressed in a homespun shirt and straw hat, and into the side of his mount. Lu's stomach dropped as both horse and rider toppled backward off the ridge and fell out of sight.

"My lord!" he whispered. "Did you see all that blood?"

Sadie grabbed one of Lu's hands and squeezed. Lu thought she looked a trifle green.

"Another horse," she said. "That's all we ever do, shoot horses."

"What about the man on it? He looked mighty young."

Sadie nodded. The horror was plain in her eyes.

Lu wondered about the part of the battle they couldn't see. He remembered the way the deer had been blasted open when he shot it, one of its front legs having been sheered clean away. And how Cody's neck had spurted blood like a fountain until he'd sunk beneath the surface of the lake. He thought about the buffalo Henry shot, the slug driving right through its enormous skull. From where they crouched, Lu couldn't see Henry at all, but he could hear the boom of his rifle, and knew all too well the sort of damage it might do. All at once, he didn't want to be there any longer. Sadie's orders or no, he was going back to the horses.

"I don't want to see any more," he whispered.

Sadie nodded. "Me either."

They began to scoot back through the trees. But before they'd gone even five feet, Sadie grabbed Lu's arm. "Look!" she squealed.

Ahead of them, and just a hair to their right, a group of men was attempting to climb over the ridge. Lu could just see their eyes, and the brims of their hats, as they raised up, took a quick gander along the edge of the rock outcropping, and then ducked back down. They were only about ten yards from MacLemore, but for some reason he hadn't noticed them. Maybe they'd found a blind spot, Lu guessed. He knew he had to do something, and fast. Any second, one of those men was liable to rise up with a gun in his hand. MacLemore would be dead where he sat.

Lu didn't want to do it, but could see no other way. He drew his revolver, thumbed back the hammer, making sure as he did that there was a bullet in the next chamber, and took careful aim on the rocks over which the Saints were trying to sneak. He was just about to pull the trigger when the memory of the last time he'd fired the gun leapt to his mind.

"Hold my shoulders," he whispered to Sadie.

"What?"

"Last time, the kick knocked me off my feet."

"This is ridiculous," Sadie muttered, but did as he asked. Lu could feel her breath on the back of his neck.

"I'm going to shoot now," he warned.

"Just do it. And hurry." One of the Danites had just stuck his head over the tops of the rocks again, and this time he made no move to duck back down.

Lu squeezed the trigger and his pistol gave its deafening boom. The recoil tore through his elbows and shoulders, and even into Sadie, who lost her grip and fell against Lu's back. She'd added sufficient weight to keep him from going over backward, however, and so Lu got to see what became of the bullet he'd fired.

It was a bad shot. Lu missed the Danite by a good two feet, hitting instead a piece of the stone ridge. But the results were amazing. A chunk of granite as big around as a dinner plate exploded, sending bits of stone flying in every direction. Lu might not have done so much damage if he'd used dynamite. More importantly, the blast drew MacLemore's attention while it sent his attackers scrambling for safety.

"Let's get out of here," Sadie said.

Lu didn't need to be asked twice. He leapt to his feet, slid his pistol back into its holster, and ran.

They crashed through the underbrush, bouncing off the trunks of trees and tripping over old logs, but somehow managed to keep their balance long enough to reach the path. Sadie was a swift runner, but Lu matched her step for step. By the time they reached the horses, both were out of breath.

"My Lord," Sadie wheezed. "When Daddy said you had a cannon, I thought he was just foolin'. But that pistol of yours puts Henry's rifle to shame. You must've put the fear of God in them."

"Not Higbee," Lu muttered. His ears were ringing again, just like last time.

"What?"

For some reason, Lu knew, as sure as if he'd seen the man's face, that Higbee had been amongst the group of men trying to climb over the ridge and take MacLemore unawares. How he knew that, Lu had no way to tell. It was just a thought that had burrowed its way into the back of his mind. And it wasn't the only one. He also knew that the other Danites were by no means excited to be on this adventure. In fact, a few had already suggested going home. One had come right out and said that this whole enterprise was nothing more than lust gone wild. Again, those weren't statements Lu had heard. He just *knew* them.

"Higbee was one of those trying to climb over the cliff," Lu said.

"I didn't see him," Sadie replied. "And I'd bet my eyes against yours any day."

"He was there."

"And just how do you know that?"

"The bullet." The words popped out of their own volition. They felt true, but still not the sort of thing a body ought to say. In fact, if Lu had known he was about to say something so outlandish, he'd have come up with a lie.

"I'm serious," he continued, then clapped a hand over his mouth. For some reason, the truth was just boiling to come out, whether he willed it or not.

"The kick on that pistol has rattled your brains," Sadie said. "You sure it didn't come up and bonk you in the head?"

"I'm sure. Those men. Their thoughts. Even their memories. The bullet put it all in my mind." He tried to cover his mouth with his hands again, but it didn't help. Every word came out as clear as air.

Sadie laughed. "If those are magic bullets, why didn't you *know* anything the last time you shot one? Why didn't you hear what that javelina was thinking?"

Lu shook his head. He had no answer for that. "Maybe it wasn't thinking anything," he said.

But Sadie wasn't listening. A hush had descended over the forest. "What do you think's happening now?" she asked.

"The Danites are scared."

"Is that more bullet talk?"

Lu shrugged.

Just then, they heard the sound of running feet. Someone was coming up the path. Sadie reached into her jacket pocket for her own little revolver. Lu lifted his gun out of its holster again. Both of them came close to shooting Henry as he loped into sight.

"What's happening?" Sadie asked.

"The Danites seem to have given up," Henry said. "And I thought they were just about to get us, too."

A moment later, MacLemore came huffing and puffing through the trees. "We heard your gun," he said to Lu. "Are you all right?"

"Higbee was trying to lead some men around behind you," Lu explained.

"Did you shoot him?"

Lu shook his head.

"Too bad. Would've served him right, the old pirate."

"Where's Chino?" Sadie asked.

"Here." Chino trotted into the clearing.

"What are they doing now?" Henry asked him.

"Trying to catch their horses. What few they have left. Something really put the terror into them."

"I'd guess it was Lu's shot," Sadie remarked. "His are *magic* bullets, you know."

"Was that what we heard? I thought the mountain had been struck by lightning." Chino grinned at Lu. "Magic bullets, eh?

What do they do? Other than blast things all to kingdom come."

Lu ground his teeth. He didn't want to say.

"Well?" Chino asked.

"They tell the truth," Lu said. "All of it."

"Enough," Henry said. "The Danites may decide to go home, or they may not. I don't intend to wait around to see which they choose."

For the next hour they rode, keeping to a fast trot as much as possible. Henry and Chino stayed at the rear, just in case their pursuers elected to follow. Lu didn't think they would, but couldn't say for sure. Whatever insight the bullet had given him was used up.

"How much farther do you think it'll be before we strike the river?" MacLemore asked. "I sort of think I hear something."

"Looks like there's a clearing ahead," Lu replied. "Just through those trees."

MacLemore led them to the edge of a shallow basin, surrounded by pines.

"Lord of mercy," he said, stopping cold.

The entire basin was filled, front to back and edge to edge, with skeletons. A path had been swept through the center, but all the rest was bone. If a person was of a particularly twisted mind, he might skip from one side of the depression to the other and never step on anything but death.

They rode through in silence, passing the weathered remains of women, children, horses and men. Here and there they saw the moldered scraps of old dresses, shirts and trousers. Near the opposite end of the basin lay a team of oxen. Their yoke had been either stolen or rotted away, but the necks that wore them—the neck-bones, at least—were still there, tied together in death for all eternity.

"Doyle said we'd pass through some of his handiwork," MacLemore said, as they climbed out of the basin on the other side, "but I didn't pay him much attention."

"Did you see all the little ones?" Sadie whimpered. "Someone mashed their little skulls in with an axe."

Lu had nothing to add. The bones spoke for themselves. These settlers had suffered across the desert, maybe across the terrible Lago del Fuego itself, only to be gunned down and butchered in what should have been the welcoming embrace of the forest. And with a stream of fresh water just a stone's throw away, too.

Henry suggested they stop and water the horses.

"What about the Danites?" MacLemore asked.

"Something tells me they'll hesitate a good long while before crossing through that meadow back there."

"What makes you say that? Aren't they the ones that did it?"

"That's why they'll hesitate."

"Did you notice the ground under those bones?" Chino asked. "Burnt. Just as though there'd been a fire. I didn't see any char on the trees though."

"Let's not talk about it," Lu said. He felt as though darkness was closing on them with every word.

"I agree," MacLemore said. "I don't want to talk about it either."

They waited until their horses were finished drinking, then pushed on.

It was getting toward sundown, two days later, when they came around a bend in the river and saw the remains of a log cabin. One of the walls was caved in and the rest leaned perilously to the side. Most of the logs were rotten, the windows had all been smashed, and the front door hung by a single hinge. A crow, easily the largest Lu had ever seen, sat on the roof, or what little remained of it, eyeing them warily. As the riders approached, it stuck its head out and delivered a throaty croak.

"I know this place," MacLemore said. "I've been here." He looked through one of the windows, careful not to cut himself on any of the glass. "This used to be a miner's cabin. Old Joe McShane built it."

"How far is it from here to Silver City?" Henry asked. They'd finished Mrs. Hammond's goat sandwiches the day before and were once again hungry. All but the horses, who'd put back some of the considerable weight they'd lost in the desert.

"Can't be an hour's ride. We ought to see lots more cabins soon enough."

"I hope one or two are still lived in," Chino remarked. "Never met the miner yet that didn't keep a jug. I could stand to wet my whistle."

"Look over here," Lu called.

Lying a dozen or so yards beyond the deserted cabin was a sign. It had once stood beside the road, but the post onto which it'd been affixed was rotten, and the sign had fallen down.

"What's it say?" Chino asked.

Lu read aloud:

"Welcome to Silver City.
Population 122 and Growing.
No Irish."

"No Irish? That's certainly new," MacLemore said.

Henry peered down the road ahead. Another burned-out old hulk of a cabin was just visible amidst the shadows. "I don't think anything here is new," he muttered.

"This is where I was born?" Sadie asked as they rode down the main street, passing the first in a long series of boarded-up shops. "No wonder Mama hated it."

Lu understood her disappointment. They were all disappointed. After weeks and months of travel, they'd finally made it to Silver City. But rather than a cozy village, offering comforts to both body and soul, they'd instead discovered a dusty, flea-bit, broken-down, knock-kneed, misery of a town. Lu had expected a growing community, made wealthy by mining. What he saw was a village with but one resource in abundance, and that was frowns. Lu felt the corners of his own mouth tug steadily downward as they passed by the boarded-up front of what had once been a fine general store. A gang of young hooligans loitered out front, sitting on empty nail-kegs and overturned produce crates. Their leader, a redheaded boy of no more than sixteen, had an old musket slung across one knee, and a one-eyed bulldog on a chain. The other four boys carried knives. What they thought they might like to do with those blades was as clear as if they'd written it out on their shirts.

"Did you say they had opera?" Sadie asked her father. "In this town?"

"Used to be a fine stage in the Grange Hall," MacLemore said. "Your mother and I once watched a pair of ladies from San

Pablo sing French for two solid hours."

Chino pointed down the street. "In *that* Grange Hall?"

Most of the paint had long since peeled off, and those rare bits of faded yellow that were still visible along the undersides of the roof eaves and windowsills hung like strips of dead skin after a bad sunburn. The plank sidewalk had been mostly torn up, and the wood steps leading up to the Grange Hall door appeared rotten. The door itself was still in place, amazingly, although it looked as if someone had taken a few swipes at it with an axe. Worst of all were the plywood walls. They were so riddled with bullet-holes that Lu half-expected to see the entire building come crashing down any second.

"This whole town is falling apart." MacLemore shook his head in what Lu took to be sorrow and confusion.

"One structure is in good repair," Henry said, pointing.

Catty-corner from the Grange Hall, toward the back of a vacant lot, stood a gallows.

It was an impressive bit of carpentry, Lu had to admit. The wood platform looked brand new, and the stairs leading up to it were wide and even. Fanciest of all were the copper hinges on the trap-door. Each had been polished until it shone like a penny in the sun. The cross-bar even sported a noose of fine horsehair rope.

Next door to the gallows, directly across the street from the Grange Hall, was a saloon. Unlike the other shops in Silver City, it was open and doing business. From between the swinging doors they could hear the chatter of voices, accompanied by the plink and plunk of a tuneless piano. Lu wondered if Chino would want to go inside.

He was about to ask when all of a sudden the whole interior of the saloon came tumbling out into the street. Drunkards piled through the batwing doors, some so sloppy they could scarcely walk. One old tramp, his long white hair hanging in his eyes, stumbled across the raised wood sidewalk, tripped over a hitching rail and fell headfirst into a puddle of horse urine. Only a handful of his fellow revelers even seemed to notice, and those that did merely laughed. None showed the slightest interest in helping him up.

Last out of the saloon came a man in a three-piece suit. He had a handlebar mustache, and was flanked on either side by gunmen. A trio of saloon girls, decked out in their revealing best, marched ahead of him, shoving stragglers off of the plank sidewalk, clearing a path for their boss. As the gentleman sauntered out, he raised one hand to the crowd. The rabble in the street stared up at him in hushed awe.

"Three cheers for Pitt and Sawyer!" the suited gentleman called.

The townsfolk answered with a chorus of hips, hoorays, and loud whistles. Lu watched closely, and after the third cheer he guessed he knew which of the men were Pitt and Sawyer. He wasn't impressed. Judging by their expressions, those two were about the drunkest of the bunch.

"These two fine boys," the suited gentleman continued, "have come all the way from San Pablo. Apparently, they heard about our Yankee problem, and have come to lend us a hand. What do you think? Can they do it?"

Another loud cheer exploded from the crowd. Pitt and Sawyer each shook hands with at least a dozen men. One of the saloon girls gave each of them a kiss on the cheek.

Lu glanced at his employer. He expected MacLemore to call out, or go riding through the crowd. The whole town was gathered. This seemed as good a time to reveal himself as any. But MacLemore didn't so much as shift in his saddle.

The man in the three-piece suit held up his hand again, once more quieting the crowd.

"I don't mind saying, on behalf of the whole citizenry of Silver City, that you boys are among the best, the bravest, the most prepared adventurers we've seen to date." He smoothed the ends of his mustache, grinning all the while. "And with any luck, you'll be the last we ever do see. I have no doubt at all that, come the end of the week, you'll be striding through our little town again, rich as Sheiks, with the MacLemore gold in tow." He laughed. "If I was a betting man, I'd reckon that a sure thing. So now tell us gents, what'll you do with all that treasure? Invest in one of our fine and profitable mining claims, no doubt."

Suddenly, and for no apparent reason, Pitt and Sawyer jerked the pistols from their belts and began firing wildly at each other. Horrified townsfolk dodged and dove in every direction. Lu ducked as low over Crash's neck as he could.

Fortunately, only one man was shot in the gunfight. Lu didn't know whether it was Pitt or Sawyer—he hadn't figured out which was which yet—but he could see that the bullets the man had absorbed were likely to kill him. There was a hole in the man's belly, and another in his chest. Blood poured out by the quart. One of the saloon ladies—the very same one that'd kissed both men just moments before—bent over him, hoping to staunch the flow by pressing her fingers into the holes. But the effort was a waste.

"Pitt's dead," she said.

The crowd buzzed. They sounded excited. Lu wondered what could possibly happen next. Things happened fast in Silver City, it seemed, and without much reason. Lu still didn't even know why they'd fought.

"Well, that certainly was one of the shortest expeditions on record," the three-piece gentleman muttered, straightening his tie. "Dern fools never even got out of town."

"I seen him do the shootin'," one of the saloon ladies offered, pointing at Sawyer.

At the moment, Sawyer was being held down by no fewer than five men. The very same five that'd accompanied the suited gentleman out of the saloon, Lu observed.

"Plenty of witnesses," their boss agreed. "No need to belabor the point. I guess we all know what this means." For the third time that afternoon, the assemblage cheered. "That's right," the suited gentleman said. "To the gallows!"

The men hauled Sawyer to his feet, bound his hands behind his back, and marched him to the vacant lot next door. They didn't even pause before hauling him up onto the platform.

Lu glanced at his friends. "Can you believe this?' he whispered.

No one responded. Sadie and her father watched the proceedings with blank expressions. Chino appeared neither surprised nor disturbed. Henry looked to be disgusted with the whole affair. Lu guessed that Chino and Henry had both seen this sort of justice before.

As soon as Sawyer was standing on the trap-door, the man in the three-piece suit reached into his jacket-pocket and pulled out a Bible. He chose a scripture apparently at random, and then read it through as quickly as he possibly could. Sawyer didn't listen. Nor, seemingly, did anyone else.

"Can we take their stuff yet?" one of the saloon ladies asked as soon as the reading was over. "Their horses are tied up out front. And Pitt had a fine watch."

"Don't I get to say nothin'?" Sawyer demanded.

The men holding him looked to their boss.

"What do you want to say?" the man in the suit asked.

Sawyer cleared his throat. "I only want to say one thing. I'm damn glad I got the chance to shoot my old partner, Joe Pitt. Just this very morning, Joe said he thought he'd like to open another saloon, right here in Silver City. He reckoned this town was fit to grow. I told him I'd shoot him dead 'fore I'd ever agree to spend my life in a town such as this. And by jings, I meant it."

The crowd waited, expecting the doomed adventurer to continue. But apparently, that was all Sawyer had to say.

In the meantime, a pair of local toughs—Lu recognized them as two members of the gang he'd seen lazing in front of the boarded-up general store—had shimmied their way up onto the crossbar. While Sawyer talked, they'd shortened the hang rope until there wasn't even a foot of slack.

"Now then, Mr. Sawyer," the man in the suit said. "You did your shooting, and it's time to pay the price. In Silver City, as you may or may not know, we like nothing better than a dance. So that'll be the price of your crime. A dance."

"I guess I can do a pretty fair jig," Sawyer muttered.

"I'll bet you can. Unfortunately, we prefer another dance." He nodded to one of the attendants, who gave the trap-door lever a sharp pull.

Sawyer fell just far enough for the rope to pinch off his windpipe, but not nearly far enough to snap his neck. It was a gruesome spectacle, watching him twist and flop like a fish on a line, and lasted almost five minutes. As he suffocated, Sawyer's face went from white to red to purple. When it started going white again, one of the saloon girls went to inspect the body.

"Show's over," she announced. "He's dead."

A few of the citizens cheered, but most just marched back to the saloon. It was sort of anticlimactic, Lu had to admit. Sawyer had only really struggled hard for a few seconds. His death, whenever it came, was utterly silent. It might've been something else entirely if anyone had cared for the dying man. But no one did. There was no begging. No tears for a life wasted. No feeling of any kind.

Once the street had mostly cleared, two of the saloon ladies went through the dead men's pockets, Pitt and Sawyer both, followed by their saddle-bags. The women only pocketed whatever they reckoned valuable. Everything else they flung into the street. Pickings didn't seem to be good.

Eventually one of them found Pitt's watch and an argument ensued. The woman who'd found it figured it was hers, while the other woman thought they ought to share. Listening to them bicker made Lu sick. That these men's lives had been reduced to the value of a watch seemed to him truly awful.

Lu wanted to move on, and was just about to say so, when a youngish fellow with a wispy mustache sprouting from his lip strode up to MacLemore.

"You fellers in the army or somethin'?" he asked.

"Pardon?" MacLemore glared down at him.

"Them matching shirts. Don't look like army duds to me, but I figured I'd ask. Nobody 'round here likes the army much."

"We're not in the army," MacLemore assured him.

"Well, that's good. Say, ain't you folks comin'?"

"Coming where?"

"Why, to the saloon, o' course."

"I don't believe we will."

"What's wrong? You Irish or somethin'?"

"Scotch."

This caused a certain amount of pause, as the young man considered the word MacLemore had just used.

"Scotch?" he said at last. "Ain't that some sort of Injun?"

"In my case it's a form of southerner."

"Reb? Well hell, that's no reason to stay outside. We don't mind Rebs 'round here. You can even bring in your darkie, so long as he stays right with you. We had one in just last week. Tried to chat up one of the girls and Mayor Strong hung him. But that ain't typical. Most coons know their place, I guess. Now the Irish, that's different."

"Mayor Strong. Was that the man in the suit?" Sadie asked.

"And proprietor of the saloon. After a hangin', Mayor Strong buys the whole city a round. Always turns to a party. Sometimes it gets so dern wild we have another hangin' later that same night."

"I believe we'll pass," MacLemore said. "But so long as I have you here, maybe you could answer a couple of questions?"

"I don't know. If I fiddle 'round too long, I might miss my free drink."

"Just one question then."

"Well, all right. But just the one."

"I thought this was a mining town," MacLemore said. "But nobody seems to be doing any mining. The hardware store doesn't even seem to be open. How come no one's working?"

"Not workin'? Shucks, I guess just about everybody's workin'. All you have to do is go into the saloon and ask for Mr. Moss. He'll take you right over to the hardware store and sell you whatever you want. Unless he's playin' cards, of course. Or drunk."

"Of course," Chino said.

"As for minin', heck, I'm in the minin' game myself." He reached into his pants pockets, pulling out a half-dozen rocks, each about the size of a man's thumb. "These here are samples from my claim." He handed one of the rocks to MacLemore. "See that mica?"

"What of it?"

"Why, every fool knows mica and gold are just like this." He crossed his fingers. "And these ain't even my best specimens neither."

"If your claim's so rich, why aren't you working it?" MacLemore asked.

"No investors. If I could just get a stake together—say five hundred dollars—why, I'd be rich in no time flat. What about you folks? You lookin' to invest?"

MacLemore handed him back his rock. "Maybe later."

"Well, if you are, just come on into the saloon. I'm there most ever' day. Just ask for Mike. That's my name. Mike Dunleavy."

"Isn't that an Irish name?" Sadie asked.

"Irish?" Mike was shocked. "Course it ain't Irish! It's American! Just like me."

"Thanks for your help," MacLemore said. "But you'd best get along now if you're going to get your free drink."

"Dang, you're right." Mike hastened away, leaving Lu and his friends alone.

They sat where they were for a few minutes. The piano resumed its tinkling and the chatter of voices in the saloon grew more boisterous. Every other building in town was dark.

"This is quite a town," Chino said at last. "We've been here less than an hour, and already seen both a shootin' and a hangin'. Stick round long enough and we're like to see a war."

"We still need supplies," Henry said, obviously disgusted. "Apparently that means a trip to the saloon."

"I figured you'd jump at the chance," Sadie remarked. "You were excited to visit the one in Fort Jeb Stuart."

"This is different."

"How?"

"You remember those army boys? The ones that took offense at your father's choice of tunes?"

Sadie said she remembered.

"Well, this whole town smells of boys like those."

"Maybe we ought to find someplace to spend the night," Chino suggested. "Supplies can wait 'til morning. You know anyone that might put us up?"

"I used to know the blacksmith," MacLemore said. "He had a fine house north of town. We could see if he's still there."

They rode to the far end of town and a quarter-mile past,

finally stopping in front of a two-story white-washed cottage. Sunflowers grew to either side and a steady stream of smoke poured from the stone chimney.

"His name is Dell Lower," MacLemore said, climbing down from his mule. "But folks all call him J.D. His wife Pearl was a good friend to my Daisy."

MacLemore strode up onto the front porch and knocked. No one answered.

"Maybe they didn't hear you," Sadie suggested.

He knocked again, harder this time. Still nothing.

"Could be they're out back in the shop," MacLemore said, and started around the side of the house. "Hey Pearl! J.D.! Anybody home?"

He'd just rounded the corner when the front door swung open. The room behind was dark, but not so dark that Lu missed seeing the rifle barrel that poked out at them.

"Don't anybody move," the rifle's owner said. "I'll cut down the first son-of-a-bitch that so much as sneezes."

"J.D.?" MacLemore asked. "Is that you?"

The rifle eased through the door, followed by a tall man with straight black hair. He looked like a blacksmith. Even through his shirt Lu could see the muscles in his shoulders and upper arms.

"Come on out from there," he said. "And keep your hands where I can see 'em."

MacLemore did as he was told.

"Who are you?" J.D. Lower asked.

"John MacLemore."

"MacLemore? He left town fifteen years ago. Everybody knows that."

"Well I've come back. That's my girl." He gestured at Sadie. "Daisy's daughter."

Lower glanced over at her, but kept his rifle at the ready.

"Where's Pearl?" MacLemore asked. "She might recognize me."

"Hey, Pearl!" J.D. called. "Come to the door a minute."

A woman, dark hair curling from under her bonnet, shuffled outside. She gripped the door-frame for an instant, steadying herself before cautiously stepping over the threshold. As she crossed the porch, she stretched both hands in front of her. At first, Lu thought she was finding it hard to navigate the darkened house. But that wasn't it at all. Pearl Lower was blind.

"My Lord, Pearl," MacLemore said. "What's happened to you?"

"Well, I'll be jiggered," she said. "I never thought to hear that voice again." Pearl stretched her hands toward him. "Come closer, John."

MacLemore stepped onto the porch.

"Give me your hands," she said. "Why, your knuckles are near as tough as J.D.'s. You've aged, John MacLemore."

"What happened to you, Pearl?"

"It was the influenza. Struck most every Irish family in town. Killed off most of 'em. All four of us had it, of course. I'm the only one that was struck blind, thank God."

"Four?"

"We've got two girls now. Hazel and Claire. Girls!" she shouted. "Girls! Get out here and meet one of your mother's friends!"

"It'll take them a second," J.D. confided. "I expect they were hidin' in the crawl-space under the pantry."

Lu, Henry, Chino and Sadie took that opportunity to dismount. As they did, the two Lower girls came stumbling onto the porch.

"Ma!" the younger of the two exclaimed. "You wouldn't believe it. The whole yard's full of coloreds. There's even a China-man, only he's just a kid."

"Claire!"

"And they're all wearin' the same shirts, too."

"That's quite enough out of you, missy. Keep it up and I'll have your father wallop you. Besides, these men all look the same to me."

"Oh, Ma," the older girl said. "Everybody looks the same to you."

Henry stretched his hand out to the girls. "Pleased to meet you," he said. "My name is Henry. That's Chino. And this is Lu."

"Go on," J.D. said. "Shake the man's hand."

Both girls did as their father commanded. When her turn was

over, Claire peered down at her little fingers as though surprised to find them all present and accounted for.

"Now, about this girl of yours," Pearl said to MacLemore. "Where is she?"

"I'm here." Sadie climbed onto the porch beside her father.

Pearl took Sadie's hand. "Gracious honey, you're a full grown woman. How old are you now? Sixteen?"

"Yes, ma'am. I'll be seventeen next March."

"Is she as pretty as her mother was?"

"She favors Daisy," MacLemore said. "Thank God."

"You must be a vision." Pearl beamed. "And I'll bet you're hungry, too."

"I sure am."

"How about the rest of you? Anyone else hungry?"

"We don't mean to put you out," MacLemore said.

"Nonsense, John MacLemore. It'd put me out if you didn't stay the night. I can't imagine what Daisy would say if I let her only daughter sleep in a room at the saloon. Even you have more sense than to take your teenage daughter there, John."

"I figured we'd just camp out."

"You'll do nothing of the sort. We don't have tons of room, but we've got enough for five."

Pearl turned to her husband. "J.D., help these men with their horses while I find out where John and Sadie have been all these years. Claire and Hazel can put on the kettle. I hope you men like stew, because that's what we're having."

"Yes, ma'am," Lu said.

Once their stock had been released into the corral, and their saddles and other equipment were locked inside his blacksmith shop, J.D. escorted Henry, Lu, and Chino into the house.

They entered through the back door, which led directly into the Lowers' kitchen. As they crossed the threshold, Hazel and Claire handed each of them a bowl of stew, a slab of dark bread with butter and honey, and a cup of strong black tea. Lu took a deep breath from his own cup and nearly giggled. Until this very instant, he'd never realized how much he missed having tea with his own family back home.

The Lowers had only one small table, barely large enough for the four of them to sit at comfortably, though they did manage to squeeze in two extra chairs for the MacLemores. Lu, Henry, and Chino leaned against the wall, stew bowls balanced in their hands and teacups resting on the windowsill.

"You'll be after the gold," J.D. remarked.

"High time, too," Pearl said. "When I think of that dirty Yankee in Daisy's house, well, I'm near tempted to cuss. When do you plan to head out?"

"We need supplies," MacLemore said. "Explosives mostly. Assuming the hardware store really is open, we should be able to get everything in town."

"Hope you brought plenty of money," J.D. said. "No one 'round here's likely to extend credit. Too many folks have gone broke offering credit to fortune-hunters."

"What do you mean?"

J.D. told them about all the expeditions that had been mounted over the years. Most were just adventurers out for easy money. The MacLemore gold was an enormous draw. Folks had come hundreds of miles, each and every one of them hoping to kill the Yankee and steal it away. For the most part they were rank amateurs, relying on nerve and luck to see them through. But a few were more organized. One of the most serious expeditions had even come armed with a Gatling gun. The town had high hopes for that group. But they'd soon disappeared, same as all the others.

"For a while I'd say we averaged as many as two expeditions a month," J.D. said. "It's trickled off some over the years, of course, but there are still a few show up every summer. The last expedition set out today. Two reckless young fellers by the name of Sawyer and Pitt. Don't have much hope for 'em myself. All the time I was shoeing their horses, those rascals were arguing about how to spend their money."

"They didn't make it," Henry said.

"No?"

"Sawyer shot Pitt just after we rode into town, and Mayor Strong hung Sawyer not five minutes later."

J.D. sighed. "Dang. I've shod a passel of horses that never came back, but I never knew of an expedition that died out before it even left town."

"Is this Yankee really so tough?" MacLemore asked him.

"Must be. Though so far as I can tell, no one's even got a clear view of the man. Leastways, none have and lived to tell about it. There are tales, of course. But I never put much stock in them."

"Tales? Like what?"

"Foolishness mostly. Some folks say he's got a whole army of fire demons watching over his gold. Others say it's him that's the demon, and that he's out there all by himself, limping 'round your old house on a gimpy leg, setting booby traps for anyone foolish enough to wander by." J.D. shrugged. "One or two old-timers claimed to have come across him in the woods, but their stories never added up to much. They couldn't even agree on whether he was old or young, black or white." He pointed at his daughters and scoffed. "Kids around town have this idea—I don't know where it comes from exactly—that the Yankee can only be defeated by an American."

"That's true!" Hazel said.

Claire nodded in agreement. "Pete Wisniewski's father even said so, before they decided to move away."

"See?" J.D. shook his head. "If you ask me, this has got something to do with Mayor Strong. He's the one that started all the no-Irish bunk, too. As if folks in this town needed an excuse to act ugly to each other. Besides, we've had scores of Americans give it a try, and not a one successful. If you want to know the honest truth, no one knows a thing about the Yankee. Not for certain, anyhow."

"We do," Lu said. "We have a book."

"A book? About the Yankee?"

"It's more of a notebook, really," Sadie said. "But Jack Straw told us it was important."

Lu described the contents of the notebook to Mr. Lower, beginning with the story of the missing schoolmaster and running clear through the death notice. Henry and Chino both chimed in here and there, reminding Lu of important bits he skipped over.

They did their very best, but for some reason not one of the three could remember the names of either the notebook's writer or the man he'd met in the hotel.

"Knickerbocker," Sadie said at last. "That was the writer's name."

"That's right," Henry agreed. "Diedrich Knickerbocker. Do you remember the name of the man he met?"

Sadie shook her head.

"Where is this notebook?" J.D. asked.

"It's in one of my saddle-bags," Lu said.

"Out in the shop? Well hell, son, let's go get it. I'd like to read this story myself."

The path to J.D.'s blacksmith shop led through a small vegetable garden. Earlier, J.D. had told them that it was Pearl's pride and joy, and that her green beans were generally reckoned the best in town. As they passed through again, this time in the dark, Lu wondered aloud how she possibly managed to do her gardening blind.

"I guess she can tell a cucumber from a green bean by the feel," J.D. said. "What I'd like to know is how she does her sewing. Pearl made Hazel a fine quilt for her birthday, and never got a single square of fabric out of place."

"Maybe Claire helped her," Lu suggested.

"That's exactly what I said." J.D laughed. "Pearl was so mad she didn't talk to me for a week. Here." He thrust the lantern he'd been using to light their path into Lu's hands. "Your saddles are on a table in the back."

J.D. waited outside while Lu went in search of the notebook. The smells in the blacksmith shop were deep and earthy—a mixture of ash, horse, and manly sweat. But it wasn't a bad smell. In fact, there was something about it that reminded Lu of his grandfather's sanctum. For some reason, thinking about home made the nerves in Lu's spine tingle. At least that's what he thought.

"I like your shop," he said, as he stepped back outside and J.D. locked the door behind him. "It reminds me—"

He didn't finish.

In the sky, directly over the Lower house, hung a streak of orange fire. Lu had seen a blaze like this just once before, months ago, while on the plains leading to Fort Jeb Stuart.

Demons.

Back then, the flames had been miles away, and too small to make out clearly. This time, Lu could see the demons' fiery expressions and hear the clatter of their hooves. Every inch of their bodies was engulfed in flame. Their eyes were white hot and radiant. Their lips twisted grins of molten flesh.

Lu was still gazing up at them, his whole body gone rigid from shock and terror, when the rear door to the cottage banged open and Sadie came running out, followed by Hazel and Claire.

"What in the hell was that?" Sadie asked. "Sounded almost like there were horses on the roof."

Lu pointed.

Sadie gasped. "What are they?"

"Ghost-riders."

Lu winced as the demons turned and headed back toward them, skimming once more over the cottage roof, missing the stone chimney by mere inches. They were so close now that Lu could hear the ghost-riders' voices, the vile curses they leveled at their flaming mounts. He saw their whips land, over and over, on their horses' flanks. He flinched as sparks burst from their hooves.

The ghost-riders urged their mounts higher and faster, laughing as they set the whole sky ablaze. In an instant they'd reached the nearest mountain, a prodigious peak capped by snowy-white rock, and went burning across its upper face. From the pinnacle they leapt skyward, passing through the center of a dark cloud, illuminating it from the inside like a bolt of lightning. Then they shot over the other side of the mountain range and were gone.

Lu took a deep breath. The tingling in his spine began to subside. "Is everyone all right?" he asked. His voice shook.

Sadie nodded, though Lu could see that she too was trembling. The Lower girls only stared, mouths agape, saying nothing.

"Shooting stars," J.D. muttered. "First saw 'em just as you went into the shop. Mighty pretty, but nothin' to get worked up about."

"What are you talking about?" Sadie asked. "Those weren't shooting stars!"

"He can't see them," Lu said.

"Can't see them? Why not?"

"Jack says only the innocent and the damned can see them."

"Didn't you see the riders, Pa?" Hazel asked. "They went right over our house."

"Just shooting stars," J.D. said again. "Nothin' to worry about."

Lu looked at the notebook in his hand. It was still bound in its silk covering, but his grandfather's dragon charm was gone.

"Look," he said to Sadie.

"Where's the dragon?" she asked.

"It must've fallen off."

J.D. unlocked the door to the shop again, and Lu went in search of the missing amulet. He found it in the bottom of his saddlebag.

"Got it," Lu said as he stepped back through the door. He was glad to see that the sky was free of demons.

"For heaven's sake, tie it back on," Sadie said. "And hurry!"

As soon as the charm touched the white silk, a flash of blue light burst from the dragon. Sadie and the Lower girls both leaned close, their faces illuminated for a moment in the mysterious glow. Hazel's teeth shone like pearls in the ghostly light.

"Is it on tight this time?" Sadie asked.

"I double-knotted it," Lu said.

"Good." Sadie sighed. "Never let that charm fall off again!"

"Never," Lu agreed.

"Let's go inside," J.D. suggested. "I'm anxious to read this tale. And it's time you girls got ready for bed."

"But we want to read it, too!" Claire moaned. "Can't we?"

"No one's going to read this story," Lu said, notebook clutched to his chest. "Not tonight. We shouldn't even have been talking about it." He looked at the mountain over which the demons had disappeared. "The ghost-riders must've heard us. That's how they knew we were here."

"That's right," Sadie whispered. "And that means *he*'ll know we're coming."

"Who'll hear?" J.D. asked. "Who'll know?"

"The Yankee," said Lu.

IT WAS A GLUM CREW that sat around Pearl Lower's kitchen that night, drinking tea and pondering their next move. J.D. and MacLemore were both inclined to ignore the ghost-riders—neither believed in them anyway, Lu suspected—and read the notebook through just as though no one had seen a thing. But they were in the minority.

"Look here," J.D. said at last. "If no one is going to read the blasted thing, we may as well go to bed. Nothing more we can do tonight."

"I'll walk down to the saloon first thing tomorrow," MacLemore said. "We still need those explosives. A bit of provender wouldn't hurt either."

"As to that," Pearl said, "you'll have fresh vegetables from my garden. Beans. Carrots. I hope you all like squash."

"How are you going to pay for the explosives?" Henry wanted to know. "Chino and I have a dollar or two, but nothing close to what you'll need to buy blasting powder."

"I'll strike a deal."

"Who with?"

"We've got some money saved," Pearl said. "Nearly thirty dollars. It's not much, but you can sure have it."

"I'd pay you back," MacLemore promised, "with interest. Just as soon as we get the gold."

"Oh, I know you *would*," J.D. muttered. "*If* you get it."

✪

The next morning, MacLemore got up before sunrise. He washed his face, borrowed a clean shirt from J.D., and rapidly ate the oatmeal Pearl made for breakfast. While he was in town, J.D. planned to shoe their mounts. One or two of the horses had probably never worn shoes, Crash among them. Lu wondered how he'd take it. Chino, who'd done some blacksmithing himself in years past, offered to help.

"Maybe I ought to go with you," Henry said to MacLemore.

"The fewer of us the better, I think." MacLemore put a hand on Lu's shoulder. "Besides, the two of us ought to be able to carry back everything we'll need."

"You want *me* to come?" Lu asked.

"You're our explosives expert. I guess you'll know what's needed to do the job."

"But I don't even know what the job is."

"Doesn't hardly matter. You can do it, I've no doubt. We've all come to have a mighty high opinion of your skills, Lu. Jack was right to hire you."

Lu looked at the other members of their party. Henry and Chino were standing in their usual spots beside the kitchen window. Sadie sat with the Lower girls at the table. All three smiled at him. Lu couldn't help blushing.

Hazel and Claire walked with them as far as the edge of Silver City, but returned home as soon as they got within sight of the first broken-down building. The Lower girls weren't allowed to go into town. In fact, J.D. didn't much like their getting out of sight of the house. But Pearl insisted they be given at least a bit of freedom. And Pearl generally got her way.

"What was the name of that hardware store owner again?" MacLemore asked, as they approached the saloon. A few early-risers were already bellied up to the bar. Lu could see their feet beneath the batwing doors.

"Moss," he replied.

"That's right. Moss. I sure hope he's here."

They pushed their way inside.

The remains of the previous night's party lay scattered throughout the tavern. It was awful. Glass from a half-dozen broken bottles was littered over the floor, along with at least one deck of playing cards, dozens upon dozens of empty brass shell-casings, and the ruins of one thoroughly smashed chair. The human garbage was even more sickening. A handful of the very worst drunkards were still there, passed out in the corner or collapsed face-down on a table. One pitiful fellow had somehow managed to slide out of his chair and was lying spread-eagle in front of the piano, an empty whisky bottle still clutched in his fist. Only one saloon-girl was visible, slumped unconscious at the bottom of a rickety staircase. Her dress was partially unbuttoned, showing the lacy top of a cotton shift. As they picked their way through the wreckage, Lu looked around for Mike Dunleavy, the young prospector they'd met the evening before, but didn't see him anywhere. He was glad of that. For some reason, Lu had sort of liked Mike.

The men standing at the bar were the very same bunch of hard-cases that'd hung Sawyer the previous afternoon. They were dirty and unshaven, their eyes bloodshot. Lu doubted that any of them had slept a wink.

Mayor Strong stood behind the bar, still dressed up in his three-piece suit, wiping tobacco spittle from the bottom of a long line of shot glasses. He smiled at MacLemore as they sidled up.

"You Irish?" he asked.

"Scotch," MacLemore replied.

"Is that right?" He whistled. "Hey Della!"

The girl at the bottom of the stairs stirred, but her eyes remained closed.

"Damned Scotch lush," Strong muttered. "If you're looking for a whore, I guess you'll have to wait 'til noon. We ought to have a few American girls up by then."

"We're not really interested in whores," MacLemore said.

"No? So then what can I get you?"

"Let's start with a whiskey."

"You can bring your coolie into the bar," Mayor Strong said, pointing at Lu. "But he can't drink out of my glasses."

"That's all right," Lu said. "I don't want one anyway."

Strong picked up one of the glasses he'd just wiped clean, slammed it down on the bar, and filled it to the rim with brown liquor. "That'll be four bits," he said.

MacLemore handed over a dollar, picked up the glass, and downed the whole shot at a single gulp. "Guess I'll have another," he said.

The second glass disappeared as quickly as the first.

"More?" Strong offered.

"Not just yet. We're looking for a Mr. Moss. He owns the hardware store, isn't that right?"

"You plan on doing some mining? Or are you fortune hunters?"

"Miners."

Strong squinted at them. "What did you say your name was again?"

"You can call me John." MacLemore held out his hand for the Mayor to shake, but Strong ignored the offer.

"That's Moss there." He nodded at one of the men slumped over the tables. "He doesn't usually wake up for an hour or two yet."

"Think he'd be offended if we woke him?"

"Does it matter?"

"Not really." MacLemore strode over to the drunk in question and tapped him on the shoulder. Moss didn't even stir.

"He's a touch sleepy yet," Strong said.

Lu rapped on the tabletop with his knuckles. "Mr. Moss!" he called.

The drunkard's head came up as though shot from a cannon. He had a long reddish-brown beard, reaching halfway to his belt buckle. Judging by the spots on the front of his shirt, Lu guessed that he'd missed his mouth with roughly half the whiskey he'd drunk the night before. Either that or he'd found it hard to keep down. His beard was soaking wet.

"Get outta' my house!" Moss yelled, bug-eyed and trembling.

"You aren't in your house," Strong said. The men at the bar laughed. "You're sleeping in my saloon again."

Moss looked shocked. He gazed around him, as though never having seen the saloon before. His mouth fell open.

"Mr. Moss," MacLemore said. "We'd like to buy some supplies."

"Supplies?" He looked up at MacLemore, mouth working like a landed fish. "I've got to get home. Esther will be looking out for me."

Moss leapt for the door. It was so sudden a burst of activity that Lu and MacLemore could only stare at each other in mute dismay as the batwing doors swung on their hinges.

"He was sure in a hurry," Lu said.

"He'll be darned lucky if that wife of his doesn't skin him alive," Strong said. "She's not much for drinking. Which is funny, because drinking is about the only thing Franklin Moss does."

"Where do they live?" MacLemore asked.

"In a little room over his store."

"C'mon Lu, let's get over there."

"What sort of tools are you looking for?" Strong asked.

"Nothing out of the ordinary. A hammer. Picks and shovels. That sort of thing."

"Explosives?"

MacLemore stopped cold. "Why?"

"Miners are always wanting to blast away at some dang thing or other. That sound like something you might be interested in?"

"We might. Do you know where we can buy powder?"

"Not from Moss, that's for sure."

"Where then?"

Mayor Strong grinned. "How much you boys looking for?"

"How much should we get?" MacLemore asked Lu.

"He's your man, is he?" Strong didn't look surprised. "Been a while since I saw a coolie blast-man. This one looks awful young to me. But it's your head. Where'd you learn your trade son?"

"My grandfather is an expert. He even taught Jack Straw."

"Jack Straw." Strong looked impressed. "Haven't seen Jack Straw around here in years, have we boys?" He looked at the men lined up at the bar. They shook their heads, but otherwise kept silent.

"What's your granddad's name?" Strong asked.

"Master K'ung."

"Master? Can't say as I've heard that one. Only famous Chink I ever knew was Yen Hui."

"Yen Hui was my father," Lu said.

"Is that right? Dang boys, this here's Yen Hui's son. You remember me telling about him? Old Hui blew himself to smithereens digging a well for some wetbacks south of San Pablo. Can you beat that? Climbs down the shaft, sets the charge, and those damned Mexicans refuse to haul him back up. Just goes to show, it never pays to help a Mexican. They're almost as bad as the Irish." Strong licked his lips. "I tell you boys, I'd hang all four of them Lowers today, little girls included, if that damned J.D. weren't the only blacksmith in town. Hells bells, I may do it anyway. I do hate to be held in check by an Irishman. Maybe we ought to see if we can't get us a new blacksmith. I hear they have a fine man down at Corto, and there's always—"

"We'd like that powder now," MacLemore said, cutting Strong off mid-sentence. "Enough for five charges. Have you got it or not?"

Strong glared at him. "Five charges," he said. "That'll cost you."

"How much?"

"Ten dollars a charge."

"Ten?" MacLemore was incensed. "Why, that's robbery."

"That's your price. Just this morning it was five. But I do hate to be interrupted when I'm lecturing my boys. Rudeness is a thing I can't stand. You'd be wise to keep that in mind, John. I hate it so much I could just about hang a feller over it."

MacLemore took out his wallet and peered inside. "I've only got thirty," he said.

"That's enough for two charges," Strong said.

"Two? But you just said it was ten dollars a charge."

"I suppose you'll want fuses. Powder ain't worth shucks without a fuse."

MacLemore ground his teeth audibly, but handed over the thirty dollars.

"Hey, Joe." Strong folded the money into his pocket. "Get these boys two tins of blasting powder from the storeroom. And a loop of fuse long enough to set it off with."

One of his men shuffled across the saloon and through a door under the stairs. He was in dire need of a haircut, but otherwise in remarkably good condition. Lu glanced down the bar, toward where he'd been standing, and saw that instead of liquor Joe was drinking coffee. In fact, not one of the men parked at the bar was drinking whiskey. And every last one of them was armed. In addition to his revolver, Joe carried a bowie knife. Seeing it, Lu was reminded of Gokhlayeh, and of the younger hooligans they'd seen at the hanging the night before. Lu wondered if Sawyer was still dangling at the end of his noose, or if someone had the good sense to cut him down. Somehow, Lu doubted it. Good sense didn't seem to hold much sway in Silver City. He'd be glad to leave it behind once and for all.

"This is good powder?" MacLemore asked, as Joe placed two cans and a length of greasy fuse down on the bar.

"If it isn't," Strong said, "you just come on back and I'll give you another tin."

"Fine." MacLemore signaled to Lu that it was time to go.

"Another whiskey?" Strong offered. "It's on the house."

But MacLemore wasn't interested. He motioned for Lu to grab the powder.

As soon as they were out of earshot, MacLemore exploded into curse. He let loose with a string of swear vile enough to have made Chino jealous. Lu was mighty glad the Lower girls hadn't waited to walk them home. Youngsters oughtn't to hear such filth. MacLemore's description of the honorable Mayor Strong was particularly awful, and potentially dangerous. If Strong considered interruption rude, this would've got MacLemore hung for sure.

"I hate to mention it," Lu said, once the profanity had abated sufficiently for him to get a word in edgewise, "but this powder is worthless without a hole to put it in."

MacLemore stopped dead in his tracks. "What do you mean?"

"We need tools. Both a hammer and a bit."

"And just where are we supposed to get those?"

"Don't we have any more money at all?"

"One dollar."

"Well, let's try the hardware store. Maybe we can get a drill bit at least. The Lowers may have a hammer we can borrow."

They turned and headed back through town, passing once more in front of the saloon. Joe stood beside the doorway, smoking a cigarette. Lu pointed him out to MacLemore, but received only a grunt in return.

The hardware store was directly across the street from the gallows. Sawyer was still dangling, just as Lu feared he would be, though someone had stolen his boots, and his pants were lying in a heap on the ground. A crow sat perched on the dead man's shoulder, pecking at his eye.

"You think this is the right place?" MacLemore asked, gazing up at the peeling sign. "Looks deserted to me."

Lu tried the door. The hardware store was locked tight, its windows boarded over. It was hard to imagine buying tools in such a place, but they decided to knock anyway.

"Who's there?" a woman called. She didn't sound old enough to be a man's wife, let alone so ragged a specter as Franklin Moss.

"Is Mr. Moss in?" MacLemore asked.

"He's out back. What do you want?"

"Tools."

The lock gave a sickening clunk and the door swung open.

Inside, the store was clean and orderly, if poorly stocked. There were a handful of dusty gold pans, some shovels, a few picks and rakes. There were also axe-handles, mostly gone to dry-rot, an open nail keg filled with rust, a hammer with one claw broken off, and a shelf loaded with various odds and ends. Mrs. Moss stood behind the door, fists on her hips. She was barely five feet tall, with a head of tight brown curls and spectacles as thick as the bottom of a whisky bottle. There was just enough of a swell in her dress for Lu to think she might be pregnant.

"We ain't well stocked," she said.

"Neither are we." MacLemore held out the single dollar they had left. "But we aim to do some blasting and need a hammer and bit."

Esther eyed the dollar bill as though it were a poisonous snake. "Bits cost two dollars. A twelve pound maul will run you three. We don't got hammers lighter 'n that."

"I'd gladly give you ten if I had that much. Unfortunately, we just got robbed by Mayor Strong."

"Mayor Strong? Well now, that's different." Esther took the dollar from MacLemore and folded it into her apron. "Whatever bits we have left are on that shelf. Take whichever you want."

Lu began searching through the odds and ends. He found the drill bits right away, though they were all a good deal shorter than the one he and Jack had used. After looking them over, he settled on a medium-length bit. It was only about a foot and a half long, but it had one quality that Lu particularly liked. The driving end was slightly bigger around than the rest of the shaft, providing a nice broad target for the hammer. Lu didn't know who'd be wielding the sledge during their upcoming adventure, but felt certain he'd be holding the bit. He wanted it to be as broad a target as possible.

While he searched the shelf, Esther Moss retired to a back room, returning a few seconds later with a sledgehammer. It was as large as the one Jack had brought from St. Frances, and then some.

"Are you sure this will be all right with your husband?" MacLemore asked. "These are expensive tools."

"I don't guess he'll know." Esther handed the sledge to MacLemore, who came close to dropping it on his foot. "Need anything else?"

"We don't have any more money," MacLemore said.

"That's all right. I'd be happy to extend credit."

"Why? I don't mean to be rude, but you don't even know our names."

"You're against Strong. That's good enough for me." She pointed at the tins of blasting powder Lu had set on the shelf while searching for a bit. "Those used to be ours. My husband gave 'em to Strong as a payment on his tab. Another month or two and Strong will own this whole store. But I don't aim to let that happen."

"Looks like you're near cleaned out now," MacLemore said.

"Yep. And when the last tool's gone, I plan to open a café." She smiled. "Pearl Lower promised to give me some vegetables from her garden, and I been talking to the Saints that bring Strong's beeves. They promised they'd sell me a couple of cows the next time they come. So now I just have to save up some money. I figure forty dollars would just about cover it." She patted the dollar she'd just gotten from McLemore. "Make that thirty-nine."

"Tell you what," MacLemore said. "If we find any gold, I'll give you fifty. You can buy some decent tables and chairs."

"I won't hold my breath," Esther muttered. "Only gold ever found round here is in that mountain behind the old MacLemore house. And no one's gettin' any of that."

"My offer still stands."

Esther escorted them to the door. "Well, good luck to you." She shook their hands. Lu was astonished at the woman's grip. "I hope you find your gold."

As soon as they were outside, Mrs. Moss slammed the door closed behind them.

Their horses were all shod, the food packed and ready to go, by the time Lu and MacLemore sauntered back into the Lowers' front yard. Hazel and Claire sat on the front porch, swinging their feet and sewing squares of fabric together for a quilt.

"How'd you do?" Hazel asked them.

MacLemore held up their new sledgehammer.

"Get that from Esther Moss?"

"For one dollar. Bit included."

"Our Pa has a bigger one," Claire said.

"Where are Henry and Chino?"

"'Round back with Pa," Hazel said. "Sadie's inside with Ma."

"What's she doing?" Lu asked.

"Talkin'."

"What about?"

Hazel shrugged. The girls went back to their sewing.

Lu and MacLemore walked around to the rear of the house. They found Chino and Henry in the corral with the horses, checking the saddles to make sure they were tight. Crash was kicking one of his brand new shoes against a stone. He looked irritated.

"These Indian horses don't much like shoes," J.D. said. He stood in the open door of his shop, blacksmith's apron tied around his waist. "They're good animals, though. At first I didn't think much of that plug of yours," he said to Lu. "Then he leaned against me and I saw he was as strong as a bull. I reckon he could carry you clear back to China, if you could find a trail."

"We're ready to go any time," Henry added.

"Good. I want to be gone by the end of the hour." MacLemore handed the sledgehammer and bit to Chino. "Where's my guitar?"

"Still in the house," Chino answered.

"Go and get it for me, will you Lu?"

Lu set the cans of blasting powder on the top rail of the corral, and then ran to the back door. He found Sadie sitting at the kitchen table, watching Pearl roll out dough for a fruit pie. A dish of huckleberries sat to one side, glistening like wet sapphires.

"Your father would like to get out of here," Lu told Sadie.

"After lunch," Pearl said. "I've got fried chicken and mashed potatoes all ready."

"Has Carrot been shod?" Sadie asked.

Lu nodded. "Though I don't guess he likes it much."

"Tell Daddy I'll be out in a minute. We can eat in the garden."

"Do you know where his guitar is? He asked me to find it for him."

"It's on the couch in the front room."

Pearl was just setting the lower crust into her pie pan as Lu hurried back through the kitchen, guitar in hand.

"No," she said to Sadie, "Daisy wasn't much interested in cooking. Your Mammy did most of that, I guess. Daisy was a fine seamstress, though. Liked making all her own dresses. Why, your Daddy must have bought a bolt of fabric a month . . ."

Sadie was unusually quiet as they rode away from the Lower house, though in truth no one had much to say. Henry was at the front, as usual, his keen eyes fixed on the road ahead. MacLemore was still stewing over his encounter with Mayor Strong. Even a picnic in the garden hadn't taken the bad taste out of his mouth. Chino studied the bushes and trees that lined the path, but didn't care to share his insights.

They rode due north, right along the edge of the Paiute River, between mountains as high and sheer as castle walls. It was hot and dusty in the gorge. Few birds sang, and those that did sounded more alarmed than joyous.

At last, long after the sun had gone down and it was almost too dark to see the trail ahead, Henry called a reluctant halt.

"Aren't we going to build a fire?" Lu asked. They'd tethered their horses close to camp, ready to grab and run should the need arise.

"Not tonight," Henry said.

"No more fires, amigo," Chino explained. "We're trying to sneak up on him."

He handed Lu a piece of cold chicken. Pearl Lower had given them the leftovers from their picnic lunch. Lu liked the chicken now even better than he had that afternoon. It was tougher, but more flavorful. And the skin wasn't so greasy. There were no mashed potatoes, but Lu guessed he could do without. He didn't much like cold mashed potatoes anyhow.

"I guess the Yankee must know we're comin'," Sadie muttered. "What with the ghost-riders and all."

A shiver ran up Lu's spine.

"He must," Henry agreed. "But I still don't see any reason to advertise."

"Kind of makes you wonder, don't it?"

"How do you mean?"

"Well, is any of us American enough to send him packing?"

"What are you talking about?" Henry asked.

"Don't you remember what J.D. told us?" Sadie looked at the men seated around her. "Kids in Silver City say he can only be defeated by an American. This isn't exactly the whitest bunch in the whole world."

"You don't believe all that guff, do you?" her father asked.

Sadie shrugged. "I reckon not."

"Good. Because I haven't come all this way to fail."

"Me either," Chino said. "By this time next week, I plan to be living in a fine hotel, with a white servant and indoor plumbing. At first they won't want me. But once they see the gold in my purse . . ." He grinned. "And if they still don't want me? I guess I'll just buy the hotel."

"I don't plan to quit either," Henry said. "But I still can't help wishing we'd got more ammunition. I'm down to just two boxes of shells."

"That's true." Chino slid one of his six-shooters from its holster and spun the cylinder. "Then again, one bullet could do the job I figure." He pointed his pistol into the darkness. "If it was aimed just right."

CHAPTER 19

FRIENDS IN NEED

"IS THERE ANY MORE CHICKEN?" MacLemore asked.

Chino dug through the bag of provisions Pearl Lower had packed for them. He found carrots, celery, and snap peas, but no more chicken. "Want a carrot?"

"I guess."

"Give me one, too," Henry said.

Before long, all five of them were munching carrots, and Lu had begun to eye the snap peas as well. He wasn't really hungry, but he wasn't tired either. Mostly he felt agitated. Thoughts buzzed through his mind like yellow-jackets in a paper nest. If it'd been light, Lu might have run around or tried to climb a tree. As it was, he had nothing to occupy him but his thoughts, and they were a frightening lot.

"I'll tell you what I'll do with my share of the gold," Sadie said at last, tossing the bushy remains of her carrot to the horses. Lucky pounced on it like a dog on a bone. "Rent a stateroom on the first ship out of San Pablo."

"What for?" Lu asked her.

"Why, to see the world of course. What'll you do with your share, Daddy?"

"I owe a good bit to your uncle. I suppose I'll have to pay that off. And I aim to keep my pledge to Mrs. Moss. After that, I guess I'll just settle down somewhere, live high on the hog."

This was just the sort of talk a nervous band of adventurers liked best. They went all around the circle, discussing how they'd spend their money, just as though the Yankee was already defeated and the gold in sacks on the way to the bank. Chino had the most vivid ideas. In addition to life in a fancy hotel, Chino thought he might like to start an overland stage company. His idea was to hire a teamster to drive the horses, but to ride shotgun himself, just so he could give his six-shooters a "work-out" on occasion. Sadie thought she'd like to see Africa. She wanted to shoot a lion. Lu suggested she might like to practice by shooting a bear, right here in America, but she said that was just "fool talk." The one animal she said she'd never shoot, however, was a giraffe. She had a passion for giraffes. Henry hadn't fully decided how he'd spend his share, though he planned to build a church, complete with hand-carved pews, for some former slaves that'd come out to the Pacific coast after the war. He thought that if they had a decent church, more folks would want to come. Henry figured they could build a nice little town in no time.

When it was his turn to speak, Lu discovered that he hadn't the foggiest notion as to how his share of the gold ought to be spent. He might like to live in a hotel for a while, he supposed, but thought that might get awfully stuffy before long. Seeing the world would be nice, and Sadie did speak eloquently about giraffes, but Lu wondered if wandering around all the time wouldn't get lonely. And of course, there were any number of ways he might help the folks back in St. Frances, but nothing that set his imagination ablaze.

"I guess I'll just give the gold to my grandfather," he said at last. "He'll know what to do."

Sadie stared at him, as did her father. Chino burst out laughing.

"That's the worst plan I ever heard of," he said. "Your grandfather will spend the whole thing on potions and scrolls."

"No he won't," Lu said. "My grandfather is a wise man."

"Isn't there anything you'd like for yourself?" Henry asked. "A new pistol maybe?"

Lu looked down at his old brass revolver and shrugged. If he were honest, he'd have to say that he had just about everything he wanted now. Never in his life had he been so happy. While traveling with Henry, Chino, Sadie, and Mr. MacLemore, Lu had done things and met people he never thought he would. It was just like living one of his favorite story-books. And the things he'd learned? Why, he'd never have such a chance again. In fact, Lu had only one wish, and that was to keep the adventure going for as long as possible. But he didn't think that was the sort of thing he ought to say out loud.

"I wonder what Jack will do with his share," he said instead.

"*I* wonder if he'll ever show up to claim it," MacLemore muttered.

"Jack will show up eventually," Henry said. "He always does."

There was a lull in the conversation after that. Lu took another carrot, and was just about to pull the stem off, when he noticed that the trees around them were beginning to sway.

A stiff breeze had picked up while they talked. It hadn't reached far enough into the gorge to muss their hair yet, but the trees felt it. Branches were knocking back and forth, especially high up on the yellow and ponderosa pines. The summer-dry needles made a rustling sound, like a man walking through a meadow of tall grass.

"It's getting windy," Lu observed, pointing up at the swaying giants.

"A storm is comin'," Chino said. "There are clouds in front of the moon."

Moments later, they felt the first gust of arctic wind come whistling through the forest. It was strong enough to send Henry's hat tumbling down the road. Chino's might have gone as well, but he grabbed it by the crown and held on.

The horses pawed nervously as the wind picked up. Thick clouds descended over the gorge. In no time, what had been a starry night turned to pitchy dark. Lu could barely see his friends' faces, even though they were huddled close around him. Sadie, who sat on his left, grabbed Lu's hand and squeezed.

"Think it'll rain?" Henry had to shout to be heard over the howling wind.

"Sure could," Chino replied.

Lu shivered. The ferocity of the mounting tempest reminded him of another storm, in another canyon, not so long ago. And of a whole line of mules falling to their deaths in a blast of rock and fire.

"Maybe we ought to find shelter," he suggested.

"Don't worry," Henry said. "This will blow over in no time."

But he was wrong. For more than an hour they sat, heads lowered, as gusts of icy wind blasted up the backs of their shirts. Lu was shivering cold. They all were. Henry would've built a fire, and stealth be damned, except that there was no hope whatever of striking a match.

"What's that sound?" MacLemore asked, cocking his ear to the wind.

Lu listened, but heard only the trees, moaning as they fought to maintain their toeholds in the sandy earth.

"Sounds like music," MacLemore continued. "Don't any of you hear it?"

This time, Lu thought he did. It was a strange tune, high-pitched and sort of warbling. Under other circumstances he might've taken it for a bird. But no bird was fool enough to come out in weather like this.

"It's a flute," Henry said at last. "No, a fife. Camp boys played them during the war."

"It's Yankee Doodle," MacLemore said. "That's what it is. Yankee Doodle." He sang, "*I'm a Yankee Doodle Dandy, Yankee Doodle do or die. A real live nephew of my Uncle Sam, born on the Fourth of July. . . .* Don't you hear it?"

"I guess it sounds a little bit like Yankee Doodle," Sadie said. "But not really."

"What does it sound like to you?" Henry asked her.

"I don't know, exactly. It's familiar though."

Lu thought so, too. To him, it sounded just like a song his mother used to sing, whenever she thought no one was paying attention. It was an old farmers' song, one Master K'ung had taught her when she was just a little girl in China. As he listened, Lu became convinced.

"It's a Chinese song," he said.

"Nope, Spanish," Chino corrected him.

"You're both wrong," Henry said. "It's an old slave hymn. We used to sing it while picking cotton in the fields."

"You're all crazy," MacLemore said. "It's Yankee Doodle, clear as water."

Their debate was ended by a sudden blast of wind, the strongest they'd felt thus far. Lu crossed his arms over his chest. He'd never heard of anyone's shirt getting torn off by a storm, but he wasn't taking any chances. That was soon the least of his worries, however, as one of the big trees perched at the edge of the river cracked. Even from forty feet back, Lu and his friends were drenched by spray as the whole upper third of the trunk splashed into the river.

"Let's move!" MacLemore shouted.

They needed no further encouragement. Lu crawled on hands and knees toward where he'd left his saddle. He had a hard time locating it. Ever more clouds settled in front of the moon, blanketing the gorge in shadow. It was so dark that Lu and Sadie knocked heads.

Saddle in hand, Lu stumbled toward the sound of the pawing, whinnying horses. He bumped into people, animals, and bushes, as he searched for his lost mount. And still the darkness seemed to thicken. Before long, Lu could no longer even see the outlines of the surrounding trees, giants though they were, to say nothing of his friends. He despaired of ever finding the right horse. In the end, Crash found him, grabbing a hold of Lu's shirt sleeve with his teeth.

It took only a minute for Lu to have his horse saddled and ready to go. He cinched the girth down tight, though he had no way of knowing whether the saddle was on straight. It hardly mattered, as they couldn't possibly ride in such impenetrable darkness anyway.

They walked their animals north as best they could reckon it, without sight of stars or river to guide them. Henry tried his hardest to find the road, calling out every few seconds to make sure no one got left behind.

And still the night grew darker.

About ten minutes into their hike, Henry gave a shout. "I think I see a light!"

"Where?" MacLemore called back. "I can't see anything."

"It's right there in front of us." Henry's voice sounded remarkably far off now. "Just keep coming."

Lu hurried to catch up, but still saw no light of any kind.

"Henry!" Sadie shouted. "Henry, slow down!"

But there was no answer.

"Well, I'd call that irresponsible!" MacLemore shouted. "Did anyone see where he went? Chino?"

Again, they got no response.

"Damn!" MacLemore cursed. "Now we've lost him, too. We have to try to stick together."

"Where are you, Daddy?" Sadie sounded close to panic.

"I'll just stand still. You two come toward the sound of my voice."

"But where's Lu?"

"I'm here!" he shouted. "I'm coming! Keep talking so I can hear you."

"Sadie!" MacLemore called. "Sadie!"

Lu froze. This time, MacLemore's voice seemed to be coming from directly behind him.

"Where are you?" Lu screamed.

"Daddy!" Sadie sounded like she was about a thousand miles ahead, her voice reaching back to him only because it was being carried on the wind.

"Sadie?" Lu called after her. "Mister MacLemore? Wait for me!"

The wind howled, the trees crackled and moaned, but no human voice penetrated the inky black.

Lu called and called, but there was no answer. At last he gave up. Lu was all alone.

It was the Hell Mouth all over again. Lu felt as though he wanted to cry. But instead, he pressed his face into Crash's neck. "You'll stick with me. Won't you, boy?"

Crash shook out his mane. Lu took that as a "yes."

"Well, I guess we ought to keep moving. Do you know which way?"

Crash took a cautious step forward and stopped.

"Me neither." Lu grabbed on to Crash's lead, just an inch or two below his chin. "I think I last heard Sadie from this direction." They began to walk.

At first, the going was surprisingly good. We must be on the road, Lu thought. But it didn't last. They'd only been walking for about fifteen minutes when Lu wandered directly into a wall of thorns. If he hadn't had his arm stretched out in front of him, he might've stumbled right into the middle of it. That would have been a nightmare. It was hard enough just getting the barbs to let go of his shirt sleeve.

Clearly, this wasn't the way to go. So Lu made a right turn. He felt no thorn bushes that way, and took one cautious step.

It was a good thing he hadn't stepped boldly. His stomach lurched into his mouth as his foot descended through open air. If he hadn't had a good grip on Crash, he'd have fallen for sure.

Somehow, Lu had wandered to the edge of a precipice. In all likelihood, the river was directly below him, though how far below he couldn't guess. Fortunately, that was one question Lu would never have to answer. At the last minute, Crash managed to drag him back from the edge.

"That was close," Lu said, patting his horse on the muzzle. "But at least now we know where we are."

Lu made another right turn, exactly ninety degrees from the direction he'd been facing a moment before, and reached out with his foot. Horribly, he felt the same sickening drop.

"Where should we go?" he asked Crash.

The horse started off in a direction exactly opposite of the way in which Lu thought they ought to be traveling. He didn't complain however, as Crash did manage to avoid falling in the river or striding into the teeth of a briar patch, a feat Lu might not have accomplished if he'd tried all night.

After an hour of further wandering, during which they neither saw nor heard any sign of their missing friends, Lu decided that there was no point in going on. If some old snag wanted to break off in the storm and kill them, so be it. But he wouldn't go searching for it. The snag would darn well have to come to them.

As they stood, shivering and wishing for morning, Lu began to wonder about the darkness that surrounded them. There was something not quite right about it. For one thing, it didn't feel entirely real. Lu had been in his grandfather's basement with the lamps turned off at least a dozen times, and still there'd always been a ghost of light that managed to filter down the stairs. It wasn't enough to see by, maybe, but it was there. Now, here he was outside and the blackness was so complete as to give him the impression of having had his head wrapped up in a burlap sack. It was too much. Even with clouds obscuring the moon and stars, he ought not to feel as though black paint had been slathered over his eyeballs. And that's exactly what he did feel like. Lu rubbed his eyes, but the sensation wouldn't go away. And then he thought about the ghost-riders, passing by over the Lowers' house, and wondered if this darkness couldn't be the result of sorcery.

Lu reached for his saddlebags. He wanted to strike a flame, just for a second, to test his suspicions. But no matter how he dug, he couldn't find a match. And with all that wind, he wasn't entirely sure that there would even be a spark anyway. Then another idea struck him. He could fire his pistol. The muzzle-flash ought to be visible enough.

Lu grabbed his gun, and was about to thumb back the hammer, when he saw something glimmering through the trees. It was bright red, and looked for all the world like a camp-fire. Relieved, Lu jammed his gun back into his holster. He couldn't see how anyone might possibly build a fire in this hurricane, but didn't much care. Henry had mentioned seeing a light just before he'd disappeared, Lu remembered. This must have been what he'd meant.

Tree limbs clawed and scratched at his arms and face as Lu dragged Crash toward the flickering light. He felt certain that his friends would be there, waiting for him. So certain, in fact, that Lu didn't even bother looking at the figure crouched over the fire before bulling his way through a last bit of brush and into the clearing.

"I found you!" Lu said, joyously.

But none of his friends were there. Only one person was sitting by the fire, and he looked less than thrilled at being so rudely interrupted. Lu found himself staring down the barrel of a six-shooter, and the finger on the trigger belonged to a man he'd never seen before.

"Who in the hell are you?" the man asked.

He cut a dashing figure. A shock of blond hair poked out from under what looked to be a brand new Stetson, black to match his high-heeled riding boots and crisscrossing gun-belts. Round his neck was a kerchief, clean and blue as a winter's sky. His cheeks, recently shaven, were like polished alabaster.

"I'm sorry," Lu stammered. "I thought you were somebody else."

The man lowered his pistol a hair, training it on Lu's chest rather than his forehead. "What's your name?" he asked.

"Lu."

"Lu what?"

"Tzu-lu."

"And just who were you looking for out here, Tzu-lu?"

"I lost my friends. We got separated in the storm."

"More Chinks?" He squinted, obviously searching for any sign of a lie.

Lu shook his head. "I'm the only one."

The man lowered his gun another inch. "You out here after the MacLemore gold?"

"Yes, sir."

"Figures." He gestured for Lu to sit down across from him.

A boulder, easily as large as Master K'ung's store, formed a natural barrier on their northern side, breaking the wind enough to allow for the small fire. Even so, the flames were having a hard time sticking to the bits of log and kindling.

"My name's Phillip," the man continued. "But you can call me Phil."

"Pleased to meet you," Lu said, and shuddered.

There was a sort of ruthlessness in Phil's gaze, and in the set of his jaw, that froze Lu clear to the soul. In a way, Phil reminded

Lu of Jack Straw, only much colder. With Jack, the ruthlessness was tempered by a streak of justice. If there was anything decent in Phil, Lu hadn't yet seen it.

"Who are you with?" Phil asked him.

"There are five of us," Lu said. "Henry, Chino, John, Sadie and me."

"Sadie? A girl? Well now, that's a new one. How long you been on the trail?"

"Months. We started in St. Frances."

"Is that right? Didn't think anyone had heard of the MacLemores as far away as that. You hear all the legends?"

"Some of them."

"So, did you bring any Americans to help you kill that old Yankee devil?"

Lu shook his head. "We never heard about that 'til we got to Silver City."

"Who told you?"

"J.D. Lower."

"The Irish blacksmith?" Phil smirked. "It'll serve him right when Mayor Strong finally hangs him. Some folks don't know when to mind their own business."

"He was nice to us," Lu said.

"I'll bet he was. Just like him to befriend a Chink. Who else you got with you? No wait, let me guess. You got a nigger, and a Mexican and . . . a Jew."

"Southerner," Lu corrected him.

"A Reb? Hell, boy. You might as well have given up on this treasure back in Silver City. You haven't got one decent American amongst you."

"We . . . we don't believe in that legend," Lu said.

"You'd best start. 'Cause there ain't nobody to roust that old devil but a genuine American. Hear me? And that's going to be yours truly."

Lu nodded.

"Still, you've come a long way. So I'll tell you what I'm gonna do." As he talked, Phil brought his pistol up so that it pointed at Lu's face again. "I need someone to help me carry my gold. You agree to join up and I'll give you five percent."

"But I have a contract with—"

"Now you've got a new contract. Hear? And you'd best hold to it."

"But my other contract was going to pay me a full share."

"Now you'll get five percent. But cheer up, that's five percent more than you'd have got riding with them mongrels. Speakin' o' which, it's time we got movin'."

"Right now?"

"Don't want your old pards beatin' us to the house, do we? No reason to rile that old Yank 'til we're ready to plug 'im." Phil gestured at Lu with his pistol. "Go on, get ready to ride."

Lu checked Crash's saddle while Phil fetched his own horse. It was an American quarter-horse, a lot like Sadie's old mare Cinnamon, but even bigger.

"You take the lead," Phil said, pistol still trained on Lu.

"What about the storm?"

"I guess it's just about blowed out."

Lu looked around and saw that he was right. A few of the bigger trees were still swaying, but the gusts they'd had earlier were more or less gone. Even the dark clouds were clearing.

"Which way?" Lu asked.

"Head 'round this here boulder. You'll see the road soon enough. After that it's just a short ride to the house."

"You've seen it?"

Phil scoffed. "Only a fool would ride in without scoutin' first."

"What about the mine? Have you seen that?"

"Mine? Pshaw. We're after easy money, boy. I don't aim to do no work. Not more 'n what I can do with my shootin' irons anyway. Now git."

Lu did as he was told. As they passed around the boulder he had half a mind to give Crash a kick, and trust him to outrun Phil's oversize quarter-horse amongst the trees. But Lu felt certain that Phil would shoot him in the back if he did.

They found the road easily enough, and Lu turned what he

thought was north. He must have been right because Phil let him go. For the next hour they rode in total silence.

Eventually Phil must've gotten bored, because all at once he rode up alongside Lu and began asking him questions.

"Tell me 'bout this girl you're ridin' with," he began.

"Sadie?"

"Naw. T'other one."

"But there's only just the one," Lu said.

"Then tell me about her. Jeeminy you're dense."

"What do you want to know?"

"What's she look like?"

Lu gave a full description, beginning with Sadie's dress habits and ending with her tendency to furrow her brow when she was angry, all the while downplaying what he considered her best attributes. The last thing he wanted was for Phil to decide they ought to try to find her.

"Don't sound like much to me," Phil said. "You ever seen her naked?"

Lu shook his head.

"You'd like to though. Am I right?"

"No!"

"Sure you would." Phil guffawed. "Tell you what. Soon as we're finished with this here Yankee, we'll see if we can't find your girl. Who knows? Maybe she'll be so impressed with your five percent that she'll just strip naked for you on the spot."

"Don't talk about her that way," Lu said.

Phil grinned. "What'll you get with your share of the gold?" he asked.

The question reminded Lu of the last conversation he'd had with his friends. Back then it'd seemed like innocent fun, speculating as to how they might spend their money. Now it seemed dirty.

"You still want it, don't you?" Phil asked.

"I guess."

"Say you could have anything—anything in the whole world—what'd it be?"

Lu thought about it. He honestly didn't know. One thing he knew for sure, though. He wanted nothing more to do with Phil.

Suddenly, Lu felt certain that he'd heard that name somewhere else, and not so very long ago. "Phil. Phillip." Had he heard it back in Silver City? At the saloon perhaps? The answer was right on the tip of his tongue. But he was darned if he could find a way to spit it out.

"What brought you all the way out here from St. Frances?" Phil asked him.

"My grandfather made me come."

"Maybe you'd like to be free of your grandfather. Ever wish he was dead?"

"No!" Lu said. "I love my grandfather. I would like to be free, though. Just to do whatever I want. Go wherever I want to go. Be whoever I want to be." Then the answer hit him. "I guess what I want most is . . . I want to be an American."

Phil laughed so hard that Lu thought he might fall off his horse. "Now that's one thing you'll never be," he said at last. "Never in a million years. It's a good wish though. After all, if you was an American, you wouldn't need me."

"I don't need you," Lu muttered under his breath.

"How's that?" Phil asked.

"I said, I guess five percent isn't so bad."

"That's the spirit." Phil gave him a hearty clap on the back. "Knew you'd come around. After all, who wouldn't want five percent of the MacLemore gold?"

The house turned out to be everything Lu had envisioned. It was two stories, with tall dormer windows on the second floor, shutters painted forest green, a wrap-around porch, and a copper roof that glowed orange in the moonlight. There were even flowers in the garden, planted in neat orderly rows.

"Nice, ain't it?" Phil said. "Got to hand it to the Yank. He sure kept the place up."

"What'll we do now?" Lu asked him.

"Y'know, I've been wondering that very thing."

"And?"

"And I reckon you ought to just go right up and knock on the front door."

Lu was shocked. "But he'll kill me for sure."

"Don't worry, I'll be right here. If he makes a move, bang." Phil thrust his pistol toward Lu. "'Sides, you haven't got a choice. If you don't do it, I'll kill you."

"Can I take my gun out at least?" Lu asked.

"I think you'd best leave it set." Phil grinned. "Some folks get nervous when they see a weapon. I'd hate to see you get shot on accident."

"What'll I do if no one answers?"

"You just go right on in. But don't take too long. I'd hate to have to come in after you." He gestured at Lu to get moving.

Seeing no way out, Lu gave Crash a swift kick, and started toward the house. It stood at the center of a mountain meadow, about a hundred yards from the nearest tree. No cover, he realized. Phil could shoot him any time he felt like it.

Lu was almost to the front porch when he got the urge to look behind him. Just as he'd figured, Phil was nowhere to be seen. Someone else had been along that way recently, however. Lu noticed hoof marks on the path. And there were boot prints on the front steps. Whoever made them had smallish feet.

After tying Crash's lead to the porch rail, Lu started up the stairs, careful not to make any noise. He was just about to knock when he heard strange voices from within.

On impulse, Lu reached for his gun. He did so fully expecting to hear a pistol shot from the direction of the trees, followed by an explosion of pain, probably in the back. But nothing happened. If Phil was still watching, and Lu guessed that he must be, he'd decided to allow Lu to draw his gun after all.

Heart racing, Lu reached for the door. He was about to grab the knob, but decided it might really be better to knock. It was lucky he did. The second his knuckles struck the plywood, a gun began firing wildly from inside the cottage.

Shards of door speckled his face and hair as the bullets crashed past him, one of them flying so close he could feel the air sizzling as it spun past his ear.

Instinctively, Lu crouched down. As he did, he brought his

own pistol up, cocking it with his thumb. He didn't bother to aim, just pointed it at the door and fired.

Lu had no time to brace himself against the recoil, and so was thrown backward off the porch. The wind was knocked out of him by the ferocity of his landing, but he still managed to sit up and watch as the door to the cottage, now riddled with a half-dozen tiny holes, and one great enormous one, swung open.

Sadie stepped out, both arms shaking. The look on her face was pure horror. Her tiny revolver was still clutched in her fist, smoke pouring from the barrel. It took her only a moment to spot Lu, lying in the dirt at the bottom of the stairs. And when she did, her eyes went as wide as silver dollars.

Lu watched in mute terror as she raised her gun, aimed it at him for a moment, and then dropped it at her feet.

"My God!" she said. Lu could only just barely hear her over the ringing in his ears. "I nearly shot you. I thought you were . . . But then your bullet . . ." Sadie put a trembling hand over her mouth. "It *is* magic. It *does* tell the truth. I'm sorry, Lu, I—"

She was cut off mid-sentence by another volley of gunshots, this time being fired from somewhere behind the house.

"What's happening?" Sadie asked, grabbing Lu by the hand and dragging him to his feet. "What's going on?"

"It was all lies," Lu tried to say. But he still hadn't recovered from his fall, and so couldn't do much more than mouth the words. And he didn't have time to try again. He knew exactly what was happening, and who was on the other side of that house. If he was going to get there in time, he had to go now.

Wheezing, feeling as though a pair of enormous iron bands were fastened over his lungs, Lu started to run. Sadie chased after him as he raced around to the other side of the cottage. They passed not one, but two horses, tied to the front porch, though Lu barely paid them any mind. Nor did he look at the rotten and broken down porch railing, the weathered walls and peeling paint, or the grave stones set in their orderly rows—just as the flowers had *seemed* to be, only moments before. Lu had to hurry. He *knew* what was coming.

They bounded around the side of the cottage, arriving just in time to see Henry, sitting tall astride his military charger, galloping down a narrow pathway. His rifle was cocked and ready. Lu also saw Chino, crouched behind the walls of a broken-down old outhouse, a pistol in either fist. They were ready for each other, Lu understood. Prepared to gun each other into oblivion. Another moment and one of them, maybe both, would be blasted to bits. He could think of only one way to stop it. The sorcery had to be broken, the lies dispelled. He had to show his friends the truth.

Lu lifted his pistol once more, aiming at a spot directly between both men, and squeezed the trigger.

It all happened so fast that Lu didn't even manage to straighten his elbow before the recoil took over. His pistol kicked straight backward, in spite of his hand being wrapped around the grip, and struck him square in the forehead.

The last thing Lu saw, as he lay face up on the barren field, was a flash of orange hell-fire, as of a shooting star lancing across the night sky.

"Ghost-riders," he thought, as the demons disappeared over the mountains. "Phillip Traum."

Then Lu closed his eyes, and knew nothing more until sunup.

CHAPTER 20

A GOOD LONG SOAK

LU FELT SOMETHING wet plop down on his forehead.

"Wake up now, son. It's time for you to get up."

"Henry?" Lu opened his eyes to see the face of his friend, surrounded by a fantastic blue sky. "I don't want to shoot the rifle today, Henry. I'm tired. And my head hurts."

"Don't you go back to sleep on me." With one arm, Henry lifted Lu into a sitting position. "I know it's hard, but you've got to try and stay awake."

Lu reached up to discover a cool rag had been placed over his forehead. "What happened, Henry?"

"That pistol of yours, that's what. Got you right above the eyebrow. Dug a trench near to the bone. It'll scar, I'm afraid. Won't look too bad, though. A man can't go through life without a few scars."

"Is Chino all right? And Sadie?"

"Both fine, thanks to you."

"What about Mr. MacLemore?"

The look on Henry's face was unlike any Lu had yet seen.

"Is he dead?" Lu asked.

"Not yet."

"But he's hurt."

"Shot in the stomach."

"Where is he?"

"Sadie and Chino carried him into the house. He's in his old room."

"Can we see him?"

Henry nodded.

With his friend's help, Lu managed to stand up and make the short walk around to the front door. His head was throbbing so hard that he found it difficult to maintain any sort of balance. Henry held his hand the whole way.

The inside of the house was in even worse shape than the exterior. Mold grew on the remains of an old kitchen table. Whole chunks of flooring had been ripped up. Even the stove had been smashed to bits and scattered. Worst of all was the blood. A trail of it led from the front door, across the room, and up the stairs.

MacLemore had been placed in one of the second floor bedrooms, on what remained of an old gray mattress. Generous portions of the ticking had been torn out and strung across the floor, along with the broken remains of a wood bed-frame. Sadie sat in the corner, watching her father's chest rise and fall. There were lines of dirt running down both of her cheeks, but she wasn't crying now.

"How is he?" Henry asked.

"Asleep," Sadie said.

Lu stumbled toward the mattress, still clutching the damp cloth to his forehead. When he saw what remained of Mr. MacLemore, he nearly passed out. The man's face was as pale and yellow as an old boiled shirt. Blood poured from a bullet wound in his gut, the color of tar. Lu was amazed that he'd lived this long. He didn't think a person had that much blood in them.

"Is there anything we can do?" he asked.

Henry shook his head. "The bullet went through his liver," he explained. "There's nothing anyone could do."

"Where's Chino?"

"Scouring the woods. He's hoping to find some sign of our Yankee."

"Phillip Traum."

Henry and Sadie both started.

"That's his name," Lu said. "Same as it was in the notebook Jack gave us. We should have remembered it better."

"Shut up," Sadie growled. "Just shut up about your damned notebook."

"What's all this?" MacLemore whispered. "No reason to be mean to the boy."

"Daddy?" Sadie rushed to his bedside. "Oh Daddy, I'm so sorry. We never should have got separated in the woods."

"Not your fault. No one's fault but Traum's." MacLemore coughed. "He made Chino and me think we were enemies. I'd have sworn Chino was the very Yankee we were after. Even took a shot at him." He chuckled. "Chino was too fast for me . . . Too fast for your old man."

"What exactly happened out there?" Henry asked him.

"Not long after I lost y'all, I came across a fine upstanding southern boy. Good manners. Said his name was Phillip." MacLemore took a deep breath. "He told me he knew where the Yankee was hiding, even offered to guide me to the house."

He paused to let out a long, chest rattling cough.

"You don't have to say any more," Sadie whispered. "Save your strength."

"I need to." MacLemore smiled feebly. "It doesn't really hurt. I just can't seem to catch my breath."

"Take your time," Henry said.

MacLemore continued—"So Traum asked me what I wanted with the Yankee, and I said I wanted to shoot him. More than anything in the world I wanted to get a shot at that Yankee." He patted Sadie on the knee. "It was really for your mother all the time, you know."

"I know it, Daddy. I know it."

"I wish you could have known her," MacLemore said.

Tears rolled down Sadie's cheeks.

"You'd have loved your mother. And she'd have loved you."

"But I'm not womanly," Sadie said. "I don't make clothes or like opera."

"She wouldn't have cared. Your mother was a strong woman. Had to be, living all the way out here with me." MacLemore took his daughter's hand. Lu could tell he was trying to squeeze it, but his muscles didn't seem to have the strength. "Nothing wrong with a woman knowing what she wants from life," he continued. "I wouldn't change a thing about you for all the world."

Sadie couldn't hold back a moment longer. She put her face against her father's chest and bawled. Lu felt tears beginning to well up in his own eyes, and quickly wiped them away. Even Henry was moved. He grabbed Lu by the forearm and gently pulled him toward the door. "Let's leave them be," he whispered.

They went downstairs to the front porch, where they sat eating Pearl Lower's vegetables and watching the surrounding trees for any sign of Chino. Lu's head was beginning to feel better.

"So what did you see out there?" Lu asked Henry.

"In the forest?" Henry picked up a snap pea and popped open the husk. "Well, I saw a sort of bright red light, like from a campfire. I thought you were all right behind me, so I went for it. But when I reached the clearing, I was all alone." He dropped the peas into his mouth and flung the husk away. "There was an old man sitting beside the fire. He said he was a preacher, heading for San Pablo."

"Phillip Traum."

Henry nodded. "I told him we were after this Yankee, and he said he'd pray for our safety. I told him he ought not to travel in such a place by himself, and he asked if I wouldn't help him cross the river. So, I rode him across. All the time he's asking about my hopes and dreams. He seemed like a kindly old preacher, knew his Bible forward and back. I told him how I'd like to start my own church. He said that sounded fine, and tells me he hopes I rid the world of this Yankee once and for all.

"Next thing I know, I'm riding down a back road, headed toward an old house. There's a blond-haired devil, pistol drawn and firing on you, Chino, and Sadie. I swear I could hear you calling to me for help. So I pulled out my rifle. I had him in my sights, ready to shoot, when all of a sudden I hear the most awful explosion, and fear unlike anything I ever knew goes all through me." He looked at Lu. "It was like seeing my every sin, hearing my every petty thought, all at once. It was so terrible I dropped my gun. Lucky that I did, too. Because when I looked up again, I saw it wasn't a blond man hiding out behind that old outhouse, but Chino. And him looking near as scared as me."

"How is Chino?" Lu asked.

"Furious. With himself as much as anything else."

"But it wasn't his fault. There was some kind of sorcery." Lu shook his head. "We should've known when we first heard that strange music. Remember how we all heard it different?"

"Chino knows we were duped, but I'm not sure that does him much good. If he could get his hands on Phillip Traum it might help him some, but . . ." Henry shrugged.

"He won't find Traum out there," Lu said. Firing that bullet yesterday had given him a number of insights into Traum's methods. "If you want to know the truth," Lu continued, "Traum never really was here. No one was. This was just a sort of big elaborate trap. MacLemore's gold was the bait."

"And just how do you know all that?"

Lu was about to answer when he noticed movement from near the tree line. "Look, there's Chino," he said.

Chino had just emerged from the forest. He was on foot, leading his tall mare. The expression on his face was so tired, so full of guilt, Lu thought he looked at least ten years older.

"Find anything?" Henry asked him.

"Not a damn thing. I seen Lu's tracks. And Sadie's. I even found where you crossed the river. But no Traum. It's just as though he was never there at all." Chino tied his horse to the porch rail between Crash and Carrot, and then sat down next to Lu. "How are you, chico?"

"Pretty good."

Chino let out a long sigh. It sounded almost as if he'd been holding his breath.

They sat a while in stony silence, wondering what they ought to do next, or if they ought to do anything at all, when all at once the door behind them swung open and Sadie stumbled out.

"How's your father?" Chino asked her.

Quietly, but clearly, she said, "We need to dig a grave."

There were picks, shovels, and other mining implements in a little shed attached to the main house. Most had long since gone to rust, but a few were strong enough for an hour or two of work.

They chose a spot in the graveyard, just a few steps from the front door of the cabin. Upon inspection, they discovered that the headstones weren't stone at all, just wood, weathered until it had turned a dull gray. Not one of them had a name attached, though most had a winged skull carved into the face. Henry called it a "death's head," and said they were a common feature on grave-stones back east. Lu thought they were gruesome, and a bit scary. Into one eye socket of each skull had been placed a tiny speck of gold-dust, the only portion of the supposedly vast MacLemore horde these former adventurers would ever get. The idea was enough to make Lu shudder.

There were only two headstones without skulls. They stood side by side, one half-again larger than the other, and both of them blank. Sadie stared at them a long time, then declared that her father's grave should be dug between.

The ground was hard and rocky, making for sweaty work. But no one complained. Henry and Chino both took off their shirts. Lu didn't, mostly out of a desire to keep Sadie company. By noon they'd dug a hole four feet deep, and by unspoken con-sensus decided that would be sufficient.

Sadie said she'd like to wash her face in the river. While she was gone, Henry, Chino and Lu, wrapped her father's body up in his bedroll, leaving only his face uncovered, and carried it down to the grave. Chino filled MacLemore's water-skin with some of the mattress ticking from the second floor, and then propped it under his head for a pillow. Lu went into the woods nearest the house and picked as many wild daisies as he could find. Henry built a fire in the fireplace, and began boiling water in a cook-pot he'd found amongst the litter in the kitchen. By the time Sadie returned, all of an hour later, they had her father laid out, looking as peaceful as they could get him, and mugs of hot vegetable soup for lunch.

They sat on the front porch, chatting about nothing in par-ticular, as the sun made its lazy way across the sky. None of the men pressured her, and Sadie seemed to appreciate it. Finally, when the afternoon had faded into evening, and a sunset the color of roses hung in the notches between the surrounding mountains, Sadie said it was time.

"Would you say a word?" she asked Henry.

He nodded solemnly. From memory, he recited:

I will lift up mine eyes to the mountains,
Whence comes the source of my salvation.
My help comes from the Lord,
Who made heaven and earth.
May He save you from stumbling.
May He, your guardian, never slumber.
The Lord is your keeper, your shade,
He stands strong upon your right hand.
By day, the sun shall not smite you,
Nor the moon by night.
The Lord shall preserve you from evil.
He shall preserve your soul.
The Lord guards your comings and goings,
Both today, and forever more.

Henry paused, gazed for a moment up at the sunset, and the mountains upon which it lay, and then bowed his head. "May the Lord do as much for us all," he prayed. "Amen."

Sadie picked up a fistful of dirt. She reached out, and was about to drop it into her father's grave, but stopped. "Where's Daddy's guitar?" she asked.

"It's in the house," Lu said. "We can bury it with him if you want."

She thought about it for a moment, and then tossed her fistful of dirt into the grave. Henry immediately did the same, and Lu followed suit. When it was Chino's turn, Sadie grabbed his arm.

"Will you help me to cover him up?" she asked.

"Me?"

"You."

Chino picked up a fistful of soil from the pile and tossed it in. Then he took up one of the shovels and began filling the hole in earnest. Sadie grabbed another of the shovels and helped.

"Let's go inside," Henry said to Lu.

Sadie joined them soon after. Together, the three of them worked to set right all the damage that had been done to the cottage over the years. It seemed the best way to honor the spirit of their friend, to set his house to rights. They hauled the trash out behind the shed, replaced the ripped up floor boards, and scrubbed the mildew, blood and mold from the furniture and floors. There were a few salvageable items scattered amidst the wreckage—a carton of beeswax candles, a corncob pipe, and a silver thimble—all of which Sadie placed carefully into her saddlebags. It was past midnight before they'd finished, but the little cabin actually began to seem livable once more. Henry built a fire in the fireplace, and made a pot of coffee with grounds Pearl Lower had sent them. It was the first they'd had in months. Lu could hardly stand to drink it, the taste was so rich and full.

Finally, when they could think of nothing more to do or say to each other, they spread their blankets on the floor.

"What do you think Chino's doing out there all by himself?" Lu asked, as he crawled under his. "Not still looking for Phillip Traum?"

"Probably just keeping an eye on things," Henry said. "Making sure we're safe."

"You think he'll ever come inside?"

"He will when he's ready," Sadie replied.

The next morning, they came outside to find Chino sound asleep on the front porch. He had a hammer in one hand and a rusty chisel in the other. The two blank headstones were blank no longer. On the larger one was carved a flower, a wild daisy just like those Lu had picked the afternoon before. And beside the daisy was a guitar. On the other, smaller headstone, Chino had carved a sun, half-risen—or half-set, Lu couldn't tell which—over a mountain exactly like the one that rose up behind the MacLemores' cottage. Lu was amazed at the skill of the carvings.

Sadie woke Chino with a bear hug. Neither said a word about the epitaphs Chino had chosen. It wasn't necessary.

They ate the rest of the vegetable soup for breakfast, and then Chino said he was going back to the woods. He still hoped to find some sign of the missing Phillip Traum. Henry decided to go with him. As they saddled their horses, Sadie suggested that they might also go up to the mine. "Who knows? Maybe Traum's up there."

She told them where she guessed the opening was, and the two men rode off. Lu and Sadie stood on the porch, watching as their friends disappeared amidst the trees.

"There's no chance that they'll find anything," Sadie said. "Is there?"

Lu shook his head. "None."

"Too bad." Sadie bit her lower lip. "And they'll be gone for hours."

"What should I do?" Lu asked her.

"Follow me."

Sadie led him back into the house. "I want to show you something," she said. She bent down under the staircase and pulled up a trap door. Lu had noticed it earlier, while cleaning, and had even lifted it to look inside. A ladder went down into a deep cellar, smelling of earth. At the time, Lu had guessed there was probably nothing down there but more rubbish, and so did-n't bother to investigate. Sadie seemed to have other ideas.

She took a candle from her pocket, lit it with a match, and held it down inside the tunnel. Squinting, Lu could just barely make out the floor. As he'd figured, it was covered in trash.

"You want to clean up down there?" he asked.

"Maybe, but not right this minute." Sadie swung one foot down into the tunnel. A moment later she'd disappeared down the ladder. "Well?" she called up at Lu. "Are you comin' or not?"

Lu scrambled down the ladder as fast as he could.

"This was my mother's root cellar," Sadie explained. She waved the candle back and forth. Treasure-hunters had ran-sacked it thoroughly, though amazingly there remained one unbroken jar of what appeared to be pickled beets. There was also a door leading out of the room. Sadie turned the knob and the door swung open.

Lu followed her down the tunnel beyond. It was narrow, and they had to crouch to avoid hitting their heads on the support beams, but it did have a nice pine floor. In fact, so had the cellar. That certainly seemed odd.

"What is this?" Lu asked.

"When they were building the cabin, Daddy found a hot spring. Mother loved to soak in the tub, so he built her a bathhouse. This was how she went back and forth."

The tunnel ended on a smallish room. Never having seen a ladies' bathhouse before, Lu had no way to judge whether it was larger or smaller than normal. It was certainly luxuriant, in a strange, outlandish sort of way. To the left of the passage, as they came in, was a long wooden bench. And over that was a series of hooks. The rest of the room was taken up by the tub, which had been carved from a single mammoth sheet of dark gray stone, and then sunk so that only a couple of inches extended above the floor. A pipe jutted out of the rear wall. It had a tap on the end, so that a person could shut off the flow when the tub was full. Sadie reached over and turned it on. Immediately, steaming water began to flow into the tub and down the drain.

"Neat," Lu said.

Sadie sat down on the bench and began pulling off her boots.

"What are you doing?" Lu asked her.

"Help me clean it out."

Lu kicked his own boots into the corner, and then the two of them got down inside the tub and began swishing the water all around, washing away years of collected dust. When they were done, Lu climbed out and put his boots on. Sadie turned off the water, but stood in the tub, thinking.

"What's wrong?" Lu asked her.

"Daddy's last words to me were about the gold."

"Really?" Lu hadn't entirely forgotten about the gold, but he hadn't felt comfortable mentioning it either. It would come up when Sadie was ready, he figured. "So what's that got to do with being down here?" he asked.

"He said the gold was in Mama's tub, and told me to bring you." Sadie frowned. "But there ain't nothin' down here. Some treasure hunter must've found it after all."

"What exactly did your father say?"

"He was pretty out of it," Sadie admitted. "His breath was comin' so hard. But I could see he wanted to tell me somethin', so I leaned down. And he whispered, 'The gold is in your mother's bath.' I asked him what he meant, but he started in coughing and couldn't say. The last words he managed to get out were, 'Take Lu.'"

"Strange," Lu said.

"Yeah."

They stood looking at each other, neither saying a word. Finally, Lu had a thought. "What kind of rock is this tub made of?"

Sadie felt the rim and shrugged. "Granite, I guess."

"Is there anything shiny in it?" he asked. "Some kind of metal maybe?"

"I guess it's sort of shiny down near the bottom. But that's probably just the water."

"Maybe we ought to fill it up," Lu suggested.

They spent the next few minutes searching the room for anything they might use as a stopper. At last, Sadie found the actual stopper. It had a piece of rope tied through a loop at the top, and was dangling from a hook on the back of the bench. She pushed it down into the drain, twisting it until it seemed solid, and then turned the water back on. By the time there was three inches in the bottom of the tub, the whole room was filled with steam.

"Anything happening?" Lu asked.

Sadie shook her head.

"Well, I'm all out of ideas," Lu said. "Maybe you're just supposed to take a bath."

"Maybe." Sadie set the candle down on the arm of the bench. She frowned. "I can't exactly bathe with you here, but I guess I could soak my feet."

She rolled up her pants until the better part of both legs were visible, from the middle of the thigh down. "Here now, get your shoes off," she said to Lu, as she lowered her feet into the steaming water. "You may as well join me."

"Really?"

"Sure. It's plenty warm. Feel." She grabbed up a handful of water and flung it at him, hitting him in the chest.

"Knock it off."

Sadie laughed.

Lu sat down on the bench and began unlacing his boots. He couldn't take his eyes off Sadie's legs. They were long, white, and shapely. "See anything yet?" he asked. "Any sign of the gold?"

Sadie leaned down to inspect the sides of the tub. "Nope. Still nothing."

Lu rolled up his pants until both legs were exposed to the knee. Suddenly, he was shaking so hard he thought he might topple off the bench.

"What's wrong with you?" Sadie asked.

"Nothing."

Lu felt ridiculous as he scooted to the edge of the tub. His legs were hideously bony, and sparse black hairs grew out of his shins. As he sat down beside Sadie, the naked skin of their lower legs happened to rub together for an instant. Lu winced. He hoped she hadn't noticed, but couldn't see how such a thing was even remotely possible. To Lu, Sadie's leg felt as smooth and soft as . . . There was nothing to compare it with. He might have said they were as soft as Crash's muzzle, except that they felt utterly hairless.

For the next couple of minutes, neither of them spoke. Finally, Sadie broke the ice. "I sure wish we'd find that gold, don't you?"

Lu nodded.

"What's wrong?" Sadie asked again.

"I . . . I just never saw so much of your legs before."

Sadie scoffed. "You mean in all these months you never snuck a peek?"

Lu shook his head. "Not one. Did you?"

"One or two."

"When?"

"While you were bathing with Joseph and his people mostly."

"Which day?"

"Every day."

This was a revelation. Lu blushed so hard he felt sure his face must glow. It was hard to believe a girl would be interested in such things. Everything he thought he knew suddenly felt blown apart, like so many New Year's firecrackers.

"You spied on me?" he asked her.

"And others."

"Dang."

"Are you mad?" Sadie playfully elbowed Lu in the ribs, making him jump.

"I just wish I'd known."

"Why?"

"Well . . . I would've tried harder to spy on you, too."

Sadie laughed.

They sat there, chatting about various bits and pieces of foolishness until their feet were wrinkled beyond recognition. Lu couldn't remember when he'd had such a nice time. Sadie appeared to feel the same.

At last, by mutual agreement, they decided that they'd had enough. It'd been a good long soak, and now it was time to go back upstairs. Grabbing the rope with her toes, Sadie pulled the stopper. Slowly, the water began to sink away.

They had nothing to dry off with, so they just sat on the edge of the tub, letting their legs air-dry for a few minutes before rolling their pants back down and pulling on their boots.

"Do you think we should do this again?" Sadie asked, as the water sunk from around their toes. "It was kind of fun."

"Yeah, it was." Lu's self-consciousness was already starting to come back. "Do you want to?"

"If you want."

Lu elbowed Sadie in the ribs. "Maybe tomorrow," he said. "If Henry and Chino go off somewhere again."

"Yeah, all right."

"Who knows, maybe they'll want to look for the gold." Even as the words left his mouth, Lu was reminded of Sadie's father. What could he have meant, sending Sadie and he down here? There was no gold in this tub.

"Boy, this drain is loud," Sadie said. "Sounds like a waterfall. You'd think the water was going down a thousand feet."

Lu listened. She was right, it *was* loud. Then a new thought struck him. "Where *is* the water going?" he asked.

They both leaned down to listen as the last drops of bathwater swirled away. When it was all gone, Lu grabbed their candle and handed it to Sadie. "Here. Try looking down the drain hole," he said.

Sadie did, and gasped. "My God," she said. "It must go down twenty-five feet. What in the world?" Then she stopped. They looked at each other, smiles spread across their faces. "So that's what he meant."

"Let's go find Henry and Chino," Lu said.

They were just pulling on their boots when a realization stung Lu in the heart.

"We'll have to blow it up," he said. "That's why your father told you to bring me. That's why he hired someone familiar with explosives. He knew right from the start."

"What do you mean?"

Lu pointed at the tub. "There's no way to dig it out. I'll have to blow it up."

"Mama's bath," Sadie said, and frowned. "No more soaking our feet."

"Nope."

Sadie stared down at the tub. "But maybe we can do it again somewhere else," she said. "You think?"

"Sure." But Lu knew such a set-up would only come once in a lifetime. Even if they found a great big tub like this somewhere else, they'd never be able to sit beside it together. Out in the world, Sadie was a white woman, and Lu Chinese. Even if their enjoyment of each other was completely innocent, society wasn't likely to see it that way. Judging by the expression on her face, Sadie was having the exact same thoughts.

"Absolutely," Lu said. "We'll do it lots more times."

"How does that look?" Chino asked.

He held the drill bit while Henry swung the hammer. After having spent the whole morning engaged in what amounted to a wild goose chase, both men seemed to enjoy the work. It'd taken them the better part of the afternoon, but eventually they'd managed to pound a hole through the hard stone tub. Actually they'd drilled two, one hole almost touching the other. Lu only wanted to do this once, and so had decided to use both charges at the same time.

"Looks all right to me," he said, cutting two extra long bits of fuse and snaking them down the holes. As soon as he had the fuses placed to his satisfaction, Lu poured in the blasting powder. "Got that sand?"

Sadie brought him the cook-pot in which Henry had made vegetable soup the night before. They'd only found one old bucket in the shed, and it had a hole rusted clear through the bottom.

"The sand's got rocks in it," Sadie said. "But I can sift them out if you want."

"Don't bother." Lu piled the sand into the holes, packing it down with the back of the drill bit. When he was done, he looked at his friends. "Guess you three ought to go outside now."

"Here." Henry set one of their candles down beside the tub. "But for heaven's sake, be careful."

"Just make sure you leave the door open at the end of the tunnel, and that someone holds the trap door for me to climb out."

When all three of them were safely clear of the cellar, he lit the fuse.

Lu ran as fast as his feet would carry him. He stumbled once, halfway up the ladder, but Chino reached down, grabbed him by the wrists and hauled him out. They were racing down the front steps when they heard the explosion, and felt the whole earth shake. Timbers throughout the cabin creaked. Smoke gushed up through the trapdoor, filling the main floor, and even drifting upstairs. Thankfully, the walls and roof remained both strong and upright, and nothing caught fire.

Sadie and Henry, sitting on a pair of gravestones in the yard, waved them over.

"You blew up half the meadow," Henry said.

Indeed, an enormous pit had been opened, just a few yards beyond the cabin. The hole was easily ten feet across, and all of fifteen feet deep. Shards of the wonderful granite bathtub littered the bottom, as did the splintered remains of the pine floorboards and ceiling supports. The tunnel to the house had partially caved in.

"Anybody see any gold down there?" Chino asked.

"Not yet," Lu said. "But we will."

It took them only an hour to haul the treasure up, now that they'd found it. Lu and Sadie, being the only ones slender enough to pass through the mouth of the drain tunnel, played a quick game of rock-paper-scissors to decide who got to do the honors. Sadie won two times out of three, and they lowered her in.

At the bottom she found a stone ledge with five water-skins stacked atop it, each brim-full of gold dust and weighing more than forty pounds. One by one she tied the skins to the end of the rope, and Henry, Lu, and Chino hauled them up.

They were just snaking the rope back into the pit to haul out Sadie herself, when she said she'd found something else. Quick as they could, the men dragged it to the surface.

It turned out to be an old trunk. They waited until Sadie was topside, and then opened it up.

Inside, along with a china-doll, some ladies' dress combs, a tin-type portrait of a young couple sitting on a porch swing, and an empty perfume bottle, they found a dress and a pair of matching shoes. They also discovered, at the very bottom, an old notebook. The cover had been doodled over with butterflies, flowers, and other bits of girlish malarkey. Sadie opened it up, read the first page to herself, and then placed it gingerly back in the trunk.

Lu didn't ask her what was inside, nor did Henry or Chino. From the look in her eyes, such questions were absolutely unnecessary. A man would have to be a fool not to know what was in that book, and an even bigger fool to ask.

"I guess we may as well haul this all back to the house," Henry said.

Lu picked up one of the gold-filled water-skins, Henry and Chino each took two, and Sadie carried the trunk. It was the lightest thing they had, and the men figured she would want to carry that treasure herself.

They were right.

CHAPTER 21

INNOCENTS LOST

LU WOKE THE NEXT MORNING to find Sadie gone. Her blanket was balled up in its usual spot, but she was nowhere to be seen.

Henry was crouched in front of the fireplace, stirring a pot of strong coffee. Chino was still fast asleep.

"Where is she?" Lu whispered.

Henry pointed at the door.

Lu went to the window and peered out. Sadie was sitting on her father's grave talking a mile a minute, but Lu couldn't hear what she said. All four horses were groomed, saddled, and tied to the porch rail. Lucky too. Strangely, the mule was wearing Chino's old army saddle.

"Come away from there," Henry said. "Leave the girl alone."

Lu sat down on the floor beside Henry. The heat rising from the fire felt good. Mornings in the high mountains were cool, even in late summer.

"Any idea what month this is?" Lu asked.

"Must be September," Henry said.

"Do you think the kids in St. Frances are at school?"

"Unless it's Saturday or Sunday. I can't tell you that."

"Sadie saddled our horses. Do you think that means she's ready to leave?"

"I'm sure she'll tell us when she's ready."

Chino got up a few minutes later. "Where's Sadie?" he asked.

Henry handed him a cup of coffee. "She's talking to her father."

"Maybe I ought to take her a cup."

"Not just yet."

Sadie came in soon after. She plunked herself down by the fire and stretched her hands to the heat. "What's for breakfast?" she asked.

"Coffee," Henry said.

"Nothin' else?"

"Vegetables, if you want 'em."

Sadie shook her head. "I'm sick of vegetables. Let's get out of here."

They packed up the remaining provisions, placed the five sacks of gold dust into the bottom of Sadie's trunk, and hauled it all outside. Chino and Henry shouldered the heavy trunk up and onto Lucky's saddle, and Sadie strapped it down tight. They had no more need of a sledgehammer or drill bit, so Lu tossed them in the shed.

"Well," Chino said, "I guess that about does it."

"There's just one more thing," Sadie said. "I want you to have Daddy's saddle."

Chino was taken aback. "I couldn't."

"What'll I do with an extra saddle? And you need something better 'n that old army thing you've been ridin'."

She didn't wait to hear his thanks before turning to address Lu.

"And I want you to take his guitar." Lu tried to protest, but Sadie wouldn't listen. "You enjoyed his playin' more than any of us. If you'd learn to strum a bit, I know he'd be honored."

"I'll try," Lu promised.

"Good enough."

Finally, Sadie turned to Henry. "I'd like to give you Daddy's boots. I did some lookin' while you were asleep, and I reckon they might fit." She took the boots from her saddle bags and handed them to Henry. They were dusty and scuffed, no longer the ebony mirrors Lu had first observed back in the doorway of the Stars and Bars in St. Frances, but they were still among the finest pieces of leather he'd ever seen.

"Daddy always liked a man that cared for his shoes," Sadie said.

Henry sat down on the porch, kicked off his old boots and pulled on the new. "Fit like they were made for me," he said. "Soft as butter."

Sadie beamed.

They rode into Silver City just after noon the following day, and went directly to the house of Pearl and J.D. Lower. Their girls, Hazel and Claire, were sitting on the front porch, shucking corn. As soon as they saw who was coming, they screamed for their mother and father to "come out front" and "see who's here." The noise they made was high-pitched enough to wake sleeping dogs the world over. Their mother burst through the front door a moment later, no doubt wondering who'd got murdered. J.D. came loping around the side of the house, still wearing his blacksmith's apron.

"We're back!" Sadie said. "And I reckon we'll repay that loan now."

"John?" Pearl called. "Are you there, John MacLemore? Someone has come lookin' for you."

"Who is it?" Sadie asked.

But before Pearl could answer, a man strode through the open door behind her, his spurs jangling on the wood porch.

"I hear you folks have had some adventures," Jack Straw said.

He looked even more ragged and woebegone than Lu remembered. His cheeks were sallow and unshaven, his mustache long and greasy. The skin on his hands was chapped and blistered. Even his coat, Jack's lone piece of decent clothing, was damaged almost beyond repair. There was a bullet-hole in the right breast, and the cuffs of both sleeves had been scorched black. He was even missing a few brass buttons.

"Are you all right?" Lu asked him.

"Fine," Jack said. "Some Confederates were trying to sneak across the border. We told them they couldn't, and they took it amiss." He grinned. "Don't worry, they went back eventually, one way or another."

"Daddy was killed," Sadie said.

"Lord!" Pearl Lower moaned. J.D. hugged her to his chest.

"How'd it happen?" Jack asked.

For the next three hours they talked, first in the front yard, and then over meatloaf sandwiches Hazel and Claire served in the garden. Sadie told every last detail of their ride across the Lago del Fuego, even reciting whole conversations word for word. When she got tired, Henry took over. He told Jack all about their encounter with the Saints, and their subsequent flight from the Sons of Dan. Lu told about the hanging they'd witnessed in Silver City, and how he and MacLemore had purchased blasting powder and tools. They left it up to Chino to describe the storm, their separation, and MacLemore's death. Lu could see it pained him, but Chino left nothing out. Sadie finished by explaining how they'd buried her father and discovered the gold under her mother's tub.

When the story was all told, Jack took a cigarette from his breast pocket and lit it with a match. "So what's your plan now?" he asked.

"I can't speak for the others," Chino replied. "But as for me, I aim to hunt Phillip Traum to the ends of the earth."

"You can speak for me," Henry said.

"And me." Sadie glowered so terribly that Lu could barely stand to look at her.

"Oh, I don't think you'll have to go that far," Jack said. "Will they, Lu?"

Lu shook his head. "Traum is in the saloon. Right where he's been this whole time."

The sun was setting as they rode into town, passing between the boarded up store-fronts and abandoned houses.

It felt strange, Lu thought, and a bit spooky, not to have his bedroll with him, or his saddlebags. Everything they'd hauled across country was now hidden, right along with Sadie's trunk, in the crawlspace beneath Pearl Lower's pantry. They'd only brought one type of equipment on this adventure—guns.

It was quiet in Silver City, the streets all but deserted. Even the saloon was wrapped in a ghostly hush. The usual plink and plunk of the barroom piano was conspicuously absent, as was the chatter and hum of half-drunken voices.

A pair of saloon girls were rifling through the saddlebags of a half-starved, sway-backed old plug, tied to a hitching-rail across the street from the saloon. It was a poor fortune they had to pick through, judging by the quality of items Lu saw lying in the mud. An empty whiskey bottle, a broken hairbrush, some rusty shell-casings for a scattergun Lu suspected had been pawned long since, and bag after bag of worthless gray rocks. Lu wouldn't have given a penny for the whole lot. Even so, the saloon girls didn't quit digging until they'd turned both saddlebags inside out. Finally, empty-handed and grumbling, they led the horse down the street and through the open doors of what had once been a livery stable. Lu wondered what they planned to do with it.

"We've seen all this before," Henry remarked. "Right after they hung Sawyer."

Sure enough, a fresh body was dangling from the gallows next door to the saloon. It was Mike Dunleavy, the very same young prospector they'd met after the previous hanging. A third saloon girl, the most slovenly of the bunch, was going through the hanged man's pockets. She'd discovered the mica samples from his claim, but apparently didn't think nearly as much of them as Mike Dunleavy had. The glassy stones littered the ground beneath his still swinging feet.

"I can't stand this," Chino said, climbing down from his mare. He strode over to the gallows and marched up the steps. When he'd reached the top, he pulled out his knife and began sawing at the noose.

"And just what in the hell do you think you're doin'?" the saloon girl asked. "This here's an *Irish*man. Mayor don't like 'em cut down for at least a day and a night."

"You'd best get out of the way," Chino warned.

The girl stepped aside as the body fell.

"That's your death!" she shouted. "Mayor Strong is going to hear about this, just you bet. And I'll tell him who did it, too. I

guess he'll use one of you as a replacement. You damned turds!"
She finished with an obscene gesture, and then sprinted off
toward the front of the saloon.

"Strong is liable to be upset," Henry said.

"Yep," Jack agreed. "He'll be fightin' mad all right."

"So let's go meet him," Sadie suggested.

Quick as they could, they tied their horses, all but Jack's
appaloosa, to a hitching rail in front of the boarded up dry goods
emporium. Henry said they'd be out of danger there, and Lu
hoped he was right. That done, Jack told Chino and Henry to get
inside the Grange Hall, directly across the street from the tavern,
and to be ready for action.

Jack stationed Sadie at the southern corner of the saloon.
There were no windows on that side of the building, which meant
that no one was liable to get the drop on her from behind. And
by peeking around, she could easily see anyone that might try to
come out the front door.

Lu was told to crouch down behind a watering trough,
directly in front of Franklin Moss's hardware store. From there he
could look over the top of the trough or around either side, and
so keep a watch over everything that happened. It also gave him
a good vantage point from which to use his revolver, when the
time came.

Jack remained in the street, seated atop his appaloosa.

They waited.

From his hiding spot, Lu watched as Sadie reached into her
jacket pockets, lifting out both her own tiny revolver and her
father's somewhat larger model. Her hands shook violently. Lu
could see her trembling even from twenty yards away. But his
hands weren't doing much better. He nearly dropped his pistol
as he lifted it from his holster, and holding it steady was next
to impossible. Lu tried aiming at the saloon doors, but for
some reason the tip of his gun dipped and bounced with every
breath he took.

He was scared. Terrified.

Lu had yet to hit anything with his strange brass revolver, and
he didn't guess he'd fare much better this time unless he figured

out some way of controlling his nerves. Lu tried to breathe deeply and relax, as Henry had taught him, but it was no use. The pistol seemed to have a will of its own. He squeezed the grip as hard as he could, but that just made the jumping worse.

Finally, after what seemed hours, the saloon doors swung wide and Mayor Strong, dressed in his usual three-piece suit, strutted out. His boot heels echoed on the board sidewalk.

"Who cut down the Irishman?" Strong roared. He had a pistol in his hand, the largest Lu had ever seen, and looked more than ready to use it.

"I did!" Chino called through the open door of the Grange.

"What did you want to do that for?"

"Maybe he figured it'd make you mad," Jack said.

Strong looked at the gunfighter and sneered.

Jack was the only one of them who had yet to draw his weapons. In fact, he wasn't even sitting up in the saddle. He sort of slouched with one elbow resting on the horn. Lu thought he looked bored, but guessed that must just be playacting.

"Who are you?" Strong asked.

"You know me," Jack said. "Know me all too well, I'd say."

"So what do you want?"

"It's time you left this town and let it die in peace. The gold's gone. No more roughnecks will be coming after it. No more adventurers. Your time in Silver City is at an end."

"No one knows it's gone," Strong said. "Besides, it wasn't the gold they wanted. It was what the gold could *buy*. Glory. Fame. Women. Some even thought it could buy freedom."

"They'll know it's gone soon enough." Jack motioned toward Sadie, peering out from behind the corner of the saloon. "When that girl deposits her share in the treasury at San Pablo, word'll get out."

"Good point. So why would I let her do that?"

"No choice. As usual, you'll be off licking your wounds in some cave."

Strong grimaced. "Not this time."

"No?" Jack sat bolt upright. "Well, let's see what you've got."

Strong turned and leapt back through the swinging doors of

his tavern. As he did, the windows all along the second floor slid upward, and gun barrels of every description jutted out, all of them pointing down at Jack.

Jack went for his pistols, but it was too late. The guns in the upstairs window fired. Spooked, Jack's appaloosa reared, sending him toppling out of his saddle.

Lu could scarcely believe his eyes. Quick as thought their gunfighter was down. Lu couldn't tell whether Jack had been shot and killed, broke something in the fall, or was knocked unconscious. Whatever it was, he made no move to get up. And his appaloosa tore off down the street, disappearing in the gathering dusk.

Stunned, Lu watched as bullet after bullet cascaded down and into the corpse of his friend. It was the most gruesome thing he'd ever witnessed. And without Jack, Lu supposed they were as good as dead, too. He was so sure of it, in fact, that he very nearly gave himself up. And he would have, if not for the earsplitting roar of Henry's rifle.

A thrill of hope raced up Lu's spine as smoke and muzzle-fire belched from the open door of the bullet riddled Grange Hall, smashing in one of the saloon windows across the street.

Not to be outdone, Chino peppered the saloon with a full dozen slugs, managing to break all of the remaining upstairs windows and sending hot lead careening through the rooms beyond.

Mayor Strong and his men replied.

Soon, the air was filled with the clattering zip and boom of bullets being fired back and forth across the road, and over the prostrate form of the downed gunfighter, Jack Straw.

The speed of the attacks, the reloading and emptying of the guns on both sides, beggared description. Three times Lu tried to stick his head up and over the lip of the trough, intending to enter the battle. He never did see any faces in the saloon windows, but figured a bullet or two from his own pistol, even if he missed, might help his friends.

But every time he tried, the vast majority of the melee would suddenly be directed at him. Lead slugs crashed into the trough in front of him, splintered the wood sidewalk behind him, and tore holes through the front of Moss's store. Lu couldn't possibly get a shot off. Not without having his head sheared clean from his shoulders.

Sadie appeared to be having similar difficulties. Around the side of the trough, Lu could see her. Every few seconds she'd lean out from the corner of the saloon, aiming shots at the second story windows. None did much good, unfortunately. Sadie's angle was all wrong. From that position she had no chance whatever of hitting Strong's gunmen. Worse, every time she fired Strong himself would lean through the batwing doors and send a bullet toward Sadie's head. Somehow, he always managed to miss. But Lu didn't guess that could go on forever. Sooner or later, Strong was sure to get lucky.

Finally, after as many as a hundred shots had been fired in either direction, one of Chino's slugs found a target. With a cry, a gunman collapsed through the middle upstairs window and went tumbling to the wood-plank sidewalk below. His pistol clattered across the boards and into the street. Lu saw no blood, but judging by the way he'd landed, he guessed the man's neck must've been broken.

Unfortunately, the gunman refused to stay dead.

All at once, they heard the rolling thunder of a galloping horse. It was so loud, so unexpected, that for a moment it sucked the will right out of the combatants. Sadie paused in her battle with Mayor Strong. The gunmen in the upstairs windows ceased their rain of death. Even Henry and Chino were quiet.

Lu, wondering where the sound could possibly be coming from, gazed skyward. What he saw froze his blood.

It was one of the ghost-riders. Or its mount, anyway. The fiery beast shot the whole length of the town, leaving a trail of blazing hoof-prints in its wake.

When it reached the downed gunman, the demon horse stopped. It pawed the ground, setting even the mud in front of the plank sidewalk aflame. Tongues of hell-fire, some ten feet tall, leapt from its mane. Its coat was a roiling boil of liquid steel.

The dead gunman lurched to his feet. His skin and clothes scorched under the heat, then burned off as he climbed into the saddle.

With a curse and a howl of vicious laughter, the ghost-rider spurred his horse, whipping it up and over the town.

As they gained altitude, Henry shot wildly upward, his rifle sending what should have been certain death and destruction into the very heart of the flaming demon. But nothing could unseat him from his horse.

Just as Lu began to hope that he was leaving for good, the ghost-rider set his spurs, yanked his reins, and turned straight back around, diving hell-bent-for-leather toward the Grange. Like a comet he streaked earthward, crashing through the roof of the rickety old Hall, laughing as it exploded into flames.

Chino and Henry fled into the street, their clothes and hair smoldering, but still blasting away at both the saloon and the ghost-rider. Lu screamed at them, telling them to take cover. But it did no good. They had nowhere to hide. Without the meager protection that the Grange Hall provided, Henry and Chino were quickly shot to bits by Mayor Strong's gunmen. Tears coursed down Lu's face as his friends collapsed in the street beside Jack Straw.

Lu sat up, no longer caring whether he was killed, and aimed his revolver at the saloon. He hoped against hope that Mayor Strong would lean out just once more, so he could get a shot at him before being killed himself.

But Mayor Strong never did stick his head out. Instead, four more fiery horses appeared at the edge of town. Still sitting bolt upright, Lu watched in mute horror as they flew to the second-story windows of the saloon, pausing for only an instant as their riders, now stripped of their human forms, leapt into the saddle.

Cursing and whipping their mounts, the ghost-riders burned the town. With a mere flick of their tales, the slightest touch of their hooves, the demons set fire to everything. In moments, the whole of Silver City was consumed by hell-fire. All but the saloon and the gallows, both of which they left standing.

Lu sat in front of Moss's store, watching the flames race along the dry shakes of rooftops, shoot through abandoned doors, and leap out of chimneys. He felt the heat. Soon, even the plank sidewalks would burn. At that point, he'd have no choice but to abandon the middling safety of his watering trough and move into the street.

He was just about to make a run for it and hope for the best, when their horses went galloping past. They'd broken their bonds, and were fleeing the burning town. Crash was in the lead. Lu was glad to see him go. He didn't want his horse to die, too.

As he contemplated his own death, Lu saw one of the ghost-riders come swooping down over the gallows, heading straight for Sadie. Lu screamed himself hoarse as the demon chased Sadie across the street, finally latching onto the blond pony-tail that stuck out from under her flowered bonnet.

Sadie burst into flame as the ghost-rider lifted her onto his horse, setting her on the saddle in front of him. Her mouth opened wide, howling in agony. And then the ghost-rider leapt skyward once more, disappearing up and through the flames of the former Grange Hall, lost amid the holocaust of Silver City.

Lu put a hand over his eyes. He couldn't stand to see any more. Any second now, Lu expected to be set on fire, his clothes first melting to his flesh, and then his whole body bursting into unholy flame. He only hoped it would kill him quickly.

Suddenly, above the crackling of the fires, Lu heard a voice. It wasn't the voice of his own thoughts, which he'd heard every moment of his life, but it was familiar. He listened, trying to make out words. After a few seconds, he came to realize that the voice was saying only one word, over and over.

"*Shoot*," it said. "*Shoot*."

"Jack?" Lu called, recognizing the voice at last.

"*Shoot!*"

All of a sudden, Lu realized that he was still holding his revolver. He lifted it, eyes still shut tight, and pointed at what he hoped was the saloon.

His pistol gave its normal stunning roar.

Lu would've been blasted over backward, except that he was sitting with his back propped against the wood sidewalk in front of Moss's store. As usual, he hadn't managed to hit anything. So far as Lu could tell, his bullet had shot straight over the top of the saloon, headed for the infinities of space.

But that hardly made any difference.

Instantly, everything Lu thought he'd seen over the last couple of minutes was gone. All the lies and illusions had been whisked away.

Henry and Chino stood in front of the Grange, firing up at the second floor of the saloon as fast as they could reload their guns. Sadie leaned out from behind the corner, aiming up at those same windows, and then darting back. But most amazing of all, Jack sat astride his appaloosa, right in the middle of the street.

The ghost-riders, seeing that their illusions had been pierced, made one final impotent turn over the town, their laughter and curses now turned to wails of torment, and retreated behind the nearest mountain.

"It was all lies," Lu muttered to himself. "Again. Just lies."

As the reality of their situation sank in, Henry gave up shooting. Chino quit soon after. And Sadie stumbled from around the corner of the saloon, pistol still in hand, but no longer bothering to aim or pull the trigger.

Lu gazed at them, his ears ringing until he thought his head might crack in two, tears of joy running down his cheeks. He saw the whole truth now, recognized the entirety of what they'd faced.

The danger had never come from Mayor Strong, or Phillip Traum, or whatever else you might like to call him. It had always been *them*—Henry, Sadie, Chino, and even Lu himself—they were the *real* danger. Even tonight, Traum's only hope had been that they would flee their hiding places, give in to anger and hatred. In the confusion, he thought he could fool them into gunning each other down. It was the same trick he'd been using forever. The same use of illusion. No different from when Chino had accidentally killed Mister MacLemore. Or Sawyer had murdered Pitt. Traum had done it time after time, year after year. The body count was enormous.

"Just lies," Lu said again, and felt sick to his stomach.

The hell-fires that had bounded from the surfaces of the surrounding buildings were nowhere to be seen. There wasn't even a puff of smoke. In fact, the only danger that remained was Phillip Traum himself, who stood in front of his now battered saloon, dressed in Mayor Strong's three-piece suit, face wrinkled up in disgust.

"There's your Phillip Traum!" Lu said, standing up and pointing. "There he is! The Prince of Lies!"

"Guess you couldn't fool the boy," Jack said.

They walked toward him, cautiously at first, guns raised in case of danger.

Traum glared. His three-piece suit was in tatters. The cuffs of his pants were shredded to ribbons. The pockets of his jacket had been torn open and were hanging by mere threads. His chin was no longer clean-shaven, but bristling with whiskers parted cleanly down the center. In his hand, rather than the pistol Lu would've sworn he'd seen there earlier, was a reed flute.

"Goddamn each and every last one of you to hell," Traum said. His voice was odd. To Lu he sounded like an actor, trying to mimic some European king. "You're nothing but a pack of filthy mongrels," Traum continued. "True sons of—"

He didn't finish the thought. Sadie shot him in the side of the head, and Traum went spinning off the plank sidewalk.

Screaming at the top of her lungs, Sadie ran toward him. When she was at point-blank range, she emptied her revolver into Traum's body. As soon as that gun was empty, she fired the remaining bullets from her father's pistol.

Henry went after her, tried to stop her, but she shoved him away.

"That's enough," he whispered. "It won't do any—"

"Let her go," Jack said.

Sadie looked at them, wild-eyed. "Give me your guns," she said to Chino.

Dutifully, he handed her his pistols. Sadie emptied both into the motionless body of Phillip Traum. After that she demanded Henry's rifle, and quickly shot it empty as well. Finally, she looked at Lu.

"No," Lu said. "You've got to quit."

Sadie bit her lip. She looked at Jack Straw.

"Feel any better?" he asked.

She shook her head. "No. No, I don't."

"Small wonder," Phillip Traum said. He sat up, brushed off the front of his suit, now even more torn and dirty than before, and slowly climbed to his feet. He was favoring one leg, Lu noticed. "Still, we all enjoyed the effort."

"Old Scratch," Jack said. "Good to see you in the flesh."

"I say, you've always been a bother, Jack Straw," Traum replied. "Even back in the old country, you always made a point of meddling in the affairs of your betters."

"Betters? I don't suppose you'd care to settle this once and for all?"

Traum grimaced. His teeth were as brown as tobacco leaves, but still looked strong enough to bite through hardened steel. "And just what did you have in mind, Jack?"

"The usual."

Revolvers leapt into Jack's hands, faster than sight, faster than thought, and in an instant he'd fired both empty.

Traum cart-wheeled backward. Chunks of flesh, muscle and bone ripped from his body. Lu winced as a section of Traum's skull tore open, his brains bursting outward like a child's jack-in-the-box.

When he was done, Jack dropped his pistols into their holsters and went back to leaning on his saddle-horn.

For a moment, Traum seemed finally to be dead. Blood spurted from a dozen wounds. Most were in his chest and stomach, but the ring-finger of one hand had been shorn off as well, and coils of purplish brain waggled from the hole in his skull.

"Is that it?" Sadie asked, hopefully. "Is he finally—"

Jack pointed. "Look."

Traum turned toward them. He winked. "Guess I'll be seeing you, old boy," he said to Jack. "Here and there and everywhere."

And with that, Traum raised the flute to his lips. The notes he played seemed to Lu as familiar as any he'd ever heard, though he couldn't place the tune.

He was about to say as much when a shooting star pierced the inky dark above the tavern, causing Lu to glance upward. As he did, a flash of brilliant red fire shot past. For an instant, Lu was blinded. When he looked again, Phillip Traum was gone.

"Where'd he go?" Sadie asked.

"Ghost-riders took him," Jack said.

"I didn't see them." Sadie looked at Henry and Chino. Both shook their heads.

"I saw something," Lu said. "There was a flash, and then—"

"Nope, I don't guess you would have seen them," Jack said. "Not anymore." He looked at Lu. "Do you remember what I told you about the ghost-riders?"

A shiver ran up Lu's spine. "Only the innocent and the damned can see them."

Jack nodded.

"But why'd you let him get away?" Sadie demanded. "Why did you let him go?"

"Don't worry, Traum's hurt plenty. Might take him years to put himself all back together. That's about as much as we could've hoped."

Henry sighed. "So he really was the Devil after all? Lucifer himself."

"Not Lucifer," Jack said. "Not by half."

"Jesus y Santa Maria." Chino made the sign of the cross. "I could use a drink."

Jack laughed. "What's your poison?"

"Tonight? Whiskey, straight, and lots of it."

"Good idea." Jack led them into the saloon.

Franklin Moss lay slumped over his usual table, an empty bottle beside his elbow. There was also one saloon girl, sitting in a straight-backed chair at the bottom of the stairs, passed-out drunk. All the rest of the saloon was deserted.

Jack reached over the bar, grabbed a bottle of brown whiskey by the neck, and slammed it down on the nearest table.

"Have as much as you like," he said. "Tonight, drinks are on the house."

CHAPTER 22

HOME AGAIN, HOME AGAIN, JIGGETY-JIG.

IT TOOK JUST TWO DAYS to conclude their business in Silver City. Sadie paid back the money her father had borrowed from the Lowers, plus about a thousand percent interest, and gave sufficient gold to Esther Moss to open five cafés. Jack set fire to the saloon and gallows, and then went ahead and torched the old Grange Hall for good measure. When she wasn't chatting with Sadie, Pearl taught Lu how to bake pies. It was a pleasant sort of apprenticeship. Even his mistakes were delicious.

The trip to San Pablo lasted only a little more than a week. Not because they were in a hurry—there just wasn't that much land left to cross. Along the way they passed through some spectacular forests, where they saw trees with trunks as large as twenty feet in diameter. Waterfalls seemed to spill out of every rock. And there was plenty of game, too. Not one of them was ever hungry, thirsty or tired.

It was during the afternoon of their ninth day that Lu got his first view of the Pacific. All his life Lu had heard men talk about oceans, and calling them "big." Now he knew those men for the rascals they were. "Big" wasn't the word. It wasn't descriptive enough by half. The Pacific was enormous. Gargantuan. Everywhere Lu looked was ocean. The encounter with Old Scratch had inflated Lu's ego somewhat—he'd even begun to wonder how he would be seen by history—but one look at the Pacific cured him. Staring at those unending waters he felt just as small and paltry as ever. What was a gunfight, after all, compared with all of that?

San Pablo was a pretty town, with white-washed buildings that shone in the morning, and enough restaurants so that a person might eat in a different one each night for a month, and never have to suffer the same victuals twice. There was even a fairly good Chinese establishment. Lu took his friends there one night, introducing them to the joys of crispy duck. Fine hotels were sprinkled in nearly every street, where even the bedrooms had wall-paper, and a man didn't have to go outside if he should feel the need to make water in the night, but could use a basin that was cleaned fresh every morning and sat waiting just under the bed.

Sadie deposited all five bags of gold at the bank, and ten days later received an accounting of its value. The total came to just under three hundred and twenty thousand dollars. Lu's share amounted to forty thousand—enough to build a brand new stern-wheel river steamer, stock it with coal, and hire all of his old school friends to pilot it up and down the Old Man River back home. It was a heady sum for anyone, but especially for a fifteen-year-old boy from St. Frances. The first thing he did was to buy a full suit of clothes, just for going to dinner in. The suit came with a beaver top hat, but Lu wore that all the time. It was too classy to keep only for evenings. He wanted people to be able to *see* it.

And clothes weren't the only things he bought. Once he'd got the full sense of his fortune, Lu found that the world was alive with activities and experiences he'd never even heard of, but could no longer bear to imagine going without. By the end of his first week back in civilization, Lu had spent upwards of one hundred and fifty dollars. That was a good deal more than the average Chinese man could earn if he worked a year, and but for his fine suit of clothes, Lu hadn't a thing to show for it.

Eventually, Henry and Chino decided they'd had enough civilizing, and were ready to push on. Henry still wanted to open a church, and Chino decided he'd keep his friend company by opening a saloon next door. At first, Henry was annoyed. But

Chino promised to keep his establishment locked tight until after services on Sunday, and that suited Henry fine.

The day they left, Henry gave Lu a bear hug. Chino kissed him on both cheeks. Lu was so choked up he could barely say goodbye.

Sadie spent the bulk of her waking hours meeting with mining interests. She had no intention of ever going back to Silver City to live, and but for her parents' graves, no interest in owning a house or property of any kind. Unfortunately, selling off her father's mining rights proved surprisingly difficult. The companies she met with all demanded an opportunity to survey the ground, a point on which they steadfastly refused to budge. They were equally unpleasant with regards to Sadie herself. Apparently, the vast majority of them considered it a personal affront to have to deal with a sixteen-year-old girl in men's trousers. At last, Sadie had to consent to hiring an agent, or she never would have got anything accomplished. The agent demanded five percent of the final sale price, which warmed Sadie under the collar, but she calmed down once she saw the success her man was enjoying. If things went as Lu thought they probably would, Sadie would soon be the richest woman in San Pablo. The richest *single* woman anyway, a fact that drew bachelors to her like flies.

October came and went as they waited for the sale to be finalized. Finally, Jack decided that they'd waited long enough, and booked passage for Lu and himself on a steamer bound for the tropics. They were scheduled to leave on the last Friday in November. Their plan was to disembark in Central America and ride across that narrow spit of land to the Caribbean. It was time to go home. And since the land route would shortly be inundated in snow, they would go by sea.

As a going away present, Sadie treated them to dinner at the finest restaurant in San Pablo. Lu wore his fancy duds. Jack still wore his tired old army coat, and miserable gray boots. Lu might have been ashamed except that Sadie met them at the front door in trousers.

The dining room was chock-full of Americans. Just a few years back, the President had declared this to be a special day of

Thanksgiving. Seeing an opportunity for profit, the chef had prepared a fine meal of goose-liver pate and oysters on the half-shell, followed by either a fricassee of salmon or roast turkey and dressing.

Sadie and Jack both chose to skip the appetizer altogether—neither of the choices were fit for human consumption, they said—and go straight on to the roast turkey. Lu chose the salmon, but was sorry he did. Twice he tried to convince Sadie to switch with him, but she held steadfast.

For desert they all enjoyed a slice of pumpkin pie. Lu felt certain that Pearl Lower could've showed the chef a thing or two about pie-crusts. But Jack thought he'd better hold his tongue, so Lu choked down the mealy crust as best he could, and kept his mouth shut.

When dinner was over, Sadie shook Jack's hand, gave Lu a kiss on the cheek, and went off to meet her agent. Jack and Lu moseyed down to the wharf, checked to make sure their horses were well-provisioned in the ship's hold, met the captain—a grizzled old salt with a wooden leg, who shook Jack's hand and said to call him Ishmael—and then retired to their cabin. There were only a handful of passenger berths available, so they had to share. Lu went right to sleep. He was excited to weigh anchor the next morning, and wanted to be wide awake in time to enjoy his first breath of sea air. Jack spent the first few hours lying atop his bunk, smoking and reading a book he'd bought in town.

They steamed out of port just after sunrise the following morning, and were not even spitting distance from shore before Lu began to feel the first pangs of sea-sickness. By the time they were out of sight of land, he'd cast the whole contents of his stomach to the waves. The worst if it was, Jack had no symptoms of any kind, and even seemed to be enjoying Lu's agony. If he could have figured a way, Lu might have poisoned Jack's food. Not enough to kill him, of course. Just enough to get him good and throw-upy.

After a solid week of sea-sickness, Lu had just begun to feel better, and was even learning to enjoy certain aspects of the trip, when Captain Ishmael announced that they'd arrive the following day at the town of San Juan del Sur, and that he'd be leaving Jack and Lu there.

Their ride across Central America afforded them many more adventures, and Jack proved unable to leave without sampling them all. They were barely off the steamer before he'd involved them in a conflict over log-wood rights, being fought on the one side by a tribe of jungle Indians, and on the other by a company of Spanish mahogany hunters. Jack and Lu sided with the Indians, of course.

Then, once they'd got that all sorted out, they joined those very same Spaniards in a battle to protect their eastern ports from pirates. Lu considered that a disaster, but the local shippers must have seen it differently. They were so grateful for Jack's help that they offered both he and Lu free passage on the next steamer bound for Jamaica.

Suffice to say, Lu had a marvelous time, though he only got to shoot his revolver once more. And that was just to scare off a howler monkey that'd stolen his beaver hat.

It was on April the Twenty-Fifth, two weeks less than a full year since they'd first set out in a covered wagon bound for the territories, that Lu stepped from the deck of a luxury paddle-wheeler and found himself in St. Frances once more.

"Home again, home again," Lu sighed.

The docks were just as he remembered them. Only now, instead of huge and bustling, they seemed small and quaint.

They saddled their horses—Crash was as much a source of wonder and merriment here as he had been everywhere else—and hurried toward Chinatown.

The bell over the door tinkled as Lu stepped into his grandfather's shop.

Madame Yen shuffled out from behind the counter. "How may I help you?"

"It's me," Lu said. "I'm back."

"Tzu-lu!" She grabbed Lu by the back of the neck and pulled him into her bosom.

When she'd nearly wrung the life out of him, she held him at arm's length. "It *is* you," she exclaimed. "You're dirty."

"It's been a long trip," Lu explained.

"I'll put some water on the stove. You can have a bath before dinner." She reached behind Jack and turned the lock on the door. It was the first time Lu had ever known K'ung's Store to close early. He got the feeling his mother did it as much to keep him from slipping away as to keep thieves from getting in.

"Master K'ung in?" Jack asked.

"He's downstairs." Lu's mother was already bustling toward the kitchen.

Jack marched around to the basement door.

"You coming?" he asked.

Lu nodded. "I'm going downstairs with Jack," he called after his mother.

"Good. Your grandfather will be anxious to see you."

"Enter," Master K'ung said, in response to Jack's knock.

Lu pushed the door open. <<Grandfather,>> he said. <<We're back!>>

Master K'ung rose from his chair. <<Successfully?>>

Lu took the bank draft from his pocket and handed it to his grandfather.

<<What do you plan to do with all this money?>> he asked.

"I don't know," Lu said. <<I'd hoped you might help me decide.>>

<<What would you like to do?>>

Very carefully, Lu took one of the scrolls down from his grandfather's shelves and ran his thumb over the symbols stamped upon it. "First, I'd like to learn to read."

"And after?"

Lu shrugged.

Master K'ung smiled. <<Can I offer you tea?>> he asked Jack. <<Thank you,>> Jack said, and bowed.

Master K'ung poured three bowls from the kettle on his desk.

"Where's Lion-dog?" Lu asked.

Master K'ung shook his head. "She was struck by a wagon and killed. I'm sorry."

Lu took a sip from the bowl his grandfather handed him. He was shocked. It had never occurred to him that his loved ones might be in danger. Certainly not that any of them might be killed.

"Before I forget." Master K'ung picked an envelope up off his desk. "This came for you."

He handed the envelope to Lu, who quickly tore it open and pulled out the letter inside. It was from Sadie.

While Jack told Master K'ung all about their adventures, Lu read Sadie's note.

> *March 18. San Pablo.*
> *Dear Lu,*
> *Well, I finally booked passage on a ship bound for Asia. But I wanted to send you a note before I go. My plan is to go round the world. Can't give no more details than that. Don't got any. In the future, I may come to America again. If so, I'd like to see how you're getting on. I think about you, and hope you're well. We had a good time, I'd say, despite everything. I hope you feel the same.*
> *If you ever feel like getting in touch, just contact my agent in San Pablo. He'll know where to find me. Maybe we could hunt them lions? But not giraffes. I'd shoot any man that hurt a giraffe.*
> *Come to Africa with me and I promise you a first class adventure. Lord knows there were plenty of scoundrels in San Pablo barking after me to come. But not a one was interested in anything other than money.*
> *Say hello to your mother and grandfather. And to Jack Straw, if you see him.*
> *Your friend,*
> *Sadie*

As he read the note, tears welled up in Lu's eyes. It didn't say much, but there was a feeling behind the words that Lu never could have got from Sadie's mouth if he'd talked to her a month.

"Can I ask you something?" he said.

Jack had just come to the part of their story where they'd entered the Hell Mouth, but Lu couldn't wait for him to finish.

"Go on," Jack replied.

"When I was with him, out in the forest, Traum said no one could defeat him but a true American."

"So?"

"He seemed convinced. Was it true?"

Jack smiled. "He's not called the Prince of Lies for nothing."

Lu nodded. "No, I guess not."

"What's wrong?" Jack asked.

"I guess I was just hoping . . ." He looked at the gunslinger. "I mean, I helped to chase him away, didn't I?"

Jack looked surprised. "Of course you did."

"But I'm not an American."

"What makes you say that?"

"Well, look at me."

"Let me tell you something, Lu. Being American isn't in your blood, or your skin, or your hair."

"Then where is it?"

"It's in your mind. A person's an American because he wants to be. That's all."

"I'm not sure I understand."

"America isn't a place, exactly. And it's not a people either. It's an idea. If you believe in it, then you're an American."

"But that would mean everybody's an American," Lu complained. "Anybody can believe."

"Anybody *can*," Jack agreed. "But not many do. It isn't always the easiest thing to believe in. America falls short about as often as it succeeds. More often, some would say. But that doesn't mean it's worthless."

"Is Sadie an American?" Lu asked.

"What do you think?"

"I guess she must be."

Lu was going to ask about Chino and Henry, and Mr. MacLemore, but just then his mother called to them from the top of the stairs. Dinner was almost ready, and Lu still needed to wash up.

"I wonder what we're having," he said.

"Spicy beef," his grandfather replied. "With mashed potatoes and gravy."

"Mashed potatoes?" Lu couldn't remember ever having seen his grandfather eat a potato, mashed or otherwise. So far as he knew, Master K'ung ate rice with every meal.

"Your mother has been cooking them a lot lately," his grandfather explained. "Baked, fried, mashed. I guess I've developed a taste for potatoes. I'm trying to get her to learn to make potato salad."

"Potato salad?" Lu was astonished. "But that's not Chinese. It's not traditional. It's not . . . *you.*"

Master K'ung shrugged. "I like it," he said. "Traditional or not, I like it."

ACKNOWLEDGMENTS

THE GREAT MAN THEORY OF HISTORY has been under attack of late. Schools throughout the country now spout an endless stream of nauseating filth upon the heads of such long-revered fathers as Christopher Columbus, Robert E. Lee and Henry Ford. Charges of racism, sexism, meanness of all shades, have been leveled against these gentlemen with a degree of rabid hatred possibly never before seen. Anyone caught admiring them is sure to be defrocked, disbarred or burned alive. As for me, I offer them no defense. First, there's no percentage in it. And second, no use. My kind are whipped. I know it, and you know it. So I say— "To heck with Albert Einstein, Robert Kennedy and Abraham Lincoln." Their time is over. I'll not thank them or their sons. Not for anything. Instead I'll lay credit for this book on a less controversial bunch—*American Women.*

American women remain unsurpassed, probably unequaled, by any group in the world. Their strength, fortitude, and spirit sit at the very heart of what it means to be an American. Over the course of the preceding pages you've come to know a handful of these American women, including such powerhouses as Eliza Jane Hammond, Hazel and Pearl Lower, and Esther Moss. Each is major a hero to my characters, the sort of person who fights back death and despair just when you think things couldn't possibly get any worse. But each of these women also happens to be one of my great-grandmothers. So my debt to them includes my very life.

There are also, of course, innumerable women who, though they don't appear in name, embody the very spirit of what I have tried to do with this book. Chief among these are my grandmothers, Jeane Hammond and Ada Allen Mills, and of course my own mother-dear, Karleane.

Then there are those women without whom this book could never have seen print. My agent and friend, Katherine Fausset, is a stalwart and a champion I do not deserve, but am ever thankful to have in my corner.

Outside of the bounds of the book, though no less important, are Joan Mitchell, whose marshalling of support from the great state of Alabama has been immeasurable, and Anna Mitchell, matriarch of "the folks" in Mississippi. Also of enormous influence and support has been the great Idaho horsewoman, Carol MacGregor. You might be interested to know that hers is the saddle Sadie rides.

Finally, a big open-mouthed kiss to the first girl I ever loved with all my heart—Sadie. If you knew her, you loved her. That's all there is to it.

To each of these women, and to all American women, I offer my thanks.

But there is one American woman who for me stands above all others. My wife, partner, first reader, stalwart, and the best friend a boy named Lu could ever have—Day Mitchell. As I have said before and will say again, this book is as much hers as it is mine.